T0024308

CASTING LACEY

By the Author

Forget Her Not

Casting Lacey

CASTING LACEY

by

Elle Spencer

2018

CASTING LACEY

ISBN 13: 978-1-63555-412-0

This Trade Paperback Original Is Published By
Bold Strokes Books, Inc.
P.O. Box 249
Valley Falls, NY 12185

First Bold Strokes Edition: August 2018

CREDITS
PRODUCTION DESIGN: STACIA SEAMAN
COVER DESIGN BY STREETLIGHT GRAPHICS

For my wife—my love, my forever.

CHAPTER ONE

"I don't want to do this, Jack."
Jack Harris put the car in park and turned toward Quinn. "We've talked about this. It's the best way to get what you want."

"And keep what I have. I know, Jack. You've mentioned it at least a thousand times." Quinn Kincaid shook her head in disbelief. She'd been doing that a lot lately, ever since she'd decided to entertain Jack's ridiculous idea.

Jack reached for her hand and gave it a little squeeze. "Besides, she's perfect." He beamed with pride. "I've completely outdone myself."

Quinn pulled her hand back and turned away in a dramatic huff. "How do you manage to be the publicist who gives all the other publicists a bad name? Do you know how hard that is?"

"What can I say?" He gave her an insincere shrug. "I'm a winner."

Quinn lowered her sunglasses and shot him a glare. "I'm serious, Jack. I really don't want to do this."

"Just give me five minutes. I haven't even told you about her yet." He unrolled Quinn's heavily tinted window. The anticipation was killing him. He had to know what she would think of his choice for her. "The one at the end, with the long brown hair."

"Dammit, Ja—" Quinn froze, her mouth hanging open.

Jack wanted to laugh out loud at Quinn's reaction, but he covered it up with a clearing of his throat. If he wasn't sure before—and by God he wasn't—he certainly was now. Quinn Kincaid was indeed gay. He leaned over and looked out the car window with her. "I expect a week at your Aspen condo. *Peak* season. Not friggin' late April. That's just insulting."

Quinn kept her eyes on the woman. "Remind me again why I have to pay your retainer *and* give you my condo in exchange for carrying out your dumb-ass idea?"

"Because I'm that good." Jack grinned, entirely too pleased with himself. "Now then, would you like the *lowdown* before you *go down*, Quinn darling?"

"Late April, just for saying that. Maybe even May."

"And here I thought we were friends." Jack put his reading glasses on and opened a file folder. "Her name is Lacey Matthews. Thirty years old. Lives in New York—"

"New York? Then why is she sitting at a Starbucks in West Hollywood?"

"She comes here every day. Gets her out of that shitty little hotel she's staying in. Now, can I give you her history without any more interruptions, please?"

Quinn waved a dismissive hand while she kept her eyes on the brunette. "Please do. We both have better places to be."

"She came up in the business. Spent her childhood on a daytime soap, went to college, then back on the soap. Left the show last year, so she's in L.A.—going to every audition she can. She really needs the work."

"Any luck?"

"She's good, Quinn. She has a couple of Daytime Emmys, but nothing so far."

"I've never heard of her." Quinn impatiently looked at her watch.

"Does it matter? And by the way, anyone who watches soaps would know who she is."

"So, she's like this generation's Susan Lucci?"

Jack chuckled. "So, you *do* watch soaps."

"You know me better than that, Jack."

He closed the folder and opened his iPad. "Shall we YouTube her?"

"No. Just tell me about her love life." Quinn glanced at her watch again and then lowered the car window a little more.

"Broke up with her ex about six months ago. Word is, the stress of coming out was too much for them."

Quinn stilled herself and slowly turned to Jack, glancing at him quickly before turning to the window again. Looking the woman up and down, her eyes widened. "She's gay?"

Jack smiled, feeling so very proud of himself. "Perfect, right?" Quinn didn't reply. "Quinn?"

She gave him a nod. "Okay. I'll need a face-to-face before we make an offer."

"Well, as you can see, she's alone. Just don't get into any specifics until we have a signed nondisclosure agreement."

"Great," Quinn replied. "I was ready to open with 'Hey, good lookin', want to hear my publicist's half-cocked plan?' Now I need another pick-up line."

"Cockblocker by day, publicist by night. Just doing my job!"

Quinn shot him an indignant glare and then looked away. "I don't know, Jack. I'm having second thoughts about this."

"Quinn." He put a reassuring hand on her shoulder. "How many times have you told me you can't do this alone?" His tough publicist façade gave way to the face of a friend, because the truth was, he and Quinn *were* friends. She trusted him more than anyone else in the business and with good reason. He'd been by her side through a very tough time. The last thing he wanted to do was break that trust. "You've always said you need someone on your arm when you announce it to the world."

"Always?" Quinn scoffed. "I mentioned it once—after two glasses of wine, I might add. And then you came up with this crazy idea."

"It's not crazy, it's smart. This way, we control it." And the publicist was back, pushing every one of Quinn's buttons. "We control the whole thing. And nobody loses anything."

Quinn shook her head in disgust. "I can't believe I have to do this. I mean, seriously?"

"I still can't believe you're gay, and neither will the rest of the world. They'll think it's some sort of stunt to boost ratings, and then they'll hound you relentlessly until they get a photo of your girlfriend, so forget about dating for real, Quinn. No woman would put herself through that. Not even for you."

"So, what you're telling me is, I have to live a lie, or the world won't believe me?"

Jack reached across her and opened her door. "Welcome to show business, baby."

"No, Dad. Nothing yet." Lacey rubbed her forehead. These daily phone calls from her father were getting tedious. "Yes, I used the security bar on my door." She sighed. "Dad, I grew up in New York. I think I can handle L.A." Her eyes widened in surprise as she tracked a woman who had just made herself at home at her small table. "Dad, I have to go. Talk soon. Love you."

"Sorry for interrupting. I hope this seat isn't taken."

Lacey slowly shook her head. "No." She'd had soap fans insinuate themselves into her personal space before, usually to praise her for standing up to that TV husband of hers, or because they desperately wanted to give her advice on how the storyline should go, as if she had any control over that sort of thing. But this time, Lacey was pretty sure she was looking at Jordan Ellis. No, not Jordan Ellis. That was her character's name on that law show. She was looking at—

"Quinn Kincaid."

Why the hell had Quinn Kincaid just plopped down at her table? Was she a soap fan? Lacey reached across the table and took the offered hand. "Lacey Matthews."

"Actor?" Quinn pointed at Lacey's iPad. "I noticed you're looking for auditions."

Not a fan, apparently. Then again, no one was anymore. Two more rejections just this morning had cemented that fact. Lacey tossed the iPad onto the table. "Yeah, I guess I am," she said, with a tinge of frustration in her voice.

"Anything interesting?"

"Absolutely…not…a damn thing," Lacey answered, frowning.

"Sorry. It's tough out there right now."

"Not that you would know." Lacey leaned back in her chair. It was a small table and she felt the need to regain some of her personal space.

"I got lucky five years ago," Quinn said. "I was in the right place at the right time and I got the gig of a lifetime. I'll deny it if you quote me. I tell the whole world how hard it is, but it's mostly luck."

"Oh, well that's great news," Lacey sarcastically replied, throwing her hands in the air. "And here I was, thinking that owning the ten o'clock slot on Thursday nights had something to do with talent." Was it really all about luck? Had Lacey been working hard every day, honing her craft, becoming the best at what she did, only to be told it all came down to fucking luck?

Quinn's smile brightened. "I take it you watch *Jordan's Appeal*?"

Hell, no, Lacey didn't watch the show. Why would she watch the woman her ex-girlfriend fawned over every Thursday night? Yeah, they would joke about Dani's crush, but it irritated Lacey more than anything else, since Dani couldn't ever seem to find the time to watch

Lacey's soap. But saying that out loud didn't seem appropriate. "My ex watched it. Religiously."

"I see. And what about you? What do you think of the show?"

Lacey shrugged. "Honestly, I was memorizing my lines while she watched, but she thinks you're amazing." She huffed out a breath, wishing she hadn't said that last part. Dani and her damn celebrity crushes. And they were never women who looked anything like Lacey. Always blond, California girls. Dani had a type. Jesus! Why hadn't Lacey ever figured that out until right now?

Quinn pushed her sunglasses up on top of her head, giving Lacey a close-up view of those ice-blue eyes she was so famous for. "Will you tell the network that? I keep asking for a raise and they keep shooting me down," she joked.

Lacey smirked. "What, from one million per episode to two? I'm sure you're doing just fine."

Quinn's eyes widened in surprise. "Am I really sitting here arguing with a stranger about my pay?"

Lacey leaned forward and picked up her cup of coffee. "I introduced myself. Lacey Matthews, remember?" She took a sip and held the cup close to her mouth, peering at Quinn over her cup.

"How could I forget?" Quinn picked up the coffee she'd ordered before sitting down at the table. She took a sip and they stared at each other for a few long seconds before she said, "Now that we've established how unfair this business is—"

"I'm sorry," Lacey interrupted. "I guess I'm just a little bit bitter about the huge pay gap between daytime and prime-time actors."

Lacey was bitter about a lot of things, and sitting here looking at Quinn Kincaid wasn't helping. The woman had it all; a great career, a great marriage to some other A-lister, enough money to last her two lifetimes, Lacey guessed. And yet, here she sat, flirting with those blue eyes like there was no tomorrow. With a total stranger. A *female* stranger.

Lacey glanced around, wondering if she was being punked.

"Look," Quinn started. "It's like I said before, it's all about being in the right place at the right time, which is a perfect segue into asking you if you'd like to come to a party at my place tonight. I could introduce you to some industry people, because it's also all about *who* you know. And now you know me, so…"

Lacey's brow knitted as she folded her arms. "Weird."

"What's weird?"

"I'm a New Yorker. I don't take people at face value, and this is weird." She glanced around again.

Quinn glanced around too. "What are you looking for?"

"Hidden cameras," Lacey replied, with all seriousness.

Quinn leaned back and laughed. Few people were famous for their laughs. Quinn was one of the few. It wasn't a laugh that you heard across a crowded room. It was a little subtler than that, but it made you want to laugh right along with her, even if you hadn't heard the joke. "I promise there are no hidden cameras. Well, paparazzi maybe, but not like one of those hidden camera shows. So, can I ask what you find so weird about this?"

Lacey leaned forward and lowered her voice. "Well, for one thing, I'm getting a gay vibe from Quinn Kincaid, who everyone knows is married to..." Lacey looked away for a second. "God, what's his name..."

"Divorced. We're divorced."

"Are you?" Lacey was genuinely surprised, not that she kept up with celebrity gossip. That was more Dani's thing, but she'd never mentioned that her celebrity crush had gotten a divorce. "I guess I should read the tabloids more often."

Quinn chuckled. "Well, if you read those, you would know that the divorce was due to the fact that I'm infertile." She put up her finger. "Oh, and also, I was too fat for him."

"What a pig," Lacey said, still leaning forward on the table. Their eyes locked on each other for a few seconds, and then Lacey asked, "When was the last time you plopped down at someone's table in West Hollywood?"

"I don't make a habit of it," Quinn admitted. "And you can question the weirdness of it all day long, since you have so much time on your hands. Or you can graciously accept an invitation to my party tonight." She didn't wait for a reply. She grabbed a napkin and quickly wrote down the address. She slid it across the table and smiled. "See you later."

Quinn didn't make it out of Starbucks before someone stopped her, wanting a selfie and autograph. She gave the woman both and then turned back around. Lacey was staring at her with her arms folded, looking rather perplexed. Quinn gave her a little wave and left.

❖

Jack opened the door from the inside and Quinn slid into the passenger seat. "Well? How did it go?"

"You're right, she's gorgeous."

Jack grinned. "I knew you'd think so. Brunette. Big, brown eyes. Legs that go on forever."

"Okay, settle down there, big guy." Quinn watched Lacey collect her things and get up to leave. "She's not a fan, but I kind of like that."

"She didn't fawn over you?"

Quinn almost snorted. "I'd say it was the opposite of fawning."

"Hey, as long as the camera likes the two of you..." Jack handed his camera over to Quinn. "I took a few shots. The blonde, brunette thing is killer. You already look like a couple. She's even scowling at you in one of the shots."

Quinn scrolled through the photos, and sure enough, Jack was right. They did look good together. "We'll see how it goes tonight. She might not even show up."

"Oh, she'll show up. She'd be a fool not to."

Quinn handed the camera back and looked out the window just in time to see Lacey walking down the sidewalk to her car. She couldn't help but smile because, goddamn, Lacey Matthews had it all in the looks department. And yes, Jack was right—her legs looked fabulous in those shorts she was wearing. And truth be told, Quinn Kincaid had a thing for brunettes. "Good work, Jack."

Finally, the praise Jack knew he deserved. "My wife says Presidents' Day weekend would be perfect."

"For what?"

"Aspen."

Quinn shook her head at him for the hundredth time. Jack was nothing if not pushy. "Fine. Tell Amy to pencil you in." She raised her window and rested her head on the back of the leather seat. "If this doesn't blow up in my face before then."

CHAPTER TWO

Lacey stood in front of the huge wooden door wondering where the hell the doorbell was. It was one of those ultra-modern homes where all the essentials like light switches and the damn handle to flush the toilet were hidden. She'd been in a home like that in New York—some unnecessary party she and the rest of the cast had been invited to. Needless to say, that particular toilet went unflushed.

And why did she have to find the doorbell anyway? Quinn had already let her in the security gate. She was probably watching her on a security camera from inside the house. Lacey pounded on the door. She considered flipping off the camera on the overhang with her spare hand, but she thought better of it.

Quinn opened the door with a smile. "Hi."

Lacey pushed her hands into her pockets. Feeling awkward and slightly annoyed, she forced herself to smile back. "Hi."

Quinn opened the door wider. "Come in."

Lacey took a quick look around but didn't see any other guests. "Either I'm early, or this isn't a party at all."

"A party of three," Quinn said. "Me, you, and if things go well, eventually my publicist."

Lacey spun around. "So, I was right. When we met this morning, I was right?"

"Which part?" Quinn led Lacey into a meticulously decorated room. A long, white sofa faced floor-to-ceiling windows that looked out onto a large swimming pool. Lacey was pretty sure she got her period just looking at the sofa.

As living rooms go, this one was a blatant display of wealth. Lacey wasn't impressed. And even if she was, she'd never admit it. She'd met a few A-list actors in her time, and rarely did she come away believing they were anything but self-absorbed, egotistical—and okay, yes, they were usually gorgeous to look at, but God they could be shallow pricks.

Quinn asked again. "Which part were you right about, Lacey? The gay vibe or the not so random plop down?"

Feeling like she'd been played, Lacey didn't bother with pleasantries as her eyes lingered on Quinn's tits. That dress was certainly hugging her in all the right places, and clearly the moment called for just the right blend of bitchy and coy. "Play your cards right and maybe I'll tell you."

Quinn didn't acknowledge the comment. She sat in a chair and motioned for Lacey to sit on the sofa. A bottle and two glasses were perfectly placed on the coffee table. "Wine?"

Lacey sat down and leaned forward, resting her elbows on her knees. "Trying to get me drunk?"

Quinn suppressed a grin. "You're not a pushover. I like that."

"I'm a little jaded." Lacey stared at Quinn intently, trying to read her expression. In other words, trying to figure out why the hell she was there. The house was empty. Dead quiet, except for some depressing classical music playing in the background. And so tidy, she wondered if anyone actually lived there.

"I don't blame you. Child actor. Smart. A bit of a has-been—"

"Five minutes off camera and I'm a has-been?" *God, this woman!* Quinn offered Lacey a glass. "It's been a year, hasn't it?"

"A hard year." Lacey took a large sip of wine, almost emptying the glass. Then she tilted her head and frowned. "And now I have to wonder how you know that. Surely you have better things to do than watch soaps all day."

"That was my mother. Still is, I'm sure."

"So, you didn't grow up watching the soaps with your mom?"

"I was too busy studying and playing the piano and trying to be the perfect daughter."

"Oh." Lacey seemed to have hit a nerve. She could've commented on how Quinn had succeeded by the looks of it. She was perfectly dressed in her, what was that color called? Oh yeah, *cornflower* summer dress with matching sandals, sitting like such a lady with her hands clasped on legs crossed at the ankle. Instead, she leaned forward and held her glass out for a refill. "Nice wine."

"Glad you like it." Quinn filled the glass and resumed her ladylike position.

Lacey wondered if they still had finishing schools. If so, surely

Quinn had been, you know, finished at one. She noticed that a blush was working its way up Quinn's chest, probably due to the awkward silence that was, if Lacey had to guess, going on forty-five seconds now. It looked as though Quinn was trying to come up with a good way to say what was really on her mind. Lacey didn't have time for that. "Maybe we could talk about why I'm here?"

Almost seeming relieved by the suggestion, Quinn's shoulders relaxed slightly. "I have a proposition for you."

"Are you going to save my career?"

"Maybe," Quinn said. "Quite possibly. Most likely." She gave a firm nod. "Yes."

Lacey didn't hesitate. "All of those work for me."

"I can guarantee you'll get a lot of publicity. What you do with it is completely up to you."

"Guess I didn't need all that college to figure out Quinn Kincaid introducing herself at Starbucks probably wasn't a random encounter." Lacey tried to hide her smile by taking a sip of wine. Whatever this was, it was starting to get interesting.

Their eyes met for a few seconds and then Quinn said, "Look, you were right. I don't frequent West Hollywood or even Starbucks. I guess it's just easier to make coffee with my"—she gestured toward the kitchen—"Robospresso 3000 or whatever the hell it is."

Lacey looked over her shoulder, and sure enough, there was a rather large stainless-steel espresso machine sitting on the kitchen counter. She tried not to let her envy show. "And it's easier to pretend you're straight when you're not hanging out in West Hollywood?"

"Nah, I just can't deal with the traffic on La Cienega." Quinn averted her eyes, killing her chances of selling the joke.

Lacey stared intently until Quinn finally met her gaze. *Oh. Good. God.* She kept herself from squealing with pride at being right.

"Are you willing to sign a nondisclosure before I make you an offer?" Quinn asked.

And there it was. Lacey chuckled. "I'm not going to out you, if that's what you're asking."

Quinn slid the nondisclosure contract across the coffee table, along with a pen. Lacey took a look at it and rolled her eyes. With a big sigh, she leaned forward and quickly signed on the dotted line. Quinn looked at the signature and scowled. "Is that really how you sign your name? It looks like Larry…May…nerd."

"I never learned to spell," Lacey quipped. "So, you're gay?"

Lacey immediately regretted asking the question. She could still hear her producers asking her the same thing with a look of horror on their faces. They blamed her firing on wanting to take the storyline in a different direction, but she knew better. She'd been fired for one reason and one reason only.

"In about four months, I'm going to make a big announcement," Quinn said.

Lacey set her glass on the table. She eyed Quinn for a moment, trying to decide how much personal information she should divulge. "Can I give you some advice?" she asked, in a serious tone.

"Only if it's constructive."

"Stay in the closet."

Quinn stiffened at the suggestion. "I can't. I want a life."

"That's what I thought too, and then my producers decided I was no longer believable playing a straight woman. I'd been Sarah *Fucking* Covington since I was ten, and now all of a sudden I'm no longer believable in that role?"

"I know," Quinn said. "Look…like I said before, this is a shitty business. But if you take this offer, maybe the jerks who fired you will regret it."

"The producers of that show were like my parents," Lacey snapped back. "I grew up with them, and they turned their backs on me." She took a deep breath, trying to fight back her emotions.

Quinn gave her a sympathetic smile. "I know the feeling. It's amazing how many people are brilliant at pretending they care about you."

"Right? And we're supposed to be the actors."

Quinn leaned forward. "But one way or another, you're going to need to move on."

"That's what I've been trying to do. It's the whole reason I'm in L.A." Lacey was losing her patience, and the last thing she wanted to do was talk about all the hurt and anger she felt about losing her job. And she still didn't know why she was there, for God's sake. So Quinn Kincaid was gay. What the hell did that have to do with her? "What's your offer?"

"I'm not going to do this coming out thing willy-nilly. It's going to be a finely tuned show that I control."

"Smart. Unlike me, who went into work one day and said 'hey, this is my girlfriend. Aren't you fucking delighted for me?'" Lacey dropped her gaze as she relived that awful moment, the fake smiles and the quick change of subject. One of the producers refused to even look her in the eye the rest of the day. It was the beginning of the end of everything. Her career, her relationship—all gone now.

The last thing Lacey wanted to do was cry in front of Quinn Kincaid in her damn mansion. She might ruin the very soft rug under her feet that looked like it was made of cotton candy. It was pretty. Azure blue. *Since when am I such an expert on shades of blue? And cornflower? Where the hell did that come from? Get a grip, Lace. Get a fucking grip.*

"My publicist thinks I have a believability issue," Quinn said. "It's his somewhat expert opinion that the media, and more importantly, the public, will be more sympathetic toward me if I have a girlfriend when I come out."

Lacey raised her head, a look of confusion written all over her face. "Wait. What?"

"My publicist—"

Lacey put up her hand. "No, I heard you." She paused for approximately 400 years. Quinn couldn't possibly be suggesting what Lacey thought she was suggesting. "You want me to pretend to be your...girlfriend?"

"Yes," Quinn said with a firm nod. "I would pay you, of course. We'd start with some photos of us out in public, not canoodling, just together having dinner or whatever. They'll be of no interest until I come out. And then, according to Jack at least, they'll be fascinating proof that we've been dating."

Lacey let a small laugh slip out of her gaping mouth. Was this woman insane? And did she seriously just use the word *canoodle*? "Well," Lacey cleared her throat and put up a finger. "There's just one problem. You see, I don't know if I could handle being out in public with *the Quinn Kincaid* and not *canoodle*."

Quinn blushed. "Come on. You know what I mean."

"Yes, I know what you mean," Lacey said. "And I'm flattered, but I don't think I can do what you're suggesting."

Quinn's shoulders straightened, looking surprised by the response. "I'm not asking for romance, if that's what you're thinking."

"And I'm not a prostitute, if that's what you're thinking." Lacey threw her hands in the air. "Why don't you just find the real thing? Start dating. *Canoodle* all you want."

"I can't control that," Quinn calmly stated. "Women are crazy, and a woman in love is even crazier. I don't want any emotion from you. This is a job and I would expect you to treat it as such."

"Women are crazy? You must have met my ex!" Lacey couldn't believe she was having this conversation. If anyone seemed crazy, it was Quinn Kincaid. She put her face in her hands and rubbed her forehead. Desperate for a paying gig, she tried to ignore how ludicrous the idea seemed to be. "What are the terms?"

"Steady pay for a year," Quinn said. "You be where I ask, when I ask. There'll be some wardrobe considerations, of course. And anything you say publicly will be tightly controlled. Most importantly, you act. I hear you're not half bad."

"You HEAR?" Feeling completely insulted, Lacey's voice raised a couple of octaves. "You've never even seen my work and you're offering me a job?"

"I trust Jack's opinion on that."

"Sure. Publicist. Casting director. What's the difference, really?" Lacey had imagined any number of scenarios on the drive to the Palisades. This craziness wasn't one of them.

"Do you want the job or not?"

This was insane. Did people really do this? Lacey grabbed her purse and stood up. "No, I don't."

Quinn also stood up. "But…you need the work."

"Not this kind of work!" Lacey said, almost shouting.

Quinn's expression changed from confusion to anger. "You're above this, is that it? Because being a soap star is so admirable?"

"I'm an actor," Lacey said, pointing at herself. "And on top of that, I'm well educated." She put her hand on her hip, furious she'd braved L.A. traffic for this nonsense. "This is just…bullshit!" she said, throwing that same hand in the air.

Quinn remained calm, even though Lacey was practically yelling at her. "Bullshit? So, tell me, Lacey, what was your last storyline before you got fired? No, let me guess. You were playing Sarah Fucking Covington and her long-lost evil twin?"

Lacey held Quinn's stare, her eyes full of anger. She was fuming and damn near burning Quinn with her glare. At least that's how it felt until she burst out laughing. "Oh God. My TV husband couldn't tell us apart. They had me doing so many love scenes with him, who knows? Maybe I really wasn't that believable anymore. As if believability is what the writers were *ever* going for on that show." She dropped her purse, sat back down, and grabbed the bottle of wine, pouring the last of it into her glass. She took a sip, her hand shaking slightly.

Quinn also sat down and picked up her glass. "Well, if it makes you feel any better, my mother would probably be thrilled if I brought you home. As my friend, of course."

Lacey looked up in surprise. "Your mom doesn't know you're gay?"

"No, not yet."

God, what a mess! Lacey groaned at herself. She should've left the second Quinn revealed her intentions. So why the hell was she still sitting here? Sure, she needed the money, but not that badly. As for the fame, Lacey was no Quinn, but she still had her fans. Plenty of them. And yet, she was still here, actually considering this absurdity. "I take it I'll be playing the part of the dumped girlfriend eventually?"

"Yes. We'll break up and we'll both move on. Everyone will know your name and I'll start dating. Maybe, if I'm lucky, I'll even find the real thing one day. It's win-win."

"And what do we tell the people close to us?" Lacey asked.

"You start now. You tell them you met me and I was super nice," Quinn said with a smile.

"So, I'd be acting right off the bat?"

Quinn's eyes widened in surprise. "Damn, you're sassy!"

Lacey set the wine glass back down. If she kept drinking, she wouldn't be able to drive back down the steep, hairpin-curved road that brought her here. "Sorry. You caught me on a bad week and this whole thing just reeks of everything I hate about this business."

"They don't call it show business for nothing," Quinn gently quipped.

Lacey looked at the ceiling and shook her head, unable to believe she was actually considering this. "If I take this *job*, as you call it, where will I live?"

"There's a guesthouse out back. I'd prefer it if you stayed there, so we can control the paparazzi. My home is very secure. The backyard is private. There's a side gate, so you can come and go as you please. I think you'd be quite comfortable here. The only thing I ask is that you don't bring any guests here."

Lacey stood up and walked over to the world's largest window. It was getting dark, but she could easily see a long, lighted pool that looked like it poured over a cliff and into the ocean. A sleek, modern-looking guesthouse sat off to one side, and a fire pit sat in the opposite corner. As for the neighbors—if there were any, you'd never know it. The property was lined with tall, narrow evergreens that created an impressive privacy hedge on each side. The whole scene called to mind exactly two words. Skinny. Dipping.

Compared to her tiny hotel room in West Hollywood, this would feel like paradise. And Quinn hadn't said Lacey couldn't keep looking for real acting jobs. It wouldn't be so bad, would it? She could swallow her damn pride for once, couldn't she?

Lacey turned back around and folded her arms. "I want everything in writing. I want an early termination bonus in case you decide you don't like me and change your mind. And I want to be able to keep auditioning."

Quinn stood up. "I already don't like you, Lacey. You have that New York bullshit attitude that rubs me the wrong way, but my publicist tells me you're a hell of an actress and that's what I need on my arm. The fact that I would never consider dating you is probably a good thing."

Lacey went back over to the sofa and grabbed her purse. "Fuck you too. And tell your publicist I want an advance," she said, walking to the door. "And a car! A nice one!" she shouted over her shoulder.

Quinn followed Lacey to the front door. "Do you think I'd let my girlfriend drive a…" Quinn looked out at the driveway. "What is that? A Hyundai?"

"It's a Sonata, thank you very much. The fancy kind of Hyundai."

Quinn laughed. "Uh-huh."

Lacey gave her a sarcastic scowl. She stepped out of the house and glanced at the white Maserati sitting in the driveway. "I prefer black," she said as she sauntered over to her rental car.

"Of course you do," Quinn muttered under her breath.

"And watch my fucking show!" Lacey yelled as she climbed into her car and slammed the door. Quinn gave her a little wave, smiling like she hadn't even heard that last request. Lacey put the key in the ignition and whispered, "What have I gotten myself into?"

CHAPTER THREE

The following afternoon, everyone seemed on edge. Quinn kept finding excuses to leave the room and Lacey...well, Jack hadn't figured Lacey out yet. She was nervous. He was sure about that much, since she kept bouncing her leg. He glanced under the table again. Yep. Still bouncing.

"Shall we cover the rules?" Jack opened the folder and put his glasses on. "No nightclubs, unless you're with Quinn. And definitely no gay clubs. No dating anyone else, obviously." Jack paused, waiting for confirmation.

Lacey shrugged. "No dating. Got it."

"In the beginning, Quinn will introduce you as her friend. You won't show any affection in public."

"Or at all," Lacey interrupted.

"Until she comes out," Jack clarified.

"And then what will be required of me?"

"Nothing you can't handle," Jack said with a smirk. "You've kissed a woman before, correct?"

Lacey sighed in frustration. "Look. I don't think I'll throw up in my mouth if I have to kiss Quinn. I'm just asking how far we'll be taking this little charade."

"Nothing inappropriate, considering you're being paid. Just things like walking arm in arm, holding hands, maybe a light kiss, and sweet little looks for the paparazzi."

Lacey shrugged again. "I can do sweet."

"Prove it," Jack mumbled as he eyed her over his reading glasses. After meeting Lacey in person, he had his doubts about her "sweet" factor. "Anyway, we'll bring in a stylist and Quinn and I will decide on your look."

"My look?"

"Yes, your look." Jack took off his glasses. "Quinn's a tastemaker. When she wears something out in public, the fashion world takes notice, photos are taken, and before you know it, everyone is copying her look. You need to complement that style without overpowering it."

Lacey looked down at herself. "I have style. I can be...stylish."

Again, Jack had his doubts. He glanced at her cropped jeans and V-neck T-shirt. There was no shortage of hotness, but she looked like a "Stars: They're Just Like Us!" magazine spread featuring Jennifer Aniston's Sunday morning trip to the Coffee Bean. And then there were the leather sandals. Or more accurately, the leather *flip-flops.* Sure, they were Tory Burch flip-flops, but flats? Really? At least her toenails were painted a pretty shade of pink.

Jack chuckled to himself as he realized, not for the first time, why so many people assumed he was gay. "If you're going to complain about a new wardrobe that you get to keep when the job is done, then maybe I was a bit hasty."

"Fine. I'll take the clothes. But I want the Range Rover too. And why is it a Range Rover? Why not a sports car?"

Jack huffed. "The last thing we need is you killing someone on PCH."

"But it's okay if I kill someone on Sunset?" Jack narrowed his eyes at her. "All right. Fine," Lacey acquiesced. "No sports cars or vehicular homicide. You drive a hard bargain."

Jack ignored her sarcasm, even though the slight curve at the corners of his lips said he kind of liked it. "I've created a cover story. You'll memorize it. And it's your job to get to know Quinn so that when you're together in public, it's believable."

"I've got this, Jack," Lacey said impatiently. "I've been doing this since I was a kid. I can look at a rock and cry because it's so damn gray, which makes me blue and reminds me of the dolly my druggie daddy never gave me as a kid, and before you know it, I've got real tears in my eyes."

"Druggie daddy?" Jack opened another folder—the one containing the research he'd done on Lacey.

"Me and him, homeless on the streets of New York. Works every time."

"Wasn't your father a college professor?"

Lacey shrugged. "Still is."

It was Jack's turn to roll his eyes. "Actors…" He closed the folder and tucked it back in his briefcase.

"Make you a wealthy man," Lacey said.

Jack leaned forward, folding his arms on the table. "Do you always have a sarcastic reply?"

Lacey's leg stopped bouncing. She opened her mouth and quickly closed it. She looked down at her hands and then met Jack's gaze again. "I've had a tough year. People I loved and trusted, they let me down. And I won't make that mistake again."

"Loving and trusting?"

"Exactly. And honestly, I'm kind of okay with having a script for my life right now." Lacey tapped the paperwork with her finger. "You know, as long as you two don't screw me over."

"Nobody's going to screw you over, Lacey. I think you'll find this to be a very lucrative arrangement, if you sell it right."

"No problem. Selling love has been my job my whole life," she said. "You want me to be the excited, giddy, high on life girlfriend? Put me in front of Oprah and I'll have her wishing she was me."

"Just don't do a Tom Cruise and jump up on the furniture," Quinn said, walking into the room. "Sorry, I had to make a quick phone call. I take it we're in business?"

Jack looked at Lacey. It was her call. And as far as he was concerned, she'd be crazy to pass up the opportunity. Her attitude could use a little adjusting, but she really was perfect for the role. He believed the two of them would make a beautiful couple and he was pretty sure all of America would agree with him. Quinn Kincaid and Lacey Matthews would soon be the "It" couple and Jack Harris would keep his best client, and possibly gain another. "Ms. Matthews?"

Lacey picked up the pen. "Show me where to sign."

"The dotted line usually works." Quinn offered her a fake smile. Lacey gave her a heated look and signed the contract.

"Well, this should be fun," Jack said, his eyes darting between the two of them.

Lacey paced in front of the window that looked out on to the pool and guesthouse that would soon be her new home. She knew she should back out of the deal right now, while she still had the chance. Just walk away. But the truth was, she was tired.

The last six months had been hell. She'd gone through almost all of her savings, traveling between the coasts, going to every audition she could manage. She was never "quite right" for the part, they'd tell her. All the career-related rejection would have been enough for anyone. Her girlfriend dumping her on top of it? Yeah, the last six months had taken its toll.

What she really needed was to find a role where all that cooped-up anger and frustration could win her an Oscar. Or at least an Emmy. Hell, a People's Choice Award would be welcome at this point. But finding that role had been an exercise in futility.

Lacey had started young in the business. Her mother saw a spark in her only child; a kid with a big personality who wasn't afraid of anything or anyone. Lacey's very first audition landed her the role of ten-year-old Sarah Covington, illegitimate heir to the Covington fortune on the long-running daytime soap opera, *Light of Day*.

She'd been playing the same character her entire career, and she'd only recently realized just how lucky she'd been. None of that changed the fact that she was a seasoned, highly trained actor (she went to Yale, for God's sake!) and this scheme with Quinn made a joke out of everything she'd worked so hard for. A joke that paid extremely well, but still—a goddamned joke.

Quinn walked back into the room after seeing Jack to the door. Lacey turned to her new, albeit fake, girlfriend. Jack was right. Quinn was a full-on style maven. Her blond hair was pulled up, a few loose strands framing her face. Because who doesn't rock a perfectly coiffed updo on a Saturday afternoon? Her faded, skintight jeans showed off her long legs, and that sheer blouse… Lacey had to work to tear her eyes away.

Okay, so the scenery wouldn't be so bad, inside the house and out. She finally forced a smile. "Jack said I'm supposed to get to know you."

"That won't be necessary," Quinn said. "And I don't want you getting cozy with my assistant, either. You'll meet her soon, but she knows nothing about this. I keep my relationship with her very professional. We don't go to movies together and she doesn't run my bath for me."

Lacey sighed. "Yeah, I never had one of those. Two decades in the business and I've never had a fucking assistant."

Quinn sat on the sofa, motioning for Lacey to do the same. "You like that word."

"The F-word? Does it offend your fragile sensibilities?" There was that sarcastic tone again. She'd have to work on that.

Quinn chuckled. "No, it doesn't offend me. And honestly, all this anger makes it really easy for me to not like you, which is probably for the best. Frankly, I'd rather *act* chummy with you than *be* chummy with you."

Lacey wanted to say it again. *Fuck you, Quinn Kincaid. Fuck you and this stupid idea and also, fuck you for thinking anyone gives a flying fuck about your fucking sexuality.* Except Lacey knew better. Of course people cared. Agents cared, producers cared, casting agents cared, the audience cared. "Sorry," she said, her eyes on her hands. "I guess I didn't realize how bitter I really am. Even I don't like being around me sometimes."

Quinn's only reaction was a slight smile. "My inner circle is small, and I'd like to keep it that way. This house is my refuge. I don't host big parties here. My family lives on the East Coast and they rarely visit. We usually meet in Aspen for the holidays. My assistant meets me on the set, so you being here is kind of a big deal."

"I'm honored," Lacey said. Her eyes wandered around the room. After she'd left the day before, she tried to remember if she'd seen any family photos in the living room. Looking around again, she didn't find any.

"No, you're not, and that's okay. The last thing I need is someone worshipping the ground I walk on and then committing suicide when I kick them out."

Lacey huffed out a laugh. "Good God. That's a bit..."

"Charming?"

"Predictable."

"Whatever," Quinn said with a wave of her hand. "I imagine you'll take the money and run without so much as a good-bye. Jack knows his stuff."

Lacey met Quinn's gaze. "Are you sure you want to do this? I mean, why not just..."

"Just what, Lacey? Keep living a lie? Why did *you* come out? Surely you knew the risks."

"Actually, I had no idea it would be as bad as it was," Lacey admitted. "And if you must know, I did it for my girlfriend. We had a good life. We were out in our private lives, just not at my work. Neither of us knew the toll it would take."

Quinn leaned forward, softening her tone. "If you're not up for this, you need to tell me. You're obviously still healing."

Healing? Lacey wasn't healing, she was surviving. Rock bottom didn't seem that far away. Or, maybe *this* was rock bottom—being Quinn Kincaid's fake—oh God, was she really going to do this? Yes. Yes, she was. And if she couldn't look herself in the mirror for a while, that was okay too. At least she wouldn't have to see the angry, bitter person she'd become. "I have nothing to lose. I've already lost it all. But with this, maybe I can get my life back." Lacey fought like hell to keep the tears at bay, but she couldn't keep her voice from quivering. "I just know so much is missing. And I need a good job. I was the breadwinner."

"Wait. Hold up. Did she leave you because you got fired?"

Lacey couldn't hold Quinn's gaze. "It's way more complicated than that."

"Is it?" Quinn asked.

Good question. Lacey didn't have the answer, and she certainly didn't want to think too hard about it. She just wanted her life back, including her girlfriend. And on top of that, she was angry at herself for divulging so much personal information. She straightened her shoulders and forced a somewhat pleasant smile. "If you don't mind, Quinn, I'd rather not talk about her."

"I probably wouldn't either."

"Excuse me? Quinn, you *literally* live in a glass house." Lacey gestured with her hand toward the massive window. "Maybe you're not in a position to make judgments about your fake girlfriend's very real ex-girlfriend."

"I'm sorry. That was out of line. Let's keep it professional." Quinn stood up and walked into the kitchen. Lacey breathed a sigh of relief and followed her. "My assistant will be told that you're traveling back and forth between coasts at the moment, so I offered you the guesthouse. This is the kitchen."

Lacey sat at the breakfast bar. She stifled a laugh at Quinn's introduction to her house and smiled brightly. "Yes, I recognize a kitchen when I see one."

Quinn put her hand on her hip. "So much for sophisticated New York humor. Are you sure you're not from New Jersey?"

Lacey waved her hand as she let the laughter go. Laughing was easier than crying. "I'm sorry. I promise I'm not always like this."

"And I promise I'm not the enemy."

"Right." Lacey pointed at Quinn and winked. "Not the enemy. I'll try to keep that in mind." She giggled again, relieving some of the pressure in the room. "Sorry. I still can't believe we're actually going to do this."

Smiling, Quinn said, "You have a cute giggle. It makes up for the…" She shook her head. "Never mind. There's something I wanted to ask you." She leaned down, resting her elbows on the other side of the breakfast bar so they were eye to eye. "You mentioned a vibe, and I've been wondering—"

"Oh, the gay vibe?" Lacey asked, interrupting her. "Yeah, you made the mistake of taking off your ever so stylish sunglasses."

"So…I looked at you wrong?"

"I wouldn't say wrong."

Quinn covered her eyes for a second. "Oh God, what did I do?"

Lacey laughed under her breath. Was Quinn really this clueless? "Well, straight girls admire earrings and hair styles, but that's not where your eyes went."

"Where did they go?"

"I'm pretty sure you know."

"I should've been more discreet." A blush started creeping up Quinn's neck. She straightened back up and tried to cover it with her hand.

"You like my lips." Lacey was having fun now. She'd found a weakness and she sure as hell was going to exploit it. "A lot."

Quinn shot her a glare. "Don't flirt with me. We're keeping this professional, remember?"

"Oh, come on, Quinn. I wouldn't be here if you didn't find me attractive. And besides, I'm not flirting. You asked, and I'm telling you what gave you away. Your eyes lingered where straight girl's eyes don't. And not like a man. Men have one focus, but women like it all… and cleavage too…but that's not the only thing they look at."

Quinn nodded sheepishly. "You have nice arms."

"Now who's flirting?" Lacey teased her.

"I'm just saying that I noticed them that day." Quinn gestured with her finger at Lacey's arms. "You were wearing a sleeveless shirt and I noticed."

Hmm…this was interesting. Quinn was full-on blushing from cheeks to chest. "And you have incredibly distracting eyes," Lacey said in a low, sexy voice she hadn't heard herself use in quite some time.

Quinn looked away again. "You wouldn't know that if I'd kept my sunglasses on. Or anything else about me."

"I couldn't stop looking at them. That's how I know where they went."

Quinn cleared her throat and put up her hand. "Okay, this conversation…"

"Scares you?"

Quinn folded her arms, standing in a protective stance. "Cards on the table?"

Lacey motioned with her hand as if she were a dealer in Vegas. "Lay 'em out."

"We're not going to fuck. Ever. Contract or not. Yes, you're beautiful, and I will have no problem selling this, but that's where it ends."

Lacey chuckled. "So you *can* say the word. And I told you, I'm in love with someone else, but once again, I find your arrogance amusing."

"I'm not arrogant." Quinn took a deep breath. "I'm scared, okay? I don't want to lose everything I've worked so hard for."

"Then don't do this coming out thing. Nobody is forcing you to risk everything. For what, Quinn? You're not even in a relationship. No one's saying, 'If you really loved me, you'd tell everyone.' "

"Are you trying to talk yourself out of a job? Because—"

Lacey put up her hands. "You're right. You know what you're doing, and like I said, I've got nothing to lose."

CHAPTER FOUR

Quinn desperately wanted to back out of the deal. Truth be told, she figured Jack wouldn't be able to find someone with the right qualities. Known, but not famous. In need of the work, but not desperate for it. Unattached. Gay. Gorgeous. Why was Jack so damn good at his job? As if anything about this was his job.

Quinn knew she needed someone who wouldn't worship the ground she walked on. Even other actors could sometimes act like rabid fans, and that would get old faster than Lacey's cynicism. What bothered her was the way this woman looked at her, with eyes that seared into her soul, reading every secret, every vulnerability she had. And then laughing at it. Mocking it with her eyes and that sly little grin. It was unnerving. It was also untrue. *Eyes that seared?* Quinn realized she was being ridiculous.

On second thought, maybe a fan was exactly what Quinn needed. Someone young in the business who would hang on her every word. Someone who would listen to her and follow instructions without hesitation because they came from the mouth of the very successful, very famous Quinn Kincaid.

Lacey Matthews was the exact opposite of that. God. Had she and Jack made the wrong choice?

Quinn stood there frozen, wondering how to end this deal here and now. She tracked Lacey as she sauntered over to the sliding glass door. A fan wouldn't saunter. She'd wait for further instruction, eyes wide like a hungry puppy dog.

Not Lacey. She opened the door and let the warm sun hit her face. "I can't wait to get out of that hotel I've been staying in," she said, leaning against the door frame.

Quinn walked over and stood next to her, her arms protectively folded like they'd been most of the morning. "Don't you have friends here?"

"I do, but as you can see, I'm a total bitch right now and I didn't want to have to be the nice houseguest. You can't just take their bedroom, you have to play with their kids and eat dinner and smile. A hotel was easier."

"You need to heal," Quinn said. Lacey looked at her with those big, brown eyes and Quinn quickly looked away. Lacey Matthews was the one for the job, whether Quinn liked it or not. Even though she rubbed Quinn the wrong way, Lacey seemed honest and forthright, not to mention strong. Yes, Lacey had been through a lot this past year, but Quinn could see her underlying strength. In fact, she found it more attractive than she would ever admit. Because that's not what this was, nor would it ever be. This was a business deal. Period.

Quinn stepped outside. "Just relax for a while. Get your bearings, and in a few months, you can take on the world again."

Lacey kicked off her sandals. She dipped a toe in the pool and then turned back around. "Cards on the table?" Quinn nodded. Lacey hesitated for a few seconds and then said, "I really need that."

Quinn could tell that was a hard thing for Lacey to admit. She was trying to hide it well, but the pain of what she'd been through was evident. Taking Lacey by the elbow, she said, "Good. Come with me. I think you'll like your new digs." She led Lacey past the pool to a small guesthouse. "You'll have complete privacy out here, and everything is brand new. You'll be the first one to stay out here since it was renovated a while back."

Lacey walked in, her eyes wide with shock. "This is bigger than my apartment in New York. And a full kitchen too? I love to cook."

"That makes one of us. I'm a terrible cook." Quinn stood back, feeling proud of the renovation. She'd worked closely with the designer to make the house, including the guesthouse, more her style: clean and modern. She'd purchased the house purely for its privacy and security, not because she loved it. But looking at it now, and seeing it through Lacey's eyes, she felt a sense of satisfaction that she'd made the right choice.

Lacey ran her fingers across the white marble countertops. "Do you have a workout room too?"

Quinn pointed over her shoulder with her thumb. "Those hills behind us. That's where I ride my bike."

"I'm more of a treadmill girl. Too much traffic in New York."

"I'll ask Amy to get right on that." Quinn pulled an index card out of her back pocket and looked at it, hesitating slightly. This was it. Once she handed this card to Lacey, it was pretty much a done deal. She looked Lacey in the eye and offered the card to her. "Here are the security codes for the doors and the gates. They're all different, so put them in your phone or something."

Lacey took the card. "Thank you for trusting me."

Quinn shook her head. "I don't. I'm scared shitless that you'll turn on me, but we're in this now and I need you." Quinn hoped Lacey could hear the sincerity in her voice and take her seriously. She hoped she'd understand just how serious this was and act accordingly. And she prayed for a good outcome.

"Are we good?" Quinn asked.

Lacey still wasn't sure why Quinn felt the need to follow through with this crazy plan, or even that it would achieve her goal. Hollywood was a very fickle town, after all. But that wasn't her concern. She took another quick glance around the guesthouse. "I need my career back, and if this is what it takes, I'm all in."

"Good!" Quinn said, looking rather relieved. "On to business, then. I start shooting season six in two weeks, so we'll go out a few times before then for photo ops."

"How do you know the paparazzi will be there?"

"Jack will handle that part."

"So, you'll let me know what to wear for those photo ops?"

Quinn looked Lacey up and down. "You'll go to my stylist this week and she'll set you up. We'll do some casual stuff and a little more formal as well. I'd like to take you to a friend's wedding this weekend, if you're up for it. Again, just as friends."

"Whatever you need," Lacey said with a smile.

Quinn eyed her skeptically. "Why so nice all of a sudden? Surely you want to give me crap about dressing you."

Lacey grinned. "Jack said I can keep the clothes."

"Ah. I knew there had to be an ulterior motive." Quinn tried not to smile back, but the effort proved impossible.

Lacey bit her lip. "And the Range Rover."

"Wow!" Quinn chuckled. "Are there any other demands I should know about?"

"Don't expect anything of me in private."

The smile quickly left Quinn's face, along with the positive energy they'd managed to have in the room for about five seconds. "Now who's being arrogant?"

"Whatever. Just…when I'm on set, so to speak, I'll shine for you. That's all I'm saying."

"And off camera, you'll be angry and bitter. Got it."

Lacey grabbed Quinn's arm as she tried to leave. "Look, I just…"

"It doesn't matter," Quinn said, shooting her a glare. "Do your thing when we're in public. That's all I ask."

"I will. I promise. And I'm sorry that I'm coming across like a complete bitch. This is just a crazy situation, you know?"

"I know," Quinn replied, softening her tone. "Look, I'm sorry I told you we'd never fuck. I mean, we won't, of course. But I'm sorry I said it like that. It was rude."

"Don't worry," Lacey said, smiling. "It hurt more when I heard we wouldn't be *canoodling* in public."

Quinn laughed. "God, you're something else." She pointed toward the door. "Should we go get your things?"

"I don't have much. Just the suitcase and carry-on I brought to the main house." She finished the sentence off with a stuffy British accent. Quinn rewarded her with a smile she was trying very hard to suppress.

They walked side by side past the pool, Lacey with her hands tucked into her pockets. Quinn was about the same height as her ex-girlfriend, so just a few inches shorter than Lacey. She could easily put her arm around her shoulders, and Quinn's arm could wrap around her waist. When the time came, that's the way they should walk for the cameras. Lacey grinned, thinking it might be rather fun to put on this little charade, blocking the scenes, right down to how they held hands. Maybe this actually could feel like real acting work.

"Is something funny?" Quinn asked.

"No." Lacey picked up both bags. "I've got this. See you in the morning?"

"I stocked the fridge for you, but the coffeemaker in the main house is much better, so feel free to come in and use it."

"Well, I do love good coffee. And I've always wanted an excuse to say 'the main house,' so you're on."

Lacey took her luggage to the guesthouse, dropped it by the bed, and then went back to the door. She leaned against the doorframe, taking in the beauty of the backyard. It looked like a resort with the gorgeous pool and lounge chairs with thick white cushions she could sink into. And why waste a single second of my time here, she thought.

It took about thirty seconds for her to change into a bikini. She'd only brought the one—a simple, black style that was comfortable and fit well enough to do laps. And this pool was certainly long enough to do laps. She'd have to go shopping for a few more swimsuit options. Maybe something more colorful, more "California."

Lacey looked at herself in the mirror. She'd always had a nice body. Long legs, flat stomach, nice ass. Even with the pressures the soap world put on women to enhance their beauty, she'd managed to stay natural. She didn't need breast implants. Her tits were fine. Not too big, not too small. One of the producers had suggested she try to plump up her lips a little bit and she all but told him to fuck off.

No, Lacey Matthews would never succumb to the pressures of producers and directors, most of whom looked like they'd never seen a green smoothie or a vitamin, or even a salad in their lifetimes. Assholes.

Lacey walked outside and threw a towel on one of the lounge chairs. She stood at the edge of the pool, staring down into the calm water. "This could be the easiest job I've ever had," she said to herself, right before diving into the pool.

CHAPTER FIVE

Lacey didn't want to get out of bed. She couldn't remember the last time she'd slept straight through until morning. It was eerily silent. No car alarms or garbage trucks or horns honking—the sounds that punctuated her memories of growing up in New York City. Not even the sound of gardeners, which seemed to be L.A.'s unique soundtrack. Just silence. Oh, and a bird chirping somewhere in the distance.

She'd left the privacy curtains open, giving her a view of the pool through the French doors. What a view to wake up to, she thought. She rolled over and checked her phone. The first thing she saw was a text from Jack.

We're at the hospital. Beverly & San Vincente. Get here as soon as you can.

What the fuck? She quickly typed a reply and then jumped in the shower. She'd planned on spending the day in her swimsuit while she caught up on her laundry. Everything was dirty. "Shit!"

What the hell was she going to wear? She got out of the shower and dug through her suitcase. The only clean thing she had was a blue, flowery skirt she'd yet to wear, mostly because she hated it. It was too high-waisted, but she'd brought it just in case...actually, she had no idea why she'd brought it. *Shit.*

She put on the skirt and a bra and went into the main house. She had no idea where Quinn's bedroom was. She scanned the main floor and decided it had to be upstairs. She opened the first door and found what was obviously a guest room. It looked too sterile to actually be lived in. She closed that door and went to the next. *Bingo.*

Immediately drawn to the floor-to-ceiling windows on the far side of the room, Lacey pushed a white sheer curtain to the side and discovered a balcony with a breathtaking view of the ocean. She wanted to step out onto that balcony, but she stopped when she remembered she wasn't yet fully clothed. That, and she was expected to be at the hospital soon. She turned back around and scanned the room. The bed was made up, the feather duvet carefully tucked in at the ends. Huh. That seemed strange since as far as Lacey knew, Quinn didn't have a live-in housekeeper. Were those hospital corners the work of Quinn Kincaid herself? "God, she's tidy."

Lacey went into the bathroom. It smelled like Quinn; soft vanilla-ish something or other, and it was just as tidy as the bedroom. The only thing sitting on the two-sink countertop was a toothbrush resting on a neatly folded white towel with the toothpaste tube evenly lined up next to it. On the other side of the room was a huge bathtub that Lacey eyed with envy, since it was a luxury few New Yorkers had.

She flipped the light switch on for the closet and the whole room lit up. "Holy shit!" Shoes were neatly stacked on special lighted shelves. The clothes seemed to be color coordinated and separated according to season. *Jesus, Quinn. OCD much?*

She rifled haphazardly through a rack that seemed to be strictly summer blouses and found a short-sleeved white gypsy-style blouse. She quickly put it on and shrugged at herself in the mirror. It didn't look great with the skirt, but it would have to do. She looked at the rack again and noticed the mess she'd made. Most of the blouses had been pushed to one side and were no longer equally spaced. She tried to separate them but quickly gave up. "Aw, screw it." She didn't have the patience for such ridiculous perfection. Besides, it might do Quinn some good to see a shirt or two askew.

She went back into the bathroom and looked in the mirror. No makeup. Wet hair. She opened a drawer and found more perfection. "Who the hell keeps their makeup drawer so organized?" She picked up a blush brush and ran it over her cheeks, then tied her long, wet hair up into a ponytail. Again, it would have to do.

Fucking traffic. By the time Lacey walked into the hospital, she was frazzled and hungry and in desperate need of a cup of coffee. She saw Jack sitting in the lobby and headed in his direction. "What happened?" she impatiently asked.

Jack took her by the arm and led her to the elevators. "Quinn broke her arm this morning, mountain biking. It's pretty gruesome."

"Oh my God." Lacey stopped dead in her tracks.

Jack took her arm again and kept walking. "She's just come out of surgery and we have her on a private floor. I'm going to put out a statement in about an hour."

"Jack, you didn't need to call me down here to tell me the deal's off. It's cool. I get it." Lacey hadn't even unpacked yet, unless you counted all the clothes she'd tossed around looking for something clean to wear. God, if Quinn saw her guesthouse right now, she'd be horrified. Actually, if Quinn saw her own closet right now, she'd be even more horrified. Lacey suddenly felt like a kid whose mom was about to find out she'd broken the lamp.

"Our deal's not off," Jack said. "Not yet, anyway. I'm still going over our options, but we figured we better have you here for the show in case we decide to go forward with this."

"You can't be serious, Jack. She needs to focus on getting better, not on some fantasy you invented."

Jack held the elevator door open. "Oh, for God's sake, Lacey, it's a broken arm, not the end of the world. Just come up with me and we'll work it out. Trust me, she wants you here."

Lacey stared at him, not sure what to do. He motioned with his head for her to get in the elevator. Against her better judgment, she did.

Two hours later, Lacey was still sitting in the waiting room. Jack walked in and waved her over. "She'll see you now."

Three cups of bad hospital coffee, a dying phone battery, and an uncomfortable chair had made Lacey cranky. And on top of that, none of this made any sense. She got up and brushed past him, walking down the hall faster than necessary. "This is ridiculous. She has no business worrying about coming out of the damn closet right now."

Jack grabbed Lacey by the arm. "Slow down, honey, and if you don't mind keeping your voice down just a little, that would be great."

Lacey pulled her arm away. "I'm not your honey, Jack. And I thought you said this was a private floor."

"Private. Not empty."

Lacey stopped and took a deep breath. "Sorry. Where is she?"

Jack opened the door to Quinn's room. "Just hear her out and then let me know your decision."

Lacey slowly walked into the room and stood at the foot of the bed. She put her hand over her mouth to stifle a gasp. Quinn looked like hell. She had scratches on her face, a black eye, and a big friggin' cast on her arm that was being propped up with pillows. This wasn't good, and Lacey felt like an intruder. She took a few steps back, hoping to get out of there without being noticed, but Quinn opened her eyes. Well, one eye. "Hi," Lacey said, giving her a little wave.

Quinn motioned that she wanted Lacey to come closer with a very limp wave of her hand. Lacey stood at the side of the bed, gripping the safety bar. It was even worse up close. Quinn's left eye was swollen shut and she had several nasty-looking bruises on her good arm. Lacey wasn't sure what to say. She swallowed hard and was about to make a joke to lighten the moment when Quinn said. "Do I look as bad as your face says I look?"

"Worse," Lacey said, giving her a sympathetic smile.

"Fabulous." Quinn pointed at the lighted x-ray on the wall with her thumb. "Check that out."

Lacey grimaced. "Oh my God! Is that your arm?"

"What's left of it," Quinn slurred. "I hit sand and went head first over my bike, right onto a pile of boulders. Smashed my humerus. I'm lucky I didn't break my neck."

"I'm so sorry."

"Me too. Not the best timing."

Lacey reached out to touch Quinn but pulled her hand back. "Look, I totally understand if you want to back out of our deal. My feelings won't be hurt at all."

Quinn tried to laugh, but it came out as more of a drunk groan. "You have feelings?"

Lacey smirked. "Okay, I guess I deserved that."

Quinn closed her eyes, a faint smile on her lips. "These drugs are fantastic. And that blouse looks better on you than it does on me."

Wow, she doesn't miss a thing. "I, um, I was going to do laundry today, but something came up. Hope you don't mind that I found something in your closet. I promise I didn't move anything."

"No, that's…" Quinn's head slowly drooped to one side as she fell asleep mid-sentence.

Lacey plopped down into a chair and settled in to watch Quinn sleep. She was pretty sure the drugs were the only reason she didn't get reamed for going through Quinn's closet. She looked at the clock and then focused on her phone. She needed to start looking for auditions again. Surely Quinn's family, her friends, the people closest to her would descend on her house, leaving no room for Lacey or this stupid plan. She groaned when her phone took its last breath and went dark.

❖

"Hi, I'm Stephanie, Ms. Kincaid's nurse."

Lacey looked at the clock again. She'd been sitting there for half an hour. "Hi, Stephanie. I'm Quinn's...I'm Lacey."

Stephanie administered more pain meds and ran down her checklist. "Everything looks good, so I'll be back in thirty minutes."

Lacey stood up. "You'll make sure she stays medicated, right? You won't let the meds wear off?"

"I only have two patients today, so it won't be a problem."

"Thank you. I watched my mom suffer."

Stephanie nodded her understanding. "I won't let that happen."

There really wasn't any reason for Lacey to stay, since Quinn was so heavily medicated. And if there was one thing in this world Lacey hated, it was hospitals. Quinn was in good hands. Except why were there goose bumps on her arms? Was she cold? Lacey glanced around, looking for another blanket. She found one, along with a set of sheets and a pillow sitting on a recliner. Oh, God. They didn't expect her to sleep the night here, did they?

Lacey unfolded the blanket enough to cover Quinn's shoulders and arms.

"Thank you," Quinn whispered, her one good eye barely opening enough to focus on Lacey.

Her throat sounded so dry, Lacey picked up the mug of water and rested the straw on Quinn's lips. "Take a sip of water."

Quinn took a couple of sips and immediately fell back to sleep again. Lacey set the mug down and stood motionless for a moment. She couldn't be here. It brought back too many bad memories of her mother, lying helpless in a hospital bed, slowly dying.

Quinn wasn't dying. Lacey knew that. Still, it was too much. She wanted to say something. Some words of comfort. At least, a good-bye. But her own throat had dried up. "You'll be fine," she whispered, and then quickly left the room.

She went down to the cafeteria and poured herself a tall cup of coffee to take with her in the car. She wasn't about to go back into heavy traffic without one. She saw Jack sitting in a chair in the lobby as she was walking out. "She's too medicated to talk. I'll come back tomorrow," she told him without stopping.

Jack stood up. "Lacey, keep this under wraps, okay?"

Lacey stopped and turned around. She was angry that he'd forced her to be here when Quinn was obviously in no condition to even talk, let alone make a major decision. "Jesus, Jack. We still have a contract. I'm pretty sure that covers broken arms. Besides, who am I going to tell?"

Jack put up his hands. "Just sit tight until we figure out the next step."

Lacey stepped into his personal space and lowered her voice. "If you're really as good as you say you are, you'll convince your client that this whole thing is a bad idea. Especially now."

Lacey walked away but Jack followed her. "It's a good idea, Lacey. Hell, it's an even better idea now. And it's not over, so get back on board and earn your money."

Money. Lacey definitely needed some of that. The first payment wasn't supposed to hit her account for three more days. She stopped just outside the door and pulled the keys to her new Range Rover out of her purse. She stared at them for a second and then at Jack. She needed this gig whether she liked it or not. "What do you need from me? And please don't tell me I have to sleep in that damn recliner all night." She put her hand on her hip and chided herself. It was a selfish thing to say out loud and she knew it. "Is that what you need? What Quinn needs?"

"When you come to pick Quinn up in a few days and take her home, wear something nice." Jack looked her up and down. "Nicer than this. There will be cameras."

Lacey looked down at her ill-fitting skirt and worn-out leather sandals. She made a mental note to find the business card Quinn had given her with her stylist's phone number on it. Maybe it would be fun getting a new wardrobe. Maybe the stylist could give her a new attitude too. "Fine," she said. "Anything else?"

"Just be a good friend and drive her home in your fancy new car, okay?" He made little finger quotes around the word *friend.*

"Friend. Snazzy dresser. Got it." She headed toward her fancy new car and waved behind her. "Bye, Jack."

Lacey pulled into the driveway of her new home, the gate closing behind her, blocking out the whole world. She sat there for a moment, wondering how the hell she got here. She should be out there, getting in front of every casting director in town. Getting a name for herself in L.A.—not wasting precious time behind the walls of this mansion. Quinn could wake up and decide exactly what she *should* decide—

that this was a stupid plan concocted by her publicist and she should abandon it and fire him.

Lacey had it in writing, she reminded herself. An early termination bonus, plus the car. But Quinn would have to be the one to terminate the contract, not her. That meant she'd be sticking around for at least a few more days, so she might as well enjoy it. "Swimming pool, here I come," she mumbled as she got out of the car.

After putting her laundry in the fanciest washing machine she'd ever seen, Lacey turned a lounge chair toward the sun and sank into it, sighing deeply as her head hit the soft cushion, determined to enjoy the sun before it got too low in the sky.

On the drive back up the hill, Lacey had taken note of the neighbors' homes. She couldn't really see the actual homes, just the tall walls and secured gates. From her viewpoint in the backyard, she couldn't see any houses or rooflines peeking through the trees. It was completely private. "Well, in that case…" She untied her bikini top and took it off, grinning at herself for being so brave.

She lay there for a few minutes, taking in the heat of the sun and enjoying the peace and quiet. After her morning of heavy traffic and the long wait at the hospital, it felt heavenly. Her phone rang, pulling her out of her reverie. "Shit," she said, looking at the caller ID. She quickly grabbed her top and tried to cover herself, as if the person calling could see her lying there, topless. "Hey, Dad."

"Hi, honey. Just checking in. Any luck today?"

"Um…maybe." She got up and made her way into the guesthouse, throwing on a bathrobe.

"It's always maybe with those people. Always, we'll get back to you."

"I know, but this might be different. I mean, it is different, but there's been a slight glitch, so I can't really confirm yet."

"I don't understand," her dad said, his voice tightening.

"I can't really say anything more yet. I signed a nondisclosure."

"Oh. Well, that sounds promising. I guess if you're sworn to secrecy, I'd better find something else to talk about." He paused. "How's the weather out there?"

Lacey laughed. "It's nice. Really nice." She figured it wouldn't hurt to start working on the cover story. "And I made a friend. Do you watch *Jordan's Appeal*? It's that law show on Thursday nights."

"Yeah, I've seen it once or twice."

Lacey smiled. Her professor father hardly ever admitted to

watching television. He wouldn't even admit to watching her soap opera, but somehow, he magically knew exactly what was happening on the show at any given moment. "Well, it's Quinn Kincaid, the woman who plays Jordan Ellis. She's super nice. In fact, I'm staying at her place for a few days."

"You're kidding."

Lacey laughed. "Nope."

"She's almost as good an actress as my daughter."

"Aww, thank you, Daddy. I love you too."

"Quinn Kincaid. Wow. Someday you'll have to introduce me."

Lacey missed her dad. She wanted to invite him right then and there to come out to L.A. but she wasn't sure what would happen in the next few days. "Maybe I'll bring her to New York sometime. I'm sure she'd love to meet my very smart, very handsome father."

Her father chuckled. "Okay, kiddo. I'm glad to hear you're staying with her. I worry about you staying in that hotel. It's not in the best neighborhood."

"Dad, we've been over this. First, you don't even know the neighborhoods in L.A. Second, I can take care of myself, so don't worry, okay?"

"It's my job as your father to worry, no matter how old you are. Get used to it. There's no woman good enough for my little girl, and there's no neighborhood safe enough." He chuckled at himself for a moment. "Oh! I've got to go. Class is starting soon. Take care, honey. Love you."

"Love you too, Dad. Bye."

Lacey went back outside and took off the bathrobe. She dipped her foot in the pool and then dove in, still topless. She came up out of the water for a breath and looked around again. There really wasn't anyplace in all of L.A. that would feel safer than Quinn Kincaid's fortress. Her dad could rest easy. And so could she.

Lacey checked her watch. It was late. She walked up to the nurse's station. "I'm here to see Quinn Kincaid."

"Your name?"

"Lacey Matthews."

The nurse looked at her clipboard. "Yes, you're on the list. I'll need to see your ID."

Thank God, Jack had put her on the list. After lounging by the pool and making herself a fabulous dinner of salmon, roasted potatoes, and white wine, the guilt had set in. So here Lacey was, back at the hospital. She signed in and slowly made her way to Quinn's room, not even sure she was doing the right thing. Would Quinn even want her there?

The room was dark, except for a dim light coming from the bathroom. Quinn was whimpering in her sleep. Lacey leaned over the bed, trying to get a closer look. "Are you in pain?" she whispered.

Quinn stilled and opened her eyes. Well, only one eye actually opened. "No," she whispered back. "Bad dream, I think."

Laccy went to the sink and wet down a washcloth with cold water. She dabbed Quinn's sweaty forehead and red cheeks.

"Thank you," Quinn whispered. "That feels good." She reached up and tried to touch her blackened eye. "Why won't my eye open?"

Laccy took her hand and held onto it. "You have a shiner. Don't touch it, okay?"

"A shiner? You sound like you're in *West Side Story*." Quinn laughed, but it quickly turned into tears. "Oh, God. Really?"

"Hey, it's cool," Lacey said, giving Quinn's hand a gentle squeeze. "You look like Rocky."

Quinn opened her good eye wide, taking a long look at Lacey. "You're that woman."

"I beg your pardon?" Quinn was heavily medicated, but did she really not recognize her?

"Yo, Lacey," Quinn said, imitating Rocky. She smiled and closed her good eye. Within seconds, she was asleep again.

Lacey laughed under her breath as she sat on the edge of the bed, her hand still firmly wrapped around Quinn's. She could let go, but Quinn's hand felt cold, so she covered it with both of hers. Startled, she jumped when the nurse walked in. "Hi. I was just...um..." She gently set Quinn's hand on her stomach and backed away from the bed. She didn't belong here. Not really. Someone else should be holding Quinn's hand, not her. "She likes a cold washcloth," she blurted out in a loud whisper. "On her forehead. It...you know...soothes her."

The nurse nodded. "Okay. Maybe when she wakes up."

Lacey took a final look at Quinn. She was resting peacefully. That was good. She could go back to the mansion now, and maybe get some guilt-free rest. "Take care," she whispered.

CHAPTER SIX

Quinn read the last card and put it back in the envelope. Her hospital room was full of bouquets and balloons from the cast and crew, friends and acquaintances, and even a few fans. Her assistant, Amy, had stopped by several times, relaying everyone's messages of love and concern. She appreciated all of it, but she didn't want visitors and she'd told Amy so. Just keep everyone away, she'd told her. Maybe it was rude, but she just wanted to go home and regain some of her privacy. She felt vulnerable in this hospital room. Even though it was a private floor, anyone could get in if they really wanted to.

"Wow," Lacey exclaimed as she walked into the room. "It looks like someone bought out the florist downstairs."

Quinn grinned from ear to ear. "You're certainly a sight for sore eyes." She motioned with her hand up and down Lacey's body. "Is all that for me?" It was obvious Lacey had taken some time in the mirror. Her hair was blown straight, she had soft "daytime" makeup on, and her white skinny jeans fit her like a glove, hugging her in all the right places.

"You know why I'm dressed up."

Quinn tried to sit up a little bit, but she had no strength. "Actually, I don't even know why you're here. But you look fantastic."

Lacey furrowed her brow. "I'm taking you home. Jack asked me—oh my God, do you two even talk?"

"I've been a little under the weather the last few days. And high on cocaine, or whatever it is they've been shooting into my arm."

Lacey pulled up a chair and sat next to the bed. Her eyes scanned Quinn's face. "You're looking a little better. Both eyes are working… sort of. And your color is back. How are you feeling?"

Quinn didn't want to think about how torn up her face was. She hadn't looked in a mirror yet, but she knew it was bad just by the way Jack and Amy had looked at her. She knew one eye was black because Jack had referred to it as a shiner. She was pretty sure she'd had a dream about Lacey saying the same thing.

She could feel the small lacerations on her cheeks and forehead, probably from the prickly bushes she'd landed in. She figured she could look in the mirror and cry about it once she was back home. In the meantime, she wanted to turn her attention back to her fake girlfriend. "You look tan. Have you been sipping drinks poolside?"

Lacey glanced at her bare arms. "Maybe. And clothes shopping," she said with a shrug. "I'm a Kardashian now. It's what we do. That, and sunbathe naked in Quinn Kincaid's backyard."

Quinn's good eye widened in surprise. "No." Her mouth hung open for a second. "What about drones?" She hardly ever used her backyard, but being naked back there would absolutely never ever happen. With her luck, a drone would fly overhead and her tits would be plastered all over the internet within hours.

"Drones?" Lacey got a quizzical look on her face. "You think people fly drones over your house? Isn't that illegal?"

"You never know. Better safe than sorry."

"Well," Lacey wagged her eyebrows, "they've had a great show the last few days."

Quinn smiled. Lacey seemed more relaxed. Maybe even…happy. "Did you say you're taking me home?"

"Yes. I got a text from Jack."

Quinn let her eyes wander down Lacey's body. The first two buttons on the sleeveless black silk blouse were undone, allowing a little bit of cleavage to show. "Will you be my nurse too?"

Lacey rolled her eyes and laughed. "Oh, God. You *must* be feeling better."

"Well, I'm not hallucinating anymore. I mean, seriously, what is the appeal with heavy drugs? I felt like I was losing my mind. And they make my face itch."

"I really couldn't tell you. I was a good girl."

"Oh yeah?" Quinn asked with a raised eyebrow. "You're destroying my image of child stars. I thought you were all doing acid by the age of ten."

Lacey shook her head. "Nope. For me, it was work, not play. I have a very strict father."

"What about your mother?"

"What about getting you out of here?" Lacey asked, trying to change the subject. "That's what I'm here for, although I never imagined my career track would lead to being a chauffeur."

"They should be here any minute to discharge me." Quinn casually wiped the sweat from her brow. Just trying to find a comfortable position for her broken arm completely wore her out, but she was trying her best to hide it. She was still on heavy pain meds, but not so heavy that they knocked her completely out.

"And what about at home?" Lacey asked. "Do you have a nurse lined up? Your mom? A sister, maybe?"

Quinn bit her lip and smiled. "I was hoping..."

Lacey's eyes widened. "Oh, no. No, no, no, Quinn. I'm not a fu— I'm not a nurse."

Quinn shook her finger at Lacey. "You were going to use that word again."

"I know. I'm working on trying not to sound so harsh. This is California, not New York."

Quinn laughed, which made her grimace in pain. "Good luck with that."

Lacey leaned forward in her chair, grabbing the safety bar on the bed. "Seriously, Quinn. You need to hire a nurse. Or what about family? Let's just put everything on hold and you can have your mother come and stay with you."

Quinn huffed. "My mother and her politics would drive me crazy. Come on, Lacey. I need you. I'll pay extra."

"I'm not a nurse!" Lacey said, throwing her hands in the air. "You need someone who knows what they're doing! Someone who cares about you!"

Quinn turned away.

"Oh, God." Lacey rested her hand on Quinn's shoulder. "That came out wrong. Look, I'm an actor. I'm not a nurse."

"But you played one on TV. Maybe you could act like you have *some* capacity for empathy."

"See, this is exactly why I shouldn't be your nursemaid. The level of care would be...not up to par."

"I disagree," Quinn said. "I think given the right incentive, I'd be very well taken care of."

Lacey shook her head. "Quinn..."

"You're smart, Lacey. Sassy as hell, with a chip on your shoulder the size of Texas, but smart. So why don't you come up with a way that makes this a win-win, because I really don't want to hold up progress on our plan just because I broke my arm. And I sure as hell don't want more houseguests."

"I'm sorry, but how are you even going to start shooting the next season? You've got what…a week and a half?"

Quinn was worried about that too. She needed to heal up. And fast. "They'll write it into the script. I'm always beating the crap out of that pissy little DA. Maybe he returns the favor. Literally. Anyway, I can't delay it."

Lacey bit her thumbnail as she thought about it. "But will you be ready?" She glanced over at the X-rays that were still hanging on the wall, the new one displaying several screws and two metal rods holding Quinn's bone together. "It's a pretty bad break."

"See, Lacey, you're practically a radiologist already," Quinn quipped. "Just give it a shot. You know how I feel about strangers in my home."

Lacey stood up and started pacing. "You're so paranoid."

"I have my reasons. And if someone like my mom is in the house, you'll have to move out for the plan to work. And it looks to me like you've become accustomed to a certain lifestyle these past few days."

Lacey paced for another minute, glancing at Quinn every so often. Eventually, she walked over to the bed and leaned down so they were face-to-face. "I'll do it on one condition. And it's a pretty big goddamned condition."

Quinn smiled up at her. "That didn't take long. And you smell good, by the way."

"Shut up and listen, because the only thing that would make it worth me babysitting your sorry ass is you getting your producers to give me a part on your show."

"Wow, you're even smarter than I thought you were. Done."

"I'm not finished. I have a story idea, but let me flesh it out before I pitch it to you."

"Just get me out of here first." Quinn put out her hand so Lacey could help her get out of bed. "You can flesh all you want poolside."

Lacey didn't take Quinn's outstretched hand. She wanted more assurances. "Tell me you have enough pull to make this happen."

"Look, I can't make any promises. You know that's not how it works. Actors don't write storylines." Quinn dropped her hand. She didn't have the strength to keep it up in the air. "That having been said, it's my show, Lace. Does anyone call you Lace? I don't have enough strength to add the *y* on."

"You can call me whatever the hell you want if you can make this happen, but my producers never let me pitch anything—"

"Thank God," Quinn said, interrupting her. "I'd hate to think you had anything to do with that storyline."

Lacey wagged her finger at Quinn. "So, you *have* seen it! Should I be flattered?"

"I watched a few episodes on YouTube last night. Fascinating stuff."

Lacey rolled her eyes. "Yeah, yeah, everyone's a damn critic."

"I was looking at the acting, not the storyline."

Lacey hesitated to ask. "And?"

"Sarah Fucking Covington is one messed-up bitch, but you, Lacey, are—"

Quinn was interrupted by the nurse rolling in a wheelchair. "Who's ready to leave this joint?"

Quinn looked at Lacey and smiled as she finished her sentence. "A brilliant actor."

Lacey sprang into action, pulling the blankets back and helping Quinn sit up. "Sarah Fucking Covington is actually a doctor, thank you very much, but she did start out as a nurse. You'll be delighted to know I even have a uniform."

Quinn grimaced as she tried to work her way to the edge of the bed. "Will you wear it for me?"

Lacey helped Quinn to her feet. "Hell, no. I was just making conversation."

Quinn pointed to the bathroom and started shuffling in that direction. "You're a bitch sometimes, you know that?"

The nurse laughed at their conversation. "You two are a hoot!"

Lacey turned around and smiled as she helped Quinn into the bathroom. "This is us on a good day!"

The nurse tilted her head and pointed at Lacey. "Aren't you...?"

"Sarah Fucking Covington," Quinn said. "Nurse, doctor, brain surgeon, identical twin—"

"I knew it!" the nurse exclaimed.

Lacey pulled Quinn's gown up to help her onto the toilet. Quinn swatted her hand away. "I broke my arm, Nurse Covington, but I'm pretty sure I can pee on my own." She tried to sit down on her own and quickly grabbed Lacey's hand. "Okay, so maybe I do need help."

"Good God, this is going to cost you."

"Good thing I'm rich." Quinn closed her eyes and sighed as she relieved herself. "Whatever you want. It's yours."

Once Quinn was out of the bathroom, Lacey opened her large purse and pulled a few items out. "I tried to find something with big arm holes." She held up a ribbed tank top. Quinn nodded her approval. Lacey handed it to the nurse and turned away, giving them some privacy. When Quinn was dressed and the nurse gone, she turned back around and pulled a baseball cap out of her purse. It was a Yankees hat she'd had since she was in high school. "I couldn't find a hat anywhere, but I thought you might want one since your hair is kind of...destroyed."

Quinn ran her hand over her blond hair, trying to smooth it down, but it was no use. Only a shower and some good conditioner would take care of those knots. "Yeah, I guess I'll need it."

"Don't lose it. It's my lucky hat." Lacey handed it to her and folded her arms, waiting for Quinn to put it on.

Quinn looked at the worn-out hat and grimaced. "Maybe I'll get it dry cleaned before I give it back to you."

Jack burst into the room. "Hello, ladies." He looked Lacey up and down and said, "Wow. A little effort goes a long way."

Lacey resisted the urge to flip him off.

He looked at Quinn, who was now sporting an old Yankees cap and a cast that went from her hand to her upper arm. "Maybe we should've had the stylist swing by the hospital room."

Quinn actually did flip him off. "Shut up, Jack." She looked up at Lacey with pleading eyes. "Can we do this, please?"

"Which part," Lacey asked. "The fake girlfriend, or..."

Quinn grabbed her hand and gave it a gentle squeeze. "Can you please take me home?"

"Yes," Lacey said with a nod. She wanted to make another joke about how much it would cost, but seeing the pleading look in Quinn's eyes stopped her. "Let's do this."

The sliding glass doors opened and cameras started flashing. They were all yelling for Quinn to look their way. Someone shouted, "Who's your friend, Quinn?" She kept her head down, letting the brim of the baseball cap cover her eyes as she gave them a little wave and thumbs-up.

Lacey looked shell-shocked at first, the cameras flashing in her eyes. Jack touched her arm, getting her attention. "You're blocked in. Let's get her in my car."

Even though Lacey had spent her life in the business, she'd never experienced any kind of paparazzi before. She quickly recovered and pushed the wheelchair to Jack's black Escalade and helped Quinn into the back seat. She buckled Quinn's seat belt and patted her hand. "I'll see you at home, okay?"

Quinn winced in pain as she tried to find a comfortable position for her arm. Lacey reached across her and put the middle armrest down. "Maybe this will help."

"Thank you." Quinn's faced contorted in pain as she moved her arm onto the rest. "God, it hurts," she whispered.

"Do you have your pain meds?"

Quinn winced again. "The scrip is in my pocket."

"Are you going to tell me which one or do I need to..." Lacey ran her hand up Quinn's jean-clad leg to her front pocket.

"Back pocket."

Their eyes met for a second and Lacey quickly moved her hand. "Right." She reached behind her and pulled out the prescription. "Got it."

"I'd make a joke about you enjoying that a little too much but I don't have the energy."

Lacey smirked. "Yeah, you're so damn sexy right now, with your greasy hair and...what is that smell?"

"Okay, ladies." Jack motioned with his head at the cameras.

Quinn reached for Lacey's arm. "See you at home?"

Quinn looked frightened. And honestly, she should be, considering she was going home to an empty house, with no one there to take care of her except Lacey. It was crazy. But Lacey had agreed to it, and she'd hold up her end of the deal. "Yeah. See you at home."

CHAPTER SEVEN

Jack stepped out the front door as Lacey pulled into the driveway. She got out of the car with the filled prescription in hand. "Sorry. The pharmacy was busy."

"She's on the sofa." Jack looked back at the house and paused for a moment, a look of concern evident in his eyes.

"What's wrong, Jack? Is she okay?" Lacey started to panic a little bit. "You can't leave me here alone with her if she's not okay. I have no idea what I'm doing."

"Calm down. She'll be fine," Jack assured her. "Quinn is a very private person. The only reason I'm here is because I'm one of the few people she really trusts in this world. And apparently, now she trusts you too."

Lacey slowly shook her head. "I have no idea why."

"Neither do I, quite frankly. She hardly knows you. And a signed nondisclosure hardly makes you qualified to take care of her."

"That's what I tried to tell her! Will you try to talk some sense into her?"

"It's not my decision." Jack pulled his keys out of his pocket and nervously shook them in his hand. "Look, if you need anything, call me first. I'll have groceries delivered tomorrow and I'll check in every so often, but I really think she wants to recover in private. No visitors. And don't take any photos of her face, even if it's just for fun. We don't need someone hacking your phone and selling them to the highest bidder."

"Got it. But what if family shows up?" Surely Quinn had family who would want to be involved in her recovery, or at least stop by to check on her well-being. Lacey didn't feel comfortable turning family away.

"She's an only child," Jack said. "Her parents are divorced. She's not very close to her dad. We've given them the heads-up, but she's putting her mother off, hoping she'll stay away." He opened his car door. "I'll call later tonight and see how it's going."

Lacey waited until the gate closed behind Jack's car and then went into the house. She found Quinn resting on the sofa. She sat on the coffee table and inspected Quinn closely, taking in her coloring and her chest rising and falling. She seemed to be resting well at the moment. Just when she was about to stand up, Quinn opened her eyes. "Do you need anything?" Lacey asked. "A glass of water? A blanket? Turn back time?"

Quinn didn't know where to start. She needed food so she could take more meds. She needed a bath. She needed to wash her hair. She needed to cry. "I stink," she whispered.

"Yeah, you do. I can smell you from here." Lacey jokingly put her finger under her nose.

"Will you help me?" Quinn's voice sounded weaker than it had in the hospital. She'd tried to be brave and act stronger than she really was, just so she could get out of there and come home. She was so happy to be home, but she had no strength to do anything except breathe, and even that hurt.

"Hmm…" Lacey said, considering the options. "What if I taped a trash bag to your arm and helped you shower?"

Quinn nodded, tears forming in her eyes. She wasn't sure if she was up to it, but she desperately wanted to be clean again. The nurses had done their best, but she still had dirt under her fingernails from the fall and she felt sticky all over. Not to mention her matted, greasy hair. "Let's give it a try."

The shower worked out okay. Quinn quickly had to accept the fact that Lacey would see her naked. There was no getting around it. Truth be told, with all of the bumps and bruises, it probably wasn't much of a show anyway. She tried to keep her back to Lacey as much as possible, letting her wash her hair and soap down her backside. They worked in silence, neither one in the mood to make jokes.

Lacey took a pair of scissors to an oversized T-shirt she found in the closet, cutting open the neck and sleeve so it was easier to put on. By the time Quinn got settled in bed, she was in a cold sweat again. Every move took all of her energy. Once she was truly settled and seemed to be comfortable, Lacey went back downstairs and heated up a can of soup and toasted a couple of slices of bread.

They ate together on Quinn's huge bed, watching *The Not So Late Show with Johnny Falcon.* "Have you met him?" Lacey asked.

"Yeah, I've been on his show a few times. He's always sweet to me."

Quinn was struggling to eat with her left hand. Lacey noticed and took over. "God, I even have to hand-feed you. What's next? Wiping your ass?"

"Would you rather clean up the mess I make from trying to wipe my ass with my left hand or just do it yourself?"

Lacey pulled the spoon away. "Are you serious?"

Quinn slowly nodded. "I'll pay you a thousand dollars to wipe my ass."

Lacey dropped the spoon in the soup. "I have my limits, you know. You can't just throw money at me and expect that I'll…"

"A million."

"Charmin or Cottonelle?"

"See? Everyone has a price."

Lacey shook her head in disbelief. "You realize there are nurses for this shit. Literally, a nurse would come here and do that for you for like…I don't know…fifty dollars."

Quinn just stared at her.

Lacey sighed. "Okay, fine. I don't know what the going rate is for ass wiping, but I'm pretty sure a real nurse would charge less than a thousand dollars."

"Give me another spoonful of soup. I need to take a pill."

Lacey reluctantly did as she was told. "I really don't understand why you don't want a professional. Is this some sort of power play?"

Emotion welled up in Quinn's eyes. "No. I promise, it's not." She knew none of this made any sense, but she wasn't sure she could explain how she felt without revealing too much of her life to Lacey, and she wasn't ready for that. "This house is the only place in this world I feel truly safe. I don't want strangers in my bedroom. I don't want people poking around. And one day I might not have a choice about that. But today, I do."

"But…I'm a stranger," Lacey said. "I poked around your closet and stole a blouse. You didn't even flinch when you saw me wearing it."

"Well, I was pretty high. Besides, you needed a blouse," Quinn said with a shrug. "Keep it. It looks cute on you."

Lacey shook her head in disbelief. "I don't understand you, but whatever. Open up." She filled the spoon and held it in front of Quinn's mouth. "And just so you know, I plan to charge per wipe."

Lacey was right. Had it been anyone else, Quinn would have been horrified, wondering which drawers had been rifled through and what photos had been taken of her underthings. She couldn't put into words how she felt when she fell off her bike and broke her arm. Someone saw it happen and called the ambulance for her. They found her phone in her pocket and asked who they could call. Her first thought was Lacey, but she hadn't memorized her number and Quinn sure as hell wasn't giving a total stranger the password to her phone.

As much as she didn't want to trust Lacey, as much as she wanted to keep her at a distance out in the guesthouse, something inside told her Lacey wouldn't betray her trust. Yes, she was a colossal pain in the ass, but her gut told her Lacey wouldn't take advantage of her. And Quinn had learned to trust her gut.

Lacey awoke with a start and sat up on the sofa. *Three a.m. Shit.* She was an hour late. She ran up the stairs to Quinn's room and opened the door. Even with the low lighting in the room she could see that Quinn's face was covered in sweat. "Thank God," Quinn whispered. She was shaking, almost like she was shivering.

"I'm sorry," Lacey said, grabbing the pain pills and filling a glass with water from the bathroom sink. She sat on the edge of the bed. "I'm so sorry," she said again, grabbing a packet of soda crackers. She broke a cracker in two and watched as Quinn ate it. Once Quinn had swallowed, she put the pills in Quinn's hand, but she was too shaky to do anything with them.

"Oh, God." Lacey took them back and put them in Quinn's mouth. She held the glass for her to drink and then blotted her forehead with a towel.

Quinn swallowed the pills and tried to settle her breathing. "Don't touch me. Don't move the bed," she breathed out, closing her eyes. "God, it hurts."

Lacey sat as still as she could, her heart pounding in her chest. She berated herself for thinking she could watch television and not fall asleep. "I'll set an alarm on my phone," she whispered.

"I couldn't reach my phone to call you. I think it fell off the bed," Quinn said, pointing at the floor.

"I'm so sorry," Lacey said again. "You need a real nurse, Quinn." No matter what the situation, Lacey couldn't stand seeing anyone in pain. Especially when it could be avoided.

Quinn rested her hand on Lacey's leg and closed her eyes. "No. I need you. Please stay."

Lacey waited until Quinn's breathing evened out before she dared move. She carefully stood up and backed away, a look of fear in her eyes and a big ball of guilt sitting heavy in her gut. She sat in an overstuffed chair in the corner, setting her alarm before she wrapped a quilt around herself.

She'd have a much-needed conversation with Quinn in the morning.

Lacey took the breakfast tray away and sat on the edge of the bed. They both had dark circles under their eyes from a lack of sleep, but Quinn was well medicated and seemed to be experiencing less pain at the moment.

"I'm going to try one more time to convince you to get a real nurse," Lacey said. Quinn tried to sit up. "But," Lacey put her hand on Quinn's good shoulder, keeping her where she was, "if you're so fucking determined to put us both through this hell," she set a folder on Quinn's lap, "then you're going to have to keep up your end of the bargain."

"What's this?"

"The idea I told you about in the hospital. You pitch this to your producers and you won't have to do this big coming out thing because you'll already be out and America will love it."

Quinn eyed Lacey suspiciously for a few seconds, then opened the folder. At the top of the page was written *A Story Arc for Jordan's Appeal*. Quinn read a few lines and smiled. "Shrewd. You're very shrewd."

"You like it?" Lacey's eyes were full of hope.

"I didn't say that. And this isn't a bit part for you, it's a recurring role."

"Okay, stop reading." Lacey grabbed the folder and held it against her chest. "Let me pitch it to you. Jordan is working on a big case when she has an accident. Car...bike...whatever...she breaks her arm. Turns her into a complete bitch."

Quinn cleared her throat and raised an eyebrow.

"What? It's fiction." Lacey tossed the folder on the bed and continued. "Now she needs help with everything. She can't drive, she can't type, she can't even get her fancy courtroom suit jackets on. So she picks a first-year associate in her firm to take on the job of being her little helper."

Quinn pointed at Lacey. "Your character."

"Yes. Only my character isn't flattered about being the chosen one. She's a Harvard Law grad and this is beneath her. She thinks one of the paralegals should be changing bandages, not someone who made fucking Law Review."

"So your character swears as much as you do? Sounds familiar. Let me guess. They bicker about it, which the audience loves, and Jordan says, either you help me or you're gone?"

"Exactly," Lacey replied, pointing a finger. "Except for the swearing. This is network TV. But there's this energy between them. This love-hate thing."

Quinn took the folder and opened it again. "More love than hate, from the look of things."

Feeling excited that Quinn could see her vision for the storyline, Lacey scooted a little closer and put her hand on Quinn's leg. "Here's the thing. We do this without the producers knowing it's coming, because then they'll think it's their idea. They'll see the chemistry between us… America will see it…and they'll want more."

Quinn chuckled. "Tell me more about this chemistry you think we have."

"Shut up. It's acting, remember? You're not the only one who watched YouTube. Turns out you're not half bad either."

"Not half bad?" Quinn huffed. "I believe I said you were brilliant, and all I get is a *not half bad*?"

"Well, we can't all have such rich, nuanced material to work with." Lacey suppressed a giggle. "Okay, fine. You're brilliant too."

Quinn considered it for a moment. "Okay. So, I tell them it's a bit part for you while my arm heals, but we make it more, just because we can." She chuckled again. "It's totally *Rizzoli & Isles*."

"Right. But with real, live lesbians. You know we can do this," Lacey pleaded. "It'll be subtle at first. People will replay the littlest things and think to themselves, is something happening between those two?"

Quinn knew they could convince the audience of anything. She just wasn't sure it was as good a plan as Lacey thought it was. She laughed ruefully to herself. *Sure, Quinn. Because now seems as good a time as any to worry about whether a plan is a good one.*

Still, there were things to consider. Like how working together would affect living together. She relaxed against her pillow and studied Lacey, who was sitting there looking all beautiful and determined. She needed to be careful. "If I say yes, we still keep our deal. We keep it professional." Her eyes fell to Lacey's hand that was currently resting on her thigh.

Lacey pulled her hand away. "Of course."

"I just don't want you to think—"

Lacey stood up, putting some distance between them. "I assure you, I don't think anything. Nor do I want anything except an actual acting gig. Not this bullshit real life"—she waved her hand in the air— "nursing crap."

"Good." Quinn nodded her agreement. She wanted to keep the lines clear between a working relationship and a real one. She trusted Lacey, but not necessarily with her heart. "We need to keep this what it is."

"Oh my God," Lacey said with a laugh. "You realize you're not even a little bit attractive right now. And last night you informed me that I'd be wiping your ass. Trust me when I say that the last thing you need to worry about is me jumping your bones or falling in love with your sorry ass."

Quinn wasn't sure whether to laugh or cry. While it was true that she didn't want Lacey getting any romantic thoughts in her head, she by no means wanted her to be repelled by the thought of it. "Got it. Heart is in New York. Wouldn't touch me with a ten-foot pole. Definitely NOT in any way attractive right now." She absentmindedly ran her hand over her hair that was now clean, but probably looked like a rat's nest. "And just how does having you on my show help me come out?"

Lacey's excitement bubbled to the surface again. "Because you'll already be in a relationship with me on the show. So when you fall in love with your costar in real life, it won't have to be such a big mental leap for people. You won't have to announce it. It'll just be a natural progression. And more importantly, we're going to kill this thing on-screen so people will be dying for us to be together. They'll completely forget our characters aren't real." Lacey narrowed her eyes. "You know, just as soon as we do something about that hair. You can't even brush it with your left hand, can you?"

"Do you mind?"

Lacey huffed as she stood up. "You don't have to give me those sad, puppy dog eyes. Just ask."

"Well, I tried that with the ass-wiping, but I got a lot of pushback."

Lacey found a brush in the bathroom and sat back down on the edge of the bed. Quinn closed her eyes while Lacey carefully ran the brush through her hair. Finally, something felt good after days of agonizing pain. It was such a stupid accident, and the timing couldn't have been worse. Her face was a mess. Her body was a mess. How could she possibly get in front of the camera looking like this? Just thinking about it brought tears to her eyes. She squeezed them tight, hoping the tears wouldn't fall.

Lacey pulled the brush back. "What's wrong?"

"Nothing," Quinn said with a quick shake of her head. "Just…you know…pent-up stuff."

"You're not in pain, are you?" She handed Quinn a tissue.

"Like you said, I'm not exactly attractive right now. How am I supposed to…" She paused, trying to shake off her emotions.

"Oh my God. You're fishing for a compliment, aren't you?"

"What? No!" Quinn said with a firm shake of her head.

"No, I get it. You're used to being the most beautiful woman in the room." Lacey picked up the lip balm. "But your lips are chapped and your breath smells…and…"

Quinn batted Lacey's hand away, causing the lip balm to go flying across the room. "There's a reason for that, genius. I haven't brushed my teeth yet. Now, help me get up."

Lacey followed Quinn into the bathroom. "If it's any consolation, you still have the best ass in the room. All that mountain biking has really paid off."

Quinn unsuccessfully tried to pull the T-shirt down to cover her ass. She watched while Lacey put toothpaste on the toothbrush, trying not to smile. She awkwardly brushed her teeth with her left hand while Lacey tidied up the bathroom, picking up towels and wiping down the counter. The hand towel that she normally set her toothbrush on was missing. Just when she was about to go to the closet to find a replacement, a new towel was set down in front of her. "Thank you," she whispered. Quinn didn't know if she was thanking Lacey for the compliment or the towel. Probably both.

"I'll run your idea by Jack," Quinn said, looking at Lacey in the mirror. "I trust his instincts. If he likes it, I'll pitch it to the producers.

Maybe they'll be thrilled we have a solution, especially if it involves me not missing a minute of work. Just be prepared that they might not be all that interested in story ideas from the talent."

Lacey gave her an unconvincing nod. "Yeah, yeah. I got it."

"Now, can you help me to the toilet, please?"

Lacey groaned in frustration. "God, this better be worth it."

CHAPTER EIGHT

Q uinn? It's Amy. Can I come in?"
     "Come in, Amy!" Quinn yelled from the bathroom.
     Lacey wrapped a towel around Quinn's wet body. "Who's Amy?"
She grabbed another towel and ran it over her wet hair.

"My assistant. I need to get back in bed." Quinn grabbed onto
Lacey's arm. "I feel like I'm going to fall over."

"I've got you." Lacey helped Quinn out of the bathroom and back
to her bed.

Amy, a cute, petite girl with curly blond hair, was setting up what
looked to be a rather large selection of cold-pressed juices and health
supplements on the dresser. "Don't worry," she said. "I got this, Quinn.
We'll have you back on the set in no time." She looked up and saw
Lacey. "Oh!" She looked at her a little closer and furrowed her brow.
"Oh my God," she whispered. "How did you get Dr. Sarah Covington?"

"Oh, for Christ's sake," Quinn said, looking rather annoyed.

Lacey thoroughly enjoyed the look on Quinn's face. Quinn
Kincaid wasn't the only one who had fans. "Hi, Amy. I'm Lacey." She
walked over and shook Amy's hand.

Amy slapped a hand over her mouth. "My God, it's really you?
We grew up together! I wanted to *be* you!"

Desperately needing to see Quinn's reaction to her assistant being
a BIG soap fan, Lacey turned around and was greeted with an eye roll
and shake of the head. "Yes, Amy, it's really her," Quinn said. "We're
all so grateful to have daytime's most accomplished doctor here to help
me get dressed—when she's in between heart transplants, of course."

Lacey smiled. "Ignore your pain-in-the-ass boss, Amy. Quinn and
I are friends."

Amy jumped up and down and grabbed Lacey, pulling her in for a hug. "I had no idea! And my sister's going to DIE! And my mom will just completely flip out. She wanted to KILL your mother for hiding your identical twin sister all those years ago, but like Mom said, it was a different time back then, and wealthy people could get away with just about anything."

"AMY!" Quinn shouted.

Amy got a look of panic on her face. "Shoot," she whispered. "We'll talk later, okay?"

Lacey covered her mouth, trying to hold back a laugh as Amy walked over to the bed and sat on the edge. Quinn put a pillow under her arm, trying to get it in a comfortable position. "What are the rumblings?" she asked, looking pale and weak after her shower.

"Well, they're freaking out a little bit," Amy said. "The writers are trying to figure out how they can write you out of the first few episodes."

"WHAT?" Quinn shouted. "That's ridiculous! There's no way. That's a breach of contract. Get my agent on the phone. Or my lawyer. Or someone!"

"Boris is already on it. And don't worry, there's no way they're writing you out. It'd be like writing Olivia Pope out of *Scandal*." Amy looked over at Lacey. "Or when they wrote Dr. Sarah Covington out of *Light of Day*. The show hasn't been the same since."

"Thank you, Amy. That's nice of you to say." Lacey bit her lip to keep from laughing. She turned away from them, suddenly finding interest in the cold-pressed juices Amy had brought. She picked a bottle up and grimaced as she read the ingredients.

Amy tore her loving gaze from Lacey and focused on Quinn again. "I know how you are about your privacy, but don't worry. I'm a certified nurse's aide and I dabble in homeopathy."

Lacey's eyes widened in surprise. She whipped her head around. "You're a CNA?"

Amy almost swooned at Lacey. "Yeah. I wanted to be a doctor like you, but," she glanced at Quinn, "life got in the way."

Lacey moved closer, standing at the end of the bed. "Quinn, Amy's a CNA. She could—"

Quinn put up her hand. "Amy, I appreciate your concern, but Lacey's staying in the guesthouse, so—"

"Yeah, but," Lacey interrupted, "Amy could help with the heavy lifting."

Quinn shot her a glare. "Heavy lifting?"

Amy gazed at Lacey with a look that said she'd died and gone to heaven. "You're staying in the guesthouse? Here? At Quinn's?"

Quinn sat up a little straighter in bed, grimacing in pain as she did so. "Okay, both of you just shut up and listen. Amy, no one is writing me off the show. I'll be ready. Got it?"

Amy nodded. "Got it."

"And I'll let you know when I need something, but Lacey will be doing most of the 'heavy lifting,' as she puts it." Quinn made a finger quote with her good hand. "Since she has so much experience being a nurse or a doctor or whatever."

Lacey guffawed. "Yeah, and Quinn will defend me in court when I go insane and commit a heinous crime due to all the heavy lifting."

"Or maybe I'll just sue your ass for malpractice," Quinn snapped back.

It took Amy a second but then she laughed. "Because Quinn plays a lawyer...I get it." She stood up. "Okay, well I know you're in very good hands, Quinn." She turned to Lacey, getting that dreamy look on her face again. "I'll leave my CNA kit if you want. Stethoscope, blood pressure cuff, thermometer, pretty much everything you'll need."

Lacey gave her a swift nod. "Absolutely. I'll need all of that."

Amy hugged Lacey again, gripping her shoulders as she pulled away. "I can't wait to tell my mom I met you. And we're all praying for you to come back to *Light of Day*. They didn't kill you off, so there's still hope."

"Ha! Like that ever stopped them," Quinn said. "You're never really dead in the soap world, are you?"

Lacey smirked at Amy. "She's suddenly an expert now?"

Amy gave her a knowing smirk back. "She doesn't know what she's missing. Maybe she and her mom would be closer if they watched *Light of Day* together."

"I can hear you, Amy," Quinn said. "I may look like the walking dead, but my ears work just fine."

Amy bit her lip. "Okay, then! Call if you need me!" She winked at Lacey and went to the door.

After seeing Amy out, Lacey went back into Quinn's room, pulled a chair up to the bed, and sat down. Quinn opened her eyes and closed them again. "I don't want to hear it."

"You let me think you had no one to take care of you and here's Amy, ready and willing. Not to mention the fact that your phone rings nonstop with your mom and everyone at work calling."

Quinn turned away from her.

"What is it with you?" Lacey asked in frustration. "Why would you rather have a stranger take care of you?"

"That stranger's a doctor. And a good one, I hear. Brain surgeon or something, but if that thermometer comes anywhere near my ass…"

Lacey sighed. She obviously wasn't going to get a straight answer out of Quinn now or probably ever. "You're obsessed with your own ass. You know that, right?" She sighed again. "Okay, it's time for your meds. And you can drink that shit Amy brought or I can make you some real food."

Quinn closed her eyes and breathed a sigh of relief. "Oh, thank God. Real food."

CHAPTER NINE

L acey sat cross-legged on Quinn's bed, looking rather anxious as she sipped her coffee. Quinn took a final bite of the omelet and wiped her mouth with a napkin. "I feel like such a klutz eating left-handed."

"That's because you are a klutz." Lacey tucked the towel she'd used to soak up spilled orange juice behind her. "When we find you a real girlfriend, she'll have to like your money because ambidexterity sure isn't a selling point."

Quinn laughed and attempted to hit Lacey with her napkin. "Fuck you."

"Never." Lacey winked.

"Well, your next real girlfriend can love you for your cooking. That omelet was—"

"Stop messing with me. Just tell me," Lacey interrupted.

Quinn tried to hide her amusement, her lips curling up at the corners. She knew Lacey was going all kinds of crazy, wondering if Jack had liked her idea. Getting on a prime-time show would change everything for her, even if it turned out to be a short-term gig. Quinn cleared her throat and pursed her lips together, trying to look serious. "He didn't like your pitch."

"He didn't?" Lacey's shoulders fell. "Dammit," she whispered.

"No. He didn't like it at all."

"I thought for sure..."

Quinn held back a giggle. She wanted to keep up the charade, but Lacey looked so downtrodden she just didn't have the heart. "He didn't like it, he loved it."

Lacey's eyes widened. "You are *such* an asshole!" she said, throwing the wet towel at Quinn.

Quinn burst out giggling. "Sorry. Your face, though."

"Shut up. So, for real? And you like the idea too?"

"It's the sixth season. We need to shake things up a bit, so this is kind of perfect."

The idea wasn't just growing on Quinn, she was fully embracing it. Lacey was right—Quinn wouldn't have to make such a big deal of her coming out process, and that alone would lift a huge weight off her shoulders. If this worked, it would be seamless. No interviews, just a natural process that would slowly unfold in front of America's eyes. It was brilliant.

"Can you make sure they give the part to me and not someone else?" Lacey asked.

Quinn sensed the fear and insecurity in Lacey's voice, afraid that she'd somehow be left out of the equation. It was understandable, since it happened all the time in Hollywood. Actors were at the mercy of directors and producers and their little whims. One day, you're their favorite and the next, you don't have a job.

"Don't worry about that," Quinn said, trying to reassure her. "They'll think they're doing me a favor by casting you in a few episodes. After that, it's up to us to get the audience invested in looks that linger a little too long and banter that seems just a bit too flirty."

"So, you're all in?" Lacey waited expectantly for an answer.

Quinn gave her a nod. "Yeah. All in."

"YAY!" Lacey shouted as she threw herself back on the bed and kicked her legs in the air. She sat back up and jumped off the bed. "I'll be right back." She came back in the room a few seconds later holding a black marker in her hand.

"Um…" Quinn tilted her head. "What do you plan on doing with that?"

"I'm going to sign your cast. Who knows, my autograph might be worth something someday."

"Uh, no." Quinn covered her cast with her other arm. "I've seen how you sign your name. Your autograph sucks."

Lacey sat on the bed and took the cap off the marker. "Come on, Quinn. I had a cast when I was eleven and all my friends signed it. If you have a signature-less cast, people might think you have no friends."

"Oooor, maybe they'll take an even bigger leap and assume that I'm an adult." Lacey pouted, so Quinn reluctantly moved her arm. "Fine. But you're the only one who signs my cast."

Lacey leaned in and furrowed her brow as if she were really

focusing hard on her task. "Laaaceeeey...Matthewwws." She sat back and gave an affirming nod. "Perfect. You now have one friend."

Quinn smiled, wondering if Lacey really meant it.

The next few days went smoothly. They had the routine down by then. Breakfast first, so Quinn could take her pain meds. After that, Lacey would put the laptop in front of her so she could check her emails. Sometimes it took too long for her to reply with only one working hand, so Lacey would type while Quinn dictated.

After that, Quinn would rest and watch one of the cable news channels while Lacey did the household chores. Then, about an hour before lunch, Lacey would go back up to the bedroom and get Quinn showered and dressed in clean pajamas.

"Ready to shower?"

Quinn waved Lacey into her bedroom. "Please, I'm so hot. And open a window. This room is stifling."

"You are, actually...kind of hot...you know...for an..." Lacey pulled the curtains back and opened the sliding glass door, letting a cool breeze in.

"Were you going to say older woman? Because I'm only a few years older than you." Quinn winced as she tried to stand up. "Okay, maybe several," she mumbled under her breath.

"Helpless...middle aged...muscles are melting away with every passing second...woman."

"My tits are still good, though, right?" Quinn pushed her chest out and immediately bent over in pain. "Damn."

Lacey grabbed Quinn's good arm. "What's wrong?"

Quinn slowly straightened back up, pain racking her entire body. "I'm just so sore from all this lying around. My back is killing me. My neck is killing me. Everything hurts."

"I know what you need." Lacey went to the closet and came back out with a bathing suit hanging from one finger. "There's a perfectly good hot tub out back."

Quinn stood at the edge of the hot tub with her cast covered in plastic. "Are you sure? A shower is one thing, but this?"

Lacey took off her robe, revealing a little black bikini. She stepped in first and turned around, holding her hands out. "Jump to me, baby."

Quinn stuck a toe in. "I'm not jumping."

Lacey took a step back, feeling glad that she could make Quinn laugh through the pain. "Fine. Do it your way," she said as she admired Quinn's very toned body. Her eyes wandered up to Quinn's bikini top, which wasn't covering much. Soft, luscious cleavage was trying hard to burst out the top and a little bit was even showing underneath. Lacey folded her arms and waited. There was nothing wrong with looking, was there? And even though the woman aggravated her no end, Lacey's fake girlfriend/roommate/patient was still hot.

"Are you sure this plastic bag is going to hold?" Quinn hesitantly put one foot in the water.

Lacey offered her hand as Quinn took another step. "I used waterproof tape and wrapped it solid. Just trust me, okay?"

Quinn took Lacey's hand and lowered herself into the hot tub. "Oh my God, that feels good."

Lacey helped Quinn sit against one of the jets. "You good?" She didn't let go of Quinn's hand until she was sure she was stable.

"Yeah. So good." Quinn closed her eyes. "Oh my God, this is heaven." She scooted down a little bit so her neck was fully submerged.

Lacey sat on the opposite side, her arms out of the water, resting on the edge. She watched carefully, ready to pounce if Quinn sank too low in the water. "See? You should listen to me once in a while."

"I listen to your annoying voice all day long. Do this. Eat that. Take your meds. Wipe your own ass, Quinn."

"It's for your own good, especially the ass wiping. As for the meds, you can't let that shit wear off, or have you forgotten how bad the pain can get?"

"Almost." Quinn smiled, keeping her eyes shut. "Thanks to you."

"You're welcome." Lacey leaned back and closed her eyes too. She was grateful that they'd managed to find a good rhythm. Quinn was healing, and she felt comfortable and safe with Lacey in her home. She'd earned Quinn's trust, and that made Lacey happy.

After soaking for ten minutes, Lacey had Quinn sit on the end of one of the lounge chairs so she could rub her back. She straddled the chair behind her and poured some lotion into her hand.

"Why are you being so nice to me today?" Quinn suppressed a moan when Lacey's warm hand ran up her back and over her shoulders.

"Oh, please. I've been nice to you this whole time and besides, I need you up and moving so we can get to work. The good kind of work, with a script and a camera."

"That's assuming the producers are okay with adding you." Quinn leaned forward as much as she could without hurting her arm so Lacey could reach her lower back.

"Yeah, or all of this kindness was for nothing."

Quinn stiffened at the comment and tried to stand up, but Lacey held her down. "I'm kidding." She rested her chin on Quinn's shoulder. "Tell me you know I'm kidding."

Quinn nodded. She wasn't sure why the comment bothered her so much. That's what she'd hired Lacey for, wasn't it? She needed a *FAKE* girlfriend, not a real one. She needed emotional detachment. This stupid accident didn't have to change that, did it? As if all of a sudden, she's so vulnerable and needy that her hired girlfriend needs to show genuine concern?

Bullshit.

Lacey was doing her job, including the rubbing of Quinn's good arm. God, it felt nice. Magical. Quinn accidentally moaned out loud.

Lacey dug in a little deeper on her back muscles, eliciting another moan. She worked the muscles as best she could and then ran her hands up and down Quinn's entire back a few more times. Her hands landed on Quinn's waist and froze there for a moment. "Feel a little better?" she asked, a gentleness in her voice that wasn't usually there.

"Yeah, thanks. That was wonderful."

"Why don't you go take a shower while you still have the wrap on your cast."

Lacey's hands hadn't moved. Quinn could feel the goose bumps forming on her skin, under Lacey's hands and all over her body. It had been a long time since someone, anyone, had touched her this much. Actually, no one in recent memory had touched her this much, or this thoroughly.

With all of the caregiving, where had Lacey *not* touched her in the last two weeks? Well, one place. But pretty much everywhere else. Well, also not her breasts. Two places hadn't been touched. But close. Her hands had come close a couple of times.

It wasn't awful.

Quinn wondered if maybe it was asking too much of someone who was also gay. Was it possible that Lacey was enjoying all of this touching? And how should Quinn feel about it if she was? Then she remembered all the indignities that went into being Quinn's caregiver. Shit. Lacey was definitely not getting off on this.

"You okay?" Lacey asked.

The hands on Quinn's waist slowly moved to her shoulders and gave a little squeeze. She put her face in her hand and started to cry.

"Hey. What's wrong?" Lacey asked.

Quinn shook her head. "This must suck so hard for you. I'm sorry you have to do every goddamn little thing for me." She looked at the sky and let out a big sob. "God, I'm such an asshole! A helpless fucking asshole."

"Hey now," Lacey pulled Quinn into her arms. "You are not an asshole. You're just hurting and tired and, yes, being helpless sucks."

Quinn sobbed even harder.

Freshly showered and wrapped in a fluffy white towel, Quinn sat on the edge of the bed. "Thank you."

Lacey carefully pulled off the waterproof tape. "You've been through a lot. It's okay to cry it out sometimes."

She'd held Quinn for a good ten minutes while she sobbed out her pain and frustration. She hadn't realized just how hard the situation was for Quinn. She wasn't reveling in being waited on hand and foot. She hated every second of it. She hated having to ask for help. Hated being at the mercy of someone else. She felt out of control and it made her angry.

Knowing that made things a little easier for Lacey. This wasn't a power play, even though it sometimes felt that way. "Almost got it." She pulled the plastic bag off and wadded up the tape. "Okay, you're all set."

"Thank you," Quinn said, meeting Lacey's gaze. She gave her a slow, easy smile. "I feel so much better. Almost human again."

Lacey smiled back. Quinn looked so contrite and so cute with her black eye that had turned a purplish-greenish color. Her eyes fell to Quinn's lips. They were no longer dry and chapped.

Moist.

Lacey quickly shook that word from her head and said, "No problem. Sarah Fucking Covington knows her shit."

"You talk to your mother with that mouth?" Quinn quipped.

Lacey's gaze fell to the floor.

"Why don't you ever talk about your mom?"

There it was; the question Lacey had been avoiding. But she couldn't avoid it forever. She sucked in air and said, "She died when I was sixteen, but I don't like to talk about it."

"I'm sorry," Quinn said. "I didn't...I shouldn't have..."

Lacey couldn't. Even if she wanted to, she couldn't talk about her mom. "Lunch will be ready soon." She quickly left the room and closed Quinn's bedroom door, leaning against it as tears made themselves known. She hastily wiped them away and went downstairs. She started pulling vegetables from the fridge to make a salad. The tears came even harder as she sliced tomatoes and cucumbers. Tears and knives weren't a good combination. She set the knife down and put both palms on the counter. A sob worked its way up her chest.

It was Lacey who had taken care of her mother those last three months of her life. She'd taken a leave from the show so she could watch the woman who gave birth to her slowly slip away. Cooking, bathing, managing meds, and taking the train with her to doctor's appointments. Everything she was doing for Quinn, she'd already done for her mother, but with a very different end result.

She'd pushed it away, the similarities, but the memories were always right there, under the surface. "I miss you," she whispered as she grated a carrot. "I miss you, Mama."

Quinn walked into the kitchen in a short gray robe. Lacey glanced up at her as she put the finishing touches on the salad. "I thought we'd eat outside."

She hoped Quinn wouldn't notice her red, puffy eyes. Who designated this National Crying Day, anyway? Jesus. They didn't even have their periods. Lacey just wanted to move on from it. She hoped Quinn did too.

"I didn't feel like getting dressed," Quinn said, stealing a cucumber slice from the bowl. "Also, I want to sleep naked tonight, so you're just going to have to deal."

Lacey snorted as she slid Quinn's pain pills across the counter. "Whatever. You're the superstar."

It didn't make sense for Lacey to sleep in the guesthouse yet. She needed to be close by in case Quinn needed anything during the night, which she often did. The sterile guest room, which wasn't so sterile anymore, had become Lacey's new home.

"I'm sick of pajamas," Quinn said. "I never wear them. And I'm sick of this fucking thing on my arm." She raised her cast, trying to make a point, but it only caused her to wince in pain.

Lacey gave her a motherly smile. "Language, honey."

Quinn grabbed her pills off the counter. "I learned it from you." She went to the sliding glass door and walked outside. "AND I WANT A GLASS OF WINE!"

Lacey breathed a sigh of relief at the outburst. Quinn was so caught up in her own frustrations she hadn't noticed that they were both emotional wrecks. She grabbed a wine glass out of the cupboard, poured sparkling water into it, and set it on the tray. Once lunch was ready, she took the tray outside and set it on the glass table.

Quinn put her phone down. "That was my mother. She says Sarah Fucking Covington is a spoiled, crazy bitch, but she still—big surprise—desperately wants to meet you."

"You know, I always try to hide my true self from the viewing audience, but sometimes it just sneaks through." Lacey sat across the round table from Quinn and took a sip of her wine.

Quinn ignored the joke and frowned at the wine glass on her tray. "This doesn't help," she said, picking up the glass. "It's still just water. And why do you get wine?"

"Because I'm stuck with you. Check the booze rider in my contract." Lacey took another sip and forced a smile.

Quinn scowled back at her. "I should have you negotiate my next deal."

"Nah, I'm a doctor, not a lawyer. At least…not yet." Lacey rested her wine glass against her lips, trying to hide her smile. She should maybe mention to Quinn that her robe had fallen open, revealing a cute little triangle of light brown hair, but she stayed quiet.

The following morning, Quinn came downstairs fully dressed in jeans and a T-shirt. She almost bumped into Lacey, who was rounding the corner with a breakfast tray. "I was just coming…how did you get dressed by yourself?" Lacey asked, looking her up and down.

"You were just coming?"

"Don't be juvenile, that's *my* thing." Lacey set the tray down so she could inspect Quinn's sling. "Your arm must be doing better."

Getting a T-shirt on had hurt like a motherfucker, but Quinn was sick of all the coddling. She wanted her independence back. "I can't be an invalid forever." She stood still while Lacey adjusted the sling. "Can't put a bra on yet, but I zipped up my own pants. Also, I have news."

Lacey's eyes landed on Quinn's chest. Her perky breasts were, of course, standing at attention under the thin, white, almost see-through V-neck that was vying for Best T-Shirt in the World. She quickly shifted her eyes upward. "Huh?"

"News. I have news." Quinn bit her lip, trying to hold back a giggle.

Lacey put a pill in Quinn's hand and gave her a glass of orange juice. "Take your meds first." She put her hands on her hips and waited.

Quinn downed the pill and the entire glass of juice. She wiped her mouth with the back of her hand and smiled brightly. "We'll have a script by tomorrow and we start filming next week!"

Lacey looked like she wanted to jump up and down and scream through the house, but she kept her cool, slowly leading Quinn to the sofa to sit down. "Tell me everything."

"Well, they're relieved that I'm not going to hold up production. They liked the pitch, and they loved the idea you had about your character. Harvard Law and all."

Lacey slapped a hand over her mouth. "Oh my God, you're kidding me!"

Quinn pulled a piece of paper out of her front pocket. "Here's the casting director's info. Your agent needs to call her right away."

Lacey grabbed Quinn's shoulders. "Quinn…"

"I know. I'm excited too. I hope we can pull it off."

"Pull it off? We're going to KILL. IT."

"And no matter what happens, you'll see the fake girlfriend thing through to the end?" Quinn needed to be sure they were still on track with the original plan. She needed to know Lacey wouldn't bail on her once she had a real acting job.

"Of course. This is going to be huge for my career, and I'm very grateful."

Their eyes locked on one another and Quinn seductively said, "How grateful?" She immediately regretted saying it and looked away, her stomach knotting up with electricity. "Just rehearsing for later." She stood up and walked over to the window. "Don't we have a doctor's appointment today?"

Lacey also stood up. "Yeah…we do…just…um…" She stumbled

over her words and cleared her throat. "Eat your breakfast while I get ready?"

Quinn turned and nodded, noticing the blush on Lacey's cheeks. "Yeah, okay." She'd obviously felt it, too, the brief moment of intensity between them. Quinn needed to be careful now that she was starting to feel better. Being flirtatious probably wasn't a good idea. They both had far too much on the line to risk having everything blow up in their faces over temporary sexual gratification.

Besides, Quinn had waited years to be with a woman. She could definitely wait a little longer for someone who wasn't a complete pain in the ass. A faint smile formed on her lips, thinking about how explosive this energy between them would be on camera, though. Her long-running hit show was about to get a big old shot of sexy.

CHAPTER TEN

W hat do you think?"
       Quinn turned her head from side to side. "You're getting good at this." Lacey had pulled Quinn's blond hair back into a low ponytail and slicked it down with hairspray so it wouldn't move. It was the best they could do without calling in reinforcements.

Lacey set the can of hairspray down with a little more force than necessary. "God, I can't wait until you can use your right hand again."

"That's what *she* said."

Lacey stared at Quinn in the mirror, refusing to crack a smile. "Really, with the sex jokes?"

Quinn picked up her blush brush and ran it across her cheeks. "You're rubbing off on me. I used to be so cultured and well mannered. My mother would be horrified."

According to Jack, it was time for their first official foray into the public domain. The bruising around Quinn's eye was almost gone. What was left of it, they'd managed to cover with foundation. The scratches had also healed up quite nicely. In fact, if you could ignore the huge cast on her right arm, Quinn Kincaid was starting to look like herself again. Pretty, Lacey thought. So pretty.

"Don't worry, you're still very cultured." Lacey watched with fascination as Quinn put the blush brush back in the drawer, adjusting it several times to make sure it lined up perfectly with the other makeup brushes. "And I don't even know what that business is," she said, waving her hand over Quinn's drawer full of OCD. "But it's my turn to get ready."

"You have thirty minutes. Thirty-five tops!" Quinn shouted as Lacey left the room.

❖

Forty-five minutes later, Lacey walked into the kitchen wearing a long-sleeved white cropped top, fitted navy blue skirt, and three-inch silver strappy heels. Her hair was straightened and pulled to one side, revealing a large silver hoop earring.

"Ready?" Quinn looked up from her phone, doing a double take. "God."

Lacey filled a glass with water. "You can thank your stylist." She set the water and a pain pill on the counter in front of Quinn.

"Jack...um..." Quinn couldn't find her words. She'd never seen Lacey this dressed up before, with full makeup and lipstick and heels. The outfit was skintight and sexy as hell, making Quinn feel tingly in unmentionable places. She cleared her throat and let her eyes wander up Lacey's body again. "Jack wants us at Nobu in Malibu. Plenty of paparazzi there tonight."

"Do they have oysters? I want oysters."

Quinn's eyes were stuck on the thin strip of skin peeking out between Lacey's skirt and top. The bright white top was the perfect contrast to her newly tanned skin, due to time spent poolside. "I...I... think so."

Lacey grinned. "Eyes up here." Once they made eye contact, she chuckled. "God, you're so gay. Now, take your pill." She pushed the glass of water across the marble countertop.

Quinn did what she was told and then held the glass in front of her mouth, trying to hide her grin. Even though it wasn't a date, she felt kind of proud that she'd be with the hottest woman in the restaurant. "We'll take the Maserati tonight."

Lacey walked away, swinging her hips a little more than usual. "Fuck yeah, we will. I didn't just spend all that time in front of the mirror for nothing."

Lacey pulled up to the valet at Nobu, feeling a little bit nervous about the attention they would most likely receive. She wasn't the only one dressed to the nines. Quinn looked hot as hell in a little sleeveless white dress that hung loosely and came up to about mid-thigh, showing off her toned, sexy legs. The neckline was high, but the fabric was sheer down to her cleavage. Broken arm or not, she would definitely turn some heads.

Lacey opened her door and was about to get out of the car when she leaned back in and said, "Just friends, right?"

Quinn gave her a quizzical look. "I told you, we will never—"

"We will never fuck. I know, Quinn. I meant for the paparazzi. What are we tonight? You're the director of this show, so direct me. Tell me how close to stand. Where to touch you, or not touch you."

"We're um…you know…" Quinn hesitated as Lacey stared at her, waiting for an answer. "Friends. Just do what a friend would do."

Lacey smirked at her, wondering why that was so hard to say. The valet opened Quinn's door and offered his hand. "Good evening, ma'am."

Quinn pointed at her broken arm and then at Lacey. "She'll help me."

Lacey sighed as she grabbed her purse. "Nurse Fuckington will be right there."

By the time they were seated, Quinn was still busy trying to explain herself. "It's awkward, getting out of the car, and you're used to it. You know where to hold me and how to shift your weight so we don't both fall. Do you know how embarrassed I'd be if I fell and someone got a shot of my bare ass? Or even worse, my…you know."

Lacey narrowed her eyes. "Are you saying you're not wearing any underwear?" She leaned in closer. "You little slut, you. And with a short dress like that?"

"No! Yes! I mean yes, of course I'm wearing…" Quinn threw her napkin on her lap. "Just…never mind."

"Fine. You're right," Lacey acquiesced, picking up the menu. "And I was right to make sure my contract covered wine."

"I'm having some too, so just deal with it." Quinn said, getting a mom-glare from Lacey. "Let's just enjoy the atmosphere and the good food and this fabulous view. The ocean is right there! Have you even looked at it?"

Lacey set her menu down and leaned forward. Lowering her voice, she said, "You know what I'm going to enjoy tonight?"

Quinn motioned with her head. "Look at the damn ocean."

"I'm going to enjoy watching…"

"Uh-uh! Look at the ocean first."

Lacey eyed Quinn for a second and then turned to her left to glance across the dining room. Everything from the floor to the tables to the ceiling was made of rich Japanese wood. The room opened up completely to a patio overlooking the ocean, and the sun was just starting to set. "Gorgeous. Now, how the hell are you going to eat sushi with chopsticks, using your left hand?"

Quinn gasped. "That's what you're going to enjoy watching tonight?"

Lacey glanced over Quinn's shoulder. "That, and Robert De Niro. He's right behind you."

"Nice guy. He owns the place. And you have an admirer."

"What?"

Quinn picked up her glass of water and nodded at someone behind Lacey. "Studio exec. All your worries would disappear in an instant."

Lacey didn't turn to look. She kept her eyes on Quinn. "Oh, yuck. Let me guess. Sixtyish. Portly and balding. Recently divorced. Or maybe still married. Probably owns the very understated white Rolls-Royce parked out front?"

"More like forty-five. Never been married, to my knowledge. Quite fit. Full head of hair. And if I'm not mistaken, *she* drives a Tesla."

Lacey tucked her hair behind her ears and clasped her hands together. "Are you ready to order?"

"You think I'm fucking with you?" Quinn whispered loudly. "I'm serious! She can't take her eyes off of you."

"I like spicy tuna," Lacey replied.

Quinn shook her head. "I'm not touching that one."

"So you've mentioned." Lacey picked the menu up again. "And oysters. I want oysters."

"Your wish is my command." Quinn looked for a waiter but didn't see one. She lifted up her cast and reached under it, letting out a frustrated sigh. "Something's not right."

Lacey stood up. "Let me look at it." She leaned over, giving Quinn a perfect view of her cleavage. "You've got the sling all twisted."

"Do I?" Quinn's voice sounded so innocent as her eyes raked over Lacey's body.

"Stop looking at my tits," Lacey whispered.

"You smell so good. What is that?" Quinn whispered back.

Lacey untwisted the strap and smoothed it down, making sure her hand grazed Quinn's breast. She kissed her head like you would a child and whispered, "It's called, we are never going to fuck, remember?"

Lacey sat back down and Quinn's eyes widened as she looked past her. "Oh, this should be fun. Studio exec coming your way."

"Quinn! So good to see you. How's the arm doing?"

Lacey watched as the woman kissed Quinn's cheek and rested her hand on her good shoulder, giving her a reassuring, though slightly melodramatic, squeeze. It was as if a director had once told the woman it was a surefire way to indicate genuine concern.

"Getting a little better every day," Quinn said. "It was such a stupid accident." She blushed and smiled nervously, not able to hold the woman's gaze.

Well, well, well. Now wasn't this interesting? Lacey narrowed her eyes and watched the interaction closely. Was Quinn's hand shaking? Were her cheeks getting redder? And was that a nervous little giggle?

"As soon as you're ready, I know a fabulous sports therapist," the woman said. "He'll have you back on your mountain bike in no time. Worked wonders on me when I had that rotator cuff nonsense."

Quinn glanced at Lacey, suddenly remembering her manners. "Ginny, this is my friend, Lacey Matthews."

Ginny turned to Lacey and offered her hand. "So pleased to meet you, Lacey. Is there any chance we've met before?"

Lacey stood up and took Ginny's hand, covering it with both of hers. "It sure feels like we have. Are you ever in New York?"

"All the time!"

"That must be it, then. I'm new to L.A."

"Lacey's an actress," Quinn interjected. "She was on *Light of Day* in New York, and she's about to make her mark here."

"Well, aren't we lucky? How 'bout I introduce Lacey to a few friends?" Ginny suggested, turning toward Quinn. "You don't mind, do you?"

Quinn seemed surprised by the suggestion but quickly shook her head. "Not at all."

Lacey wanted to ask if Quinn would be okay while she was gone, but obviously she would be. "Order an appetizer?"

Quinn nodded and forced a smile. "Yeah."

❖

Had Lacey been gone forever, or was Quinn just imagining it? And what was with Ginny stealing her away, anyway? And where did they go? Quinn had turned away long enough to order an appetizer, and when she turned back, they'd disappeared from Ginny's table.

Ginny had put her hand on Lacey's lower back as they'd slowly walked away, like she owned her or something. And once they'd sat at Ginny's table, she'd given Lacey a sip of her wine. That seemed a little too intimate. It was, wasn't it? And knowing Ginny, it was probably a $500 bottle of wine.

God, why did Quinn care? She shouldn't care. She forced herself to look at her menu, refusing to look back up.

It seemed like forever went by before Lacey slid back into her chair. "Sorry. She wanted to show me the patio. It's gorgeous out there."

Lacey looked flushed. And was that red lipstick? Quinn squinted. "Did she kiss you?"

Lacey rolled her eyes. "It's courtesy of some French actress sitting at her table. I wasn't expecting the double cheek thing and we kind of collided. Is it everywhere?"

Quinn snorted. "You mean you accidentally kissed? Because it's..." She motioned with her hand, indicating it was on the corner of Lacey's mouth.

Lacey quickly dabbed her mouth with a napkin. "Stop laughing or I won't share the very expensive bottle of red that is being uncorked for us, care of Ginny Strong."

"Oh, I'm having a glass. Don't even with the mom-look."

Lacey glanced back at Ginny. "Yeah, I need one too."

Quinn furrowed her brow. "Everything okay?"

Lacey smiled. "Yeah. Fine."

"A bottle for the ladies, courtesy of Ms. Strong." The waiter displayed the bottle, and Quinn gestured, giving him permission to pour.

They both held up their glasses to Ginny and gave her a nod of thanks. Quinn took a sip and moaned as her eyes shuttered closed. "God, that's good." She'd missed her daily glass of wine. Coming back to it with a bottle this good was heavenly. She took another sip and swirled the wine in her glass.

"She's nice," Lacey said. "Ginny is nice."

"And pretty," Quinn added, her eyes going back to Ginny's table. "And smart, and has a wicked sense of humor, and very good taste in wine."

Lacey's eyes widened. "I see. And the second you break up with your *fake* girlfriend, you'll be all over that shit?"

"Well, I'm certainly not going to flirt with her right now. With this stupid thing on my arm, I have zero sex appeal."

Lacey took another sip of wine as she eyed Quinn. "Are you fishing for compliments again?"

"Would it be arrogant of me to say I don't have to fish for fucking compliments?" Quinn snapped back.

Feeling rather amused by Quinn's frequent use of the F-word now, Lacey leaned back in her chair and smiled. "Yes."

Quinn put her glass down and focused on the menu. "They don't have oysters. Some problem with the delivery today."

"What a shame."

"And we're not even enjoying the view." Quinn set the menu back down. She didn't really care what they had for dinner. For some reason, she'd lost her appetite. She turned slightly in her seat and stared out at the water.

Lacey watched her for a moment and then said, "Why would I look at the ocean when there's an extremely fuckable woman sitting at this table?"

Quinn turned back to her and smirked. "Fuckable?"

"Hey, you wanted a compliment."

Ginny walked back over to their table as she was leaving. "So good to see you, Quinn. Let's do lunch soon." She turned to Lacey. "You have my number?"

Lacey held up the business card. "Right here."

"Good. We'll go out for oysters sometime," Ginny said with a wink.

Quinn cranked her neck around and watched Ginny walk away. "Well, she's about as subtle as a Mack truck."

Lacey leaned in. "She doesn't know you're gay. If she did… well…I wouldn't even exist in her world."

Quinn couldn't help but smile. "See? Now, *that's* a compliment."

Lacey threw her hands in the air. "What the hell is wrong with fuckable? That seems like a compliment of the highest order!"

Quinn giggled as the woman sitting behind Lacey turned around and glared at her. Lacey covered her mouth with her hands. "Sorry," she whispered.

❖

Lacey gave her ticket to the valet and walked back over to Quinn. "It's going to be a few minutes and there are two cameras across the street. What would you like me to do?"

Quinn stepped a little closer. "Just stand there, looking like my hot friend."

Lacey stepped even closer. "So…you don't want me to run my thumb over that incredibly plump bottom lip?"

Quinn bit her lip, trying to hold back her smile. "That would be a bit premature, don't you think?"

Lacey's gaze fell to Quinn's cleavage. "Yeah, I guess friends don't really do that."

Quinn looked down at her drab beige sling. "Maybe you could Bedazzle this piece of shit sling for me, so I don't feel so frumpy. That's a friend thing, isn't it?"

Lacey giggled.

"What?" Quinn asked.

The giggle turned into full-on laughter. "Nobody—and I mean nobody—is looking at your sling. Your legs…yes. Your amazing eyes…double yes. Your tits…"

"Still fuckable?" Quinn shyly asked.

"Here we are." Lacey motioned to the car as it rolled up. "And I can't believe you asked me to Bedazzle something. Do I look crafty to you?"

"What if I asked you to embroider the word *Fuck* on my sling?"

"Is there a Michael's in Malibu?" Lacey asked while getting a tip out of her purse.

"I'm pretty sure you're the only person to ever utter those words. And no, there isn't."

"Hobby Lobby?" Lacey tipped the nice young man and then held on to Quinn's good arm as she backed into the seat and swung her legs into the car. Once she was settled, Lacey pulled the seat belt out enough for Quinn to grab it. "Or how about one of those JoAnn fabric stores?" Lacey didn't wait for an answer. She shut Quinn's door and walked around the car, getting in the driver's seat.

"For someone who isn't crafty, you sure know where to shop."

"My mom—" Lacey stopped. She took a deep breath and said, "My mom was crafty. When I was young, she needed something to do when I was working, so she would sit on the set and knit these beautiful afghans. She even sold a few of them to the cast and crew. They were beautiful."

Quinn put her hand on Lacey's leg. "I wish I could've met her."

"Yeah. Me too." Lacey put the car in drive and pulled out onto the road. They drove for a while in silence, Quinn keeping her hand right where it was.

Lacey finally broke the silence. "I'm sorry I haven't talked about her. That doesn't really honor her memory. I need to be better about that."

"Did she know that you were gay?" Quinn asked. "She died when you were sixteen, so I just wondered…"

"No. I kind of knew I was different, but I didn't have the guts to talk to her about it. It's something I regret, that she never knew the real me. All of me."

"You were so young." Quinn gave Lacey's leg a gentle squeeze.

"Do you think they got a good shot of us?" Lacey asked, needing to change the subject.

"I hope so."

"Well, even if they didn't," Lacey took Quinn's hand in hers, "it was nice having dinner with you.

Quinn smiled. "Yeah, it was."

Lacey followed Quinn into her bedroom like she did every night, ready to help her get ready for bed. She'd kicked off her heels at the garage door, but she was still wearing her tight skirt and top. Quinn stood in front of the mirror and pulled her ponytail to one side, giving Lacey access to the zipper on her dress. Their eyes caught in the mirror and Lacey hesitated. Had the temperature in the room just skyrocketed? Was that a heated blush slowly creeping up her chest? Shit. It was.

It shouldn't have felt different. Not more than a couple of hours ago, Lacey had zipped this same dress up. She knew there was a lacy white bra underneath. No big surprise there. But as she tugged on the zipper, the anticipation of what she'd find made her breath catch. "You really did look beautiful tonight," she said, her voice softer than she'd meant for it to be. She didn't dare look up. Keeping her eyes on the zipper, she gently pulled. And there it was—that too-sexy-for-its-own-good bra.

Maybe it was the ride home that had Lacey feeling things she shouldn't feel. At one point, Quinn had shifted in her seat, trying to find a comfortable position for her arm, which caused her dress to ride up, showing off her mouthwatering thighs. Lacey found herself wanting to reach over and push the dress up a little farther. If Quinn were her real girlfriend, she would have. And she would've left her hand there, her fingers gently tickling Quinn's inner thigh.

"Thank you," Quinn replied. "You looked amazing too." Her eyes were firmly set on Lacey's reflection in the mirror. "Would you mind? It was hell trying to get this bra on by myself."

Their eyes locked again. Why did it feel so different? So dangerous? Was it because they'd just been on their first date? Not really a date, though. Just two friends having dinner together. Lacey broke the eye contact and focused on her task, sliding her fingers between Quinn's soft skin and the bra. She gently unhooked it and dropped her hands to her sides, fearing what else she'd touch if she didn't control herself. Sexy, Lacey thought. So sexy. "Anything else?" she quickly asked, trying to hide the fact that her heart was racing.

Quinn shook her head. "No."

"Okay, then." Lacey took a step back. "Good night."

"Good night."

Lunging forward would be a bad idea. Taking Quinn in her arms, kissing her neck, her shoulder—letting the dress fall to the floor. Quinn would gasp at the touch. She wouldn't know what to do at first—how to react. She might even enjoy the feel of Lacey's lips on her neck. But she would quickly come to her senses.

Lacey wouldn't lift Quinn onto the bathroom sink and make love to her. She wouldn't take Quinn to places she'd never been before. She wouldn't hear Quinn's bedroom voice, begging her for more. *Don't stop, Lace. Don't fucking stop.*

She wouldn't watch herself in the mirror as Quinn Kincaid rode her fingers. Quinn Kincaid, naked and sweaty and breathless. And oh so sated.

Lacey wouldn't get on her knees and bury her face between Quinn's legs. She wouldn't taste her for the first time and hear Quinn moan out her pleasure. She wouldn't stay there, teasing and licking until Quinn came again, this time, shouting profanities, mixed with Lacey's name and, of course, God's.

No. That wouldn't happen.

Quinn would push her away before that ever happened. *We have a contract*, she would say. *And it doesn't include this!*

And it didn't, of course. That would make Lacey a...

"Good night," Lacey said again. She closed the bedroom door behind her and stood in the hall for a moment, her chest heaving. She felt a little unsteady on her legs so she leaned against the wall.

She touched her cheeks to see if they were hot. *Shit. They're on fire.* She slowly made her way to her room and stood in front of the bathroom mirror, staring at herself. "You can't fall for her," she whispered.

CHAPTER ELEVEN

Lacey woke up grumpy and sexually frustrated, which is how she ended up doing yoga by the pool. She'd found a mat in the garage and a YouTube video on her iPad called *Yoga for Beginners.*

Yoga had a calming, centering effect on people, or so Lacey'd been told. This was obviously bullshit since all Lacey could do was grunt and groan her way through another plank. "Beginners...my... ass." She could barely get the words out, what with her weak core and all.

Last night had all felt a little too real. She kept telling herself it was a fake date, but once they'd gotten past the whole Ginny Strong thing and ordered their meal, they'd settled in. And it was lovely. Quinn had sat across from her looking gorgeous with her blond hair pulled back, showing off her high cheekbones and those eyes. God, those eyes. Lacey could easily get lost in them if she let herself. It had been a constant battle not to last night.

Quinn had talked about her show and how much she loved her work. *Jordan's Appeal* was a spin-off from another show. A very successful spin-off. Something she was proud of. Her eyes lit up when she talked about it. She'd done a few movies that had put her on the A-list, but she didn't consider them her best work. *Jordan's Appeal* was her best work.

For a good hour, they talked to each other, without any sarcasm. They laughed and joked about things, but it was different. It was honest. And then, on the way home in the car, Lacey had opened up about her mom. It wasn't easy, but she did it. And afterward, it felt good. She didn't regret it.

The hard part was coming back to a home that wasn't really hers, with a woman who definitely wasn't hers—and wanting the opposite.

She found herself wanting to lead Quinn to "their" bedroom and make love to her girlfriend. And the term *girlfriend* wasn't enough. It sounded fake. Probably because it was.

"Since when do you do yoga?"

Lacey collapsed onto the mat. "I'm moving out here, to the guesthouse." She didn't look up at Quinn, she just blurted the words out. She needed space. And she needed Quinn to not be standing there all bare legged. "I didn't know you were up. Are you ready for breakfast?"

Quinn set a plastic bag and a roll of tape on the patio table. "Do you mind if I soak in the hot tub while you finish your routine?"

"I'm done." Lacey wasn't really done, but the yoga wasn't exactly working either, so she saw no reason to make a fool of herself trying to stand on one leg. She turned off the video and got up, wiping the sweat from her brow with her arm. She immediately noticed the dark circles under Quinn's eyes. "How do you feel this morning?"

Quinn took her arm out of the sling. "Last night was a bitch. I couldn't get comfortable."

"You shouldn't have had that wine. And you should've called me."

"It wasn't the wine." Quinn sighed. "And the truth is, I hate waking you up in the middle of the night. I'd grow to hate someone who did that to me all the time. And apparently, you do, since you want to move out here."

"I don't hate you. The guesthouse is where I was supposed to be all along." Lacey gently put the plastic bag over Quinn's arm and tried to change the subject. "Maybe it's time for a real massage. I'm sure your entire body took a beating with that fall, not just your arm."

"That's not a bad idea, but I don't really want a stranger—"

"In your house, I know," Lacey said, a slight tug of frustration in her voice. "I could call Ginny Strong and get a referral. I'm sure she knows someone trustworthy. And she definitely struck me as the kind of person who pampers herself."

Quinn put her hand on Lacey's, stopping her from taping the bag to her arm. "You can't date Ginny Strong. You know that, right?"

Lacey swatted Quinn's hand away. "Yeah. It was pretty obvious you have a thing for her."

"That's not why."

Lacey pulled a long piece of tape off the roll and tore it with her teeth. "So, you don't have a thing for her?"

Quinn groaned in frustration. "You know why, Lacey! What if she likes you and wants to continue dating you?"

"Well, that's a given." Lacey hastily wrapped the tape and patted it down. "There you go. Now, get in the hot tub."

Fucking Ginny Strong. Like Lacey would ever date that woman. Sure, she was pretty and pleasant enough to talk to, but she was a player through and through. Why Quinn couldn't see that was beyond Lacey.

Quinn examined the bad wrap job. "If this leaks…"

Lacey folded her arms and raised an eyebrow. "What, you'll spank me? If it leaks, we'll go to the doctor and get a new cast."

Quinn huffed out her frustration and went over to the hot tub. She dropped her robe, revealing her completely naked body.

Are you fucking kidding me? Quinn couldn't bother to put on a bathing suit? Lacey couldn't take any more of this. Not today. "Oh, look!" she shouted. "A drone!"

Quinn's good arm flailed as she lost her footing, trying to look up at the sky and step into the hot tub at the same time. Then a scream of surprise. And another, much worse scream as her broken arm landed on the support bar. Then she was all the way under the water. Lacey ran. Fully clothed, she jumped into the hot tub just as Quinn came back up, sputtering in between groans of pain.

"You did that on purpose!" she shouted as tears mixed with the water streaming down her face.

"I'm sorry." Lacey tried to hold her, but Quinn pushed her away and pulled her broken arm in, holding it against her body. Lacey tried again. This time coming from behind, she wrapped her arms around Quinn's waist and whispered, "I'm so sorry," in her ear.

Quinn relaxed slightly and let Lacey pull her onto her lap. "Goddamn you."

"I'm sorry." Lacey turned Quinn, pulling her knees to the side so she could look at her. She moved the wet hair from her face and cupped her cheek. "Are you okay? Do we need to go to the doctor?"

Quinn shook her head. "No. Just stay still for a minute. It'll subside."

Just what Lacey needed—naked Quinn sitting on her lap for who knew how long. She tried not to look down, keeping her focus on Quinn's ear. But then she turned to her, and those blue eyes were right there, boring into her. Quinn seemed to be searching her eyes for something. A reason, maybe, that she would say something so stupid? A reason for wanting to move out to the guesthouse?

It's your body, Lacey wanted to say. *Your body is the reason. This shoulder that I could so easily kiss right now. Those magnificent tits that taunt me day in and day out. The narrow waist that my hand is currently resting on. Do you have any idea what you do to me, Quinn Kincaid?*

Instead of kissing that shoulder, Lacey broke the eye contact and rested her forehead on it. She couldn't look at the pain radiating from those eyes for another second. She whispered it again. "I'm so sorry."

She felt Quinn's head rest against hers. "I know."

"Last run!" Amy dropped the last of the shopping bags on top of the pile she'd already created in Quinn's bedroom.

"All that is from your stylist?" Lacey asked, looking at Quinn.

"Some of it's for you," Amy said, pointing at Lacey. "Shauna doesn't take new clients, but of course she took *the* Lacey Matthews."

Lacey's eyes fell. She didn't want to see Quinn's reaction to Amy's unwavering admiration for her. Not today. Not after what she'd done to her. "Amy, Quinn's had a rough morning. She...I..."

"I accidentally hit my arm getting in the hot tub. It's no big deal," Quinn interjected.

Lacey gave Quinn an appreciative glance. "I'm forcing her to stay in bed today. I thought we'd watch a movie. Want to join us?" Amy would be the perfect distraction. Maybe Lacey would put her right between the two of them so she wouldn't have to look at Quinn. Or catch her scent in the air. Or be tempted to hold her hand.

Amy's eyes darted between the two of them, almost as if she couldn't believe this was happening. "Awesome! I'll go make popcorn. Is there anything else I can get for either of you?"

Lacey picked up the remote and turned on the TV. She hit the menu button and somehow ended up in the DVR section. She tilted her head as she stared at the TV and then she turned around, her mouth gaping open. "You've been watching my soap!"

"What?" Quinn put out her hand. "Give me the remote."

Lacey held it behind her back. "No." She looked at Amy. "She's been *covertly* watching *Light of Day.*" She turned around and pointed at the TV. "See? All those episodes have been watched. Except yesterday's."

Amy gave Lacey the biggest nod she'd ever given. "Yep. Busted."

"What's the big deal?" Quinn asked. "I hired you...I mean... you're gonna be on my show, so it would make sense..."

Lacey giggled and shook her head. "No, it wouldn't. I'm not on that show anymore."

Amy gasped as she covered her mouth. "She got *ADDICTED!*"

"Fine!" Quinn shouted. "So I watched a few of the YouTube videos when you were on the show, and I wanted to see how certain things turned out. What's the big, hairy deal?"

Amy sat on the end of the bed and leaned in. "I totally get it. Jacob, Sarah's husband, is still pining away for her. He has a new wife, but he's so not into her, and can you blame him? She's nothing like Sarah. And besides, Sarah is the mother of their little girl, and that poor little thing misses her mama like nobody's business. This new chick doesn't have a motherly bone in her body."

Quinn also leaned forward, crossing her legs underneath her. "Jacob thinks she'll come back eventually?"

Amy glanced at Lacey. "Everyone hopes so. Did you see last week's episode where Detective Snow found Sarah's twin sister's red sweater in their father's limousine? I think they're going to bring him in for questioning soon. And if I had to guess, they're going to find Sabrina Covington being held captive in a cabin somewhere in Upper Canada."

"But..." Quinn glanced over Amy's shoulder at Lacey, who was standing there with a look of *I can't believe you watch my soap!* written all over her face. "If Sabrina comes back, that means Lacey would go back on the show."

Amy gleefully clapped her hands. "I know! Wouldn't that be great?"

"But I told you, Amy, that Lacey's going to be on my show for a while."

"I know. But you also said it's just a bit part, so once that's over, she can go back!"

Lacey threw the remote on the bed. "How about if I make the popcorn and you two can finish planning out my entire life for me." She pointed at Quinn. "And you are so busted."

A light knock on the guesthouse door forced Lacey's eyes up from the script she'd been studying. She glanced at the clock and then at the mess that surrounded her. She jumped out of bed and started picking up clothes and kicking shoes out of the way. "Give me a second!"

But it was too late. Quinn had opened the door and poked her head in. "Don't clean up on my account."

Lacey threw the pile of clothes she'd collected in a nearby hamper. "Is everything okay? Why are you up so late?"

"Can I come in?"

"Of course!" Lacey waved her in. "I was just in bed, studying lines." She looked down at herself and folded her arms over her tits. Her nightshirt was a thin material that didn't leave much to the imagination.

Quinn sat on the bed. She had the script for the first episode in her hand. "They did a great job with your character, don't you think? I like her name. Selena." She said the name with a certain amount of reverence in her voice, but her smile faltered.

Lacey sat next to her. "What's wrong?"

"I don't know if I'm ready for sixteen-hour days. You wait on me hand and foot. I haven't exercised in weeks. My stamina is shot." She turned and met Lacey's gaze. "Everyone thinks I'm tough like Jordan. Even the crew. And it's my fault. I want them to think I'm just as badass as she is." Quinn wiped a tear from her cheek. "But I'm not her. I'm just Quinn. And now, I'm broken, weak Quinn."

Lacey wiped another tear from Quinn's cheek with her thumb. "You're stronger than you give yourself credit for."

Quinn shook her head. "No. If I was strong, I wouldn't have needed you. I would've healed on my own, and I would've come out of the closet on my own."

Lacey wrapped her arms around Quinn. "Oh, honey. You can't even put on your own bra."

"Apparently neither can you." Quinn tried to break out of the embrace, but Lacey held on tight. She pressed her lips against Quinn's head, trying to hold back a giggle.

Quinn stopped struggling and relaxed into the embrace. "Shut up," she whispered unconvincingly.

"I'm here. And I'll be there tomorrow. We'll get through this together, okay?" Lacey gently kissed Quinn's head and inhaled her scent. She'd grown to love the sweet smell of Quinn's body lotion.

Quinn didn't move out of the embrace, but she scanned the room with her eyes. "Are you happier out here?"

"I wasn't unhappy in the main house. I just thought it was time to move out here, in case people want to start visiting now that you're doing a little better. Perpetuate the myth, you know? The drones need to see me going into the guesthouse, not the main house."

Quinn sat up and wiped her eyes and nose. "Yeah. I guess you're right."

Lacey nudged Quinn's leg. "You miss me, don't you?"

Quinn rolled her eyes. "Like I'll miss this cast when it's removed." She stood up and made her way to the door.

"It's okay to be scared, Quinn. And it's okay to need me...people." Lacey shrugged a shoulder. "You're still the hot, badass woman my girlfriend used to swoon over every Thursday night."

"Ex-girlfriend." Quinn gave her a smile. "And you're pretty badass yourself."

"Oh," Lacey said, slowly shaking her head. "You haven't even seen my best work."

Quinn smiled. "Tomorrow?"

"Tomorrow."

CHAPTER TWELVE

Quinn slid her script into her character's desk drawer. She started to run her hand over hair that was shellacked into a tight bun but thought better of it. A wardrobe person straightened her silk blouse and adjusted the sling. "Okay, you're good to go."

Quinn took a breath and slowly exhaled. "Ready."

Lacey stood on the other side of the office door. She smoothed down her crisply starched white blouse and threw her ponytail over her shoulder. "Ready."

"Okay, roll sound."

"Rolling."

"Mark!"

"Set."

"And action!"

Selena Scott (played by one Lacey Matthews) walked into her employer's office. "You wanted to see me, ma'am?"

Jordan Ellis gave a cursory glance. "Selena, is it?"

"You don't remember me? I interviewed last month and you hired me on the spot."

Jordan turned her attention to some paperwork on her desk. "Have a seat."

Selena noticed the sling on her employer's arm. "I heard about your accident."

"Yes, an unfortunate mishap, which is why you're here."

"I'm sorry, ma'am, but you must have me confused with someone else. I don't do personal injury. You want someone from the third floor."

"You're not here to sue anyone, Selena. You're here to be my personal assistant while I'm healing."

Selena glanced through the window, out into the main office. "I just talked to your personal assistant."

"She sits at a desk. I need someone mobile. Someone who can go to court with me and be by my side while I heal."

Selena shifted in her chair and cleared her throat. "I really think you have me confused with someone else, ma'am."

"Selena Scott. Harvard class of 2016. Had a job lined up at Hamilton and Nye until I poached you away to be the first-year associate you are today. So yes, Ms. Scott, I remember you."

"With all due respect, ma'am, you left out the part where I made Law Review. Where I worked my way through law school and busted my ass to gain the respect of not one, but two of the most prestigious firms in America. I haven't slept in three years, so you'll forgive me if I don't exactly feel honored by the chance to play caregiver...ma'am."

Fire lit up Jordan's eyes. "I'll let you know when—and if—I forgive you for that little outburst, Selena. In the meantime, did Harvard forget to tell you what first-years do? In case you missed that day, let me be clear. As a first-year associate in this esteemed firm, you do whatever the hell I tell you to do. So no, I won't forgive your little outburst. Any questions?"

Selena paused for a moment, looking rather stunned. "And if I refuse?"

Jordan raised her eyebrows. "Ms. Scott, I assume they still teach Contract Law at Harvard. You have made a commitment to this firm and I expect you to honor it." She paused for a moment. "That will be all, Ms. Scott." Selena turned around to leave. As she walked out the door, the slightest smile played on Jordan's lips. And for the most fleeting of moments, it seemed as if maybe, just maybe, Jordan's gaze had dropped down to Selena's ass.

"Cut!"

Quinn stayed in Jordan's chair. It had been a very long day and she was barely hanging on. The director walked over to her and pointed at Lacey, who was chatting with one of the cast members. "Friggin' brilliant pick, kid."

They had several directors who worked on *Jordan's Appeal*, but J.J. was Quinn's favorite. He wasn't your typical Hollywood director, he was more like a Hollywood caricature of a New England thug. He seemed like the kind of guy who would hang out with guys named Paulie, or pre-fame Afflecks and Wahlbergs, accent and all. Maybe it was because he was atypical, or maybe it was his total soft spot for Quinn. Either way, she adored the guy.

"So, everyone's happy with her?" Quinn glanced at Lacey. She already knew the answer. Lacey had stepped onto the set and instantly fit in.

"Hell yeah, everyone's happy. They love her. We're gonna add a few more scenes for tomorrow and see how things work." J.J. leaned on the desk so they were eye to eye. "How you holding up?"

Quinn forced a smile. "Can we try to get everything in two takes? That's about all I'm up for."

"You got it. And your girl seems up for it, that's for sure. I tell ya, soap actors are way underrated."

"So I've heard," Quinn mumbled, pulling her script out of the desk drawer. "And she's not my girl."

"The screen says otherwise, kid." He waved one of his assistants over. "Make sure she gets to her trailer. Superstar's gotta rest." Of course, it sounded like "supah stah," which always made Quinn laugh.

Lacey noticed a woman take Quinn's good arm to support her. She grabbed her purse and followed after them.

"Hey, Lacey!" J.J. shouted.

Lacey stopped and waited for J.J. to catch up to her while she watched Quinn with concern.

"Just wanted to say thank you, for stepping up like you did."

Lacey turned her attention to J.J. and smiled. "No problem. I'm thrilled to be here."

J.J. leaned in and lowered his voice. "She won't admit it, but I can tell Quinn's still hurtin', so we're gonna try to get everything in two takes tomorrow."

"I'm used to one, so…"

"I can tell," J.J. said with a grin. "You come to work ready to work, which is more than I can say for a lot of actors. Just do me a favor and keep an eye on Quinn for me, would ya? Let me know if we're pushing her too hard."

Lacey gestured toward the door with her thumb. "On it, boss. I'll see you tomorrow." She rushed to Quinn's trailer and knocked before she walked in. She found her alone in the trailer, sprawled out on the sofa with one foot on the floor.

"I should just stay here tonight. I'm too tired to go home." Quinn's voice sounded weak. Nothing like it had when she was in character as the talented and tough defense attorney, Jordan Ellis.

Lacey knelt down and rested her hand on Quinn's forehead, worried she had a fever. Her blouse was drenched in sweat and she looked pale. "Tomorrow will be easier. They just tried to pack as much into the first day as possible."

"Well, I can't take it," Quinn said as her lip started to quiver. "I'm sore and tired and I need my bed, and…what if I'm too scared to come out?" She bit her lip as she started to cry.

"It's going to be okay." Lacey ran her hand over Quinn's hair. "We'll go home and have dinner in bed, and take more drugs, and tomorrow, you'll still be hot and sexy and you'll probably flash your tits at me again and—"

Quinn giggled through her tears. "Shut up."

"You shut up," Lacey gently replied, smiling as she said it. She offered her hand. "Nurse Covington is back on duty. Let's get you out of these courtroom clothes."

Quinn got to her feet and waited while Lacey unbuttoned her blouse. "You were amazing today, Lace. Fierce."

"Fierce?" Lacey's eyes widened in surprise. She pushed the blouse off Quinn's shoulders and carefully maneuvered it over the cast.

"Yeah. That's the only word I can think of right now, in my current state."

Lacey moved behind Quinn and unzipped her skirt. "It's going to be fine, you know. Things aren't perfect. They're kind of messy, and I know you don't like messy, but it's going to work out. You're not going to lose your show, and one day, everything will be back to normal again." She pushed the skirt over Quinn's hips and let it drop to the floor so she could step out of it.

Normal. The truth was, nothing would ever be normal again. Not if they went through with the plan. And Quinn was scared to death. Lacey had been right all along; Quinn didn't have to do this. She lived such a private life as it was, surely she could date Ginny Strong privately.

Ginny Strong. Quinn's mad crush. She'd had her eye on the gorgeous, powerful woman for a while now. They were acquaintances who would run into each other at awards shows and premieres. Ginny was always so suave and graceful. She had an easy time talking to anyone. Quinn, on the other hand, would clam up and turn bright red when Ginny was within three feet of her. She'd forget to breathe, even. God, it was embarrassing. How the hell would she ever find the nerve to ask one of the most powerful women in Hollywood out on a date?

"Lift your foot."

"Sorry." Quinn lifted her foot and stepped into the yoga pants Lacey had packed for her.

"I found this the other day when I was shopping." Lacey pulled a sleeveless black zip-up hoodie out of the bag.

"That's perfect. Why didn't I think of that?" Quinn took the hoodie and easily slid it over her cast.

"I bought three of them. Black, white, and navy. Easy on and off." Lacey zipped it up and put her hands on Quinn's shoulders, looking her in the eye. "What you accomplished today was amazing. If anyone in this trailer is fierce, it's you. And I promise you that it'll all work out, okay?"

Quinn almost started to cry again. Lacey had been such a godsend these last few weeks. Yes, they argued at times, but it was mostly just blowing off steam. They both hated the situation. Quinn knew that. Lacey didn't want to be a caretaker and Quinn didn't want to be so dependent on her. It sucked. But they were both trying to make the best of it. And Quinn was grateful.

Before she could express her gratitude, Amy, Quinn's assistant, opened the trailer door. "I've got a cart to take you to your car." Amy stood a few feet away. "You don't look so good."

Quinn wiped her wet eyes. "I'll be fine. I just need to rest."

"Long day," Amy said with a nod. "You'll call me if you need anything?"

"J.J. said they might add some scenes for tomorrow."

"Okay. I'll send the pages over as soon as they're ready." Amy turned her attention to Lacey. "You don't have an assistant?"

"No." Lacey put her arm around Quinn's waist, holding her steady. "We should get going."

Amy stepped to the side, making room for them. "If Quinn doesn't mind, I'd be happy to act as your assistant too, Lacey."

Quinn snorted. "Of course you would. And it's fine, Amy. Do what you need to do."

Amy almost jumped up and down with glee. "Wait till my mom hears! She's gonna flip out! Ooh, can I get a business card printed? Amy Stevens, P.A. to Lacey Matthews."

As Amy verbalized her dreams, Lacey silently giggled and held on to Quinn as she made her way down the steps of the trailer. "God, I love her," she whispered.

"She's straight," Quinn whispered back. "And married, though I don't really think that matters when it comes to you."

"Maybe I'm her celebrity free pass. You know, a freebie she's allowed to…"

Quinn giggled and then winced. "Please don't make me laugh right now. And for God's sake, don't put that image in my head."

Amy locked the trailer and got behind the wheel of the cart, grinning from ear to ear as she looked at Lacey in the rearview mirror. "Everyone said you were amazing today. I told them, duh! It's Daytime Emmy Award–winning Lacey Matthews we're talking about. And then I told them all about *Light of Day* and how we grew up together."

Quinn tried to cover her giggling by resting her forehead on Lacey's shoulder. "I think she's in love with you," she whispered.

Quinn got settled in the passenger seat of Lacey's Range Rover. She took a deep breath and slowly let it out, trying to deal with the pain. Lacey reached across Quinn's body, securing her seat belt. They were eye to eye and almost nose to nose. "Thank you," Quinn said. "You really were amazing in those scenes. And at home."

Lacey gently wiped the sweat from Quinn's brow. She needed to get her home and in bed as soon as possible, since they would have to get up early and do this all over again the next day. "You're pretty amazing yourself. I've never known anyone besides my mom with your kind of strength."

"What was her name?"

Lacey's gaze fell. She didn't like saying her mother's name out loud. It hurt too much. "Daria."

"That's a beautiful name."

Lacey nodded. She didn't want to cry. She had to drive home in the heavy traffic that was pretty much a constant in L.A., no matter the time of day. She met Quinn's gaze again. They were so close, she could see the dark flecks in Quinn's blue eyes. "I took care of her before she died."

"I know."

Lacey's eyebrows rose up. "How did you—"

"You've done this before. And not on TV. In real life."

Lacey nodded again. For once, she didn't have something sarcastic or cynical to say about her new "job." "Let's get you home." She leaned in and kissed Quinn's head. She'd done it a few times. It was a sign of affection but it didn't really mean anything. At least, that's what she told herself.

❖

It was well into the early morning hours when Lacey stirred awake. She blinked a few times, trying to orient herself to her surroundings. She was in Quinn's room. And her hand was—oh God, she was spooning Quinn. She was on top of the covers, but still, her arm was wrapped around Quinn's middle. She slowly pulled away and rolled off the bed. She was headed to the door when Quinn said, "Could you bring me some water?" Her voice sounded gravelly and weak.

Lacey walked around the bed and knelt down. She touched Quinn's forehead, a habit she'd gotten into. "Did you get any sleep?"

"Not much."

Fuck. That meant Quinn was fully aware of Lacey's cuddling mishap. She picked up the empty water glass and went into the bathroom. She felt embarrassed, humiliated that she'd somehow ended up in that position. The last thing she remembered was that they were watching the news together. Quinn had asked her to fluff her pillow. Lacey had scooted closer to do just that and she must've stayed there, close enough to fall asleep and eventually end up spooning.

She filled the glass and set it on the bedside table. "Try to get some sleep. I'll wake you up when it's time." She quickly left the room before Quinn could say anything else, shutting the door behind her.

CHAPTER THIRTEEN

Lacey practically pranced into the bedroom, all smiles and happiness. "Day two!" she said, hoping her joyful attitude would overshadow what had happened a few hours earlier.

Quinn rolled onto her back and gave Lacey a sleepy smile. "Someone's happy to be working again."

"So happy." Lacey set a glass of orange juice on the bedside table. "You don't even know how bad it was out there in audition wasteland. I was this close to becoming an alcoholic."

Quinn smiled at the obvious exaggeration. "Sitting in that motel room in Hollywood, shooing away an annoying fly while you read the classifieds. Smoking your last cigarette and downing the last drop of vodka."

"Yes!" Lacey helped Quinn sit up and tucked a pillow behind her. "And then I throw the empty bottle against the wall because I'm so goddamned at the end of my rope, and someone on the other side yells at me, telling me to shut the hell up."

"And by nightfall, you're hooking on Sunset Boulevard."

"Waiting for Richard Gere to collect me so I can glamorize hooking to a whole new generation of young girls. Wait, is it really called hooking?" Lacey asked, her finger tapping her lips.

"I'd go with Lady of the Evening-ing." Quinn took a sip of the orange juice, and in a more serious tone she said, "Thank you, for taking care of me last night, and for staying with me."

Lacey waved a hand. "Babysitting your ass is my job, right?" She wasn't going to let herself blush, and if Quinn thought she could bring up the cuddling thing, well, that wasn't going to happen. She pulled the covers back and put out her hand. "Now, let's get moving."

"No problem, snugglebug." Quinn giggled and headed toward the bathroom.

J.J. took a final look at the camera placement. "Okay, ladies, let's see how well you fight."

Quinn found her mark on the elevator floor. "Oh, we're super good at that."

Lacey stood on her mark next to Quinn, holding a large file box. "Bring it."

The assistant director ran through the protocol and J.J. shouted "Action!"

As they exited the elevator, Jordan put her briefcase on top of the heavy file box Selena carried, weighing her down even more. "Pick up my dry cleaning tonight. I'll need my black suit for court tomorrow."

They entered Jordan's office and Selena dropped the box on the floor. "Why am I here, Jordan? All I do is schlep and drive and make coffee and get dirty looks from practically everyone in this office."

Jordan sat at her desk and thumbed through her pile of messages. "You amuse me."

"I amuse you?"

"Yes. I find your attitude…amusing."

Selena glared at Jordan. "So, I'm just here to humor you? You want to see how much grunt work you can make the Harvard grad do, is that it?" Selena leaned on Jordan's desk, getting in her face. "My mother cleaned toilets until the day she died. And I worked my ass off to make sure I didn't follow in her footsteps, so you'll have to excuse me if I don't want to carry your crap around and open your door and help you put on your damn pantyhose! That's not me paying my dues, Ms. Ellis. That's being your damn slave, and I'm done. And, FYI, no one wears pantyhose anymore!"

Selena stomped out of Jordan's office.

"Selena!"

Selena stopped and squeezed her eyes shut as she shook her head. She slowly turned around and was surprised to be face-to-face with Jordan.

"The privilege of sitting next to me in a courtroom—and it is a privilege—is reserved for those who have something exceptional to contribute. No first-year gets that chance. Not ever. But I knew you were talented and I didn't want to wait. So, a broken arm created an opportunity for you. And as far as those dirty looks you're receiving goes—they're jealous, Selena. They all get it, so why don't you?"

Selena stared at her, dumbfounded. "I guess I didn't—"

Jordan didn't let her finish. "If helping me out of my skirt is so terrible, then you're welcome to go back to your little cubicle on the second floor and do whatever it is you do in there."

Jordan sauntered back to her office and slammed the door.

"And cut! Let's reset." J.J. walked over to Lacey. "You nailed it, Lacey. You freakin' nailed it."

"Thanks, J.J. Not too much?"

J.J. chuckled. "You're holding your own with Quinn Kincaid. If you haven't noticed, she nails her lines every time." J.J. motioned with his head toward Brock Tennison, the actor who played Jordan's archnemesis, the district attorney, John Dent. "I'm only telling you this because I don't want you falling prey to him, but he's the one who slows us down. If he tries to get you to change what you're doing to suit his pace, tell him to…you know."

Lacey nodded. "Got it."

Quinn came out of the office grinning from ear to ear. She waited for J.J. to walk away and then went over to Lacey. "So, that scene felt familiar. Kind of like how it went the first day I met you."

"Oh?" Lacey smirked. "Did I upstage you that day too?"

"Yeah, speaking of that, will you pick up my dry cleaning? I'm going to need…no, stop!" Quinn squealed as Lacey tried to tickle her.

"And action!"

As they exited the courtroom, Jordan handed her briefcase to Selena, instead of throwing it on top of the file box she always seemed to be carrying. "You saved my ass back there, Selena. You pulled that precedent out of thin air."

"Glad to help. And now you can save mine by letting me off early today."

"Why would I do that?"

"I have something personal to take care of," Selena said.

"Whatever it is, I'm sure no one's life is at stake."

"Maybe not literally, but figuratively. Please, Jordan, can you help me out here?"

"Is this a millennial thing? You have one good idea and expect the day off?"

Selena stopped walking and pursed her lips together. She let out a big sigh as she ran to catch up with Jordan.

"Cut!"

Quinn slumped against the wall, holding onto her arm. Lacey dropped the file box and went to her. "Get you home?"

Quinn nodded, hoping no one would notice how exhausted she was. "Please."

Lacey glanced around to see if anyone was watching them. "You know, you could just tell them to cut back a little."

"I've never missed a day of work in five seasons. I'm not going to start now." Quinn pushed herself off of the wall and stood up straight, cradling her arm in her hand. "This is where you nod your understanding instead of arguing your point."

"Yeah," Lacey said with a huff. "Like you ever listen to me anyway." She held Quinn's elbow as they walked to the door.

"I'll make it up to you with Chinese take-out. I know how much you love eggrolls."

"Yeah? What else do you know about me?"

Quinn paused at the door and faced Lacey. "I know you're hardworking, just like me. We both take our jobs seriously, and that's why I know you understand where I'm coming from."

Lacey smiled. "This is where I nod my agreement, knowing you'll make good on those eggrolls."

"And action!"

Jordan and Selena sat at a small table. Jordan looked very relaxed as she twirled the olives in her martini glass. Selena took a sip of her wine and looked around. "Really? Lunch at a hotel bar?"

"Would you rather be sitting in Joe's, listening to all the overworked ADAs complain about their paychecks?"

Selena swirled the wine in her glass and inhaled the bouquet. "They should've worked harder in law school."

"No sympathy. I like it." Jordan sucked the vodka off an olive and dipped it back in her drink.

Selena sighed and looked at her watch. Jordan tilted her head, trying to find where the shaking was coming from. Selena's leg was bouncing up and down under the table. "Silly of me to think we could relax and get to know each other outside of work. You're free to go. Anything to stop the shaking."

Selena stood up. "Thank you. And it's not you."

"Oh, I can assure you, I wouldn't care if it was." Jordan forced a tight smile.

"I mean, it's not your company. It's just...I really need to buy a birthday present for my girlfriend and, you know, actually plan something for tonight."

"Girlfriend?" Jordan asked, her eyebrows rising in surprise.

"Yes, girlfriend. For now, at least. We're on shaky ground. I can't afford to miss another special occasion." Selena glanced at her watch again.

Jordan put up her hand. "Say no more. And buy her something twice as expensive as last year. Works like a charm."

Selena breathed a sigh of relief. "Thanks. I'll do that." She picked up her purse. "See you tomorrow."

Jordan watched Selena walk away. "Selena?"

"Yes?"

"Speak up next time. You're allowed to have a personal life, you know."

"No, I'm not."

Jordan laughed. "Touché."

Selena walked back and stood in front of Jordan, looking pensive. "Oh God. You have no idea what to get this girl of yours, do you?"

Selena shook her head.

"Looks like we're going to Barney's," Jordan said as she motioned for the check.

"Cut!" J.J. tipped his baseball cap. "Well done, ladies. I think we got it. Hopefully tomorrow won't be such a long day. Quinn, you rocked the hostile witness scene. Can't wait to see what the editors do with it."

"Thanks, J.J."

Lacey offered her hand. "I'm thinking leftovers."

Quinn took her hand and stood up. "Fine with me. I'll probably sleep in the car."

"And action!"

Jordan picked up a bottle of perfume and smelled it. "Tell me about this girlfriend of yours."

Selena picked up another bottle and winced at the smell. "Uh... she likes nice things, I guess."

"Don't we all? I need more than that. Is she an attorney?"

"God, no. If she were an attorney, she'd understand."

"Understand what?"

"My life. Or lack thereof." Selena picked up another bottle and took a sniff.

"It won't always be like this. Does she get that?"

"The only thing she gets is more bitter by the day."

"You're in the right store, then. And definitely with the right shopping partner. I have my share of experience with gifts that replace... you know..."

"Being there?"

"Exactly. So, what do you want this gift to say?" Jordan asked.

"Sorry for putting my career before you and your, I mean our..." Jordan turned to Selena and lifted an eyebrow, waiting for her to continue. "...cat."

"Oh, thank God," Jordan said, clutching her chest. "I thought you were going to tell me you have a child."

Selena laughed. "I barely know the cat's name. Trigger or Terry or something."

Jordan gave her a sideways glance. "You're worse than I am, Selena Scott."

"That's not possible. You don't even have a houseplant in that high-rise apartment of yours."

Jordan sighed as they walked up to the jewelry counter. "Yes, that's true. If it can't water itself or feed itself, it won't last long in my world." She pointed at a very expensive-looking gold watch. "That should do the trick."

Selena leaned down, peering into the glass display case. "That's beautiful. How much is it?"

Jordan put out her hand. "Don't ask. If you'd like to keep your girlfriend, and the cat, of course...just hand over your credit card."

"And cut! That's a wrap, everyone!"

J.J.'s eyes followed Lacey as she walked away. "Is she okay, Quinn?"

It was close to midnight. It had been an extra-long day thanks to a few technical glitches, but Quinn hadn't noticed anything unusual about Lacey's demeanor. They were all tired. "What are you seeing?"

J.J. shrugged. "Eh, maybe she's just that good at playing the overworked, deep in law school debt, having to placate Jordan Ellis, first-year associate. Seems like the character's staying with her today.

Anyway, you ladies go get some rest. You'll be glad to know we worked in a late call for you tomorrow."

J.J.'s words kept playing in Quinn's mind on the drive home. It was unfair, everything she'd put squarely on Lacey's shoulders. She was doing it all—the laundry, cooking, cleaning, errands, doctor's appointments, physical therapy sessions. And on top of that, now they were working fourteen-hour days. She glanced over at Lacey, and now that she was looking for it, the fatigue was so obvious, she had to look away. What was she thinking, putting it all on one person?

Once they were inside and the house was secured, Quinn stopped Lacey at the stairs. "I can take care of myself tonight. You go to bed."

"Nonsense." Lacey pushed past her and headed up the stairs. "You know you'll sleep better if you have a hot bath." She went into the master bathroom and turned on the water, then squeezed a dollop of bubble bath into the tub.

Quinn stood in the doorway. "I can do this on my own now."

Lacey huffed. "It takes you ten minutes to get your shirt off. Come here."

She took off the sling first, with Quinn watching her every move and breathing in her scent. She loved the way Lacey smelled. Even after a long day, it was a nice mix of her natural scent, shampoo, and just a hint of perfume. "I'm going to get help," Quinn exclaimed out of nowhere.

"Put your arm up. And good. I'm glad you're finally taking my advice."

"Not that kind of help. I don't need a shrink."

Lacey smirked. "The jury's still out on that one."

"Being fastidious about one's life is not a mental weakness," Quinn retorted.

"Fine." Lacey made a circling motion with her finger. "Turn around." She unhooked Quinn's bra and pushed her panties down to the floor. "All set." She smacked Quinn's bare bottom. "Get in and I'll wash your hair."

"I'm serious about the help." Quinn stepped into the tub and sank down in the water, resting her cast on a towel Lacey had placed on the ledge. "Would you prefer a cook or a housekeeper or both?"

Lacey came out of the walk-in closet holding a bathrobe, stopping dead in her tracks when she heard the words. "Am I not taking care of you well enough?"

"God, no." Quinn fervently shook her head. "No, that's not it."

Lacey knelt by the tub. She filled a pitcher with water and poured it over Quinn's hair. "You don't like people in your house."

"That's true, I don't. But it's not fair, expecting you to take care of absolutely everything now that we're working these long days. It's too much for one person."

"It's a lot, but I can handle it. You're paying me to handle it."

"Not enough." Quinn turned to Lacey, looking her in the eye. "The thing is, as long as you're here with me, I think I'll feel safe, even with strangers in the house."

Lacey stopped what she was doing. "You *are* safe. I wouldn't let anyone hurt you. Ever."

Quinn nodded and looked away. She believed Lacey. With her whole heart, she believed her. "Thank you, for everything."

Lacey put shampoo in her hand. She leaned over the tub and massaged it into Quinn's hair. "I hate cleaning toilets. Maybe you could hire someone to come in once a week. I'll deal with them. You don't even have to meet them if you don't want to. And as far as the other thing goes, unless you're trying to tell me that you hate my cooking..."

"I love your cooking."

Lacey smiled. "Just the housekeeper, then. And I get to keep the title of...um...what do they call the person who bathes the lady of the house?"

Quinn giggled. "I believe her title is lady's maid."

"Oh. I guess that makes perfect sense." She scooped water into the pitcher and rinsed Quinn's hair until all of the shampoo was gone. "Am I rockin' being a lady's maid or what?"

"Mmm...where have you been all my life?"

Lacey didn't answer. Instead, she got up and set a fresh towel by the tub. "I'll come back up and check on you once I've showered."

Quinn soaked for a little longer and then got into bed naked, pulling the sheet up and tucking it under her arms. She looked at her phone one last time and set it on the bedside table. She was ready to turn her light off, but she'd gotten used to Lacey's nightly habit of checking on her before she went to bed—one final check to see if she needed anything. She usually didn't, and she didn't really need anything tonight, either. That didn't matter. It comforted her.

Quinn's orderly brain liked consistency, and if she was honest,

Lacey's hands inspecting and touching her felt good too. She'd never had such tender care in her life. Lacey may have a sharp tongue, but her hands were a different story. They were soft, warm and gentle.

Quinn found herself craving the attention, and that worried her some. But tonight, if Lacey came back into her room, she'd set her fears aside and let herself bask in the touch. No jokes. No sarcastic comebacks. Those could wait.

"Sorry. The hot water felt so good, I let it run on my back a little longer than normal." Lacey's wet hair was piled on top of her head. She had on pink flannel pajama bottoms and a purple tank top. Quinn smiled, trying to guess where Lacey would touch her first. Her eyes widened when she saw the banana in her hand. Lacey laughed at Quinn's expression. "Oh my. Where did your dirty little mind just go?"

Quinn demurred. "Nowhere."

"Uh-huh." Lacey placed the banana next to a glass of water. "I'm leaving this here for you in case I sleep in. Eat it with your morning pill, okay?"

Quinn gave her a salute. "Okay, boss."

Lacey sat on the edge of the bed. Her hand went to a red spot on Quinn's upper arm that was poking out from under the cast. She gently ran her finger over the spot. "What's going on here?"

"Irritation." Quinn pointed to a spot by her fingers. "There's some down here too." She knew what would happen. More touching.

Lacey inspected the fingers. "God, Quinn, this can't be good." She pulled the bedside table drawer open and took a tube of antiseptic cream out. "Just in case."

Quinn watched intently, all of her senses firing and her brain free-falling into a state of Zen. Lacey's voice, her touch, her freshly showered scent, all seeping into every pore of her body.

"What about the other side?" Lacey waited for Quinn to lift her arm. She tsk'd when she saw more redness on the inside of her arm. "Why didn't you tell me your cast was irritating you?"

"We've been busy."

Lacey leaned forward even more, rubbing the cream in. "We're not so busy that we can't get you a new cast." She tossed the cream on the table and set her eyes on Quinn. "You're in enough pain. You don't need more." She reached out and pushed a lock of damp hair behind Quinn's ear. "Don't suffer needlessly, okay?"

Quinn nodded, anticipating the next touch. It came in a long, reassuring stroke up and down her thigh. She wanted to throw the covers off and let Lacey do it again on her bare skin, but she was naked. The hand made its way back down her leg to her foot. A little squeeze and then back up, coming to rest just above her knee.

"The bath helped," Lacey said.

Quinn lifted her eyebrows in question.

"You're relaxed now. You seemed tense on the drive home, like you were worried about something."

"You," Quinn said. "I was worried about you." She wanted to reach out and touch Lacey's fingers that were resting on her leg, but she didn't. Instead, she held Lacey's stare.

"I'm good."

"Are you, Lace?" They studied each other for a moment. "I mean, are you really?" Quinn ran her hand down her own leg until her fingertips touched Lacey's. "Whatever you need...you'll tell me, right?"

Lacey didn't answer immediately. Her eyes fell to their fingers that were barely touching. "Yeah." It came as a whisper, so she said it again. "I mean, yeah." She let her middle finger inch up a little bit so it covered Quinn's. "I know we're both under a lot of pressure right now, and I know we fight sometimes, but I'm good."

Again, Quinn resisted her urges. Instead of leaning forward and intertwining their fingers, she just nodded. But the air between them was getting warmer with each passing second.

Lacey did lean forward, her hand ending up on Quinn's cheek. "Are *you* good? Am I giving you everything you need?"

The question hung in the air, their eyes locked on one another. Quinn covered Lacey's hand with her own. She wanted to turn and kiss Lacey's palm. She wanted to pull her closer and tell her *No, I need more. Kiss me. Touch me. Be with me.*

"What do you need?" Lacey's eyes bore into Quinn's, looking for answers. Quinn's heart skipped a beat when those same eyes dropped to her chest. Had the sheet fallen? Was she showing more cleavage than she'd intended? Did it matter?

It didn't matter, because they were never supposed to be lovers. They had a contract. And that trumped everything. With a quick inhale of air and a motherly pat on Lacey's hand, she pushed her feelings away "I'm good. Now, go get some rest. You need it."

"Oh God," Lacey groaned. "Please don't say I look haggard."

"What? Did someone say that to you?"

Lacey's wet hair started to fall out of the bun she'd haphazardly put it in. She let it fall and pulled it all to one side, running her fingers through it. "That jackass who plays the judge said I looked haggard today."

"Bill?" Quinn scoffed. "A sixty-year-old man with bags under his eyes the size of grapes had the nerve to tell you..." She let her head fall back against the headboard. "What an asshole."

"Is he right?"

Quinn's eyes widened as she leaned forward. She knew she shouldn't do it, but her hand made its way to Lacey's hair, her fingers running through the long mane. "My God, no. Lace, you're..." *Gorgeous. Smart. Sexy.* It was a long list. But saying those things out loud... "Wait a second. Are you fishing for compliments?"

Lacey pushed Quinn's hand away and went to the door. "Nah, I'm too haggard to fish for compliments. See you in the morning."

The door closed and Quinn let her head fall back against the headboard. "Fuck."

CHAPTER FOURTEEN

"And action!"

Jordan and Selena sat across the table from each other, Selena working on her laptop and Jordan jotting down notes for her client's upcoming testimony.

Selena stopped typing and said, "How do you do it, Jordan? How do you shut it all off in the courtroom?"

"As a woman, you'll find out pretty quickly you don't have a choice. Men can whine all day about how the judge hurt their feelings with a denied motion. If I pulled that crap I'd be labeled hysterical." Jordan set her pen down. "If I'm caught up in my own stuff—which I never am—it's tough to see when a witness is about to crack. Or when a first-year is about to crack."

Selena's eyes widened. "How did you know?"

Jordan sat back in her chair and studied Selena. "Well, for starters, you didn't laugh at my joke this morning."

"You made a joke?"

Jordan shrugged. "It was funny too. About the judge's robes?"

Selena shook her head.

"It's too late now. You were so busy trying to pretend that everything's fine—so wrapped up in making sure I didn't notice how sad you are. But thanks to my keen ability to completely turn off all emotion, I'm able to see right through you."

Selena lowered her gaze. "Wow. Really?"

Jordan waved her hand. "No. I saw the watch we bought when you opened your briefcase."

Selena glanced down at her open briefcase. "Yeah, um…I didn't wish her a happy birthday before I left for work yesterday. She assumed I'd forgotten, which I had, until I got to work and looked at the calendar."

"Did she break up with you?"

Selena couldn't answer immediately. Tears welled up in her eyes. "Yes," she finally whispered.

"I'm so sorry. Selena, you know you can tell me these things, don't you?"

Selena wiped a tear from her eye and nodded. A knock on the door interrupted them. Jordan quickly stood up. "I'll handle it." She lingered for a few seconds, looking like she wanted to say more, and then she left the room.

"And cut! Great job with the tears, Lacey." J.J. leaned on the table next to her. "Just one more take to make sure."

Lacey patted her eyes dry. "No problem. Just give me a minute."

Quinn sat back down at the table. "How did she do it?"

"What?" Lacey asked, confused by the question.

"Those tears weren't hard to come by. How did she break up with you?"

"You're talking about Dani, my ex?"

Quinn slowly nodded. "Yeah."

Lacey chuckled, trying to laugh off the pain. "Second worst day of my life. No warning. But if you want these tears on cue, I can't use them up right now."

"And action!"

Jordan had a satisfied grin on her face as she exited the courtroom. "Our afternoon just opened up. What should we do?"

Selena put her own satchel strap on one shoulder and Jordan's on the other. "I can't believe you got her to dismiss the case. You're a genius!"

"And you questioned being my slave." Jordan laughed. "We're a good team, you and I."

"Do you really think so, or are you just being extra nice to me today because you feel sorry for me?"

"Empathy, not pity." Jordan pushed the down button on the elevator. "I can relate. It's been a while, but your ex, with all of her emotional needs and birthday expectations, totally reminds me of mine."

Selena's mouth dropped open. "You? With a woman?"

"No, but a breakup's a breakup. Though I'm sure if I *were* with a woman, I wouldn't get my sorry ass dumped."

They stepped into the elevator and stood side by side. "Another joke. It was a good one."

"I thought so," Jordan said, looking awfully smug.

"Cut! Let's break for lunch."

Lacey dropped both briefcases where she stood. "Do these really have to be so heavy?"

Quinn stepped out of her high heels and slipped on a pair of flip-flops she kept close by. "Authenticity, Lace. I hate it when actresses walk around with such obviously empty purses that they're practically caving in on themselves."

"Oh, great! So I have you to thank for that heavy file box I've carried around for weeks?"

"Yep. But as you can see, Selena is getting more efficient with what she carries into the courtroom."

Lacey scowled as they walked off the set. "You're buying lunch."

Lacey liked having a personal assistant. She sat cross-legged on the sofa in Quinn's trailer, hungrily chowing down on the lo mein Amy had just delivered. "I have a theory."

"It's not polite to talk with your mouth full?" Quinn guessed.

"That's not my theory, but okay." Lacey finished chewing and then took a sip of her soda. "Don't you find the script changes interesting?"

Quinn took off her reading glasses, giving Lacey her full attention. "You think they're onto us?"

"What's with the last-minute scene? Selena thinks Jordan was with a woman? Seriously?"

"I know. I wondered about that too. I mean, the fact they made Selena gay in the first place. No one pitched that."

Lacey set her food down, looking rather worried. "What if they're too far ahead of us? What if they want Jordan in a gay relationship, just not with Selena? Selena's only a first-year associate and I'm just a soap actress."

Quinn closed her laptop. "First of all, you may be a soap actress, but you're a brilliant soap actress. As for Selena, she's smart and she challenges Jordan. She's also very easy on the eyes. I can't imagine them bringing in some big-name—"

Lacey put up a finger. "Wait, what was that last thing you said?"

"I can't imagine—"

"No. Right before that."

Quinn bit her lip to keep from smiling. "I'm not sure what I said before that."

Lacey grinned. "Come on. Say it again. I'm feeling vulnerable here. They could replace me at any moment with some super actress."

"That's not a thing," Quinn quipped. "But super *model* is a thing. Maybe someone like—"

"Shut up." Lacey threw herself back on the sofa, staring up at the ceiling. "I can't compete with that. I'm just a first-year associate you found on the second floor huddled in her little cubicle writing writs of habeas...whatever."

Quinn giggled. "A first-year associate who is very easy on the eyes. And Jordan can be shallow, so don't worry about it."

Lacey smiled. She knew Quinn found her attractive. She'd noticed the lingering looks every now and then, but it was still nice to hear her say it. "I just don't want to get dumped before I get a chance to show them what I can do."

"We won't let them."

Lacey rolled onto her side, facing Quinn. "What do you mean?"

Quinn lowered her voice. No one else was in the trailer with them, but she wanted to make sure she wasn't overheard by a passerby. "If they really are seeing something already, that means we're doing our job with the slow and subtle buildup. Now, maybe we should turn up the heat. Show them what fabulous chemistry we have. They'd be insane to give Jordan another love interest after they see that."

Lacey's eyes lit up. "Really?"

"Starting today." She pointed at Lacey's lo mein. "Now, stop talking and eat your lunch."

"Are you this bossy in bed?"

"No, but I bet you are."

Lacey purposely took a big bite of food and mumbled, "I plead the Fifth." Her phone started vibrating on the table. Quinn looked at the screen.

"It's your father."

Lacey put up a finger and tried to quickly chew her food. Quinn picked up the phone and in her most friendly voice said, "Hello, Professor Matthews, this is Quinn Kincaid. Lacey is just trying to swallow a big bite of food." She winked at Lacey. "Yes, it's so nice to talk to you too. Oh, you saw the season premiere? Yes, it's going great. We're just finishing up episode four. Well, thank you, Professor Matthews, that's nice of you to say. Okay, Ben it is. It looks like Lacey's ready for you now. Hope to meet you sometime soon, Ben." Quinn looked up in surprise. "This weekend?"

Lacey grabbed the phone and put it on speaker. "Hey, Dad. What's up?"

"Quinn sounds nice. I can't wait to meet her. Hey, I know it's late notice, but I want to fly out there this weekend."

Lacey looked at Quinn and scowled. "Um...Dad, the shooting schedule is grueling right now. I wouldn't be a good host. I couldn't show you L.A. I couldn't—"

Ben chuckled. "I don't expect you to show me L.A., honey. I just need to see my only daughter in person. Make sure she's okay. Your mother would be so disappointed if she knew we'd gone this long without contact. Her last words were—"

Lacey quickly grabbed the phone off the table and turned off the speaker. She turned away from Quinn as she put the phone to her ear. "I know what her last words were," she whispered. "Stay in the same city, same neighborhood..." Lacey and her father said the last part together. "Same house if you can." She turned back toward Quinn. "Yes, Dad. It is a long time."

All of the air left Lacey's body and was replaced with a heavy dose of guilt. It was the longest she'd ever been away from her father. Normally, they made time for each other at least once a week, sharing a coffee or lunch on the weekends. Now was simply not a good time. They used the weekends to catch up on sleep and errands and anything else that got neglected during the week. This definitely wasn't like shooting a daytime soap where you made it home for dinner every night. This was a heavy grind, especially for Quinn, being the star of the show and in practically every scene.

But Lacey couldn't just outright tell him no. "I'll have to check with Quinn."

Quinn stood up. "No, you don't. Tell him it's fine. Tell him I'm looking forward to meeting him."

Lacey gave Quinn a grateful smile. "Okay, Dad. Email your flight info. And Quinn says she's looking forward to meeting you." She ended the call and threw her hands up in despair.

"It's fine," Quinn said, her eyes lighting up. "Maybe I'll cook."

"Oh God, no."

"Hey! You haven't even..." Quinn thought about it for a second. "Oh, yeah. The French toast," she said, referring to the one time she'd tried to cook for Lacey.

"It's called the French Toast Incident, and who the hell ruins French toast?" Lacey didn't wait for a reply. "Never mind. We'll grill something."

Ben wrapped his arm around his daughter as they slowly made their way to the fire pit. Lacey leaned in and rested her hand on his chest. "It's good to have you here, Dad."

A tall man, with thinning hair and glasses, Ben Matthews looked like your typical history professor. Lacey got her long legs from him, along with her affectionate nature. Ben was never stingy with hugs and kisses when it came to his little girl. "It's good to be here, honey. And as always, you cooked way too much delicious food for your dear old dad."

"I'd send you home with the leftovers if I could."

Ben stopped and turned toward the view, keeping his arm firmly wrapped around Lacey. "My gosh, what a view."

"Yeah, it's pretty amazing."

"Quinn is pretty amazing too. Any chance there could be something between you two?"

Lacey wasn't sure how to answer that. Her father didn't know about Quinn's plans to come out of the closet. He also didn't know anything about their contract. Her first inclination was to be truthful and scoff at the idea. Tell him just how incompatible they seemed to be. But she quickly squelched those feelings in favor of the lie they would soon tell the whole world. "Maybe," she said with a shrug.

Ben chuckled.

Lacey pulled away from him. "What? Why are you laughing?"

"Because my daughter is glowing."

Lacey folded her arms and scowled at him. "I am not. And even if I was, it's just because I live in this mansion with a view of that." She waved her hand at the beautiful sunset. "And because I'm on one of the best shows on TV. Not because"—she glanced back at the house—"of her."

Ben tucked his hands in his pockets and rocked on his feet, a huge grin plastered across his face. "Okay."

"Okay? What does that mean, okay?" She grabbed the two bottles of beer they'd brought out and headed for the fire pit. She opened a bottle for herself and took a big swig. Then opened one for him and handed it to him when he walked up.

"This looks cozy." Ben took a sip of his beer and sat in a lounge chair. Lacey sat on a love seat on the other side of the fire.

"Very different from New York, where we all live on top of each other in little boxes." Lacey set her beer on the arm of the chair and picked at the label. Her brow was furrowed like she was deep in thought.

"It suits you," Ben said, smiling at his daughter.

Lacey shook her head. "Daddy—"

"I won't say anything in front of her, if that's what you're worried about." He leaned forward in his chair. "You're not a parent yet, so you might not be able to understand the joy I feel right now." He put his hand on his chest. "My heart is full because I can see that you're happy out here. You're thriving. And you can tell me all day long that it has absolutely nothing to do with that magnificent woman..." Ben stopped and stood up when he saw Quinn walking toward them with something tucked under her good arm. He reached out to help her. "Here, let me take that."

"It's cooling down pretty fast out here, so I brought us a couple of blankets."

Ben set one on his chair and waited for Quinn to sit next to Lacey before he laid one over their laps. "There you go." He winked at Lacey and went back to his chair and sat down. "We were just talking about this amazing view you have." He gestured with his beer at the ocean view that was quickly fading as the sun disappeared on the horizon.

Quinn tucked her legs to the side and leaned in toward Lacey. "Honestly, Ben, I never fully appreciated it until Lacey moved in. She loves it out here, don't you, Lace?"

Lacey shrugged. "It's okay." She looked at her dad and giggled.

Ben shook his head and laughed with her. "You probably don't know this, Quinn, but when Lacey was a little girl, she was a handful. She had so much energy and so many opinions, her mother and I were exhausted most of the time, just trying to keep up with her."

Quinn nudged Lacey's shoulder. "That doesn't surprise me at all."

"Anyway, we'd saved up all year for her Christmas present; a trip to Disneyworld. We had a great time. Took a ton of pictures. Ate junk food the whole time. Any kid's dream, right?"

Quinn started to giggle. "Oh God, where is this going?"

Ben shook his finger at Lacey. "We get back home and we ask her, so what did you think of your Christmas present? And she said, 'It was okay,' with the biggest shrug that a ten-year-old could manage."

Quinn covered her mouth with her hand. "Oh, God."

"Yeah," Ben said in agreement. "And, as you can imagine, that didn't sit well with Daria, so she turned it around on Lacey."

"My mom started shrugging a lot," Lacey said. "I got straight A's and I got a shrug. She opened a Mother's Day present and I got a shrug and an 'It's okay,' even when it was something I'd worked really hard on, like TWO crocheted hot pads." Lacey held up two fingers to emphasize her point.

"Aww…" Quinn rubbed Lacey's leg. "Did you learn to appreciate what your parents did for you after that?"

"It went on for a few months," Ben said. "And one day, Lacey couldn't take it anymore. She broke down crying, begging for forgiveness, which Daria quickly gave her, and after that, it became a running joke in our family. The last time I said it to Lacey, she'd just given me a retouched, beautifully framed photo of Daria's and my engagement picture. I cried and shrugged my shoulders."

Quinn still had her hand on Lacey's leg. She gave her a sympathetic smile, then turned back to their guest. "It's been so nice having you here, Ben. I hope you know you're always welcome."

"Thank you. And I'll be happy to take you up on that when you girls are on hiatus. As it is, I'm flying back out in the morning."

Lacey sat up. "What? You just got here."

Ben put up his hand. "No arguments. I know how busy you both are, and I appreciate you taking time for me today. I just needed to see that you're safe and happy so I could stop worrying." He stood up and looked at his watch. "It's midnight my time. Do you mind if I call it a night?"

Lacey and Quinn both stood up. "Sorry, Dad. I forgot how late it is for you."

Ben offered his hand. "I'd give you a hug, Quinn, but I don't want to crush your arm." He quickly took his hand back and chuckled. "Well, you can't exactly shake my hand, either."

"I'll take a hug." Quinn stood on her tiptoes and wrapped her arm around his shoulders.

Ben hugged her as gently as he could and then took Quinn's left hand in his. "Take care of my girl. She's feisty, but she has a heart of gold."

Quinn laughed. "Yes, she is. And don't worry. She's safe here."

❖

Lacey got her father settled in the guesthouse and then knocked on Quinn's bedroom door. "You still up?" she asked, poking her head in.

Quinn took off her reading glasses and tossed them on the bed next to her. "A car will be here at nine to pick up your dad."

"Thank you for taking care of that." Lacey sat on the edge of the bed and crossed her legs. "You were fidgety at dinner."

"Nothing gets by you." Quinn leaned back, resting on the headboard. "My skin is itchy under the cast, and I didn't want to pull out the knitting needle to scratch it at the dinner table."

"Oh, no. That would've been terrible," Lacey mocked.

"My mother would tell you so." Quinn smiled. "Your dad seems like a lovely man."

"Yeah," Lacey returned the smile. "He's one of the good guys."

"Unlike my father." Quinn looked away. She'd never told Lacey the story, and she wasn't sure she wanted to now, but Lacey sat there, patiently waiting for more. "He waited until I'd gone off to college to tell my mom that he'd been having an affair with his much younger assistant. He thought if he waited until I wasn't there to witness it all, it would save our relationship. Well, he was wrong."

"Is that why you go by your mother's maiden name? Kincaid?"

"How did you know that?"

"Everybody knows that, Quinn. It's on your wiki page."

"Oh, right." Quinn kept her eyes on her hands. "As their only child, I was expected to live up to these impossible standards. Meanwhile, he'd been doing whatever the hell he wanted. He probably fucked her and then came home and reprimanded me at the dinner table for getting a B in...whatever." She took a deep breath. "When I found out about it, I decided to start living my life for me. I moved out here, and no, I did not want to go by his name."

"They didn't want you to go into acting?"

Quinn scoffed. "My mother is reluctantly proud of me. And my father...he's dead to me."

Lacey shook her head. "Don't say that."

Quinn looked her in the eye. "It's true."

Lacey pursed her lips together and sighed. She paused for a moment before she said, "I was a bratty teenager when my mom got sick. You've never seen someone sober up so quickly, but I still have regrets. I still think about all the times I could've said more, done more for her. And she wasn't perfect. She had a temper. She didn't always think before she spoke. But she was my mom, you know? And I'd give anything to have just one more day with her." She looked at Quinn, waiting for a reply. All she got was a nod. "Anyway, the cast might come off next week." She reached for the knitting needle sitting on the bedside table and held it up. "In the meantime…"

Quinn took the needle and Lacey stood up. She leaned over Quinn and kissed her forehead. "Sleep well."

Quinn grabbed Lacey's hand. She held on to it for a few seconds, looking like she had something important to say. All that came out was, "You too," as she let go.

CHAPTER FIFTEEN

"Okay, Quinn. Everything looks good, so let's get that cast off."
"Yay!" Lacey clapped her hands. "No more being your lady's maid."

The doctor laughed. He'd met Lacey once before during a check-up, and enjoyed her humor. "She'll still have to take it easy, except in therapy. In therapy, I expect you to kick her butt."

"Will do, Doc. No worries there. I've always wanted to play a female drill sergeant who's both hated and loved by her new recruits."

"I think it's mostly just hate those poor kids feel," Quinn said.

"Whatever. We'll hit the Army surplus on the way home and get me a drill sergeant's hat. Maybe the whole outfit."

Quinn groaned. "Good God, Doc. You've created a monster."

A few minutes later, a nurse stepped into the room with a cast saw. "This won't take but a minute and you'll be free again."

Quinn put her hand on the nurse's arm, stopping her. "Will you save the autograph? I think it might be valuable someday." Quinn's eyes met Lacey's. They shared a smile. Quinn looked away first, her cheeks reddening. "Do you watch soaps?" she asked the nurse.

"Yes! I have to record them and then catch up on my days off. Who signed your cast?"

"Lacey Matthews." She pointed across the room. "Over there in the corner."

The nurse immediately stopped what she was doing and turned around. "Sarah Covington!"

Lacey gave her a little wave. "Hi."

Quinn grinned from ear to ear, happy to give the spotlight to the woman who had cared for her so well. The woman who would soon be thrown into a very big spotlight.

❖

"Lift those beans, Quinn Kincaid!" Lacey was pushing Quinn to finish a set of exercises with nothing but a small bean bag in her hand. "Are you telling me you can't lift beans?"

"Fuck you." Quinn threw the bean bag with her good arm. It didn't even come close to hitting Lacey, landing in the deep end of the pool.

"Fuck me? Yeah, you're way too weak and you obviously aren't so proficient with your left hand." Lacey shook her head dramatically. "Such a pity." She motioned with her head toward the pool. "That bean bag isn't going to save itself."

"I hate you so much sometimes," Quinn said with a scowl.

"No. You hate being weak. You hate being out of control. You hate that you can't get on your bike and ride up that mountain, so take your clothes off and save that bean bag!"

"Take off my clothes? Ha! Nice try, drill sergeant." Quinn plopped into a chair at the table and drank from her bottle of water.

Lacey sauntered over to the table. "Hey, that's what Jillian Michaels would tell you to do. She'd say, Quinn Kincaid, you hot motherfucker, take off your damn clothes and save that fucking bean bag!"

"I'm tired. And you're bossy as hell. It's getting old." She unconsciously rubbed her sore arm.

"Fine." Lacey pulled up a chair. "You can have a break, but we have to do these exercises before dinner." She grabbed a bottle of lotion off the table and gently massaged Quinn's arm.

"Is the housekeeper done yet?"

"She has a name. It's Vera, and she'll be done in a few minutes."

Quinn closed her eyes and moaned, clearly enjoying the way Lacey was working her muscles. "Are you sure she hasn't taken any photos of the house?"

"Positive. It's a very reputable company she works for. And she does a great job. Much better than I do. Compared to you, I'm a total slob."

"I had a stalker," Quinn blurted out.

Lacey looked completely thrown off. "What?"

"I had a stalker. That's why I'm so obsessed with privacy."

Lacey's hand ran down Quinn's arm to her hand. "God. That must've been…"

"Greer never understood my fears. He never respected our privacy. I hated him for that."

It was the first time Lacey had heard Quinn say her ex-husband's name out loud. She wasn't sure what to say, so she stayed quiet.

"It happened when Greer was shooting a movie in Montana. The guy got into my bedroom when I was asleep. I'd left the balcony door open by accident, and when I woke up, he was standing over me, taking photos on his phone."

"Oh, God." Lacey squeezed Quinn's hand.

"It turns out the guy had been watching me for years. They found all sorts of pictures and crazy love letters in his apartment."

"Jesus. It's no wonder…"

"I don't trust anyone, Lace. I know it's wrong. I know I'm keeping everyone at bay now. Even people who used to be close friends." Quinn shook her head at herself. "I renovated this house, and none of the cast and crew have ever seen it. The people I work with every day don't even know where I live."

"I'm so sorry." Lacey said it again, unsure what else to say.

"I know that doesn't jive with you waltzing into my life and me just letting you move right in. Will you keep rubbing my arm? It feels so good."

Lacey poured more lotion into her hands. "Or letting me, of all people, take care of you when you were your most vulnerable."

"I know," Quinn agreed. "It was a feeling. And really, it was either you or a stranger. So, I went with my gut."

Vera poked her head out of the door. "I'm done, Ms. Matthews. May I have my phone back?"

Lacey shot Quinn a sly grin as she stood up and wiped her hands off on a towel. "Apparently, I don't trust anyone, either," she whispered. She walked over to Vera, pulling a phone out of her back pocket. "Here you go. I'll walk you out."

"Gut feeling," Quinn said with a smile.

"And action!"

"I can't believe you!" Selena followed Jordan into her office and slammed the door behind her.

Jordan tossed a file on her desk and sat down. "I thought it went well."

"You were flirting with opposing counsel during a deposition! Is that what you'd like me to learn from you?"

"You're exaggerating."

"AM I?" Selena shouted.

Jordan noticed her assistant turn and look at them so she got up and closed the blinds. "Calm down," she warned. "He's a friend."

"Oh! He's a friend! So that must make it okay?"

"What is this really about, Selena?"

"It's unprofessional. And you'll be lucky if the judge doesn't notice you and your...sex eyes!"

"Sex eyes?" Jordan asked in amusement. She sauntered over to Selena. "And just what are my sex eyes saying to you right now?"

Selena tried to hold Jordan's gaze but had to look away. Her chest was heaving with anger as she made eye contact again. "He's an ass. You deserve better."

Jordan went back to her desk, keeping her back to Selena. "We're done for the day. You can go." She kept her back turned until Selena left. Then she turned around and leaned on her desk while she stared at the closed door.

"Cut!" J.J. took his copy of the script out of his back pocket. "Was *sex eyes* in the script?"

The script supervisor stepped forward, reading from the script. "It's unprofessional and you'll be lucky if the judge doesn't notice your *antics*. Yeah, nothing about sex eyes."

Lacey threw her hands up in the air. "She has sex eyes, okay? It just came out!"

"Attention, everyone!" Quinn waved at the crew, trying to get their attention. "If anyone calls me Sex Eyes, they're fired!"

J.J. laughed. "Hey, maybe we'll keep the sex eyes, but let's do another take, just in case."

Quinn turned to Lacey and whispered, "Good one."

"Oh, I wasn't making that up," Lacey replied. "They say you wanna fuck me."

Quinn's mouth hung open.

"You asked what your sex eyes are saying to me, and that's what they're saying. You desperately want to bend me over that desk and—"

Quinn folded her good arm over the fake cast she now had to wear and smiled at Lacey, waiting for her to finish. Lacey didn't know that the makeup artist was standing right behind her, waiting to pat the shine off her forehead. Laura cleared her throat, causing Lacey to close her eyes in embarrassment. She turned around. "Sorry, Laura."

Laura usually kept her South Carolina accent in check for the Hollywood crowd, but at that moment it managed to come out in full force as she laughed. "Honey, don't you dare be sorry. Whatever this thing is that you two have, it's hot, hot, hot. Not to mention funny. Ratings are gonna shoot through the roof and that means I'll still have a job next year. So you two can sex eyes each other till you get glaucoma and I won't be anything but grateful."

The following day, J.J. was giving Lacey direction as they prepared for a scene. "You're going for gentle here. Selena is feeling contrite about their argument and Jordan needs to sense that. She needs to believe Selena's starting to care about not only her job, but also her."

Lacey put on her character's coat. "A turning point?"

J.J. pointed his script at her and winked. "Perfect turn of phrase."

J.J. walked away and Quinn took his place. "This is the one we need to kill," she whispered. "Make it sexy."

Lacey winked at her. "Try not to get turned on."

J.J. clapped his hands. "Quiet, everyone. We're rolling!"

"And action!"

Selena rang Jordan's doorbell. Jordan opened the door but didn't greet her. She turned around, walked into the kitchen, and poured herself a cup of coffee. Selena took her coat off and set her purse by the door. She walked up behind Jordan and paused for a second. "Good morning." Her greeting was soft and apologetic.

Jordan turned around and held out her arm. "Good morning," she said, mimicking Selena's soft tone.

As Selena buttoned Jordan's cuff, she noticed that her blouse was misbuttoned. She pointed at it. "You're…"

Jordan looked down. "Oh, God."

"I've got it," Selena slowly and gently unbuttoned the shirt, revealing Jordan's black bra. Her breath caught as she rebuttoned the blouse. Jordan's chest heaved as if she was having trouble breathing.

"You usually wear your cross with this blouse," Selena said.

"The chain broke."

Selena made eye contact. "I'm sorry."

"It's just a chain." Jordan turned back around and poured cream into her coffee.

Selena noticed that Jordan's skirt still needed to be zipped up. She took a step forward. "No, I mean I'm sorry…for last night," she said as she zipped up the skirt.

Jordan turned slightly, looking over her shoulder. "Do-over?"

"Yeah," Selena replied, relief evident in her voice. "There's this little place I found when I first moved here. Great margaritas. We could…maybe sometime…"

Jordan turned back around and smiled. "Cute glasses." She took a sip of her coffee, keeping her eyes firmly set on Selena.

Selena touched her black glasses, feeling shy that she was wearing them. "My eyes…they're too dry for contacts today."

Jordan held the stare a little longer than any normal person would. After what seemed like an eternity, she broke the connection, turning to get another cup out of the cupboard. She poured more coffee and said, "Let's work here until lunch."

Selena breathed another sigh of relief and took the cup from Jordan. "Yeah. I'd like that."

"And cut! Reset." J.J. paused a minute to make sure his direction was heard and then turned to Lacey. "That last line…"

"Right," Lacey said. "Sorry. It was supposed to be 'sounds good,' right? My bad. I'll hit it on the next take."

"No, no. It's good. Your way is good. Keep it. And, ladies?" Quinn and Lacey both turned to J.J.

"Great scene." J.J. quickly abandoned the conversation, moving on to managing the crew.

Quinn turned her attention back to Lacey. "You look adorable in those glasses."

"Really?" Lacey playfully replied. "Because I could totally wear them to bed for you…you know…when we…"

"Hush!" Quinn said in a loud whisper as she looked around. "People will think—"

"Isn't that what we're going for? People thinking something that's not true?"

"Not yet. The characters first. Then us."

Lacey nodded her understanding. "Got it. I'm kind of getting a complex, though. You're the only woman who's ever had to fake it with me."

"Yes, well…" Quinn tried hard to suppress her smile, not wanting to give Lacey the satisfaction of a laugh at her joke. "I actually have no comeback for that."

"You're thinking about it, aren't you? How good it could be? I see that blush on your cheeks," Lacey teased.

Quinn shook her head as she walked away. Since they'd decided to turn up the heat with Jordan and Selena, Lacey had turned it up in real life as well. Quinn reminded herself that Lacey had a tendency to stay in character. Then she reminded herself again.

CHAPTER SIXTEEN

Quinn gave Lacey a reassuring look. Dan, one of the producers for *Jordan's Appeal*, had just asked the two of them to stay behind for a few minutes after a production meeting. He waited until the last person had closed the door behind them before he turned to them. "Thanks for staying. I just have something I need to run by you quickly." He tapped his pen on the table, eyeing them both for a moment. "As you know, the first two episodes of the season have aired and the feedback on Lacey's character has been stellar." He waited for Quinn's reaction.

"That's great!" Quinn glanced at Lacey. Was this the moment they had been waiting for? Were they going to take Jordan and Selena's relationship to a new level? All the signs were pointing in that direction. Subtle script changes, along with the whisperings on set regarding their great rapport had them both feeling optimistic.

"Brock has been pushing for a romantic arc between John and Selena," Dan said, still tapping his pen and looking apprehensive.

Ugh. Brock Tennison. He was the pompous ass who played the D.A. He was a classically trained stage actor, a fact he never let anyone forget. Lacey got a sour look on her face. Quinn laughed and said, "Brock has tried to get a romantic arc with every female on the show, including me. As if Jordan would ever! She hates the man with a passion."

Dan stopped tapping his pen but didn't respond.

Quinn leaned forward in her chair. "Please tell me you're not considering this, Dan. Selena is gay, remember?"

Dan chuckled. "She didn't start out that way. The writers wrote that in after you'd shot a couple of episodes. Besides, don't you think it would be kind of fun to watch Dent try to get in Selena's..." Getting no reaction from the women but a glare, Dan cleared his throat. "I guess not." He picked up his pen and started tapping it again. "Look, you might hate the thing I really brought you in to talk about even more, but just hear me out, okay?"

Quinn leaned back in her chair, breathing a sigh of relief. For a moment there, she thought Dan was seriously considering giving in to her costar's stupid ideas. She'd seen the way Brock watched Lacey on the set. He was always right there in the background, whether he had scenes with them or not. She'd felt protective of Lacey when he was around and it might've taken a fight, but she would've done whatever it took to make sure that storyline never came to fruition. She resisted the urge to pat Lacey's hand, letting her know everything would be fine. Instead, she gave her a slight smile and turned her attention back to Dan. "We're listening."

Dan took a deep breath. "Okay. So, here's the thing. You two have amazing chemistry and our viewers are talking about it." He hesitated for a second as he eyed Quinn. "And we had a thought."

Lacey covered her mouth, trying to hide her smile while Quinn waited for Dan to tell them what they already knew.

"What if...they fall in love?" Dan narrowed his eyes, trying to read the two women.

Lacey tried to remain stoic. She turned to Quinn, giving her the chance to respond first.

"What if Jordan and Selena fall in love?" Quinn asked, her eyebrows raised.

Dan nodded, his eyes darting between the two of them. "Yes."

Quinn tried her hardest to keep a straight face. "What are you hearing from the viewers?"

"They love your chemistry," Dan said. "And honestly, I've never seen two actors smolder the way you two do. It's like you're two seconds away from jumping each other's bones at all times, even when you're yelling at each other." He chuckled. "And there's a hashtag. It started trending three days ago."

"A hashtag?" Lacey finally let herself smile. "What is it?"

"Well, there are several actually, but my favorite is hashtag #justkissalready, but there's also hashtag #getitjordan and hashtag #breakmyarm."

Quinn burst out laughing. "Hashtag #breakmyarm? Seriously?"

Dan smiled. "Seriously."

She looked at Lacey. "Apparently, we have chemistry."

"It's her sex eyes, Dan." Lacey wagged her eyebrows. "They just draw people in."

Dan laughed. "Quinn, will you please use your sex eyes to convince Lacey that this is a good idea?"

"She doesn't have to, Dan. I'm in. Quinn?"

Quinn paused for a long moment. Just when she thought Dan was about to take his suggestion back, she said, "I think it's a great idea. All I ask is that I have some say with how things unfold physically."

Dan breathed a visible sigh of relief. "You already have that, and we'll make sure you're comfortable with the storyline."

Quinn nodded her approval. "Okay. Let's see what the writers come up with."

"How's the arm?" Dan asked, his tone sounding much lighter.

"Better." Quinn instinctively rubbed her upper arm. It still hurt more than she was willing to admit to anyone. "The doctor says I can't ride yet, which is ridiculous, but I'll get there."

"Good. Lacey, we'll need to extend your contract. We'll discuss the details with your agent."

Lacey stood up and shook Dan's hand. "Thank you. It's been great working with all of you."

"You'll have a few days off, and then we'll go full speed ahead again. And in the meantime, all the usual confidentiality applies. Don't you two *dare* let this get out," he said, pointing at both of them.

Dan left the room. Quinn and Lacey looked at each other. "We should just fist bump and save the real celebration for later."

"Agreed," Quinn said, standing up and opening the door. "Just act casual."

"We'll scream when we get in the car," Lacey whispered.

"Or maybe wait until we're off the lot."

"On the freeway. We'll scream on the freeway."

Lacey held up her beer bottle for a toast. "Here's to us. So far, so good."

It was Lacey's idea to stop at a little roadside bar on the way home, not Quinn's. She didn't frequent roadside bars any more than she shopped for her own groceries. A delivery service took care of that. But Lacey went on and on about wanting to stop, so here they were, sitting in a very public place.

The realization that their plan was officially being set in motion was hitting Quinn hard, but she wasn't about to admit that she was scared to death, so she smiled and tapped Lacey's bottle. "I'm praying for a good storyline."

"We'll make sure it's good." Lacey looked around for the waiter again. "What I'm praying for right now is a taco. They make the best street tacos here."

Quinn eyed Lacey for a moment. "I bet I know what you really want."

"Oh, yeah? You're a mind reader now?" Lacey finally caught the attention of the waiter. "Yeah, half a dozen al pastor with extra green sauce on the side." She turned back to Quinn. "What were you saying?"

Quinn took another sip of beer. "Don't you want to call your ex? I mean, this is what you've been waiting for, right? A good paying job again? Get the love of your life back and all that business?"

Lacey shook her head. "I don't want any distractions. I want to make sure we do this right so you can be out and have that life you want. You deserve it."

Quinn processed the information for a moment. Then it dawned on her. "You don't trust her!"

"Look, Dani's great in a million ways. She's brilliant and beautiful and damn funny. But do I trust her? No. Not anymore. Not with my career. And not with yours. Lesson learned on that front. She can find out I'm a regular right along with the rest of America."

Quinn wasn't sure if she felt relieved or disappointed. Maybe a little bit of both. In some ways, it was easier knowing Lacey was in love with someone else. Then again, it horrified her to think that Lacey would actually take fucking Dani back. Yeah, that's right. Quinn had taken to calling Lacey's ex "fucking Dani" in her head. In a hurry, she'd just call her "FD." Lacey was as close to a best friend as Quinn had. Her instinct—and it seemed a reasonable one—was to slap the bitch who broke Lacey's heart in two.

"We should meet with Jack tonight," Quinn said, changing the subject. "Give him an update and make a plan for the next step."

Lacey's shoulders dropped. "Can't it just be us tonight? I don't want to do anything but celebrate. And besides, we have the whole weekend to make plans. Come on, Quinn. This is huge! We did it!" Lacey slapped the table a few times with excitement, drawing the attention of the people sitting a few tables over.

Quinn's happiness was overshadowed by fear. This would be a huge step for her, coming out to the world. It wasn't just the show she was worried about, it was her entire life. *Jordan's Appeal* wouldn't stay on the air forever. Every show ended eventually. And after that, what would being an out lesbian do to her career? What would it do to *her*? Had she really thought this all through? The ramifications?

The unknown scared her to death.

"Isn't it a little too soon to celebrate?" Quinn asked. "I guess I feel like we're rounding the last corner and now we have to really bring it to the finish line." She hoped Lacey would buy that, instead of having to reveal her true fears.

Lacey grabbed Quinn's hand. "And we will. Let's go home tonight and watch the first few episodes together."

"I hate watching myself on-screen. You know that."

"Why? You're a brilliant actor."

That made Quinn smile. "So are you."

"Yeah." Lacey grinned. "It's almost like I've been doing this acting thing all my life."

Quinn winced at that. "Lace, I hope you know I never meant to belittle you. I loved you from the first second I saw you."

"No kidding? At Starbucks?" Lacey asked with a touch of sarcasm.

"I mean, I loved your acting from the very first scene. I'm trying to apologize here. If I admit that I have a whole new respect for soap actors, will you forgive me for all the other stuff?"

Lacey raised an eyebrow. "Other stuff?"

"All the nursemaid stuff." Quinn felt embarrassed now, that she'd asked so much of Lacey. "It was too much to ask of you."

Lacey took a long, slow sip of her beer, keeping her gaze firmly set on Quinn. She set her beer down and leaned forward on the table. "Go home with me and watch the first two episodes, and then I'll maybe think about forgiving you."

Lacey was doing it again. Flirting with her eyes. Quinn took Lacey's beer and set it on the other side of the table. "You're driving."

"And you're a total buzzkill," Lacey said with a wink.

It unnerved Quinn when Lacey flirted, because she didn't know what was real and what wasn't. She saw the same looks from Lacey on the set, but that was acting. So, what was this? Should she flirt back, because it was all just harmless nonsense, or should she put a stop to it? Keep the lines clear and let Lacey know there are some she just couldn't cross, even if Quinn sometimes wanted her to.

Quinn decided to take a different tack and bring up the woman she'd had her eye on for a few years now. Surely, that would change the tone of their conversation. "Can I ask you a question? A serious question?"

"You took away my beer. Might as well finish the job."

"What if the women I find attractive don't feel the same way? I mean, lesbians have types, right?"

Lacey dropped her face into her hands. "Oh my God." She scrubbed her face and clasped her hands together. "What the fuck are you talking about?"

Quinn's walls immediately went up. She wanted to change the tone, but she wasn't expecting *that* reaction. "Forget I asked! I mean, God forbid I ask a sincere question."

Lacey reached across the table, resting her hand on Quinn's arm. "Okay, wait. Just…wait. Sometimes, I forget that you have no experience with women." Her eyes widened in realization. "Are we talking about Ginny Strong?"

"No." Quinn shook her head, but then she nodded. "Maybe."

"Huh." Lacey eyed her for a moment. "So, Quinn Kincaid's type is the strong, power suit? I hope you like being a bottom."

Quinn had never thought about it that way. *A bottom?* She furrowed her brow. "What?"

"Ginny's kind of like your character on the show," Lacey said. "Jordan Ellis, kicking ass and taking names. Is that what you're attracted to?"

Quinn chuckled. "I guess so."

Lacey grinned. "Is that why you don't like watching yourself on TV? You're afraid you'll turn yourself on?"

Quinn threw her napkin at Lacey. "You're such a goddamned asshole sometimes!"

"Okay, fine," Lacey said, putting up her hands. "You want a serious answer?"

"Yes! Even if it might kill you to give me one."

Lacey pulled herself together and cleared her throat. "Okay, yes. Sometimes lesbians do have types. And some lesbians are very strict about only dating those types. But honestly, I don't think you have to worry about that, Quinn."

"Why not?"

Lacey sighed so hard she almost groaned. "Okay, you're right. It might actually kill me to say this, but I think you're exactly what Ginny Strong is looking for."

"Why would it kill you to say that?"

"Because she's not good enough for you."

They stared at each other for a moment, and then Quinn shook her head in confusion. "You don't even know her."

"She's a player. I knew it the minute I met her. You don't want someone who sees you as nothing but arm candy. You want the real thing. True love. Am I wrong?"

Quinn's jaw flexed. Did Lacey really think she could ruin Quinn's image of Ginny with just a few words? And why would she want to? "Why are you telling me this?"

Lacey stood up. "Come on. If you won't let me celebrate our success here, I'm going home and getting drunk by the pool."

Quinn looked around, searching for their waiter. "You ordered tacos!"

Lacey leaned on the table and lowered her voice. "I don't fucking care about the tacos, and I don't want to talk about Ginny Strong on what will probably be the best night of my career. So, if you don't mind…"

Was that jealousy? God, was Lacey actually jealous? Quinn grabbed her hand. "Sit down. Your tacos are here."

Lacey sat back down and poured a ton of green sauce on one of the tacos. She was just about to take a bite when someone yelled, "Fucking Quinn Kincaid is in our bar!"

Lacey set the taco back down. "Shit." The whole place turned and looked at them.

A woman sitting a few tables over said, "Yep, that's them all right." She held up her phone and took a photo. "I got one of them holding hands. Wonder what I could sell it for." She laughed heartily at her joke.

The woman and her companion weren't the glamorous types that fill most people's imagination of L.A. These were bawdy gals in ill-fitting clothes—the type one might see as participants in a news program focus group of Trump voters hoping to get their coal mining jobs back. After six shots of tequila.

"Let's get out of here." Quinn dug in her purse for some cash. "Shit! I only have plastic."

"You two make a handsome couple," the woman said. "But this ain't that kind of bar."

"Why does every damn show have to go gay?" her drinking partner asked. "I've watched *Jordan's Appeal* for years and she ain't never once showed no interest in women. Now, all the sudden, she's makin' google eyes at that little loudmouth Selena what's her name. We know what's comin' down the pike and it ain't good." The woman lifted her beer and took a big swig, as if it somehow solidified her point.

Quinn looked at Lacey. They hadn't held hands, had they? A feeling of fear gripped her as she mouthed the words, *get me out of here.*

Another woman pulled a chair up to their table, turned it backward, and straddled it, blocking the other women's view. "Ignore them," she said with a lift of her chin. She took a tortilla chip off Lacey's plate and munched on it while she kept talking. "When she's good and drunk, I'll get her phone and delete the photos. I hate that paparazzi shit."

She took another chip as Lacey and Quinn stared in disbelief. "Thank you," Quinn managed to squeak out.

"Yeah, no problem." The woman took off her dirty baseball cap. In fact, most of her looked kind of dirty, fingernails and all. Much like an auto mechanic would look after a hard day's work. A closer look at the baseball cap told them that's exactly what she was. *Jim's Auto Repair.*

"Sarah Covington." The woman said the name with a wistful tone. "Generations." She said that word with a serious look directed at Lacey. "Grandma—" She put up a finger, and then another. "Mom... Aunt Claudia...my sister, Little Claudia. They're all going to shit a damn brick when I tell them who I had dinner with." She took another chip and dipped it in the green sauce. "In fact, they won't believe me."

"Shoulda' known *you'd* want to chat them up, Ruthie." The woman behind them chuckled ruefully at her joke.

Ruthie rolled her eyes and yelled, "Tom, get Charlene another drink on me, would ya?"

"No problem, Ruthie!"

"Ignore them," Ruthie said again.

Lacey put out her hand. "Ruthie, is it?"

Ruthie rubbed her hand on her jeans to clean off the tortilla chip dust. "Sorry. Pleased to meet you." She shook Lacey's hand and then reached across the table to Quinn. "Ruth MacKenzie. My friends call me Ruthie."

Quinn took her hand. "Hi, Ruthie." She glanced around, making sure she had a clear shot to the door.

Ruthie's light green eyes lit up as she smiled at Quinn, looking her in the eye for the first time. "My, you're pretty close up."

"Oh, good one, Ruthie!" One of the women cackled behind them. "Is that your best pick-up line?"

Ruthie blushed relentlessly, her pale skin turning bright red. "Tom, get Wendy a double—on me, please!"

Tom laughed, causing his belly to bounce. "Sure thing, Ruthie."

Lacey bit her lip to keep from laughing while Quinn offered a quiet, "Thank you," and quickly picked up her beer to take a sip.

"I don't know why you ladies are here…not that I mind." Ruthie gave Quinn a shy smile.

"I came here a while back for lunch," Lacey said. "Someone told me they had the best tacos in town, and they were right."

"Ah. Well, Alonzo will be glad to hear that." Ruthie motioned with her head. "He's the cook here." She glanced at the front door, where a few guys had just walked in. She leaned in, lowering her voice. "Look, lunch is one thing, but this place gets rowdy at night. Charlene and Wendy ain't nothin' compared to who'll be walkin' through that door soon."

"Thanks for the warning." Quinn glared at Lacey. She didn't have to mouth the words again, did she? Oh, screw it. She'd say them out loud this time. "Get me out of here."

Lacey grabbed her purse, looking for some cash. "Thanks, Ruthie. Do you have a business card? An address I could send a headshot to… with a nice note for the women in your family who watch *Light of Day*?"

Ruthie's eyes lit up again. "You'd do that for me? Wow!" She pulled a notepad and pen out of her cargo pants pocket and thumbed through the greasy pages looking for a clean one. "Cuz they'll just call me a straight up liar if I don't have some proof. Ruthie's head is in the clouds again, they'll say."

"Write down their names for me. Claudia, you said?"

Quinn gave her a look that screamed, *Seriously?*

"Yeah, my Aunt Claudia, and little Claudia is my sister." Ruthie finally found a clean page, but the pen didn't work. "Shit." She shook the pen, trying to get the ink to flow. "Tom, do you have a damn pen?"

Quinn gave Lacey another look that said, *Are you fucking kidding me?*

"Maybe you have a pen?" Lacey asked Quinn, pointedly.

Quinn dug through her purse and handed it across the table. Lovesick Ruthie took it and gave Quinn a swoony smile. "Thank you. I'll cherish this forever."

Lacey looked down and rubbed her forehead, trying to hide her giggles. Quinn hit her leg with her foot. This was not funny. This was getting scary. Three more burly guys had just walked in and good ol' Charlene was already pointing Lacey and Quinn out to them.

Ruthie was quite possibly the slowest writer west of the Mississippi, carefully spelling out each name. Claudia, twice of course. Quinn couldn't take it. She had to get out of there. She bolted for the door and ran right into a large gentleman twice her size. He grabbed her by the shoulders. "Slow down, little lady. Let me buy you a drink." Quinn ran for it. "Wait! We were just getting to know each other," the man yelled. He turned and laughed to his friends.

Lacey stood up. She looked at the door Quinn had just run through and then at Ruthie. "Hurry."

Ruthie also stood up. "What's wrong? Where'd she go?"

Lacey threw some money on the table. "The address, Ruthie." She held out her hand. The second Ruthie was done, Lacey ripped the page off of the notebook. "Thanks for your help."

The roar of Harley engines drowned out Lacey's call to Quinn as four guys on bikes pulled into the small parking lot, blinding her with their headlights. She hit the button on the key fob, unlocking the doors to her Range Rover, and made her way across the dark parking lot. The passenger door opened and Quinn got in, locking the doors behind her. Lacey hit the button again and got in. She took a deep breath and reached for Quinn, who was obviously shaken.

"Don't touch me."

Lacey pulled her hand back. "You're fine. Everything's fine."

Quinn's hands were shaking. "I'm not fine. You took me to a biker bar!"

"It's not a biker bar, it's just a bar. With really good tacos." Lacey kept her voice even. "And you *are* fine. Nothing happened. And P.S., there's nothing wrong with bikers."

"That was stupid and careless. What were you thinking?"

Lacey pulled out onto the main road. "I was thinking that I wanted to have a beer and tacos."

Quinn was seething inside. "One of the prices of fame, in case you hadn't noticed, is that you can't just go out into the world like normal people. You have to think things through. You have to plan an escape route. Why do you think I only go to high-end places where there's security and a valet?"

"I guess I just thought you consider yourself above it all."

Lacey said it with an amused little smile, which only angered Quinn more. "Fuck you."

"Honey..." Lacey said with a laugh. "I would've protected you."

Honey? Quinn turned away and stared out the passenger window. Where was fiery, defensive, loud-mouthed Lacey? That Lacey would be fighting back. Telling Quinn to buck up. Live in the real world. She'd be pissed off that she didn't get to take even one bite of those damned tacos she loves so much.

This version of Lacey was disconcerting. *Honey?* Since when did they have pet names for one another?

They were both tired and overworked. Maybe that was it. Maybe Lacey was just too tired to fight. And maybe Quinn had overreacted. All she wanted to do now, was get back behind those big walls and that heavy security gate and crawl into bed and watch a movie. Alone.

Unfortunately, the way traffic was moving, her bed was at least forty-five minutes away. Just as she laid her head back against the headrest, Lacey's phone rang. She picked it up before Lacey could. "Keep driving. It just says Steve."

"Steve? That's my producer in New York. Put it on speaker."

Quinn sighed. The last thing she wanted to do was listen in on a phone call. "Fine, but stay in one lane while you're talking." She reluctantly tapped the button and held the phone up.

"Steve?"

"Hey, cutie. Long time no talk."

Lacey rolled her eyes at Quinn. "Yeah, we haven't talked since you fired me."

"Well, that's why I'm calling. We want to bring you back on the show. Full arc."

Quinn's eyes widened. She stared at Lacey, waiting for a reaction.

"Why?" Lacey asked. "I'm still gay, Steve. That hasn't changed."

"We've regretted letting you go. The show isn't the same without you."

"Is that an apology?"

"It's an offer. Come back to New York and we'll have a sit-down. We want to expand your role on the show. I think you'll really like what we have in mind. We'll even let you choose the actor who will play your son."

"MY SON? Sarah doesn't have a son."

"She had him when she was eighteen. Right about the time you took a few years off to go to college. He's a teenager now. He comes to the hospital after a car accident and you operate on him, not realizing he's your son. It's only when there's an emergency and you're the only match..."

Quinn covered her mouth to keep from giggling.

"So, no apology?" Lacey deadpanned, interrupting him.

"We'll talk when you get here."

"No, Steve, we won't." Lacey motioned for Quinn to end the call.

"You're going to shut him down? Just like that?" Quinn asked. "What about your lost son?"

Lacey sighed. "Okay, yeah. A few months ago, I would've raced back to New York for that meeting and embraced that storyline with every fiber of my being."

"So, what's different?"

Lacey turned to her, looking perplexed by the question. "Everything's different. I have you, I have a prime-time show, I'm building a life here. A life I kind of like...except for this traffic."

Quinn didn't reply. She'd already destroyed Lacey's celebratory mood. If she actually articulated all the thoughts running through her confused mind, she'd obliterate their friendship. Lacey was right. Quinn was a total buzzkill.

This wasn't how it was supposed to go. None of this was part of the plan she and Jack had started with. It was supposed to be simple, straightforward. Not messy. Lacey was messy. Things could go horribly wrong. Like tonight. *A biker bar? A fucking biker bar?*

As the security gate opened and Lacey pulled into the driveway, Quinn blurted out one of the things she'd been thinking about. "You might need to move out."

"What?" Lacey put the car in park. "Why?" she asked, seemingly thrown by the suggestion. "What the hell are you talking about?"

"Won't it seem weird that you're already living in my home with me, when we're supposed to accidentally fall in love on set?"

"I don't live in your home. I live in your guesthouse, and we've already established that we're friends, not just coworkers." Lacey stared at Quinn, waiting for a reply. "What is this really about?"

Quinn shifted in her seat. She knew this wouldn't end well, but she couldn't take it back. "I just think it might be better if you move out, but I'll talk to Jack about it."

"And in the meantime, you'll tell Jack what you want, so just be honest. Why do you want me to go?"

Quinn felt confused and worried and scared. She was a jumbled-up mess of emotions and she didn't know what to do with any of them. She couldn't read Lacey. She couldn't tell what was sincere and what was fake. And she didn't dare ask. What she needed was some distance. "I don't know what I want. I just know that it feels like maybe you're getting a little too cozy."

Lacey shook her head in confusion. "Too...cozy? What does that mean? Too nice? Too helpful? Too friendly? Too what, exactly?"

Quinn shrugged. "Too close, I guess. We were going to keep this professional and you're blurring the lines."

Lacey's mouth fell open. "Why, because I wanted to go home and celebrate with you?"

"Just you and me. That's what you said."

"Which means what to you? That I want to MOUNT you on the kitchen island?"

"I don't know, DO YOU?" Quinn shouted back.

Lacey sighed in frustration as she got out of the car. "There's that arrogance again. All I meant is that I don't feel like spending the evening with a freaking publicist. I have that in common with pretty much everyone on earth."

Quinn met her at the front of the car, blocking her way. "Am I wrong?"

"You're an asshole, that's what you are," Lacey pushed her way past Quinn.

"Lacey..."

Lacey turned around. "I don't want more, Quinn! I was just starting to feel like myself again, instead of all walled up and not trusting anyone in my life. God forbid we both get a friend out of this. Maybe that came off as too cozy...and maybe the truth is...you like me angry. Is that it? You like me all bound up in a knot, ready to explode? Is that who you want me to be? It makes you feel better if I'm more fucked up than you are?"

Quinn shrugged her shoulders again. "I guess I just want you to be the person I hired to do the job."

"Yeah? Well, I don't want to be that person anymore. She was..." Lacey took a deep breath. "Never mind." She headed for the side gate instead of going into the house.

"Hey, what about celebrating?" Quinn shouted.

"Call Jack. He's the one you want to be with anyway. Or, better yet, call Ginny Strong. She's fucking perfect for you!" Lacey punched in the gate code and disappeared into the backyard.

Quinn dropped her purse at her feet and sat on the sofa. The house felt dead quiet without Lacey there. She picked up the remote and turned on some music, trying to fill the silence.

Was it a mistake to want to maintain a certain amount of distance between them? Was it cruel to want Lacey to keep her snarky, sarcastic attitude, even if it was born out of anger and frustration because her life had fallen apart?

It was easier. That's why Quinn wanted Lacey to stay the way she was. It was easier to not fall madly in love with her if every other word out of her mouth was fuck this and fuck that.

She went to the back door and grabbed the handle, thinking she should go out there and apologize, but the light in the guesthouse wasn't on. Maybe Lacey had already gone to bed. Or maybe she was showering off the biker bar. Quinn locked the door and slowly made her way upstairs. She'd apologize in the morning when Lacey had calmed down. Over coffee. Everything sounded better when coffee was involved.

Lacey sat in the dark. She wiped her eyes, frustrated with herself for crying on what should've been one of the happiest nights of her life. They'd done it. They'd actually made Jordan and Selena into a couple that the viewers loved. And Lacey was now playing what would soon be a major role on a prime-time show. Life could not have been better. So why the fuck was she crying?

Lacey picked up her phone and opened her airline app.

CHAPTER SEVENTEEN

Q uinn woke up late, feeling grumpy and sore. She sat up and stuffed a cracker in her mouth, then swallowed a pain pill. Normally, Lacey would've been in there by now, plopped on the bed next to her, asking what sounded good for breakfast. "A toasted bagel and coffee," Quinn said to the empty room.

She sat on the edge of the bed for several minutes, regretting what she'd said to Lacey the night before. It was mean, just throwing it out there the way she had—that Lacey might have to leave her home. And go where? Where would Lacey move to on such short notice? Back to that shitty hotel in Hollywood she'd stayed at before?

Quinn picked up her phone and tapped Lacey's number. No one answered, so she hung up, afraid she'd stumble over an apology and screw it up if she tried to do it over voice mail. A better plan would be to put on her bathing suit, sit in the hot tub, loosen her muscles up, drink a cup of coffee and then try to make amends.

The guesthouse door hadn't opened. Quinn stared at it from the hot tub, willing it to open. After her designated ten minutes, she got out and went to the door, knocking twice. "Lacey?" She knocked again and punched in the code on the door lock. "Lacey?"

Quinn stood there in her bikini, dripping water on the tiled floor and staring at an empty guesthouse. The bed looked like it hadn't been slept in. In fact, the place looked spotless. Usually there were clothes strewn on the floor and draped over the furniture. Lacey wasn't the tidiest person, Quinn had noticed.

She looked behind her and noticed that there were no shoes by the door. Lacey always left her flip-flops by the door. "Shit," Quinn whispered. She went into the bathroom and her shoulders fell as she let out a big sigh. She was gone. Lacey was gone. And so were all of her things.

Quinn sat on a lounger by the pool with her phone to her ear. "Hey. Where—" She sucked in air. This was affecting her far more than she thought it would. "Where are you? Call me." She tossed her phone on the table and wrapped her arms around herself. "Dammit!" she whispered. And then she said it louder. "Dammit, Lacey!"

She couldn't sit there forever in her bathing suit, waiting for a damn phone call, so she put on her bathrobe and went into the kitchen. She'd make breakfast. Maybe that toasted bagel she'd wanted when she woke up would taste good. With a super thin layer of peanut butter and honey—the way Lacey made it.

Lacey. She made everything better. Even bagels.

Quinn sat at the kitchen table, one leg tucked under the other, her head in her hand, waiting for her phone to ring. Her coffee was cold. Her bagel hadn't been touched. She'd yet to put clothes on. Why should she when no one was going to see her? But that wasn't like Quinn. She had a routine: exercise, breakfast, shower, emails, etcetera, etcetera, fucking etcetera.

The broken arm had ruined everything. And Jack's stupid idea. God! Why did she listen to him? But it wasn't all Jack. The truth was, Quinn didn't want to come out alone. She wanted someone on her arm, even if that someone wasn't necessarily in love with her, or vice versa. She was afraid of all the speculation; all the reasons people would come up with for her sudden "lifestyle" change. Was she just sick of men? Did her divorce ruin her for men? Was she just trying something new, spiraling out of control or seeking attention?

No. Quinn wanted the world's first impression of her as a lesbian to be one of having found true love, real love. Sure, it'd be temporary love, but wasn't it always in Hollywood? This wasn't Jack's fault any more than it was Lacey's. Quinn had brought this all on herself. She picked up her phone again. "Jack, I think I messed up."

As Quinn said the words, another call came through. She looked at her phone. "I'll call you back. No, just let me call you back." She stood up, pushing her chair back with her leg. "Lace. Lacey. God. Where are you?" Quinn couldn't hide the desperation in her voice. "Your stuff, it's all gone."

"Yeah. I thought I'd save you the trouble of having to mull it over with Jack. I moved out."

Quinn's eyes shuttered closed. "Where are you?" she gently asked.

"New York. I took the red-eye out last night."

Quinn's eyes popped back open. "What? I didn't hear you leave last night."

"I tried to be quiet."

"So, why are you in New York?" Quinn already knew the answer. The ex-girlfriend. She had successfully managed to push Lacey back into Dani's arms. Quinn for the win.

"I'm tying up loose ends. Renting out my apartment, seeing some friends...my dad...stuff like that."

"Oh. I see."

"What do you need, Quinn?"

"Um..." *You. Back here with me.* "Have you seen Dani?"

"Yeah, she picked me up."

Quinn went outside. She needed room to pace. "How did it go?"

"What do you mean, how did it go?"

"I mean...I don't know what I mean."

"She'd love to meet you. Huge fan of yours."

Quinn stopped pacing. "Please tell me you're not taking her back."

"Why?"

"Because it's wrong what she did, Lacey."

"Since when do you care?"

Quinn threw a hand in the air. "I care, okay? You know I care about you."

"I know you're afraid of me."

Quinn shook her head in confusion. "Whatever. Just remember what she did and how it made you feel."

"We all have weak moments."

"Weak moments? Is that what you call someone who dumps you the second you lose your show? Is it called a 'weak moment' when someone kicks you while you're down?"

"That's a bit dramatic."

"I'm a fucking actor! It's my job to be dramatic!" Quinn shouted.

Lacey got her coffee from the barista and found a quiet corner. "What do you need, Quinn? I'm kind of busy right now."

"Don't hang up. Look...I feel bad about last night. I know I hurt your feelings. And I know I said you should probably move out, but now that you're gone, it feels wrong."

"Don't worry. Nothing's changed. We're still good as far as the show goes, as well as the other thing—the contract."

"What about us?" Quinn asked. "Are we good?"

"I just told you, nothing's changed."

Quinn started pacing again. "I don't believe you. I can hear it in your voice. You're mad."

"Quinn, what do you want me to say?"

"That you'll move back in. I just panicked for a second, but I'm over it."

"Dani just walked in. I have to go."

Quinn heard a voice say, "Hello, beautiful." And then Lacey's voice. "Hey." Then the phone went dead.

"FUCK!" Quinn picked up her water bottle and threw it as hard as she could, then doubled over in pain. She plopped down on the end of a lounge chair, cradling her arm. She stared blankly as the tears started to fall.

CHAPTER EIGHTEEN

Quinn couldn't spend another day sulking around her very clean but very empty house. She'd spent the previous day scrubbing every toilet, every flat surface. Repositioning every hanger in her closet. It didn't help. She was still so fucking alone she could hear the house creak. And Lacey was with Dani. And it was all her fault. "Gawwwwd," she groaned over her cup of coffee.

Stupid. She was stupid.

Lacey just wanted to have fun at that bar. Let loose a little. Their lives were hard right now, with the heavy shooting schedule. Why couldn't Quinn have seen that? Why did she have to turn it into something underhanded, as if Lacey was some big walking ulterior motive?

She turned on the sound system, cranking it up with Lacey's playlist. *Who puts Mary J. Blige and Taylor Swift on the same playlist?* Quinn smiled as "U+Me" filtered through the speakers. She poured herself a cup of coffee and stood at the window overlooking the pool, thinking about the time she'd caught Lacey dancing in the kitchen while she wiped down the counters. Lacey wasn't embarrassed, because when did Lacey ever get embarrassed? No, she had taken Quinn's hand and danced with her, twirling her around until they were both dizzy and had to hold on to each other so they didn't fall over.

Lacey was sunshine.

Quinn blinked away her tears. And blinked harder when she saw movement in the guesthouse. She almost dropped her coffee cup when she saw Lacey step out and shuffle toward the main house in her robe and slippers.

Quinn set her cup down and stood at the table, trying to look casual. She put a hand on her hip. No, that didn't look casual. She stuffed both hands in her jeans pockets.

Lacey opened the door and stood there for a second, staring at Quinn. "You look like hell."

"So do you." Quinn furrowed her brow, because Lacey really did look like hell. "When did you...um..."

Quinn watched Lacey pour herself a cup of coffee and shuffle back outside. Her heart was beating so hard, she covered her chest with her hand. Lacey was home. And Quinn wanted to cry again—tears of joy this time. She took a few breaths and pulled the elastic out of her hair, just in case she really did look like hell. She smoothed her hair down and tied it back up again, then went outside. She knocked on Lacey's door and poked her head in. "Are you okay?"

Lacey was already back in bed, sipping on her coffee. "Don't come too close. I think I'm coming down with something."

Quinn ignored the advice. She sat on the bed and checked Lacey's temperature, resting the back of her hand on her forehead. "You're burning up."

"First class was full, and you *know* they put all the sick people in economy." Lacey shivered. "I feel cold. Do you think it could be Ebola? Or bubonic plague?"

Quinn suppressed a giggle. "Now who's being dramatic? I'll be right back." She stepped outside, smiling from ear to ear. Lacey was back and she was making her usual silly jokes. What a relief.

A few minutes later, Quinn came back with a box of supplies and Amy's medical kit. She put a temperature strip on Lacey's forehead. "What symptoms do you have? Headache? Nausea?"

"Headache, chills, achy muscles," Lacey said, using the sickliest voice she could conjure up. What do you think it is, nurse?"

Quinn looked at her watch while she pretended to check Lacey's pulse. "It's that time of year. Maybe you caught something on the plane." She took the stethoscope out of the bag and pushed Lacey's robe aside, then slid the stethoscope under her T-shirt.

Lacey looked down at her chest. "Are you trying to feel me up, nurse?"

Quinn put a finger on her mouth. "Shh..." She listened closely to Lacey's heartbeat, then took the stethoscope out of her ears and threw it around her neck. "It sounds like bacterial meningitis. You have one, maybe two days to live."

"But...I'm...pregnant."

Quinn nodded and tried not to laugh out loud. She put her hand on Lacey's shoulder. "The baby will survive, but you won't. Who should I call to collect your bastard child?"

Lacey sat up and grabbed Quinn's sleeve. "I have no one, Nurse Ratched. No one! Who will take care of my baby?"

Quinn gave Lacey a pretend slap across the face. "Calm down. You'll upset the baby. I will take care of your child. It will have a good life with me. I will love it like my own bastard child. Come to think of it, I might even be the father."

Lacey grabbed onto Quinn's shoulders. "Oh, thank you, nurse! I can die content knowing that my bastard child will have both a mother and a father!"

Quinn pushed Lacey back down onto the bed. "Just relax now, honey. I'll go get a knife."

Lacey grabbed her head and started writhing on the bed. "Ay, Dios mío!"

"Adios and sayonara to you too."

Lacey covered her mouth to stifle the giggles. Quinn picked up the cup of coffee. "I'll get you some orange juice. Coffee isn't what you need right now."

"And an extra blanket? I'm freezing."

"And something to reduce the fever." Quinn stood there for a moment. Lacey looked like hell, with her bloodshot eyes, pale skin, and chapped lips, but it didn't matter. Quinn's heart felt full again. And her big, empty house was no longer empty.

Just like Lacey had done on several occasions to her, Quinn bent down and gently kissed her forehead. "Don't go anywhere. I'll be right back."

"I'm in no condition to travel…in my condition," Lacey mumbled, her eyes slowly closing.

Once Quinn had Lacey medicated and tucked in under an extra blanket, she went to the other side of the bed and lay down next to her. She grabbed the remote off the table and turned on the television. "What'll it be? *Dr. Phil* or *Days of Our Lives?*"

Lacey rolled onto her side, facing Quinn with her eyes closed. "Neither. And you don't have to stay here with me."

Quinn rolled onto her side and ran her fingers through Lacey's hair. "How many nights did you lie next to me and talk to me until I forgot about the pain and fell asleep?"

"Many."

"Okay, then. Let me be here for you."

"You paid me to be with you."

"I'll send you a bill."

Lacey opened her eyes. "I can't afford you."

"What are you talking about? You're a regular on a hit show now. And you're getting a raise. Things are looking up."

"It'll end. They won't keep me forever, so I need to be frugal."

"Are you forgetting about all the publicity? You won't struggle to find work anymore, Lace. Hell, your old soap would take you back in a second." Quinn paused, hoping that was the opening Lacey needed to tell her what the hell happened in New York. Did she go talk to her old producer? They'd offered her what sounded like years of future work, which was more than Quinn could offer. She had no idea how long the producers would keep Lacey on *Jordan's Appeal*. For all she knew, it would only amount to the rest of this season and then they'd move on with another storyline.

Lacey closed her eyes again. "I just want to sleep." Her phone beeped, but she didn't open her eyes. "Can you look at that for me?"

Quinn grabbed the phone off the table. "You have a text. It's from Daniela. She says, 'I'll be in L.A. on Friday. I'm not giving up on us.'" Quinn's eyes widened. "Wait, is that Dani? Your ex?"

Lacey's eyes popped open and they stared at each other for a second. "Shit," she finally said.

"Double shit," Quinn added.

Lacey threw the covers back and sat up. "She could ruin everything."

Quinn grabbed the covers and urged Lacey to lie back down. "Where do you think you're going? You need to rest."

Lacey plopped back down on the bed and grabbed her forehead. "You're right. I'm in no condition to…I'm not even sure where I was going. God, my head hurts."

Quinn held Lacey's phone up. "I could text her back for you."

"And tell her what?"

"To find another sugar mama."

"It wasn't like that."

"No?" Quinn said with the raise of an eyebrow.

"We were good. Happy. Content."

"Until you lost your job."

"Isn't money why most people divorce?"

Quinn shrugged. "Yeah. Money and sex."

"Dani and I were no different. We broke in half because the financial stress was too much."

"She left you," Quinn flatly stated. "Things got difficult and she left you."

Lacey winced at that. "Thanks for reminding me."

"She walked out on you when you were at your lowest."

"She's not a bad person," Lacey said. "Stop trying to demonize her."

"Don't tell me it was complicated, because that's just..." Quinn shook her head as she tried to find the right word.

"Why do you care?" Lacey asked in frustration. "I'm not taking her back. At least not until we've completed our mission. Is that what you're worried about?"

"No, Lacey, I'm worried about you. How the hell could you ever trust her again?"

Lacey shook her head. "It never mattered. Dani was incapable of doing anything wrong in my eyes. She owned me."

"Wow." That felt like a pretty big admission. Someone *owned* Lacey Matthews? "She still does, apparently, but you're so in control with me, I can't picture you being owned by anyone."

"Dani was my first love. My first everything."

"You're thirty years old. Get over it and find someone who loves and respects you enough to stick around when the going gets tough."

Lacey closed her eyes. "Could you harass me about this later, when I can fight back?"

"No. I have a captive audience and I'm going to tell it like it is." Quinn didn't want to start another fight, but she couldn't stand the thought of Lacey being with that woman.

Lacey threw her arm over her face. "God, I hate you right now."

Quinn softened her tone. "No, you don't. You hate that I'm right."

"The divorced woman lecturing me about love? Epic."

"I can lecture you because I know all about betrayal, Lace."

"Who was she?"

Quinn rolled onto her back and sighed. "I don't remember her name, but she was an angel."

Lacey's eyes popped open. "I was talking about him, not you." She slowly blinked. "You're the one who cheated?"

It took a moment for Quinn to answer. "Not exactly."

Lacey propped herself up on her elbows and looked at Quinn. "Oh. My. God."

Quinn looked away. "Don't judge me until you hear the story."

"Who says I want to hear it? Maybe I just want to judge you without knowing." Lacey plopped back down on her back. "Fine. I'm too sick to argue. Tell the story."

Quinn hesitated. "I haven't ever told anyone the whole story. Jack knows bits and pieces, but not the details."

"It's fine," Lacey said. "I'm delirious, so I probably won't even remember it in the morning."

Quinn sat up and crossed her legs. She picked at the blanket for a moment, removing the little nubs that build up over time. "Fine. I'll tell you. My husband, and God, I hate calling him that, even though we were married for five years. Anyway, he had a big party, which is one of the reasons I never host parties now. We were all way past drunk and he brought this beautiful girl into the bedroom and I stood there, just staring at her. She was..." Quinn's voice trailed off. She squeezed her eyes shut. "He played me and I fell for it."

Lacey sat up. "What do you mean?"

"God, it's so embarrassing. I was drunk as hell but I was so into her. I remember running my fingers through her long, brown hair. It was so soft, and she was so pretty. Her skin felt like velvet and her lips..." Quinn cleared her throat. "Anyway, I knew what it meant. I'd known for a while, years probably, that I...you know...like women. The problem was, my husband also got his confirmation that night. He watched us. He watched the way I was with her. It hurt like hell to watch—that's what he told me the next day."

Lacey rested her hand on Quinn's back. "He put you in that situation so he could test you?"

"I guess he had his suspicions. Maybe he saw the way I looked at women. According to you, I'm not very discreet about it."

Lacey slowly shook her head. "No, you're not. Your sex eyes give you away."

Quinn chuckled. "I'll have to work on that." She turned to Lacey. "I want what I felt that night with her, but I also want the morning after. I want the love that goes with it. And I don't want to have to hide it."

"I understand," Lacey said. "Everything in that department has gone to hell for me, but I understand wanting it."

Quinn focused on her hands for a moment. "He's going to out me. He's just waiting for the right moment...when it will hurt me the most."

Lacey looked up at the ceiling. "So, let me get this straight. He's the one who brought a woman to your bed. And now, he's plotting out how to mess with your career? Your life?"

"He's probably writing a tell-all book as we speak, that's how much he hates me."

"You know, this may be none of my business, but your ex-husband sounds like a world-class douche bag."

Quinn laughed. "You got that right."

Lacey leaned back against the headboard and closed her eyes. A few seconds later, they popped open. "Quinn?"

"Yeah?"

"Our plan is perfect."

Quinn turned so she was facing Lacey. "How so?"

"Instead of you doing this big coming out thing, where you'll have to answer pointed questions about your past, you can just let the rumors fly and it won't matter. That woman will probably try to make a few bucks with her story, but no one will care, because YOU won't care."

That wasn't altogether true and Quinn knew it. "My mother will care. She doesn't do scandal very well."

"Your mother will get over it. Besides, mothers love me. *Especially* soap-loving mothers."

Quinn wanted to believe it was true. She wanted to believe everything would be just fine. But she knew her mother. And where did Lacey get off? "I don't understand you. I mean, you care about what happens to me and you give me advice, but I'm not allowed to do that with you?"

"It's not that," Lacey admitted. "It's just…I don't want to admit that the love of my life screwed me over, because what does that say about me?"

"The only thing it says is that you loved her with your whole heart. Not everyone can say that."

Lacey slid back down on the bed and covered her face with her arm again. "And now, I'm scarred for life."

Quinn lay down next to her, propped up on her elbow. "Yeah, I wish I could've known you before she did this to you. I'd probably like you a lot more."

"Fuck you, Quinn."

"Fuck *you*, Lacey."

Lacey took her arm away from her face. Her eyes were teary. "You really don't like me?"

If you weren't so sick, I'd kiss you. Quinn rested her hand on Lacey's stomach. She could feel the heat from her flu-riddled body emanating through the T-shirt. "Eh, you're okay," she said, gently rubbing circles on Lacey's stomach. "Just rest now, okay?"

"Promise not to murder me in my sleep?" Lacey joked.

Quinn smiled. "I'll be right here if you need me."

CHAPTER NINETEEN

Lacey didn't have the energy to do anything except lie in bed and watch TV. That was getting old, so she grabbed her laptop and typed into the search bar, *Quinn Kincaid's husband*. Greer Farris. Action movies. Way too good looking. She lost interest almost immediately, so she typed in *Quinn Kincaid's divorce*.

"Shit." Lacey had no idea it had been such a big deal. The tabloids covered it for months. Paparazzi chased them both endlessly. Everyone had an opinion about who cheated on who. "Gross!" Lacey grimaced when she read that there was speculation about Quinn and their costar, Brock Tennison.

No wonder Quinn was so private now. Lacey couldn't blame her. They'd been relentless, trying to get the real story, or any story at all, even if it was completely false.

Her phone beeped. Quinn had dinner ready. The last thing Lacey wanted to do was eat, but she pushed herself out of bed. She went into the main house wearing a big wool sweater with pajama bottoms and slippers. "Sorry, I didn't have the strength to dress for dinner."

"That's okay, I didn't cook. Which you should be grateful for." Quinn had several take-out containers lined up on the kitchen island. She pointed at the first container. "Thai coconut soup. I love this when I have a cold."

Lacey sat on a stool across the kitchen island from Quinn. "That would be fine." Nothing would taste good. She was doing this purely for Quinn, who was playing the doting nurse.

"No, you have to hear the other options." Quinn placed her hand on the next container. "Good old-fashioned chicken noodle soup."

"Dani is sick too. She's not flying out here tomorrow, thank God."

Quinn slowly blinked as she stared at Lacey. "Did you…kiss her?"

"What?"

"Why is she sick too?"

Lacey rolled her eyes. "First of all, it's not mono. And I know you see Dani as the devil incarnate and all, but it's really none of your business."

Quinn put her hand on the third container. "Chicken pot pie." She kept her eyes down and waited for a reply.

"I'll have the coconut soup with a side of jealousy."

Quinn narrowed her eyes. She pushed the container across the island and pulled a spoon out of the drawer. She slid the spoon so hard it almost flew off the other end, but Lacey caught it with both hands.

"Whoa!"

Quinn grabbed a fork and the chicken pot pie. She went into the living room and turned on the television, choosing Lacey's old soap opera from the list of recordings. She turned the volume up and pointed at the TV. "Oh look. It's your asshole husband with his new wife and kid."

Lacey shuffled over and curled up in the corner of the sofa with her soup. "Everything changes and yet somehow manages to stay exactly the same in the soap world."

"And the writers don't ever say to each other—let's be realistic?" Quinn sarcastically asked.

"And the women are all bitches."

"So you fit right in."

Lacey closed her eyes and took a deep breath. "Yeah, I guess I did."

Quinn threw the remote on the table. "Sometimes, you're like a caged animal, Lacey. You bite the hand that feeds you."

Were they going to fight again? Lacey didn't have the energy. "You're right. I'm sorry."

"I don't want that bitch in my house or anywhere near me, so you should move out."

Lacey looked up in surprise. *Seriously? Did she really just say that?* "I told you, Dani isn't coming here. And is this your thing? Every time you get angry or scared, you'll tell me to move out?"

Quinn ignored Lacey's question. She poked around the chicken pot pie with her fork and then stabbed it forcefully. "She'll come here eventually, and I want nothing to do with it."

Lacey stood up and went back into the kitchen. "Thank you for dinner."

Quinn followed her. "You barely took one bite! You need to eat or you'll never get better. And that's not really an option since we start shooting again in two days."

Lacey put the container in the fridge. "Maybe later. Right now, I'm tired, and I don't want to fight with you."

Quinn scoffed. "You love fighting with me!"

Lacey held on to the fridge door handle, keeping her back to Quinn. "I hurt you, with the jealousy comment, or with mentioning Dani, or I don't even know what hurt you. I just know I don't want to do that anymore."

Quinn gently took Lacey's arm. "It's okay. Please, just come back to the sofa and sit with me. I'll spoon-feed you some chicken pot pie."

"Will you change the fucking channel?" Lacey had no desire to see who had replaced her on the show that had been her life for so long.

Quinn took Lacey by the hand and led her back to the sofa. She turned off the television and got a small bite of the chicken pot pie on her fork. "You'll love this. It's made from scratch."

"Hmm…" Lacey gave her a thumbs-up as she chewed, trying to appear grateful.

"I know it's hard, seeing the people we love for who they really are, and I don't mean to demonize Dani, but I can see the forest for the trees better than you, because I'm not invested."

Lacey was taken aback. Sure, Quinn was being presumptuous, but Lacey had grown accustomed to that. Not invested, though? Was she really that detached? Because she sure as hell didn't act like it. "You've never even met her. How could you possibly—"

Quinn fed her another bite, shutting her up. "I'm sure she's a saint. She'd have to be, to put up with you."

Lacey stopped chewing. "Are you trying to start another fight?"

"I'm trying to feed you, so open up."

Lacey took the bite and put up her hand. "I can't eat any more."

Quinn held up another bite. "Come on, honey. A couple more bites."

"I'm not your honey."

"Thank God."

"I'm only here because—"

Quinn gave up on feeding Lacey and set the fork down. "Yes, I know. You came rushing back from New York because we have a contract."

"I came back because I have two contracts now. One with you and one with the studio. And I'll be damned if I'll let Dani mess with my career again."

"Or your heart?"

Lacey stood up and went to the door. "Don't worry. She'll never know where you live."

Quinn ran to the door and blocked Lacey's way. "That's not my only concern."

Lacey folded her arms, wanting to protect herself. "I don't have the energy for this. You're looking for a fight…or something…I don't know, I'm just confused right now."

"That's how we communicate," Quinn said, throwing her hands in the air. "We're complete assholes to each other. But we're straightforward assholes who care about each other and sometimes we even make each other laugh. I don't get any of that anywhere else. So that's something, right?"

Lacey's eyes filled with tears. "Well, right now…in my current state…I need a little bit of love more than I need a whole lot of the cold, hard truth."

Lacey waited a few painfully long seconds for Quinn to say something, but she just stood there, dumbfounded. "Yeah, I didn't think so." Lacey took her by the shoulders and physically moved her out of the way so she could go back out to the guesthouse. "And if you ever threaten to kick me out again, you better mean it, because I won't come back." She didn't wait for a reply. She went out to the guesthouse and fell back into bed.

Later that evening, Quinn took the chicken noodle soup to the guesthouse. She set the take-out container on the bedside table and crouched down, so she was eye level with Lacey. "Can we call a truce until you're feeling better? I'd hate to think I'm winning a war of words just because my opponent is weak."

Lacey opened her eyes. "You're not winning. And I kissed her hello. That's it."

Quinn went to the other side of the bed and lay on her back, leaving plenty of room between them. "Tell me about her. Tell me about Dani."

Lacey rolled onto her back and stared at the ceiling. This couldn't possibly end well, but she took a deep breath and said, "She's beautiful. So beautiful, I can't take my eyes off of her sometimes."

"What else?"

"Her family moved here from Colombia when she was a teenager. Definitely fits the image of a fiery Latina. Smart. Trilingual. English, Spanish, Portuguese. She's still studying."

"Were you putting her through school?"

"I was the reason her parents cut her off financially, so I insisted on helping her finish. But then, something changed."

"What changed?"

It wasn't easy to think about, let alone talk about. "Losing her parents' love and support changed Dani. That's a pretty fucked-up thing, you know? Having your parents take away something they're supposed to give unconditionally. It made her angry, and the fact that I wasn't out at work made her bitter. She thought I was ashamed of her. It all added up."

"Were you? Ashamed, I mean?" Quinn asked.

Lacey huffed. "God, no. If you saw a photo of her, you'd know that's not even possible. It was never about shame. It was about keeping my job. Keeping her in school. Keeping the money rolling in. I'd heard enough negative stuff…homophobic stuff at work that I just wasn't sure how people would react."

"Sounds like you were willing to do anything to keep her happy."

God, wasn't that the truth? Even as Dani got more distant and bitter, Lacey had fought like hell to keep her. And at the end, nothing she did was enough. "I honestly don't know how she's getting by now. I have no idea who's supporting her. Maybe her parents took her back when she broke up with me. I didn't ask and she didn't offer any info on that front. But she looked good. Happier. Not so bitter."

"And she wants you back," Quinn said. "That's pretty clear, right?"

Lacey didn't want to talk about that. Yes, now that she was working again, Dani wanted her back. She didn't want to tell Quinn how shitty that made her feel. "She wants to meet you. She's a fan. I think I told you that in the beginning. She'd die if she knew that you're actually gay. Probably make advances or something. She's pretty forward when she wants something."

"You didn't answer my question. And I really don't want to meet the woman who broke your heart."

"I didn't know you cared." Quinn cared. Lacey knew that. She could hear it in her voice when she'd called her in New York. That's why she'd come back so soon. If Quinn needed her, she'd be here. She was still under contract, after all.

"Bullshit."

Lacey turned and looked at Quinn. "Yeah, I guess the trifecta of comfort food says it all."

"Just be careful with Dani, okay? Don't jump in with both feet until you're sure."

"I already told you, I'm not doing *anything* until we've completed our mission."

Quinn blew air through her lips. "What was our mission again?"

Lacey huffed out a laugh. "Faking love so you can find the real thing while keeping your career intact."

"God. It seems silly now, doesn't it?"

"We can stop. Just pay me and I'll leave."

Seeming stunned by the comment, Quinn sat up. Their eyes met for a few seconds and then she got off the bed, putting some distance between them. "Just like that?"

"Fulfill the terms of the contract. That's all I ask."

Quinn put her hands on her hips. "Give you an early termination bonus. Is that what you're referring to?"

"Yep. Give me that and I'm gone."

"You know what, Lacey?" Quinn raised her voice as she backed up toward the door. "Fuck you!"

Lacey squeezed her eyes shut. Why did she push Quinn away when she needed her the most? All she really wanted was to stop this arguing, roll over, and lie in Quinn's arms all night. "Quinn?" She sat up and looked around, but Quinn was gone. "Fuck." She fell back on the bed and threw her arm over her eyes.

CHAPTER TWENTY

It was getting worse. They couldn't even talk to each other without fighting. Twice now, Quinn had told Lacey to move out. Maybe she really should. They had to work together, and even though they were both great at shutting everything else out when the director yelled action, they didn't need the entire cast and crew witnessing this tension between them.

Lacey rolled over and stared at the suitcase that she'd yet to unpack. She'd woken up feeling slightly better, but the thought of finding another place to live felt overwhelming. She regretted practically everything she'd said the night before. Of course, this wasn't exactly new territory for her. Being hurt about one thing and communicating about it by being a monumental asshole about something else was pretty much par for the course.

From the corner of her eye, she saw the notification on her phone. She instantly, and idiotically, hoped it was a message from Quinn. Not that she could think of even one good reason why Quinn might have texted her, apart from a friendly *Get the fuck out of my guesthouse.*

Her heart sank when she saw it was from Dani. It was a photo of a dreary New York day with the words *wish you were here.* She'd have loved that message on almost any other day. But today, she couldn't shake the feeling she'd thrown something important away. She stood up and started stripping her pajamas off on the way to the shower.

With her wet hair pulled up into a bun and her pride tucked firmly into her pocket, Lacey went to the main house, ready to apologize for her careless words. Ready to do and say whatever it took to make it right. Honesty. Total honesty, she kept repeating in her head. When she opened the sliding glass door, she was shocked to find a complete stranger in Quinn's kitchen.

The woman dried her hands on a towel and rushed over to Lacey. "There she is," she said as she opened her arms and pulled Lacey in for a hug. "How are you, dear? I hear you've had the flu."

"Um…much better today," Lacey answered tentatively. "Just a little weak still. Um…forgive me, but…"

"Oh! I'm so excited to meet you I'm afraid I've completely forgot my manners. I'm Margaret. Margaret Kincaid. And I've been watching you your whole life."

Quinn's mother was one of those rare, ageless creatures. She could be forty-five or sixty, depending on who you asked. Her secret wasn't surgery, although that was common in her social circle. It had more to do with the way she carried herself—like a woman who expected to be treated a certain way. Like a woman who was in complete control. It didn't hurt that her wardrobe was almost entirely bespoke.

Suffice it to say, Margaret was not the typical soap fan Lacey usually encountered. She couldn't imagine her wearing a sweatshirt with an iron-on photo of her favorite cat on it—a memorial, of course. Okay, they weren't all like that. Only one in particular that managed to corner Lacey as she left the studio. Most of her fans were sweet and ardent and had strong opinions about the show. She appreciated every one of them, even the cat lady.

"It's such a pleasure to meet you, Mrs. Kincaid."

Margaret patted Lacey's cheek. "Of course, you're still a little weak, dear. The flu can take it right out of you. That's why I'm making breakfast. Quinn said you haven't eaten much."

Lacey nodded as she backed away, trying to regain some of her personal space. "Okay, let me just go talk to Quinn for a second and I'll be right back."

Margaret followed Lacey to the stairs. "I watched you grow up on TV. It was so wonderful to see how you emerged from that gawky stage with the braces and those few extra pounds. Such a vulnerable time, you know, what with the acne and becoming a woman."

"Wow!" Lacey said with a laugh. "That's quite a picture you're painting."

"Oh, honey, you got through it like a star. I remember wishing Quinn could have seen you when she was that age. But she's a few years older than you are, of course."

Lacey smiled politely and motioned with her thumb as she took a few steps up. "Let me just…"

"Of course, dear. We'll talk later. I have a lot to say about that husband of yours." Margaret gave her a conspiratorial wink.

Lacey smiled politely again and made her way upstairs. She went into Quinn's room and shut the door behind her. "Quinn?" She walked into the bathroom and found Quinn sitting on a bench in her dressing room, hunched over. When Quinn looked up, Lacey could see tears in her eyes. "Oh God. What's wrong?"

Quinn pointed to a manila folder sitting on the bathroom counter. "I signed the early termination, so just go. The final payment will be…" Quinn couldn't finish. She broke down and put her face in her hands.

"Quinn." Lacey knelt on the floor in front of her, gently placing her hands on her knees. "I'm sorry about last night. Will you let me explain?"

"I think it's pretty clear."

"It's not. None of this is clear. It's all a muddled mess, but I guess if I'm being honest, I'm still a little pissed off about what you said about me getting too cozy."

Quinn wiped her eyes and looked at her, waiting for her to continue.

"Okay, I'm a lot pissed. It hurt. And then you wouldn't stop talking about Dani. Between that and how sick I felt, I just…"

"Morphed into a complete asshole?" Quinn helped her out.

"I was going to say I reacted badly. But yeah, yours is more accurate." Lacey looked away for a second, trying to summon the courage to be really honest. "I'm sorry," she said, making eye contact again. "Leaving you…moving out…calling everything off…is absolutely not what I want."

"Are you sure about that?" Quinn bit her lip, trying to keep it from quivering. "Because my mother showed up this morning without any warning."

"I know. She just mentioned what a gawky teenager I was."

"Let me guess," Quinn said with a huff. "She managed to make it sound like some sort of backhanded compliment."

Lacey tilted her head. "Come to think of it, she kind of did."

"That's Margaret." Quinn shook her head. "I can't believe she just showed up like this."

Lacey resisted the urge to reach out and push Quinn's hair behind her ear. "She's been worried about you. You couldn't keep her away forever."

Quinn wiped her eyes and immediately broke down again. "You don't know how scary this whole coming out thing is for me. And that woman, my mother, will not be happy about it."

"Look at it this way," Lacey said reassuringly. "When she finds out you're gay, you can tell her it's because of something she did."

"That's not funny."

"It's kind of funny." Lacey didn't stop herself this time. She reached out and held Quinn's face, gently wiping away her tears with her thumbs. "I'm not going anywhere. And you don't have to come out to your mother right now. In fact, don't. Let her watch the show like everyone else and do it on your own terms, okay?" Lacey kissed Quinn's forehead and wrapped her arms around her. "Let Dr. Covington deal with Mrs. Margaret Kincaid."

Quinn returned the hug, resting her chin on Lacey's shoulder. She held on tight, trying to get control of her emotions. Then she pulled back just enough so she could look Lacey in the eye. "This isn't just a business arrangement anymore."

Lacey's eyes widened as she wiped more tears from Quinn's cheeks. "No shit? Does that mean we're friends?"

"Would you please take me seriously for a second?"

Lacey got up off the floor and sat next to Quinn. "Okay."

Quinn wiped her nose with a tissue that had stopped being useful. Lacey grabbed the box off the counter and gave her another one. She sat closer this time, crossing her legs and wrapping an arm around Quinn's waist.

"When my mom showed up," Quinn started, "I actually considered begging you to stay, and by beg, I mean bribe. That's how hard it is for me to have her in my home. But what I really wanted was just to be able to ask you...as a friend...to be here for me and not get on the Quinn-bashing bandwagon with her."

"She has a band? Well, I have a Quinn is awesome trumpet, so we'll see who's louder."

Quinn leaned on her and let their heads touch. "Thank you."

"You owe me," Lacey joked. She quickly added, "Just kidding. Is your mom a good cook? Because she made breakfast and expects me to eat it." She turned and kissed Quinn's temple, breathing in her scent. She'd missed that scent. She'd missed being this close to Quinn. They didn't have reason to be this close anymore, now that the cast had been removed.

"My mother's good at everything. It's part of her fucking charm."

Quinn put her hand on Lacey's knee. "You're lucky you're sick, because these awful pajamas would not fly with her on any other day."

"She doesn't like Hello Kitty?" Lacey didn't want to let go. In fact, she wrapped her other arm around Quinn, locking her in an embrace. "I guess I know exactly what I'm getting you for Christmas."

"You smell better," Quinn said. "Like yourself again."

"What did I smell like before?"

"Like you'd been on a plane and hadn't showered in several days."

"HA! Should we talk about how you smelled after the hospital?" Quinn giggled. "No."

"Should we talk about how many times I wiped your—"

Quinn slammed her hand over Lacey's mouth. "My mother must never know about that."

Lacey nodded, the hand still covering her mouth.

"Swear it," Quinn said in all seriousness. She slowly removed her hand.

Lacey offered her pinky finger. "Pinky swears."

Quinn smirked and wrapped her pinky finger around Lacey's. "Pinky swears."

Lacey motioned with her head. "How about you throw that envelope away?"

Quinn got up and pulled the contract out of the envelope. She tore it into several pieces and tossed it in the trash can. They left the bathroom together and Lacey slapped Quinn on the butt as they walked to the door. "Does your mom being here mean you're not going to get in the hot tub naked anymore? Or, does it mean she'll be joining you naked in the hot tub? Because my head might explode from all that womanly-ness."

"You're disgusting."

"Hey, she has a great figure for her age!"

Quinn shrugged. "Pilates."

"Huh. Maybe I should look into that."

"Your body is just fine."

"Fine as in…just fine? Or fine as in…girl, you're lookin' fine."

They got to the stairs and Quinn turned to Lacey. "Fishing for a compliment?"

Lacey looked down at herself. "I guess Hello Kitty pajamas are kind of like a drab, dull, beige sling."

Quinn rolled her eyes and leaned in, lowering her voice. "Yes, you're still fuckable."

"But we're never, ever, not in a million years—" Lacey stopped when she saw Margaret looking up at them.

"Are you two ready for breakfast?"

Quinn motioned for Lacey to go first. "After you."

"So, you're on my daughter's show now. I have to say, you've done a marvelous job so far."

Lacey watched Margaret take an extremely graceful bite of her omelet. She'd never questioned her own table etiquette until this very moment. She set her own fork down and rested her hands in her lap, not wanting to eat while the woman's eyes were on her. "Thank you, Mrs. Kincaid. It was just a small role at first, but we recently found out they want to extend my contract."

"Well, that doesn't surprise me at all." Margaret pointed with her fork at Lacey's plate. "Eat, dear." She turned her attention to Quinn. "She'll turn your show around, honey. Mark my words."

"My show didn't need turning around. It just needed…"

"It was getting a little stale. Of course, the soaps never let that happen. They're always throwing something new at us," Margaret said with a wink directed at Lacey.

Quinn rolled her eyes. "Yeah, maybe we should give Lacey's character a multiple personality disorder, or better yet, how about an immaculate conception?"

Margaret chuckled. "Don't be ridiculous." She set her fork down and tapped her finger on her chin while she considered the idea. "But there does need to be a twist."

"She's gay." Lacey picked up her fork and took a bite while the two women stared at her in shock, Quinn's mouth literally hanging open.

"Who is, dear?"

Quinn shot Lacey a glare. "That's top-secret information, Mother. You can't tell anyone."

"How can I tell anyone when I have no idea who you're talking about?"

"It's me. I'm gay. The producers on *Light of Day* fired me when I came out of the closet." Lacey gave Quinn an apologetic look.

Margaret furrowed her brow. "Well, that was certainly their loss. I've never known a finer actress than you."

Lacey was stunned. Did Quinn's own mother really just say that? Quinn threw her napkin on the table and was about to stand up when Lacey grabbed her hand. If Margaret could've seen under the table, she'd have witnessed Lacey gently caressing Quinn's fingers, trying to console her. "Your daughter, Mrs. Kincaid, is the finest actress I've ever had the pleasure to work with. She's highly respected on the set and loved by everyone. And just being in her presence and watching her work is an honor for me."

Lacey tried to pull her hand away, but Quinn kept hold of it. She gave Lacey a smile and intertwined their fingers. "Thank you." She took a deep breath and turned her attention back to her mother. "On the show, Jordan and Selena are going to fall in love. And one might say that life has imitated art."

Margaret set her fork down. "Are you sure that's the best thing for your show? Jordan has never shown any signs of...she's only been with...men." She turned her attention to Lacey. "Please don't take this the wrong way, honey. I have no problem with gay people."

"Unless they're your daughter," Quinn said.

"Don't put words in my mouth, dear. I'm just not sure people will believe that Jordan is..." She looked at Lacey again. "Of course, if Jordan Ellis met Dr. Sarah Covington she'd be very impressed, wouldn't she?" Margaret's face lit up like she'd just had a huge revelation. "Wouldn't that be something?"

Lacey lowered her gaze and pursed her lips together, trying to hold back a giggle. She quickly sobered up when Quinn let go of her hand and covered her eyes. "I can't do this," Quinn whispered.

Quinn started shaking as the sobs worked their way up. Lacey immediately wrapped her arms around Quinn. "Shh...it's okay." She stroked Quinn's hair as she cried and whispered in her ear, "I've got you. I'm not going anywhere."

Margaret sat there, watching. "Honey," she said, getting no reply. It took her a moment, but then she said, "Oh my God. You had me so confused, but I think I understand now."

Lacey took the napkin off her lap and offered it to Quinn as she lifted her head, meeting her mother's gaze. "You do?" Quinn whispered.

Margaret sighed. "You were afraid to tell me? Why, Quinn? I'm your mother! Why am I always the last to know anything? And how could you keep the fact that you're dating Lacey Matthews from me? You know what a huge fan I am!"

Margaret got up and rounded the table. She leaned down between them and kissed Quinn's cheek and then Lacey's. "Maybe now I'll get a grandchild."

"Stop gloating."

"I'm not gloating."

Quinn plopped into a chair. "You're gloating so loud they can hear it in fucking Cincinnati."

Lacey poured Quinn a glass of wine from the bottle she'd just opened. "I'm just out here enjoying your awesome backyard. And lower your voice. You don't want your mother hearing you swear like a sailor. She'll think I'm a bad influence on you."

"You are. But my mother would never believe it. She thinks you walk on water."

Lacey pushed the glass across the table. "Are you really going to let your mother's love and admiration for my incredible acting skills keep you from enjoying the fact that you just came out to her and she still loves you?"

"For now, she loves me, but what happens when I break up with the goddess of daytime soaps? I'll just be a disappointment to her again."

Lacey quietly studied Quinn for a moment.

"What?" Quinn asked incredulously.

"You don't want to hear it."

"Are you psychoanalyzing me? Don't analyze me," Quinn said with a slow shake of her head.

Lacey put her hands up in defense. "Okay...and I'm really not gloating. I'm just relieved Margaret took it all so well, and if my being there made a difference, then I'm very glad I could help."

"Good. I don't want to fight today." Quinn put her sunglasses on and leaned back in her chair, letting the sun hit her face. "And thank you for those nice things you said. And right back atcha."

Lacey lifted her glass and smiled. "Here's to the two best actors in Hollywood."

CHAPTER TWENTY-ONE

The two best actors in Hollywood had been hard at work for months, spending virtually all of their time together. It was the same thing every day. Lacey would make the coffee, fill their travel mugs, and grab something to eat in the car. They'd work all day, often into the night, then fall into bed, and repeat it all over again the next day.

It was a rigorous schedule and Lacey loved every second of it. She was starting to believe what Quinn had said about never struggling to find work again.

"Did the coffee taste different this morning? I'm not sure I got the ratio right." Lacey stood next to Quinn. "It's a new blend I'm trying."

"I didn't notice anything different." Quinn adjusted the sling over her fake cast. "Has it always been your dream to be a barista, or just since you moved in with me?"

"How about I fill your mug with coffee from the Mr. Coffee in the guesthouse tomorrow morning?"

Quinn snorted. "I'm really not a coffee snob."

"Quiet on the set!"

Lacey leaned in and whispered, "Yeah, I noticed you're all over that canned shit at craft services."

"Are you fishing for coffee compliments?"

The director cleared his throat. "Ladies."

"Never mind," Quinn whispered.

"Roll sound."

"Rolling."

"Mark!"

"Set."

"And action!"

Selena got off the elevator in the parking garage, walking just behind Jordan. Their satchels had been replaced with a rolling briefcase. "Are we going to talk about what just happened?"

Jordan kept walking. "Not here."

"Jordan!" Selena's voice echoed through the parking garage. They both stopped and Jordan turned around.

"Do not shout at me."

"He thought I was your assistant that he could just boss around. 'Make a copy of this, sweetheart. Fetch me that file, honey.'"

"You *are* my assistant. And it didn't kill you to fetch that file. You're still alive to tell the sorry tale."

"You let him disrespect me. You didn't even tell him I'm second chair. You let him—" Selena pushed past Jordan. "Never mind. If you don't get how insulting that was, then I certainly can't explain it to you."

Jordan grabbed Selena's hand. "Wait." She stepped closer, keeping hold of her hand. Selena looked down at their joined hands and then met Jordan's gaze. "If I'm not shouting to the world who my assistant really is, it's because I don't want to let them see..." Jordan's eyes fell to Selena's lips. She corrected herself and let go of Selena's hand, taking a step back and lifting her chin. "You're right. I set the standard, and I apologize for letting him treat you that way."

"If you don't say something..."

"I know. They think it's fine to treat all women that way." Jordan glanced at her feet and then met Selena's intense gaze again. "You shouldn't have to go through what I've already been through. I'll have your back."

Selena nodded. "Okay. Are we off the clock?"

Jordan looked at her watch. "As of three minutes ago."

"Can I take you to dinner? My treat?"

Jordan smiled. "Having your back gets me dinner?"

"No." Selena shook her head. "That gets you my respect. Dinner is just...neither of us having to eat alone tonight."

"I'd love to. But I get to buy the bottle of wine. You can't afford my taste." Jordan gave her a wink as she backed away. "Not yet, anyway."

"Cut! That's it for tonight, everyone. See you tomorrow."

Lacey handed her briefcase off to an assistant. "Any interest in sushi tonight? I found a take-out with excellent reviews."

"Sounds great." Quinn grinned as she backed away. "And your coffee is stellar."

"I knew it! And you *are* a coffee snob. Just admit it."

Quinn shrugged. "Just another way you've spoiled me."

If you only knew all the ways I could spoil you. If there weren't a bunch of people milling around them, Lacey would've said it out loud, just so she could watch Quinn turn twenty different shades of red.

The next morning, Quinn moved close to Lacey as they set up to do a second take.

"Okay, everybody. Back to ones!"

As they moved back to their starting positions, Quinn whispered to Lacey. "Brock doesn't look pleased with the script."

"Pissed is more like it. But that's no excuse to blow the scene."

"Right? Because he wanted a romantic arc with Selena? What is he, twelve? God, he's as bad as his character."

"And action!"

Jordan and Selena leaned into one another and whispered while the district attorney impatiently tapped his pen on the table. After a few seconds, he stood up. "Your Honor, could you please ask counsel to stop canoodling in the courtroom?"

The judge looked over her reading glasses. "I believe that's called conferring, counsel. Take your time, ladies."

Selena shot the DA a glare and turned back to Jordan. She gave her a final nod and Jordan stood up. "Your Honor, we're ready to proceed when you are."

"Cut! Let's move on!"

"And action!"

Selena caught up to the DA in the hallway. "What the hell was that?"

John Dent looked pleased with himself. "You tell me. I mean, since when did you and your boss get so chummy? I thought you hated her as much as I do." He pushed the down button on the elevator.

"Is this because I refused to go out with you?" Selena pushed the button a few more times.

"That was before I found out you bat for the other team. I still have a tough time believing it, though it doesn't surprise me one bit that Jordan does."

"She doesn't. And what the hell is that supposed to mean, anyway?"

John chuckled. "She hates men, or are you so enamored with her that you can't see anything past those tight skirts?"

"It's just you she hates, John. And apparently, it's you who can't get past the tight skirts. Let me guess, you asked her out and she refused and now, every time she beats your ass in court, all you can think about is proving to her how manly you are. Because that's what men like you think about when you've been outplayed, isn't it? Showing powerful women your..."

"Selena." Selena turned around and found Jordan standing behind her. "While I'm dying to know what it is you think Mr. Dent wants to show me, the courthouse probably isn't the right venue." The elevator door opened and Jordan kept it open with her hand. "This one is all yours, Mr. Dent."

When the elevator doors closed, Selena lowered her gaze. "I'm sorry. That was..."

"Don't be." They turned and walked toward the stairwell. "I'm so proud of you, I can barely breathe right now."

"Cut! That's a wrap, ladies and gentleman. Enjoy your Christmas break."

Lacey took off Selena's black glasses and walked off the set with Quinn. "I'm starving."

"What time is your flight?"

"You're going to miss me, aren't you?"

Quinn took off the fake cast and handed it to a wardrobe assistant. "I'll be too busy wrangling my mother and her twin sister."

"Ah. Aunt Betty. And when do I get to meet Aunt Betty?"

"Come to Aspen with me. We'd have so much fun!"

"See?" Lacey wagged her finger at Quinn. "You *will* miss me."

Quinn kicked off Jordan's heels and slipped into her flip-flops. "You're so arrogant."

Lacey shrugged. "Maybe I just want you to say it first."

"Come to Aspen."

"I can't. Even if I wanted to..." Lacey dropped her gaze.

"You want to. Look at me. You want to."

"I can't miss Christmas with my dad."

Quinn sighed. "I know. So, what time is your flight?"

"Late—eleven thirty-five. I was just going to get a cab from here. Do you mind driving the Range Rover home?"

"Don't be ridiculous. I'll drive you."

"You don't have to do that."

"Don't make it a big deal. I'm just driving a friend to the airport. People do it all the time."

Lacey grinned. "I'm going to miss you too."

"I didn't say it."

"You didn't have to."

Quinn opened her trailer door, letting Lacey go in first. They stripped out of their work clothes and put on jeans. Lacey threw on a thick sweater so she'd be warm on the plane and pulled her hair back into a ponytail.

"You're in first, right?" Quinn took her hair out of the tight bun, shook it out, and put on a baseball cap. "Domestic first is total trash, but at least you'll be able to sleep without people sneaking selfies on the way to the bathroom."

"Yes, snobby pants, I'm in first." Lacey glanced at her and smiled as she looked away. "Am I ever going to get my Yankees cap back?"

"Buy yourself another one while you're in New York." Quinn adjusted it on her head. "I like this one."

Quinn could see the United Airlines sign up ahead. She made her way to the drop-off area a bit more slowly than she needed to.

Lacey turned in her seat. "Promise me you'll be careful in Aspen. No more broken bones. I can't stomach the thought of taking care of your sorry ass again."

Quinn laughed. "Yeah, it'd be fun to see how they'd write in a broken leg for Jordan."

"Could you imagine Selena's reaction? She'd be all, 'Are you fucking kidding me with this shit?' Either that or she'd just kill her boss."

Quinn pulled up to the curb. "Okay, get ready to jump out. You'll have about five seconds."

Lacey unbuckled her seat belt. "Speaking of broken legs." She sat up in her seat. "This is the best goddamned send-off I've ever had. So touching. So caring."

Quinn reached over and patted her leg. "Does that help?"

"No. Get your hand off of me." Lacey pointed to the people in the car in front of them. "You're like that guy. He's patting his wife's leg too. What a chump. He's never gonna get laid."

Quinn raised her eyebrows and smiled. "Say hi to your dad for me. No. Actually, give him a hug for me."

"Oh, he gets a hug? Look at this guy. He's sitting in his car while his wife—"

"Okay, Lace. We're here."

"Fine." Lacey got out and opened the back door. She grabbed her carry-on and paused long enough to look at Quinn. "Give Margaret a hug for me." She slammed the door before Quinn could reply.

CHAPTER TWENTY-TWO

Lacey was five minutes out. Eight if the driver continued to go the damn speed limit. Four days they'd been apart for the Christmas break. Four. Hideously. Long. Days.

It had been a sobering experience for Lacey. She missed Quinn more than she could've imagined. She tried to stay in the moment with her dad, doing the things they usually did together; breakfast at his favorite diner, shopping for new shirts and ties, even though he insisted that his old ones were still fine. Browsing bookstores and vintage record stores. It was nice. But something was missing. Or *someone.*

Quinn had arrived back home from Aspen a few hours earlier. She'd texted Lacey, telling her how excited she was to exchange presents later that night. Lacey couldn't wait to see her again.

"It's the big gate on the left," she told the driver. "Just push the button and tell her it's Lacey."

The driver followed the instructions and the gate opened. "Oh God," Lacey said under her breath, a huge smile plastered on her face. Quinn was standing on the porch, looking like sex and Christmas in her red Alpine sweater, black leggings, and tall, black leather boots. Like an ad for J.Crew or something. *Damn.*

Lacey jumped out of the car. "Well, don't you look cute!" She took a good long look at Quinn, grinning from ear to ear while the driver unloaded her luggage.

Quinn waited for the driver to get back in the car before she stepped off the porch. "How was New York?"

"How was Aspen?"

"Don't change the subject." Quinn stood right in front of Lacey and took hold of the sleeve of her chunky winter sweater with two fingers. "You went shopping without me."

"I did lots of things without you. Hated every second of it."

"Yeah. Me too." Quinn let go of the sleeve and tucked her hands in her pockets. "Sitting by the fire with my mom and my Aunt Betty going on and on about how that Lacey Matthews is doing *so* great on my show almost killed me."

Being away from you almost killed me. "I bet." They both grinned. "So…are you going to hug me or what?"

Quinn stepped closer. She wrapped her arms around Lacey's waist and kissed her cheek. "Welcome home."

Lacey's eyes shuttered closed as she breathed Quinn in. She smelled different. Maybe she'd bought a new perfume. She was about to mention it when her ears perked up. "Is that Christmas music?"

Quinn picked up the suitcase and took Lacey's hand, leading her into the house. "Since we still have presents to open, I thought I'd set the mood."

She'd done more than set the mood with music. Candles were lit. There was a spread of hors d'oeuvres laid out on the coffee table, along with a bottle of champagne. And caviar.

Lacey swallowed hard. "This looks incredible. Just give me a minute to freshen up from the flight."

She rolled her suitcase into the guesthouse and shut the door. She stared back at the house, wondering how the hell she'd get through this night without kissing Quinn. It wasn't fair, the extremely romantic atmosphere she'd created. And after missing her like crazy?

Lacey was screwed.

It wasn't the champagne that did Lacey in. It wasn't hearing that addictive laughter, or being hand-fed caviar on a tiny mother-of-pearl spoon while Quinn stared at her lips with those killer blue eyes.

It wasn't Quinn laying her head on Lacey's shoulder while she sang along with Karen Carpenter. And who knew Quinn was an alto?

It wasn't when the Christmas music changed to regular music. But not just any regular music. A specific song that curiously made Quinn's eyes light up, which she quickly tried to hide by grabbing the remote and fast forwarding. It didn't matter. Lacey already knew what song it was. She giggled a little.

None of those moments broke Lacey. She didn't let it slip that she had to force herself not to text Quinn every five minutes while she was in New York—not even after her third glass of champagne. She could have, but she didn't.

She didn't lean in and lick the caviar off Quinn's bottom lip when it was so obviously sitting there for that very reason. She desperately wanted to, but she didn't.

She didn't tell Quinn that her singing voice sounded like heaven—if heaven had a sound. And Lacey was suddenly sure it did.

And she didn't jump up and grab Quinn's hand before she could fast forward the song and say, "Let's dance."

Lacey had been strong. Stoic. A rock.

Until now.

"What's this?"

"Your Christmas present, silly."

Lacey pulled the white ribbon on the large, flat, Tiffany blue box. She took off the lid and pushed the tissue paper aside. Her hand found Quinn's.

"Your dad said you probably haven't seen this one in a long time," Quinn squeezed Lacey's hand. "I was so touched by the gift you gave him, I wanted to do the same for you."

Lacey bit her lip as she ran her finger over the beautiful silver frame that housed a photo of her and her mother. Lacey couldn't have been more than three or four when the photo was taken. They were on a beach—Daria holding on tight to her little girl in her pink bathing suit with white daisies.

Lacey couldn't remember ever seeing this particular photo before. She kissed her finger and touched her mother's face as a tear rolled down her cheek.

"The nail is already in the wall—in the guesthouse. I took the liberty…"

Lacey didn't have words. Quinn looked worried. Lacey still didn't have words. What could she possibly say? *Thank you* wasn't enough. *I love you* was too much. She cupped Quinn's cheek, leaned in, and gave her the softest of kisses, the edge of her lips barely grazing Quinn's. It wasn't a kiss motivated by passion or desire. It was a kiss of gratitude and understanding. Lacey barely realized she'd done it. She turned her attention back to the photo. She could feel Quinn's eyes boring into her, but she couldn't look at her. And she still couldn't talk.

They sat in silence until Lacey could pull herself together enough to say something. Something that wouldn't scare the shit out of Quinn and make her say something stupid like *you should move out*. She put the lid back on the box and stood up, putting her hand out for Quinn. "Your present is in the guesthouse."

Lacey hung the photo on the wall and stepped back. Quinn had chosen the perfect spot. She'd be able to look at the photo before she fell asleep at night and when she woke up in the morning.

It was the perfect gift.

She took a deep breath and tried to lighten the moment. "Close your eyes." She looked at Quinn. "I mean it. Close your eyes."

"Okay. Closed." Quinn put her hands over her eyes.

Lacey wheeled Quinn's gift out of the closet. "Okay, open them."

"A mountain bike?" Quinn got a little closer. "A very nice mountain bike."

"It's not for you. I mean, unless you want to upgrade."

Quinn shook her head. "I don't understand."

Lacey was glad the mountain bike was in between them. She put one hand on the seat and the other on the handlebar to steady herself. "I know you're going to want to get on your bike again soon. And I'll be worried sick, thinking about you out there all alone...unless I'm out there...wherever...with you."

"But..."

Quinn's mouth hung open. Lacey reached across the bike and put her finger under Quinn's chin, closing it. "I guess we both left each other speechless."

"You'd really ride with me?" Quinn's expression was one of complete shock.

Lacey looked at the photo on the wall. "I..." *Love you.* "Yeah. I'll really ride with you."

A small, disbelieving laugh escaped Quinn's mouth. "That's..." *Love?* "A miracle, I know."

Lacey didn't want to come around from the bike. She was hanging on to it for dear life. But Quinn tugged on her arm and pulled her into a hug. "We're going to have so much fun. I swear, you'll love it."

"Not until you're fully healed. This is for later, okay?"

Quinn stepped back and tucked her hands into her back pockets, a look on her face Lacey couldn't quite read. "Lace, I..." She took another step back, putting more space between them. "In my whole life, I've never had..."

Lacey knew what she was trying to say—she'd never had a friend who cared this much. It wasn't easy being as famous as Quinn was, always wondering what people's motives were for wanting to get close to her. She'd even seen it at work, people in the "industry" falling over themselves to get Quinn's attention.

Lacey looked at the photo hanging on the wall. It was quite possibly the sweetest gift she'd ever been given. Dani's gifts to her over the years hadn't even come close. She looked at Quinn again, standing there with her eyes on the ground and probably a lump in her throat, not able to say the words. Lacey knew the feeling. "I know."

Quinn looked up and gave her a grateful smile. "Merry Christmas, Lace."

Lacey took hold of the bike. "Let's get this in the garage."

Quinn followed behind her. "You know we're going to have to get you some riding clothes. And a helmet."

"Can't I just wear my yoga pants or something?"

Quinn scoffed. "No! You have to wear the proper gear. It's safer that way."

"It didn't save your sorry ass."

"Don't fight me on this. You'll lose."

Lacey smiled to herself. The little thank you kiss hadn't ruined everything.

Thank God.

CHAPTER TWENTY-THREE

J.J. was going over the "first kiss" scene with Quinn. "Can't say I didn't see this coming, the way you two smoke up the joint. Are you nervous? You look nervous."

Quinn shook her head as she glanced around, looking for Lacey. "I'm fine."

"You're not fine. Your hands are shaking."

Quinn spread her fingers out and sure enough, they were shaking. The last thing she wanted to do was admit she was nervous as hell about their first kiss. "Too much coffee. I'm fine."

"We'll try for two takes, but we have to get it right. Everyone, even the higher-ups, are invested in this. They want it to be perfect."

"Are you trying to make me even more nervous, J.J.? Because it's working." Quinn rolled her head back and forth, trying to loosen up her neck.

"So, you *are* nervous about the kiss."

"A little bit, yeah," Quinn admitted. "It's a big deal, don't you think?"

"Huge." J.J. put up a hand. "Sorry. I'm making it worse. You'll be fine, kid. You two have that thing that every director wants to see, so my job will be easy today." He leaned in close and lowered his voice. "Are you sure you don't want to rehearse it a few times?"

They'd rehearsed the lines and the blocking, but Quinn wanted the actual kiss to be natural. She shook her head and J.J. turned to walk away, but she reached for his arm. "J.J., about the *getting it right* thing—will you just let the camera run? Don't yell cut. Just let it flow and then maybe we can decide together how much of it makes the cut."

J.J. gave her a wink. "You got it, kid."

Quinn took off her robe and stepped onto the set, finding her mark in Jordan's dimly lit apartment. Wearing nothing but a fake cast, a black tank top, and tight boy shorts, she stood by the front door. "Ready whenever Lacey is."

Lacey found her mark on the other side of the door. "Ready."

"Okay, everyone, we're rolling." J.J. let the assistant director do his thing and then shouted, "Action!"

Jordan opened her door and leaned against it with one hand. "It's late."

Selena looked Jordan up and down, taking in her barely clothed body. "Sorry, were you asleep?"

"Just working in bed," Jordan opened the door all the way, letting Selena in. "What brings you out so late? Isn't it snowing?"

"Just a dusting." Selena took off her winter coat and hung it on the coat rack, her eyes tracking Jordan's ass as she walked into the kitchen.

"Well, I'm glad you're here, because I've been dying for a glass of wine but I can't get the cork out with one hand."

Selena took the bottle. "Here, let me get it." She nervously glanced at Jordan. "You get the glasses."

Jordan turned away and Selena's eyes went to her long, toned legs. Jordan got on her tiptoes and reached high into the cupboard, making her tank top ride up a little. Selena closed her eyes and took a deep breath.

"You didn't come here to fight with me again, did you? Or quit? It's always one or the other." Jordan set the glasses down and turned toward Selena, leaning against the counter.

Selena poured the wine and took a quick swallow. "I didn't come here to fight with you." She quickly downed a little more wine and turned to Jordan. "I came here to…" She paused for a second as their eyes met. "This…" she said as she grabbed Jordan's face and kissed her. When she didn't get a reaction, she pulled away and took a few steps back. Jordan stood there, frozen, her mouth slightly open. "I'm so sorry," Selena said. "I shouldn't have…" Jordan grabbed Selena's hand and pulled her back to her. They stared intently for a few seconds and then Jordan leaned in and kissed her back. Selena was tense at first but eventually relaxed into the kiss.

That was where the scene was supposed to end, but J.J. motioned for his crew to keep rolling instead of cutting the scene.

Jordan grabbed Selena's hips and turned her so that she was now pushed back against the counter. She kissed along Selena's jaw, working her way to her neck, kissing and sucking as she went. Selena closed her eyes and gripped Jordan's shoulders as a moan escaped her mouth. When Jordan heard the moan, she pulled back and made eye contact before going in for another kiss.

Lacey kept the kiss closed as much as she could for the cameras, but her desire to feel Quinn's tongue overwhelmed her, so she deepened the kiss. Quinn grabbed Lacey around the waist as their tongues collided. After a few seconds, Lacey pushed Quinn away and made eye contact again. Through bated breath, Quinn said, "Please tell me you got that, J.J."

Lacey and Quinn both turned to look at the crew, who were all standing there in shock. J.J. cleared his throat. "And...cut."

Quinn opened her trailer door and found Lacey standing there, waiting. "I'm fine," she said, before Lacey could ask.

"You don't sound fine."

The last thing Quinn wanted to do was admit how discombobulated she felt after that kiss. And God, she hoped it wasn't written all over her face. Was she bright red? She felt bright red. "I'm just glad that damn scene is over."

"It sucked that bad for you, huh? Having to kiss me?"

"I didn't mean it like that," Quinn snapped back. "We knew this scene was coming. Please don't make it awkward."

"The only one who's acting awkward—"

"Oh my God, Lacey, REALLY? I'M THE ONLY ONE?" Quinn winced when she saw Amy standing there, waiting with the cart. She got in the front seat. "Not a word, Amy."

Amy followed the instruction and didn't even look at her boss. That didn't stop her from giving Lacey a worried look in the rearview mirror a couple of times. When they came to a stop, Quinn jumped out and headed straight for the Range Rover.

Lacey patted her shoulder. "Thanks, Amy."

"Yeah, okay." Amy watched Quinn get in the car and shut the door. "Is she okay, Lacey? I don't get why she's so mad."

Lacey followed Amy's gaze. "She'll be fine. She's probably just nervous about the big love scene tomorrow."

"Well, if hot scenes put her in a mood like this, we're all screwed."

Lacey laughed. "Tell me about it." Quinn gave Lacey an impatient wave to get in the car. "See you tomorrow, Amy."

Lacey got in the car and slammed her door shut. She put the key in the ignition and sat back. She was about to say something, but Quinn beat her to it. "Can we please go home, now?"

"Fine." Lacey started the car. "Don't look at me. Don't talk to me. Just look out the goddamned window." Quinn opened her mouth. "I mean it." She shut her mouth again. Lacey cranked the music and screeched out of the parking lot.

Quinn stared out the sliding glass door. They'd finished early and Lacey was where she always was if they got home early enough to see the sunset—lying on a lounge chair by the pool.

Quinn was angry at herself for letting that kiss affect her the way it did. That had certainly never happened to her at work before. The kisses she'd had with the lawyers and judges Jordan had slept with were very mechanical. She'd felt nothing. Less than nothing. It was acting, pure and simple.

Taking out her frustration on Lacey was uncalled for. Juvenile. It wasn't her fault. Lacey was just doing her job. She wasn't the one who made the kiss ten times as sexy and twice as long it was supposed to be. That was all Quinn.

She opened the sliding glass door and stepped outside. She slowly walked over to where Lacey was, her hands deep in her jeans pockets, looking rather contrite. She wasn't sure what she would say, but she knew it needed to include some sort of apology. She sat on a lounge chair and motioned for Lacey to take her earbuds out. "I'm sorry I snapped at you earlier."

Lacey turned her attention back to her magazine. "You're gay, Quinn. It's okay to get turned on when a woman kisses you."

It was only the second time Quinn had ever kissed a woman. And even with people watching, cameras rolling, and the nerves roiling in her stomach, it felt magical. And that scared her. Because she couldn't control her feelings. And she desperately needed to control her feelings when it came to Lacey. Still—she wanted to know. "Were you turned on?"

"Very," Lacey said as she turned a page.

Would it hurt their working relationship to acknowledge the truth? Would Lacey even believe her if she lied? No. She'd see right through it. "Yeah, um...me too."

"There's no shame in that." Lacey turned another page. "And it doesn't have to mean anything. Hell, I've felt several boners on set, pushing against my leg. I felt so bad for them when they had to stand up, but it didn't mean they were in love with me." She met Quinn's gaze. "At least, that's not what I took it to mean."

The amusement in Lacey's eyes was very evident. Quinn gave her a knowing smirk. "You can tease me all you want. I deserve it. But I really am sorry."

"For turning me on? Because that's *not* how the scene was written. Pushing me against the counter like that?" Lacey tsk'd as she slowly shook her head. "Not in the script."

"Neither was your tongue."

Lacey giggled. "They'll probably cut that part."

"Good. Then I can pretend it never happened." Quinn stood up. "I made dinner."

"Yeah, good luck trying to forget my tongue. And, you did?" Lacey asked in surprise.

"Bought…is a more accurate word. I *bought* dinner. And I have a movie queued up that I really don't want to watch alone."

"You hate my commentary when we watch movies."

Quinn held out her hand, helping Lacey up. "I'll make popcorn. That'll keep you quiet."

Lacey folded her magazine in half and hit Quinn's butt with it. "God, you're a pain in my ass sometimes."

"Ditto."

Amy watched Laura put the final touches on Quinn's body makeup, evening out any tan lines on her arms and legs. "Can I watch?"

"No." Quinn pointed at her right shoulder. "A little more right here."

"But you're going to be making out with—"

"Amy, if you say Dr. Sarah Covington, I swear I'll fire you right now with no severance."

Amy grimaced at Laura. "She's in her hot-scene mood. It's her thing."

Laura put up her hands. "I'm just here to make her look good." She winked at Amy. "But I know what you mean."

"Are you ready?" Lacey stepped up into the trailer, wearing a bathrobe.

Amy gave her a little wave. "Oh, hey, Lace." She'd started calling her Lace after she'd heard Quinn say it.

"Hey, Amy. How's our girl holding up?"

"Kinda grumpy," Amy whispered.

"I'm not grumpy." Quinn put her arms out so Laura could help her put on a robe. "I'm also not deaf."

"Okay, you're all set." Laura turned her attention to Lacey. "You're tan all over, so you won't need much. I'll touch you up on set."

"Can you ladies give me a minute with Quinn? I'll be right there, Laura." Lacey waited until they were both gone and the door was closed before she turned to Quinn. "You haven't done much of this, have you?"

"Love scenes or women?"

"Both, actually."

Quinn took a deep breath. "A few...and no."

"They've got me on top, so I'll be doing most of the work."

"I'm not worried," Quinn said, unconvincingly.

"That's a lie. You're worried sick."

Quinn tried to walk to the door but Lacey grabbed her hand. "Quinn, I need to say something."

"If this backfires..." Quinn sighed. "You're right. I'm worried sick."

"You're not blazing a trail, here. Other shows have gay characters and gay love scenes."

Quinn shook her head. "Not my show. I could lose viewers."

"And you'll gain millions more. Who cares if those boycotting moms target you? Fuck them. They seem like shitty moms to me."

Quinn closed her robe and tightened the belt. "Let's just get this over with."

Lacey stepped closer. "Okay, but you need to trust me in there." She adjusted the collar on Quinn's robe, even though it didn't need adjusting. "I've done at least fifty love scenes. None like this, because it was daytime TV, but still...I know what I'm doing."

Knowing Lacey would be with her through this was the only thing holding Quinn together. The truth was, she hadn't really done anything beyond the typical kissing scene and then skipping to the morning after scene. This, what was about to happen, would be her first real love scene. And it would be with a woman. She took another deep breath, trying to calm the butterflies in her stomach. "I do trust you."

"Then stop trying to push me away. We're in this together. If there's tension between us, it'll show up on camera."

Lacey was right. Quinn had been in her own head for days,

worried about all of this. She put her hands on Lacey's waist, resting their foreheads together. "I know. And I'm sorry. I just have so much on my mind right now."

"Let it all go. Just for an hour."

Quinn nodded. "I'll try."

"Also, you can't be mad at me after. You were furious with me after the kissing scene, and if your panties are wet an hour from now, you can't take it out on me."

Quinn suppressed a giggle. "Okay. I won't take it out on you, but eight people will be watching us, so I don't think that'll be a problem." Yes, Quinn had counted them. She knew exactly who would be on the closed set.

Lacey opened the trailer door. "Oh, no. You're going to get so lost in my touch they're all going to say, where's Quinn? We can't see her! And then they'll look up and find you floating on cloud nine."

Quinn leaned in as they walked to the set. "So, you're even arrogant in bed? Are you also a screamer?"

"Would you like to find out?"

"And give you the satisfaction of saying you'd slept with me? I don't think so."

"You're forgetting about the gag order in my contract…and that's not the reason anyway."

"Oh, please enlighten me," Quinn said, her demeanor seeming much lighter than it was a minute ago.

Lacey tucked her hands in the pockets of her robe and straightened her shoulders. "You, Quinn Kincaid, are scared to death that if you let your guard down for even one second, you'll fall madly in love with me."

"HA!" Quinn huffed. "You're a hot mess. I couldn't possibly—"

"Well, this hot mess is about to climb on top of you and make you a fucking lesbian icon, so you're welcome." Lacey opened the stage door. "And really, Quinn? A hot mess?"

J.J. crouched down where Lacey and Quinn were kneeling on the bed, facing each other. "Okay, ladies, you know the choreography. We're going to let you two do your thing and then we'll make adjustments on the next take. Quinn, make sure you put the cast over your head once Lacey's pushed you down on the bed."

"Got it." Quinn sat in the middle of the bed with her legs out in front of her.

Lacey straddled her legs and then reached back and adjusted her lace panties, making sure they were sitting evenly on her butt. She took Quinn's left hand and placed it on her ass. "Lower? Higher?" she asked.

"Perfect," J.J. told her. "Now, Quinn, can you put your cast hand on Lacey's hip? Just rest it there gently."

"Yeah, okay. Got it." Quinn stared at her fingertips, resting on Lacey's bare skin. Even though the fake cast made it awkward, she managed a small caress with her thumb on Lacey's stomach, right above her panty line. She swallowed hard and looked up, trying to pretend her other hand wasn't on Lacey's ass.

Lacey gave her a wink. "Ready, baby?"

"I'm not your baby," Quinn whispered as she rested her forehead on Lacey's chest.

"You will be after this. Ready, J.J.!"

"We're rolling, people!" J.J. gave a nod to the assistant director. "Same as last time," he said, indicating he'd like to keep rolling beyond what the scene called for.

"Action!"

Jordan raised her head and looked up at Selena as her fingers slid up her backside under her camisole. Selena put her hands on Jordan's shoulders and urged her back onto the pillow. She ran her fingers down Jordan's chest and grazed them lightly over her tits, then down to her stomach. Selena pushed Jordan's tank top up a few inches and caressed her stomach as her eyes raked over Jordan's now hardened nipples.

Jordan reached up and slid her hand into Selena's hair, pulling her down so their lips were inches apart. Their eyes met for a few seconds before Selena leaned in just enough for their lips to lightly touch. Jordan pulled Selena into a gentle kiss that quickly turned passionate. Selena let out an almost imperceptible moan as Jordan's hand ran up her thigh and onto her ass. Selena broke the kiss and worked her way over to Jordan's ear. Jordan closed her eyes and breathed heavily as Selena sucked on her earlobe.

Selena worked her way down Jordan's chest and bit her hardened nipple, making Jordan gasp. Jordan's eyes shuttered closed when she felt Selena circle her belly button with her tongue. She moaned and raised her other arm above her head, resting it on the pillow as Selena bit her through her panties.

"And cut!" J.J.'s voice cracked ever so slightly.

Lacey sat up on her knees. "My ass was hanging out. I could feel it."

"Don't worry about it. The camera was on Quinn…and goddamn," J.J. said, and then whistled.

Quinn sat up and covered her face with her hands. "I feel like I'm shooting porn."

"Most of it will be cut, so don't worry about it," J.J. told her. "We do still have a little thing called Standards and Practices." Apparently, J.J. lacked confidence that the in-house censors would sign off on airing panty bites.

Quinn uncovered her eyes and shook her head at Lacey. "Really… with the…" she said as she pointed at her panties. That was certainly not in the script. The action was supposed to stop at her belly button.

Lacey shrugged. "What can I say, I'm a hot mess."

Lacey waited in the Range Rover, nervously tapping her thumbs on the steering wheel. They'd done three takes of the love scene, each one a little hotter, a little more intense than the last. She liked the last one best, when she felt Quinn's fingernails dig into her back.

The car door opened and Lacey held her breath, wondering if she'd be ripped into or ignored or even yelled at, like she had been right after the kissing scene. Her concerned eyes scanned Quinn, looking for clues.

"What?" Quinn put her seat belt on and took her phone out of her purse.

"Nothing." Lacey shifted the car into reverse.

"I have some calls to make, do you mind?"

"Have I ever minded?" She eyed Quinn again, but her expression was neutral, leaving no clues as to her state of mind. "Will you check the traffic first?"

"Already on it. Normal. Red everywhere. Just take the usual route."

So. They were going to ignore it. Just not talk about it. Not mention the fact that their sexual chemistry was off the charts. *Fine*, Lacey thought. *I'll go to my happy place while you make your phone calls.*

Turned out Lacey's new happy place involved a lot of fucking in the kitchen. Taking Quinn Kincaid up against the fridge. Not Jordan. Quinn.

From behind.

As Lacey walked into the kitchen and set her purse on the counter, she paused, looking at the fridge. The kitschy little palm tree magnet was where it always was, not lying on the floor in several pieces. The photo of Quinn on her mountain bike wasn't askew, and there were no palm prints on the shiny stainless steel.

"What's wrong?"

"Huh?" Lacey quickly opened the fridge and grabbed a bottle of water. "Nothing."

"You were staring at the fridge."

"It's late. Do you still want dinner?" She stood there with the fridge open, drinking the cold water, waiting for an answer and trying to cast the graphic images of Quinn's naked body writhing under her touch from her mind. It would take Lacey about 4.8 seconds to climax if she touched herself right now. "A snack?"

Quinn took Lacey's arm and turned her around. She pulled her away from the fridge and closed the door. "It's fine. I'm not freaking out this time. I'm not going to lash out at you or whatever you're worried is going to happen. We did our job. We did it well. And I've never felt more comfortable with a costar than I do with you. Okay?"

Lacey nodded. "Okay."

Quinn studied her for a few seconds. "You still look worried."

"I'm not worried. I'm just…" *Trying really hard not to fall in love with you.* She took a deep breath. "You're right. I was worried you'd be mad at me again. But if you're good, I'm good."

"I'm good." After an awkward moment of silence, Quinn tore her eyes from Lacey and backed away. "I'm tired. I think I'll just go to bed."

"How about a soak in the hot tub first?" What the hell was Lacey doing? The last thing she needed was to see Quinn in a bikini, but she didn't want the night to end this way, in awkward silence. "I was on my knees all day," she quipped. "I could use a soak."

Quinn chuckled. "Yeah, I guess you were…hovering over me…a lot."

"Hovering?" Lacey opened the fridge again. "I topped you like a pro."

"See you in the hot tub, professional topper."

Lacey turned and smiled, feeling relieved that their banter was back. Her eyes lingered on Quinn's ass until she was almost to the stairs and then she shouted, "Finally, I get the respect I've always deserved!"

Quinn closed her bedroom door and locked it. She went into her bathroom and closed that door too. She leaned against the sink and unzipped her jeans. Sliding her hand into her panties, she whimpered at the initial touch.

She thought it would matter that people were watching their love scene. She'd worried she'd be self-conscious and mechanical because of it. That feeling went away after the first take. By the third take, Quinn had completely stopped caring about anyone other than Lacey. Having her hands on Lacey's body was everything she'd imagined it would be. She was soft and curvy, and her ass—God, her ass felt so good in Quinn's hand.

It had taken all of her self-control not to get completely lost in the moment and run her hand up Lacey's side to those tits that were hanging over her, just begging to be touched. God. She'd wanted every inch of that beautiful woman in her mouth.

Quinn's eyes shuttered closed as she imagined herself pushing Lacey's bra straps down, freeing those gorgeous tits and taking one of them into her mouth. She slid a finger into her folds and felt her swollen clit. Her breath quickened and so did her hand. She moved in circles, pressing against herself. Faster and faster until she crumpled over as the orgasm overwhelmed her. She whimpered as she turned and gripped the counter, trying to regain her balance.

The orgasm hit her far quicker than she thought it would. Or frankly, than she thought she could. She turned the water on and washed her hands, catching a quick look at herself in the mirror. "Goddamn," she whispered with a smile. Then she imagined Lacey's sarcastic commentary. "I knew it! You totally turn yourself on!" She giggled quietly as she pulled her bikini out of a drawer.

Lacey was waiting for her in the hot tub. "Everything okay?"

"Yeah." Quinn couldn't help but notice Lacey's eyes had locked onto her tits. She took her time stepping down into the water. Instead of sitting, she leaned back, resting her arms on the edge and leaving the bubbles to bounce around her tits. "Are you going to share that?" She pointed at the cold beer in Lacey's hand.

"Here." Lacey offered Quinn her beer, but she didn't stretch out her arm, making Quinn come to her if she really wanted it.

Quinn did. She stood right in front of Lacey and took a long sip, her tits barely inches away from Lacey's mouth. It wouldn't take much. One bad step and she'd trip her way into Lacey's arms. She'd apologize, of course, but she'd hold on to Lacey's shoulders and not move, like they do in the movies. Lacey's hands would stay on her body, the beer bottle floating among the bubbles. "Are you okay?" Lacey would ask, always worried about Quinn's arm. Quinn would nod. And then, she'd sit on Lacey's lap. No, straddle. She'd straddle Lacey's lap. *God.* Lacey's hands would find their way to her ass. *God, Quinn. Don't. Do. It.*

"You just drank my entire beer."

Quinn took the bottle from her mouth and inspected it. "Shit. I did."

"While I watched."

Quinn leaned forward and set the bottle next to Lacey's head. "Was it as good for you as it was for me?"

"Almost."

Quinn's movement stilled. *Does she know? Could she see it in my eyes, what I was thinking? No. No way.*

"A real friend would get me another beer."

Quinn rolled her eyes. "Whatever. You just want to watch my ass." She stepped out of the hot tub and sauntered back into the house.

"Yep." Lacey tipped the bottle over her open mouth, just to make sure there wasn't any beer left. Nothing came out. "Damn, woman."

CHAPTER TWENTY-FOUR

A few weeks later, Lacey walked into the main house, phone in hand. "Quinn?" She didn't get a reply, so she ran upstairs into Quinn's bedroom. "Quinn?" She didn't find her in the office either, so she went to the garage to see if her car was there. She opened the door and found Quinn wiping down her mountain bike.

"Good morning," Quinn said with a smile.

A look of hurt washed over Lacey's face. Quinn's shoes were muddy. The bike was muddy. She even had mud stuck to the ends of her hair. Why in the hell would Quinn go riding after it had rained the day before? And why wouldn't she invite Lacey along? That's what the extra bike was for, after all.

"What's wrong?" Quinn asked.

"You went without me."

"Yeah, I um…I woke up needing to do something."

"I'm supposed to go with you, Quinn."

Quinn tossed the rag aside. "I know. And you will. But you can't go where I usually ride. You don't have the experience."

Lacey threw her hands in the air. "How hard can it be?"

Quinn chuckled. "When was the last time you got on a bike of any kind?"

Lacey pursed her lips together. "Hmm…" It had been so long, she couldn't actually remember the last time.

"Riding on dirt trails is very different from renting a bike and riding through Central Park. I've been doing it for ten years and I still managed to smash my arm."

"So, the extra bike was a pointless gift? How am I supposed to learn to ride if you leave me at home?" Lacey was finding it hard to be truly mad at Quinn because she looked so damned adorable in her tight little biking shorts. "Huh?" she added for effect.

"I promise to take you next time," Quinn said.

"Okay, but you can't come in the house like that. You're filthy." Lacey bit her lip, trying not to smile. Would Quinn take the bait and undress right here, in front of her?

"I'll use the shower out back. Oh, and can you bring me a copy of your contract when you have a second?"

"What?" Lacey was confused by the request. "Why?"

"I want to check on the part where apparently, I'm paying you to nag."

"Oooh, bitchy. But don't complain to me when your arm is aching and you can't sleep." It didn't get past Lacey that Quinn winced when she tried to pull her shoe off with her right hand.

"Okay, Dr. Fake Covington." Quinn got both of her shoes off and looked up to find Lacey walking away. "Hey, Lacey?"

"Yeah?"

"I really do appreciate your concern, and if you're up for it, I'd love to take you out to dinner tonight. Maybe make up for leaving you in the dust this morning?"

There was only one reason Quinn would want to go out to dinner. They'd hardly been out at all since the incident at the bar, usually ordering take-out or Lacey cooking at home. "A paparazzi dinner?"

"Paparazzi, and the best bottle of wine I can find."

Lacey bit her thumbnail while she considered it. "I'll need something fabulous to wear."

"Of course."

"So will you."

Quinn smiled. "I have a closet full of fabulous things."

"What's the goal?"

"Now that the first kiss episode has aired, Jack thinks it's time for a public display of affection."

Lacey leaned on the Maserati, looking worried. "That should make things interesting with…" She trailed off.

"Dani?" Quinn helped her out.

"I've been putting her off…making excuses."

"Meaning you haven't told her it's really over? Which means it must not be really over."

"It's not easy, okay? I feel like I've loved her forever." Lacey couldn't bring herself to say the words *it's really over* to Dani. They weren't communicating every day—Dani was busy with school and Lacey barely had time to think about anything but work—but they did still stay in touch via text.

"It was easy for Dani. She dumped you, remember?"

Lacey folded her arms, needing protection. "Yeah, you like to remind me of that fact every chance you get."

"Just keeping it real."

"Says the woman with the fake girlfriend."

Quinn turned around and took off her muddy T-shirt. She was about to remove her shorts when she stopped and turned back around. "You want some reality? Fine. I went on a ride this morning because I'm scared shitless right now. I'm scared to take this coming out thing all the way, and I thought a ride would calm my nerves. I took the hardest route, and now my arm is killing me, but I didn't want to tell you that because you'll rip me a new one for being so stupid. And so gutless."

Surprised by the admission, Lacey stared at Quinn, standing there in just her sports bra and shorts. Obviously feeling self-conscious, Quinn draped her shirt over her chest. Lacey snorted. "Like I haven't seen you in a bra before." She put up her hand to stop whatever retort Quinn had for her. "Just promise me you won't get on that bike without me, and I won't say a word about anyone being stupid."

Quinn acquiesced with a nod. "Thank you."

"And as far as being gutless goes…I understand your fears about coming out. I had the same fears and some of mine came true. I lost my job. I lost my girlfriend. But no amount of money could put me back in the closet. It feels too good to be free of that burden, and I think once it's done, you'll feel the same way."

Quinn dropped her gaze and nodded again. "I know. I keep telling myself everything will be fine."

"Quinn, I'm here for you. You don't have to keep quiet. You don't have to be strong. Tell me what you're feeling so I can help."

Quinn blinked back the tears that were threatening to fall. "I don't want this sterile life I've created for myself anymore. It's safe, but it's lonely. And I don't want you to be used by that woman again. You're too special."

Lacey pushed off the car and walked over to Quinn, kicking the dirty shoes aside with her foot. "We should hug this out."

Quinn tried to hold in her laughter, but it came bursting out in a stifled giggle. She opened her arms and Lacey fell into them. They stayed like that for several seconds, Quinn resting her head on Lacey's shoulder. "You're the best and most frustrating friend I've ever had."

"You too," Lacey whispered. She didn't want to let go. Having Quinn's arms wrapped around her waist felt so good and so right. But Quinn had been clear—they would never take this beyond friendship, and in those moments when she thought Quinn was maybe softening her stance, she would put her walls back up and keep Lacey at arm's length again.

Lacey sighed. "Just so you know, you're driving tonight so I can get drunk." She pulled away and held up her phone. "Oh, and your mother sent me a text. She loved the first kiss scene."

Quinn's eyes widened. "She...texted you?"

"Yeah. She does it quite often. She gives me advice on how to handle you. Tells me embarrassing things about your childhood." Lacey noticed Quinn's chest fill with air so she took a few steps back. "Like when you—" She screamed and bolted out of the garage with Quinn right behind her, grabbing for the phone. She made it to the side gate but couldn't punch in the code fast enough.

"Give me that phone." Quinn pinned her against the gate, using her full body weight.

"Oooh, that's nice. I can feel your tits." Lacey tried to slide the phone into her panties, but she missed and it slid through her shorts and hit the ground.

"AHA!" Quinn picked it up and ran back into the garage. She quickly hit the garage door button and shut the door before Lacey could get in. She sat on a bench and found her mother's name in Lacey's phone. She managed to scroll through most of the messages before Lacey ran in through the inner door. There wasn't anything too embarrassing. Only the kindest words she'd ever seen from her mother, and extremely flattering comments back from Lacey. Things like:

You're a beautiful couple on-screen and off. Did you know Quinn eloped when she married what's his name? Quinn snorted. Her mother hated Greer. She called him a "ruffian" because he always had a scruffy beard when he wasn't shooting a movie. Quinn absently rubbed her upper lip just thinking about it. She hated that beard too.

No, I didn't know that, Lacey had replied.

It was a terrible day for me. A mother needs a wedding, Lacey. And a grandchild. Do you like children?

I love children. And weddings.

"Hand it over."

Quinn looked up at Lacey, standing there with her hand out. She gently set the phone in her hand. Lacey looked at the screen and then put it in her pocket. "Just telling her what she wants to hear."

"Of course," Quinn quietly replied. She stood up as Lacey walked away. "You don't really strike me as the type, but thank you for perpetuating the myth."

"What type?" Lacey stood at the door, waiting.

"Children."

Lacey had a number in mind. Since she was seven years old, she'd talked about having two kids, a boy and a girl. She'd name the girl after her mother and the boy after her grandfather. When she realized she was gay, she'd let the dream go for a while and set her sights on other goals, like her education and her acting career. But that little girl and boy still lived in her heart.

"No, you're right. I'm not the type." Lacey opened the door and mumbled, "And weddings are a big waste of money."

Their outfits were laid out on the bed. After rifling through Quinn's closet for half an hour, Lacey had decided on neutral colors for both of them. Quinn would wear low-waisted black trousers and a sleeveless black blouse with black heels. Lacey would wear a black plaid miniskirt with a loose white blouse and black metallic heels that strapped at the ankle. The heel was dangerously high, but Lacey had discovered the word *Manolo* solved all of her high-heel hang-ups.

Quinn came out of the bathroom and raised an eyebrow as she looked at the choices. "Are you sure? I thought maybe you'd want to wear that concoction you came up with when you visited me in the hospital that day. What was it again?" Quinn tapped her chin as she stared at the ceiling. "Oh, yeah. A mom skirt and hideous sandals with a top you'd stolen from my closet."

Lacey put her hands on her hips. "Are you done? Because I chose these without the help of your stylist."

Quinn grinned and put her hand on Lacey's back, gently rubbing up and down. "You've come so far, little grasshopper. I'm so proud."

"So…you like them?"

"I love them."

"Okay, but you better be sure because the photo of 'the Day Quinn Kincaid Came Out' is about to be everywhere." Lacey used finger quotes.

"That's a good point." Quinn looked at the choices more carefully. "I tried to go with something timeless. Twenty years from now you don't want the Gay History Month lesson plan to have a photo of you with shoulder pads."

Quinn smirked. "Gay History Month, Lace?"

"Yeah, it's where kids who never knew that gay people were hated, learn about Stonewall and Harvey Milk and the inventor of flattering light." Lacey grabbed her clothes and shoes but didn't walk away. She stood there, looking pensive.

"What's wrong?" Quinn asked.

"This is it. This is the finish line, right? Goal achieved. Like when you read the last line of a book and you're so sad it's over."

"Except I'm not sad." Quinn had thought about Lacey's words while she showered. She was right, there would be no going back in the closet. No chickening out at the last minute. This was the first day of her newfound freedom, and she was ready to embrace it. "I'm happy. And I'm gay, and pretty soon the whole world will know it." She took Lacey's hand and gently squeezed it. "I can't thank you enough for being willing to help me get to this point."

"Getting you to this point was my job. And now it's up to you to let me know when you're safe and sound, because I'd like to get on with my life too."

Quinn slowly nodded her agreement. Hurt flashed across her eyes and then disappeared. "I know. And I will." She wasn't sure what Lacey was trying to say. Was she ready to move out as soon as possible? She forced a smile. "Let's do this."

Lacey looked around as Quinn pulled into a parking spot. "This, is it?"

Quinn pointed across the street at the Starbucks where they'd first met. "I thought we could get a coffee first."

"Aww...are you going to get all sappy on me, tonight? Because it just might make me cry." It wasn't sarcasm. Lacey had been feeling emotional all day. The conversation they'd had earlier about children hadn't helped. It got Lacey thinking about her future. She'd put off some pretty important things, and that needed to change. Right now the last thing she needed was a walk down memory lane.

Quinn turned in her seat so she was facing Lacey. "I've never told you this, but I sat right here with Jack and watched you that day, trying to decide if I should introduce myself, and two things were running through my head. First, that Jack is an idiot who talks me into the most ridiculous plans."

"That's true," Lacey said, nodding her agreement. She turned and met Quinn's gaze. "What was the second thing?"

"That you were so pretty. And the longer I looked at you, the smarter Jack's idea became."

Lacey's heart soared with happiness and then sank a little bit as the memories came flooding back. "I'm so glad you could see past my horrible attitude. I was such a bitch to you that day."

"A hot mess from day one." Quinn's eyes fell to Lacey's lips. She leaned in slightly and then pulled back. "Let's go."

Quinn waited at the same patio table where they'd first met while Lacey ordered coffee. She wanted tonight to be special—their last night out in public before they'd be hounded relentlessly by the paparazzi.

Like Lacey had said, this was it. Tomorrow, everything would be different. Quinn wouldn't in fact be officially out, and she didn't plan on confirming anything immediately, but the whole world would know she and Lacey, her friend and costar, were so much more than that now.

As she kept her eyes on her phone, hoping no one would notice her sitting there all alone, her lips curled up at the thought of it. *Lovers. The world will think we're lovers.*

Even with all of her fears about coming out, and all of her mixed-up emotions when it came to Lacey—even with all of that, having the whole world believe she was making love to that woman on the regular—well, that gave Quinn a thrill that almost made up for all the other stuff.

"Quinn Kincaid, right?"

A girl who looked to be in her early twenties crouched down next to Quinn's chair. "Yes?"

"Nikki Ballard." The girl offered her hand. "I'm a huge fan. Ever since Selena came on the show, I've watched it religiously."

Quinn smiled. "Ah. So, you watched Lacey on *Light of Day*?"

"No, just your show. I've always loved it, but now I'm just so grateful, you know?"

Quinn gave her a nod, not really sure exactly what this stranger was saying.

"For what you're doing," Nikki added. "People think having a few lesbian characters on cable is enough, but it's not. A lot of us have families who don't accept us, but they accept you. When you take a chance on creating a normal, successful gay character, you make my life easier. So, thank you."

Lacey walked up behind them, holding two cups. Quinn's tummy did a somersault the second she saw her. Lacey looked so beautiful, and at least for that night, she was Quinn's date. Only hers. All hers. She was speechless for a second as their eyes met. "Um…Nikki, this is Lacey Matthews."

Nikki stood up and whipped her head around. "Oh my God! Both of you are here?" She said it loud enough that a few people turned to look.

"Nice to meet you, Nikki." Lacey eyed the cameras that were coming out of purses and pockets. She gestured with her head. "We should go."

Quinn also saw what was happening around them. "Yeah." She stood up and took one of the cups from Lacey's hand. "Keep watching the show, Nikki. I think you'll like what happens."

"Oh, I will!" As they walked away, Nikki shouted, "You're both awesome!"

Lacey looked back and smiled at Nikki as she followed Quinn out. "She's cute. She has that hot, baby dyke thing going on."

"She's too young for you," Quinn whispered.

"No, she's not. She's probably Dani's age."

They got out onto the sidewalk and Quinn stopped. "Whoa. Wait a minute. Just how old is Denise again?"

"Dani, Quinn. And she's twenty-five. You know that." Lacey took her by the arm. "You also know her name, but nice try. Now, keep walking."

"No, Lacey, I did not know that. I knew she was in school, but I just assumed she was either getting a doctorate or…more likely…that she's kinda dumb and on a twenty-year plan."

"Well, you're right about the first part. She just started working on her Ph.D."

"Oh good. Maybe we can take her to Chuck E. Cheese to celebrate!" Quinn honestly had no idea Lacey had been in a relationship with someone so young. Well, she was only five years younger than Lacey, but thirteen years younger than Quinn. *Thirteen?* She suddenly felt very old.

"You're an asshole, you know that?" Lacey mumbled under her breath.

"So are you. Now, let's go show the world what a delightful couple we make."

Once they were back in the car, Quinn turned to Lacey. "All kidding aside, have I told you how beautiful you look tonight? That skirt is just..." She caressed Lacey's thigh with her finger. "And with those heels? My God."

Lacey's eyes tracked Quinn's finger as it made a small circle on her leg, giving her shivers. She wanted to say something sarcastic but her mind was blank. "I'm glad you like it," was all she could manage. She took a sip of her coffee and looked out the window, trying to ignore the goose bumps that were popping up all over her body. "Big night," she said under her breath.

"What's that?"

"Oh...I just said...it's a big night." Lacey's leg started bouncing.

"Am I making you nervous?"

"A little." She took another sip of her coffee.

"Look at me."

Lacey shook her head. "No."

"I don't think I've ever once seen you nervous. You're always in control."

Then you haven't been paying attention, Quinn. Lacey put her drink in the holder and got out of the car. Needing space, she folded her arms and paced behind the car. Quinn also got out and stood there with her arm on the door. "Is there something you want to tell me?"

"Why are you doing this?" Lacey asked, pain evident in her expression. "Why are you making it harder? Usually, you look at me like you want to devour me and then you get all pissed off about it and go pout in the corner. THAT I can handle."

She'd seen the looks. Ever since they'd filmed the love scene, Quinn would sometimes get a look in her eye. Lacey recognized it for what it was—straight up lust. She'd had a taste of a woman and she wanted more. Only problem was, she'd get mad about it and start cleaning the house with a vengeance. The house didn't need cleaning. Vera took care of that now.

Quinn walked over to Lacey and took her hand. She led her back to the car and opened her door, effectively trapping her as she put one arm on the roof and the other on the door. "I want to tell you a thousand times a day how beautiful you are, but I don't because we have to maintain a certain…and Dani…you know…it's difficult…we're in a difficult place…being on the show together…and…"

"That's a long-winded way of saying we will never fuck. Oh, fuck," Lacey's eyes scanned the small crowd that had gathered on the sidewalk, along with a telephoto lens sticking out of a car window in front of Starbucks, pointed right at them. "Don't turn around. There's a camera on us."

Quinn visibly stiffened.

"Don't move." Lacey looked at Quinn, then the camera, then back at Quinn again. If she positioned the two of them just right, they could call it a day. That sounded pretty good right about now. "Do you want to get this over with?"

"What do you mean?"

"Right now. I could kiss you right now. We don't have to wait until tonight."

Quinn took a step closer, her demeanor softening. "Do it." She took her bottom lip into her mouth to moisten it and slowly let it back out, keeping her eyes locked on Lacey's.

Good God. Seriously, Quinn? Lacey slid her arm around Quinn's waist, pulling her in a little more roughly than she'd intended. She slid her hand down a little bit so it rested just below the waistband of Quinn's pants. She waited a few seconds so the camera could get a good shot of the pose. Then she turned them slightly, smiling at Quinn the whole time, giving the cameras a better side view. Then she leaned in and let their noses touch first.

"You're good at this," Quinn whispered.

Lacey turned slightly, so Quinn's back was to the cameras again. She ran her hands down Quinn's lower back, letting her fingers barely slide into the back pockets of her trousers and leaned in so their lips touched, but she didn't actually kiss Quinn. She lingered for a few seconds and then kissed her cheek. "That should do it," she said, letting go and getting back in the car.

Quinn stood there frozen for a second, staring straight ahead. Probably stunned by what just *didn't* happen. She expected to be kissed. Her confusion, if that's what it was, was understandable. She closed Lacey's door, keeping her eyes down as she walked to her side of the car.

Lacey glanced back at the photographer as Quinn drove away. "I'm good with take-out if you just want to go home."

"But you look so cute," Quinn said. "We can't let that go to waste."

"I wore it for you and you're welcome to take it off me tonight. Fuck me the way you never planned to, but desperately want to, if you're honest with yourself." It felt good to say it out loud—what she knew Quinn had been thinking.

"After that lame-ass kiss back there? What the hell was that?"

Lacey tried not to smile. "You don't deserve my kisses."

Quinn gasped, her mouth hanging open. "You just offered to let me fuck you!"

"That's because I know you never will," Lacey calmly replied. "But you don't get to kiss me and then leave me hanging. That's just bitchy."

Quinn stopped at the red light and stared at Lacey. "Hot. Mess."

Lacey shrugged. "I changed my mind. I want dinner in a fancy restaurant tonight. Preferably one with oysters, if it isn't asking too fucking much."

"It's not," Quinn said, looking contrite. "And I'm sorry I haven't made that happen for you. I should've taken you out more." She reached over the center console as the light turned green. "Hold my hand."

Lacey didn't move.

"Not for the cameras, not for any other reason than I just want... your hand," Quinn said.

Lacey stared at the hand. She wanted to take it, but her body was already so confused. She was turned on because Quinn looked so amazing in those black trousers and heels. Her top was unbuttoned just enough to show off the cute little freckle on her left breast that always made Lacey smile when she had the pleasure of sneaking a peek at it.

She was frustrated because she wanted to kiss Quinn and never stop. And she was angry because none of this was real. Not one second of it. But the hand—those slender fingers—were waiting for her.

"Dammit, you idiot!" Quinn grabbed the steering wheel as she slammed on the brakes, trying to avoid hitting the driver that had just cut her off.

And the moment was gone. Quinn's hand was no longer waiting for her. Lacey felt the loss.

CHAPTER TWENTY-FIVE

They pulled up to the valet. Lacey glanced at Quinn and then lowered her gaze. "You look beautiful too. I don't think I've said it out loud yet. And even though it's not real, I feel pretty lucky to be your date tonight."

Quinn smiled. "I'm the lucky one. Stay right where you are." She got out and met Lacey on the other side, holding out her hand. It was the first time the roles had been reversed. Usually it was Lacey helping Quinn out of the car. "Shall we?"

Lacey's stomach was in knots as she walked into the restaurant holding Quinn's hand. This was the big moment—the reason for everything they'd done so far. She needed to get back on task and play the part. Smile for all the pretty people and whatever cameras happened to lock on them. She took a deep breath and did just that.

It took them several minutes just to get to their table as industry people stood up from their tables and greeted Quinn. She didn't introduce Lacey as her girlfriend, simply as Lacey Matthews. Everyone already knew who she was anyway, from being on the show, and because they made it their job to know. Besides, Quinn's body language said far more than her words. After every introduction, her hand made its way back to Lacey's body in one way or another, either loosely holding her hand or touching her back or caressing her arm, setting Lacey's body on fire with every touch.

It all felt very real to her. Too real. And too sad that it wasn't. But she hid her anguish behind a genuine smile every time their eyes met. And like any good actor would do, she played off her costar's improvisations, like when Quinn said to a producer, "She's getting offers left and right but I'm gonna fight like hell to keep her on my show."

Offers left and right? The only offer Lacey had received was from her old soap, but she quickly recovered from the surprise comment and leaned in close to the man. "And I always say that you gotta dance with the one that brung ya."

He laughed and gestured to Lacey with his thumb. "She's a keeper, Quinn."

They were given a table on the far side of the restaurant. Quinn sat down and immediately started apologizing. "So sorry about that. You must be starving." The waiter came up to the table and Quinn took over. "We'll have a half dozen oysters. Kumamoto, if you have them. And if we could get those right away, that would be great. Oh, and your wine list. Oh, and some bread."

Lacey noticed that Quinn's hands were shaking. She leaned in and whispered, "You're shaking. Take a breath."

Quinn reached for her glass and noticed that her hands were indeed shaking. She took a sip of water, then clasped her hands together. "It must be the coffee."

They both knew it wasn't the coffee. "You're doing great," Lacey said, encouragingly. "They're totally buying it."

Quinn reached across the table for Lacey's hand. "You do realize you won't struggle to find work again. It makes me so happy that I can give that to you, after everything you've done for me."

"Yeah, I'll forever be Quinn Kincaid's ex-girlfriend," Lacey quipped. "No one can ever take that away from me." Her eyes fell to their joined hands. She quickly looked away, fearing she'd start to tear up.

"That's not what I meant. They're all so impressed with what you've done on the show. Didn't you hear a thing they said?"

A breadbasket was set on the table. Lacey let go of Quinn's hand and buttered a roll while Quinn chose a bottle of red. She'd push her feelings aside. They could be dealt with later, when she was alone in the guesthouse, she told herself. In the meantime, she really needed to eat something, so she stuffed a small piece of the roll in her mouth and smiled while she chewed.

Quinn returned the smile. "Can I make a prediction?"

"Only if you put money on it." Lacey moaned in delight as the oysters were set on the table. "Come to mama."

"Fine. I'll bet you five grand that you get nominated for an Emmy next year."

"Aww…honey, are you trying to get in my pants? Because there are easier ways that won't cost you nearly as much money." Lacey sucked an oyster into her mouth and moaned again.

"You're already costing me a small fortune. And you're right." Quinn shrugged. "Talking about the Emmys is kind of a turn-on."

"So are these oysters." Lacey picked up another shell. "Here, honey. You simply must taste one before I down them all." Since they were putting on a show, Lacey felt comfortable using pet names. All part of the game, right?

Quinn took the offered oyster and dabbed a little bit of cocktail sauce on it. "Did you mean what you said back there, about dancing with the one that brought you?"

The question didn't surprise Lacey. "You probably think I'd bolt given the chance, don't you?" She didn't wait for a reply. "I guess you don't know me at all."

"I wasn't sure if you were just…"

"Acting?" Lacey washed the oysters down with a long sip of the wine that had just been poured. "That's what you're paying me for, right?"

Quinn tried to calm her nerves by drinking her glass of wine a little too quickly. She'd just walked through a restaurant full of industry people holding the hand of a beautiful woman. She'd just come out to the world, and that world was now coming at her a little too fast. She wanted time to absorb it all. She wanted time to enjoy the moment. She wanted to go home and sit with Lacey and talk about what it all meant.

She was just about to ask if it would be okay if they left after the oysters when Lacey's eyes bugged out and she whispered, "Well, I'll be goddamned." She stood up and said, "Ginny Strong. How good to see you." Quinn noticed that the tone in Lacey's voice wasn't at all sincere.

The wealthy producer took Lacey's hands and kissed her cheek. "Lacey Matthews. You look stunning this evening." She rested her hand on Lacey's waist and turned to Quinn. "How are you, Quinn? You're looking well."

Just well? Not stunning? Quinn chastised herself for thinking that and then stood up. "I can give you a hug this time, Ginny. No cast in the way."

Ginny accepted the hug and kissed Quinn's cheek. "You really are looking great. How's everything going with the rehab? Are you riding again?"

"I tried," Quinn said, being fully honest. "It was too soon."

"Ah. Well, I've been there. Take your time. You'll get there." Ginny glanced at the table and grinned at Lacey. "I see you got the oysters you'd been craving."

Lacey nodded. "I did. Finally."

"You should've called me. Did you lose my card?" Ginny reached into her very expensive-looking black suit with the velvet collar and pulled out another business card. "I'm giving it to you again, and this time you must call me. We're in development on a new series and I think you'd be a perfect fit for the lead." She glanced at Quinn again and then back to Lacey. "I have to say, ladies, that scene on *Jordan's Appeal?*" She made an exploding gesture with her hands. "Hottest sex scene on television. And seriously, Lacey—call me." She turned to Quinn and kissed her cheek again. "I have to run, but let's have lunch soon."

Quinn nodded. "Yeah. Good to see you, Ginny."

They both watched her leave and then sat down, neither of them saying a word. Quinn finally broke the silence. "You should call her," she said, not sounding very convincing.

Lacey gripped the card between her fingers, staring at it. "*You* should call her. Set up that lunch date. After tonight, everyone will know you're gay, right? Including your crush."

"First of all, she's not my—" Quinn stopped herself. The truth was, she'd always had a crush on Ginny Strong. She liked Ginny's style, her swagger, the way her stylish suits hugged her in all the right places. She'd had fantasies about her. Their first date. Their first kiss. All very romantic fantasies. Ginny would've been her first call. Now she wasn't sure what she wanted. "And anyway, who cares? What happened to *the player* not being good enough for me?"

Lacey picked up another oyster. "Maybe I judged her prematurely. Far be it from me to keep you from what you want."

Quinn stared at Lacey in confusion until the waiter arrived a few seconds later. He took away the empty oyster plate. Lacey had eaten five of the six and was now looking at Quinn rather sheepishly. "Sorry. I was hungry."

"They were for you," Quinn said, barely above a whisper. She took a sip of her wine and focused on the glass, turning the narrow stem between her fingers. The air around them felt thick and full of tension, and Quinn felt very vulnerable, like all of her fears and worries were hanging out there on her sleeve for the whole world to see.

The waiter interrupted them again. "Have you had a chance to look at the menu?"

Neither of them had. "I seem to have lost my appetite," Quinn said, taking another large swallow of wine. It was strange, because the last time she'd seen Ginny, she'd lost her appetite then as well. What was it? Was it having Ginny and Lacey in the same room, breathing the same air that made her feel nauseous? Or was it just seeing Ginny? Did she really have that much of an impact on Quinn? It was a silly crush for God's sake.

"Nonsense." Lacey picked up the menu. "I'll order for both of us."

"Something easy on the stomach," Quinn gently requested.

Lacey perused the menu. She pointed at some sort of nouveau mac n' cheese. "We'll have one of those and also, the soup of the day and a salad for me."

"And more wine," Quinn added, lifting her glass to the waiter.

Lacey looked at the business card sitting by her plate. "It was my dad who taught me that saying about dancing with the one who brung ya. When I got offers from other soaps, other networks, he told me that as long as *Light of Day* wanted me, I should be true to the character they'd created for me, that it would pay off in the long run." She shook her head, remembering their conversations. "He was so upset when they fired me. I think he regretted his advice." With one finger, she slid the card across the table. "You should call her."

"Don't," Quinn interrupted. "Not tonight. Tonight we're..." She turned away, feeling frustrated. *On a fake date.* God, it was all so confusing.

This would not do—this sadness that seemed to have overtaken Quinn. Lacey had to do something about it. "Okay, so we're not talking about Ginny tonight." Quinn's expression didn't change. "Or anyone else. Look at me." Quinn did, but quickly looked away. Lacey glanced around the room. Several sets of eyes were locked on them. She set her gaze on Quinn again and smiled. "I'm going to excuse myself and go to the restroom. I'm also going to lean down and kiss you as I leave, okay? Because that's what someone who's madly in love with you would do." Quinn looked at her, finally. "You know, for the room." Lacey motioned with her head and whispered, "They're watching our every move."

Quinn gave a slight nod, her expression a little brighter. "I'll probably take your hand and pull you down to me. Maybe whisper something in your ear before you kiss me."

"Perfect. Your eyes should stay on my ass as I walk away too. You know, because my ass is pretty great."

Quinn giggled, the light returning to her eyes. "I can't disagree with that."

"Of course you can't. You also can't deny that you liked gripping it with both hands during that love scene."

Quinn gasped. "I did not! I was wearing a fake cast. How could I possibly—"

"Second take." Lacey gestured with her hands, making a squeezing motion. "Tight grip. I'm going to stand up now. Ready?"

Quinn leaned back, letting her hand dangle off the arm of the chair, ready to take Lacey's. "Action, baby."

Lacey slowly stood up. Quinn's eyes traveled down her body and then back up. They got stuck on Lacey's tits for a few long seconds. Lacey casually stood next to her. "This is where you stop looking at my tits and take my hand."

Quinn did just that, pulling Lacey down to her and whispering in her ear. "You're by far the most beautiful woman in the room."

Lacey pulled back and smiled, their noses almost touching. "Second most." She leaned in for the kiss but pulled back again, her eyes falling to the floor. "Sorry," she whispered. A kiss landed on Quinn's forehead and then Lacey was off, hurrying to the restroom.

Get your shit together. Lacey stared at herself in the mirror. She couldn't do it. She couldn't kiss Quinn and not fall apart, or worse, convey everything she was feeling with that kiss. A fake kiss? Fucking impossible at this point. She was too far gone.

Where was that façade? That armor made of cynicism and sarcasm that she wore so well? A tear fell from her eye and made its way down her cheek. "Shit." She hastily wiped it away and closed her eyes, taking in several deep breaths like she'd learned from those yoga videos.

She needed something to be angry about. She could hide her true feelings with anger. But nothing came to mind. And then it came to her like a flash and she narrowed her eyes at her reflection in the mirror. She wasn't good enough. She wasn't Ginny Strong. Yeah, she was good enough to be the fake girlfriend. Good enough to be a love interest on TV. But when it came to real life, Lacey Matthews wasn't quite good enough for Quinn Kincaid.

She sucked up her emotions with a deep breath and patted her cheeks with a wet paper towel, then headed for the door.

"Sorry. That kiss was an epic fail. I'll do better next time." Lacey slid back into her chair. "Who's that asshole who can't take his eyes off me? Black sweater at your four o'clock."

"Huh?" Quinn had already finished another glass of wine. "Oh. I dated him a few times. It was years ago." Apparently, she had thought nothing of the second non-kiss. If it bothered her, she didn't have a chance to say so because the waiter arrived with their meals.

Lacey looked at the salad sitting in front of her and frowned. On any normal day, a spinach and strawberry salad with warm goat cheese would have seemed downright decadent, but somehow it lost its appeal when sitting across from a macaroni dish that looked like it had been prepared by Jesus himself. Quinn gave the first bite to Lacey. "I'd love to share with you."

Lacey took the bite and covered her mouth. "Oh my God, that's good."

Quinn took the fork back. "I can't wait to taste it." She took a bite and moaned. "Mmm...you're right." She pushed the plate into the middle of the table.

"You're a good friend." Lacey picked up her fork and took another bite.

"Yes, I am." Quinn reached across the table and set the salad aside. "And good friends don't let their BFFs eat salad when there's mac n' cheese on the table."

"BFF? Is that what I am, now?" *Better than nothing, I guess.*

Quinn picked up her glass of wine. "Here's to my best friend. Lacey Matthews."

Good God. Lacey picked up her glass and smiled. "Best friends."

After dinner, Lacey stood in front of the restaurant, waiting for the valet. Quinn came out after having used the restroom. "I can't drive," she said, slurring her words and wobbling on her heels.

Lacey took hold of her elbow, steadying her. "I know. I'm fine to drive." She'd stopped after one glass of wine when she noticed that Quinn was on her third. So much for getting drunk, but it was probably for the best. She didn't need to drunk text her "best friend" in the middle of the night, professing her undying love. Just the thought made her cringe in her Manolos. *Note to self: stay sober for the next twenty years.*

"There's a camera across the street." Lacey was getting good at spotting them.

Quinn stepped closer and put a hand on Lacey's waist. "Maybe you could hold me and whisper something sweet in my ear."

Lacey smirked. "Or you could just pretend I whispered something sweet in your ear, like any good actor would do."

Quinn shook her head. "Nah, I'm going to need the real thing so I can react properly."

"Fine." She wrapped her arm around Quinn's shoulders, leaving one hand on her waist. "How's this?" she whispered in her ear. "If there was music, we could dance like this."

"Mmm…" Quinn closed her eyes and put her hand on Lacey's shoulder.

"Do you like to dance, Ms. Kincaid? Sloooow dance?" Lacey asked, keeping her voice low.

"Yeah, I do."

Lacey turned and let her lips caress a warm cheek. "Save a dance for me, then." She wasn't sure what she meant by that. The words had just slipped from her mouth. Good thing Quinn was just this side of drunk.

Quinn's head popped up. "Oooh, there's a song I really like. I mean, it's silly. And so clichéd. How many weddings has that dumb song been played at?"

Lacey didn't want to know. It would be so much better to never know. But she couldn't help herself when they got in the car and closed the doors, shutting out the world. The silence was deafening for a moment. "What's the song?"

Quinn chuckled. "It's just a stupid love song, Lace."

"A first dance song?"

"Yeah." Quinn looked out the side window. "But I would never actually play that song at my wedding."

"Why not? If you love the song, who cares what other people think?"

"I chose it when I was a kid. It's silly. Let's go."

Lacey turned in her seat. "We'll go, right after you promise me that you'll play that damn song at your wedding."

Quinn turned and shook her finger. "Don't even try to pretend you're some hopeless romantic, Lacey Matthews. I know better."

Lacey ignored the comment. "Promise me. We're not leaving until you promise me."

Quinn threw her hands in the air. "Fine! I promise, okay?"

"Okay." Satisfied, Lacey put on her seat belt. "Since I'm your BFF now, I'll probably be there, at your wedding—the Kincaid/Strong wedding. I'll be the fucking maid of honor or something."

Quinn cracked a smile. "I'm not marrying Ginny Strong. Dating, maybe. I don't know, we'll see." She turned to Lacey again. "Would you really be my maid of honor?"

Lacey rolled her eyes. "Do I have a choice? I mean, I've never really been someone's BFF before, but I think it's a requirement. That, and taking you to Vegas for your bachelorette party. Chippendales…or some other nonsense."

"Really? Not the Thunder from Down Under?"

"Oh yuck. Now I'll have to make it as lesbian as it can be, just to get that image out of my head. Obviously, that means we scrap Vegas and go play softball in Northampton."

Quinn gave Lacey's leg a reassuring pat. "I think it's best that you not stress about it. Marriage isn't really something I want to do again anyway."

"WHAT?" They stopped at a light, Lacey's eyes firmly planted on Quinn. "What the fuck are we doing this for, then?"

"What do you mean?"

"THIS!" Lacey waved her hand between them. "The fake girlfriend thing! Coming out! What's it all for if not so you can find the love of your life?"

Quinn shrugged. "It doesn't mean I have to marry her."

Lacey's mouth hung open. "Yes, it does!"

"No, it doesn't."

Someone honked their horn when the light turned green. Lacey focused on the road, but her head was slowly shaking in disbelief.

"What is your problem?" Quinn asked. "You said yourself that Dani is the love of your life, but I'm pretty sure you never bothered to marry her."

Quinn was right. Something had always held Lacey back from ever mentioning marriage with Dani, but she wasn't going to admit it. "She's young. She wasn't ready."

"And that's for the best, right? Since she broke up with you anyway? Why go through an ugly divorce?" Quinn waved her hand in dramatic slo-mo. The words *ugly divorce* seemed to take a bit too much effort to pronounce.

"Fine." Lacey turned on some music. "We just see it differently, that's all. And I think you're a little drunk, so let's just listen to some music."

"It goes both ways, you know. If you have a wedding one day, I'll be there, standing next to you, as your maid of honor, if you want me to. Even if it's what's her name you choose to marry."

"Really?" Quinn was definitely drunk. Sober, she would never agree to such a thing. "Even if it's Dani I marry?"

Quinn offered her pinky finger. "Pinky swears."

"Pinky swears don't really count when you're three sheets to the wind."

"Whu? That's so not true, Lace. They should espesh…espesh… lee count when your best friend is drunk."

Lacey pursed her lips together and silently giggled.

Quinn came out of the bathroom and staggered to her bed. Luckily, she still had her robe on, but she didn't waste any time ditching it before she got into bed. "I drank too much tonight."

On any other night, Lacey might've chosen to enjoy the view, but with Quinn being inebriated, it felt wrong. She turned away and waited until she heard Quinn sigh in relief as her head hit the pillow. She sat on the edge of the bed with her legs crossed. "Do you want me to stay in the guest room so I'm closer?"

Quinn closed her eyes. "No, I'll be fine." Her hand landed on Lacey's bare leg. "You looked really cute in this skirt tonight." Her fingers played with the edge of the skirt. Lacey could do nothing but silently watch. "Lace?"

"Yeah, honey?" Lacey cringed. Once again, the truth came spilling out before she could stop it.

Quinn opened her eyes. "I like it when you call me that."

Shit. "Oh, I have all kinds of little pet names for you. Miss Fancy Pants, Miss OCD, Miss Pain in My Ass. I could go on and on."

Quinn rolled onto her side. "I don't have OCD."

"Yes, you do. But let's not fight tonight. Not after that lovely meal."

"I'm just very organized. There's a big difference. And I don't call you Miss Throw Shit Anywhere I Please."

Lacey laughed. "Okay, you got me there."

Quinn smiled proudly, her hand still on Lacey's thigh. "Did you know I came busting out of the closet tonight?"

"Yeah. I was there, remember?" She'd never seen Quinn quite this tipsy. It was kind of cute.

"Oh, yeah." Quinn flopped onto her back. "The not really a kiss, kiss." She abruptly sat up on her elbows. "Twice. Why did you not kiss me, twice?"

Lacey urged Quinn to lie back down with a push on her shoulder, then she ran her fingers through her hair, knowing that would relax her fairly quickly. "We've kissed on the set several times. It's not like you don't know what it feels like."

Quinn closed her eyes. "Mmm...I know what Selena feels like. Jordan likes Selena."

"Yeah. Selena likes Jordan too."

Quinn's breathing deepened. Lacey kept running her fingers through her hair until she was sure she was asleep. "Good night, love," she whispered. She ran the back of her fingers over Quinn's cheek and then stood up. She looked back one more time before she shut the door.

CHAPTER TWENTY-SIX

Jack turned on the TV. The three of them stood together in Quinn's living room. "They've been teasing it through the entire show."

Lacey nudged Quinn. "Your life will never be the same."

Jack turned to Lacey. "Do you have your own publicist? Because if anyone's life is about to change, it's yours."

"I can't afford you, Jack."

"I'll give you a deal."

Quinn pointed at the TV. "Here we go."

And the story you've been waiting for...has life imitated art? The star herself isn't talking, but a new photo might just say it all. Quinn Kincaid, star of the highly rated series Jordan's Appeal, *has spoken extensively about her character, Jordan Ellis, falling in love with a woman, played by Lacey Matthews of the daytime soap* Light of Day. *What she hasn't talked about are the rumors currently swirling around the two actors that seem to hint at a real-life romance. Is this photo taken on Saturday at a Starbucks in West Hollywood proof that Quinn Kincaid is just as in love with Lacey Matthews as Jordan is with Selena? Take a look, folks, and let us know what you think on Twitter and Facebook.*

Jack turned off the TV. "Perfect. That's exactly what we want."

"What's next?" Quinn had been here before. She knew what was next. Dating Greer Farris, then eloping, then divorcing him—the paparazzi had been relentless through it all. She shivered at the thought of what was next, but it would be worth it, she tried to tell herself. She was mostly asking the question for Lacey's sake. Jack would be more diplomatic in his descriptions.

"A paparazzi shitstorm."

Quinn's eyes shuttered closed. *So much for diplomacy, Jack.*

"You'll be hounded until they get something more concrete, which we're not going to give them. Not yet, anyway. And, Lacey, you need to warn your family. If you want any other advice from me, I have a contract out in my car."

Quinn turned to Lacey. "I don't usually say this when he's in the room, but Jack is the best, and you'll want him in front of you on this. Also, things could get a bit complicated if you were to go with someone else."

Lacey gave her a nod. "Get the contract, Jack."

"Excellent. I need an hour with both of you, right now."

As Jack walked to the front door, both Lacey and Quinn's phones started ringing. "For the next few hours, let everyone leave a voice mail!" Jack yelled back at them.

Lacey hated lying to her father. She covered her eyes with her hand.

"Honey, are you there?"

"Yeah, Dad. I'm here."

"So, are the rumors true? Are you really dating Quinn?"

"Yeah. It's um…it just happened, unexpectedly." Lacey knew her dad wouldn't be surprised by the news. He'd seen something between them. Too bad whatever he'd seen wasn't real.

"That's the best kind, when you don't see it coming. Your mother and I…"

"Dad." Lacey didn't want to cry, and if her father told her the story that she'd heard a thousand times before… "Tell me, Dad. Tell me about you and Mom."

Ben chuckled into the phone. "You know the story. And I'm so happy for you, honey. You have everything you want now, right? A job, doing what you love. A good woman. Who could ask for more?"

Lacey's heart sank. One day soon, she'd have to admit that she'd lied to him. "Yeah, I guess so."

"Do you love her, honey? You sound kind of sad."

Lacey stood in the doorway of the guesthouse. She could see Quinn in the main house, wiping down the kitchen counter, even though it wasn't dirty. "Yeah. I love her, Dad. She's amazing. Everything. My dream woman." She chuckled to herself. "I'm…you know…so gone I can barely breathe." She bent over and put a hand on her knee, trying to get some air.

"Breathe, honey. I know the feeling, but you have to keep

breathing. Keep moving. And when it feels right, you know what to do."

"Yeah, I do," Lacey gasped for air, her emotions surfacing.

"I'm so happy for you, baby." Ben's voice cracked. "I could see it when I was there, how good you two are together. It's different, you know?"

"How so?" Lacey stood back up, holding her stomach as she watched Quinn.

"I liked Dani, but to see you with someone like Quinn…so much your equal…a good partner…"

Was her dad crying? She pressed the phone to her ear. "Dad?"

"I'm fine, honey. It just makes me think of your mother and how happy she'd be for you."

Lacey couldn't take it anymore. He'd be devastated when she and Quinn broke up in a few months. God, how would she ever tell him the truth? It broke her heart, just thinking about it. "I have to go now, Dad. If anyone bothers you, just give them Jack's phone number, okay?"

"I will. Take care, honey."

Lacey sat on the end of a lounger with her phone clasped between her hands, covering her mouth, almost like she was praying. She was so deep in thought, she jumped when Quinn shouted, "Drinks outside?"

"Yeah!" she shouted back. It was an unseasonably warm evening. Not a cloud in the sky and very little breeze blowing. Lacey moved closer to the main house where two loungers were sitting next to each other with a table in between.

Quinn set the wine glasses on the table and handed the bottle to Lacey. "Will you do the honors?"

Lacey read the label before she opened it. "This looks familiar."

"Yeah. Remember the wine Ginny sent to the table at Nobu?"

"Ohhhh…I loved that wine."

"I know. And we have a lot to celebrate." Quinn lay back in the lounger, looking relaxed and happy. Pretty much the exact opposite of how Lacey was feeling. "You know," Quinn said, looking around, "I've lived in this house for a few years now, and I've never spent this much time out here. It's really quite beautiful."

Lacey twisted the corkscrew into the bottle. "I love it out here. The swimming pool is about the size of my apartment in New York, so I kind of feel like I'm on a permanent vacation."

"I'm glad you're happy here." Lacey didn't reply, so Quinn turned to her. "You are…happy here, right?"

Lacey ignored the question as she poured the wine. She held out her glass for a toast. "What are we celebrating?"

Quinn didn't pick up her glass. "What's wrong?"

"Nothing. To the good life. Now, hit my glass."

Quinn raised her glass. "To the good life. Now, tell me what's wrong."

Lacey swirled and inhaled the wine before she took a sip. "It's just Dani and my dad. He's so excited about us, he can hardly contain himself. Meanwhile, Dani is not giving up."

Quinn didn't reply, and Lacey didn't really blame her. It was a mess on her side, and Quinn couldn't fix it. No one could. "I should start house hunting," Lacey said.

"You can't afford this town." Quinn took a long sip of her wine. "God, that's good."

"Maybe not this neighborhood, but I can find something smaller."

"A smaller home in a good neighborhood will run you at least one point five million. Probably more."

"I can rent."

Quinn was silent for a minute, so Lacey leaned back on the lounger. She glanced at Quinn's short shorts and let her eyes wander down her legs. "Do you want to go for a swim?"

"Are you trying to get me naked?"

Laccy shrugged. "You go in the hot tub naked, so why not the pool?"

"You're not very subtle."

"You like that about me. Now tell me what we're celebrating." Lacey knew, but she wanted to hear it from Quinn. Get her take on how things went with her big "coming out."

Quinn turned to Lacey, excitement filling her eyes. "We're celebrating the fact that the world doesn't seem to mind that I've fallen in love with a woman." The phrasing wasn't lost on Lacey, nor was the fact that her heart skipped a beat. As usual, the joy lasted about two seconds before Quinn slapped her back into reality. Not the fake reality, but the real reality. "It's a real shame they don't give Emmys for this shit because we're selling the hell out of it."

Lacey forced a smile. "We sure are. They really seem to love it."

"I can't thank you enough, Lace. I know it's been a pain in the ass to take care of me and carry on this little charade."

"You're paying me well. I've never had so much cash in the bank."

Quinn turned onto her side, fully facing Lacey. "Is there anything else I can do for you?"

Anything else you can do for me? What is this shit? If Quinn was going to have the nerve to say it like that, all lying on her side being sexy while she said it, Lacey would let her eyes wander down Quinn's bare legs and back up to her chest again. "You know what I want." She motioned with her head toward the pool.

"And you say *I'm* gay."

Lacey downed the rest of the glass and poured herself more wine. She took a big swallow and picked up her phone. "Would you like some music? I'm sure I have a striptease on here somewhere."

Quinn didn't take her eyes off Lacey, waiting for her to make eye contact again. When she finally did, she said, "How many seconds would it take for me to seduce you?"

Lacey's eyebrows rose. "Seconds? God, you're so arrogant."

"I'm taking into account the glass and a half of wine you just drank in under a minute."

This was a trick of some kind. Lacey wouldn't fall for it. She was smarter than that. Her eyes flicked to Quinn's chest again. Since she'd rolled onto her side, even more cleavage was showing. Soft, luscious breasts that were begging to be worshipped. She pulled her eyes away and said, "You have no intention of trying to seduce me, so it's really a moot point." She lifted her glass. "Cheers."

"Thirty seconds? A minute?"

Lacey ignored the question, sipping her wine and keeping her eyes straight ahead. Quinn set her glass down and stood up. "I think all it would take is me holding out my hand."

Lacey shook her head in disgust. "You are such a—"

"You're the one who wanted to play," Quinn said, lowering her hand. "You're always flirting and blatantly catcalling and trying to get me naked, but the second I say anything—"

"I've never flirted with you." Lacey took another sip of her wine. "Not once."

"What are you talking about? Of course you have."

"Appreciated your gorgeous figure? Yes, I've definitely done that. But you got naked in front of me all on your own…and of course I'm going to look. You knew that when you stripped down to nothing."

"But you've never flirted?" Quinn asked in confusion.

Lacey shook her head. "Why would I?"

Quinn sat back down. "Why wouldn't you?"

"Because flirting is real. And we're not real. Which of course is something you constantly feel the need to remind me of. And eventually, you're going to fake break up with me and I'm going to pack my real bags and walk away from here with a shitload of real cash and another season on network prime-time fucking must-see TV. So, gratitude, yes. But flirting? No."

Quinn looked both sad and confused, like she was in the middle of being dumped. Was she really so clueless? Lacey took a deep breath and softened her tone. "Quinn, I really hope you'll call Ginny Strong when this is all over and ask her out because you deserve it. You deserve to have the real thing, and now that you're out...well, they're going to be banging down your door, because someone like you doesn't stay single for long."

"I think that's the nicest thing you've ever said to me."

Lacey raised an eyebrow. "Really? Because I thought the nicest thing I ever said to you was that your pussy felt good in my mouth."

Quinn flopped back on the lounger, laughing. "You never said that."

"Oh really? I meant to mention it after we shot our love scene. Because what I got of it felt great."

Quinn shook her head as she smiled. "You confound me. How is that not considered flirting?"

Lacey didn't have much self-control left. If this *wasn't* some sort of trick to get her to admit her feelings for Quinn, and they actually ended up having sex—Quinn would regret it so badly, she'd probably try to kick Lacey out in the morning.

Again.

And Lacey's heart would be broken.

Again.

She grabbed her phone and slid into her flip-flops. "You can't just hold out your fucking hand, Quinn. You also have to tell me you love me. And by the way...you're both the smartest and dumbest woman I've ever met if you didn't already know that." She grabbed the bottle of wine—what was left of it—and stood up. "Also, you'd fucking know it if I flirted with you for real, because you wouldn't be able to resist it, and I'd have been three fingers deep by now." She turned and sauntered to the guesthouse.

"Lace! Come back! I'm sorry if I hurt your feelings. Come back, Lace! We have to celebrate!"

Celebrate. That seemed to be something they were incapable of doing together. Lacey held up the bottle as she kept walking. "To the good life!"

CHAPTER TWENTY-SEVEN

L acey sat at her kitchen table rubbing her temples. She was trying to decide what she regretted most about last night; her words or the wine. It was the wine. Definitely the wine. But also, her words. *Three fingers deep? Who talks like that?*

All that seduction in under a minute business had Lacey in a twist. Had Quinn actually tried to get her in bed last night, or was it all just a horrible dream? A misunderstanding, maybe. That's it, Lacey had heard wrong. Hadn't she? God, her head hurt. And her stupid phone wouldn't stop ringing—some number she didn't recognize.

It rang again and this time she picked it up, ready to yell at whoever was trying to sell her something. "Yes?" She stood up, but her expression fell as she listened. "No, that can't be. No, I just talked to him yesterday. No, no, no! Oh, God!" Lacey sank back onto the bed. "Of course. Yes, I'm on my way."

Quinn opened the guesthouse door and found Lacey zipping up her suitcase. She threw a hand in the air. "Perfect. That's just perfect. And you were probably going to leave without saying good-bye."

Lacey grabbed her sweater and put it on, completely ignoring Quinn. She set her suitcase on the floor and looked at her watch. "Shit," she whispered. She finally looked up, revealing puffy, tear-stained eyes. "Is my cab here?"

Quinn softened her tone. "Okay, look…we just need to sit down and talk."

"I have to get to the airport."

"So, you're going to run away again? Well, this time I'm not going to beg you to come back."

Lacey grabbed her purse and suitcase, trying like hell to hold back the tears. She didn't have time to break down. That could wait until she was on the plane. She wheeled her carry-on outside and hurried past the pool.

Quinn followed her to the side gate. "Will you please just talk to me for a second? Let me apologize? I know what I said was inappropriate. I was just so happy and that clouded my judgment. I didn't mean to make you feel cheap, and I certainly didn't mean to assume that you would just jump into my bed."

Lacey tried to punch in the code, but her fingers were too shaky. She stepped aside and leaned against the fence, her breath becoming so shallow she was almost hyperventilating. "Please open the gate."

Quinn shook her head. "No. This is ridiculous, Lacey. You can't run away. We have to talk. We have to…"

Lacey's face contorted, a deep sob making its way up from her chest. She gasped for air and said, "My dad," before she completely broke down.

Quinn grabbed Lacey as she fell to the ground, softening the blow. She took her phone out of her back pocket, hit a button, and held it to her ear, keeping an arm wrapped around Lacey. "Answer, goddammit." Lacey grabbed Quinn's shirt and sobbed into her chest. "Dammit, Amy, answer your phone."

Quinn's assistant finally answered. "Amy! I need a jet ASAP. New York. NOW, AMY!" Quinn dropped her phone on the ground and wrapped both arms around Lacey. "I've got you, honey. Just hang on." She heard the cab honk his horn, so she picked her phone back up and punched in the code for the front gate. She kissed Lacey's head. "Stay here. I'll be right back."

She ran back into the house and grabbed a twenty from her purse. When she returned a few seconds later, she had let the driver know his services wouldn't be necessary. Then she went back to Lacey and urged her to stand up. "Come on, honey. Let's go back into the house. I'll get us to the airport."

Quinn took a few minutes to pack a bag, insisting that Lacey sit in her bedroom while she haphazardly pulled clothes from her closet. Whatever she didn't pack, she could buy in New York. She wanted to ask questions but thought better of it, since at the moment, Lacey wasn't crying. She was sitting there, twisting a tissue between her fingers and staring at the floor, her face paler than Quinn had ever seen it before.

When they got to the Santa Monica airport, Amy was there, waiting. She asked only one question. "Two or three?"

Quinn kept her arm wrapped around Lacey and mouthed the word "three." Amy nodded and picked up her emergency overnight bag, following them onto the plane.

Quinn was right behind Lacey as she unlocked the door to her father's Brooklyn apartment. He hadn't died here; that had happened at school. Quinn was relieved Lacey wouldn't have to see any remnants of his death—a chair overturned, or a spilled cup of coffee he'd dropped when the pain hit him. She wouldn't have to look at a certain spot and conjure up memories of *this is where my dad took his last breath*, and how painful that last breath must've been.

Everything seemed in order. A book sitting on the kitchen table that he'd probably read a few pages of before going off to work. A multicolored afghan was folded neatly on the sofa. One made by Daria, Quinn guessed.

The pictures on the walls were all hanging straight and the shoes by the door were evenly spaced. Ben was more like Quinn, it seemed, than his own daughter, when it came to tidiness. She could appreciate his little world. Warm and inviting, just like the man himself.

Lacey hadn't stepped very far into the apartment. Quinn stood behind her and removed Lacey's coat, then her own. She hung them on a coat rack, next to Ben's navy blue Yankees windbreaker. When she turned back around, Lacey had gone into the small galley kitchen. She stood motionless, staring at the sink. Quinn was about to say something when Lacey reached out and unplugged the coffeemaker and the toaster.

There really weren't that many dirty dishes, certainly not enough to warrant the entire sink being filled with soapy water. That didn't matter. Quinn grabbed a dish towel and stood next to Lacey, ready to dry what she'd washed. Only one plate made it into Quinn's hand, but Lacey wouldn't let it go. She gripped that plate with all of her might as the inevitable tears filled her eyes.

Quinn pried her fingers off of the plate and set it down. Lacey grabbed the edge of the counter and bent over, resting her forehead on the sink. She was gasping for air as deep, heavy sobs worked their way up from her chest. Her knees buckled and hit the floor. "Why? Why?"

Quinn tried to swallow back her own emotions as she knelt next to Lacey. She sat on the floor, leaning against the cupboard, and pulled Lacey into her arms.

Quinn sat on the edge of Ben's bed, watching Lacey's every move but also taking in the photos in the room. It was basically a shrine to Lacey's mother—a beautiful woman with long, dark hair, just like Lacey.

She heard a crashing noise, so she ran into the bathroom. The mirror was broken. Lacey was leaning over the sink, her jaw flexed and her knuckles bleeding. There were several prescription bottles lying in the sink. "He didn't tell me," Lacey ground out.

Quinn glanced at the bottles. Ben had a heart issue, and somehow, he thought not telling his daughter was the best course of action? It didn't make sense after what Lacey had already been through with her mother's death. Or maybe it did. Now was not the time to judge Ben. He obviously had his reasons, none of which Lacey would ever understand. Quinn took the bloody, shaking hand in hers. She looked at it carefully and set it back down. "Where's your dad's first aid kit?"

Lacey opened her eyes and looked around, trying to figure out where she was. She felt the throb in her hand and looked at the bandage. *Oh yeah. The mirror I smashed.*

Quinn was at the door, signing for room service and also giving an autograph. Lacey rolled over and looked around the hotel suite. She was in a king-sized bed that Quinn had obviously slept in as well. She quickly lifted the sheet to find she'd slept in the nude.

"Oh good, you're awake." Quinn rolled the table into the room.

Lacey tucked the sheet under her arms and sat up. "I'm naked. Did you undress me?"

"Oh, that. Yeah, your father died, so I decided to fuck you in your sleep."

Lacey took the offered cup of coffee from Quinn. "Sorry," she sheepishly replied.

Quinn sat on the edge of the bed and felt Lacey's forehead. "You were burning up last night, so I forced you to take a cool shower. I have a doctor coming in half an hour. I don't know if it's just stress or if you're coming down with something again." She took Lacey's bandaged hand in hers. "He'll check your hand as well."

Lacey's eyes filled with tears as she recalled the previous evening. "Thank you, for going to the morgue with me. I couldn't do it alone."

"Oh honey." Quinn wiped Lacey's tears away. "No one should ever go through that alone."

Lacey set her coffee on the bedside table and leaned back against the headboard. "I have to plan his funeral. I have to clean out his apartment. I have to—"

"No." Quinn took Lacey's hand. "Amy and I will help with the funeral, and everything else can wait until you're ready."

Lacey covered her eyes. Her body started to shake. No matter how hard she tried to hold it together, she couldn't. Because this couldn't possibly be happening to her. Not again. It was too soon. Her dad was supposed to grow old and be a grandpa one day. He never pushed Lacey to have kids, but she knew that was his dream. He would've been good at it too. The best grandpa ever. She would've had a dumb sweatshirt made that said just that. And he would've proudly worn it.

She gasped for air and managed to whisper, "He was all I had."

"That's not true." Quinn got on the bed and straddled Lacey's legs. She pulled at Lacey's hands. "Look at me." Lacey's hands flopped to her sides, but she wouldn't open her eyes. "Lacey, look at me." Quinn cupped her cheeks. "You have me. I'm here. And I'm not going anywhere." Lacey finally opened her eyes and blinked back the tears. "BFFs, Lace. Remember? BFFs."

Lacey didn't feel comforted. Nothing would comfort her right now, and if anything, Quinn's words were making it worse. She didn't need a fucking BFF. She needed her dad. Ben Matthews. Her hero. Her rock.

Her eyes flicked around the hotel room. She couldn't remember how they got there. She didn't even remember having a fever last night. Had she eaten anything? No. She couldn't eat. Probably wouldn't ever eat again. That was silly. Of course, she would eat again. Her stomach roiled and her eyes went wide. She pushed Quinn off her in one swift move and ran to the toilet.

There wasn't anything left in her stomach, but apparently her body didn't know that. She knelt over the toilet for what felt like hours, dry heaving and feeling so weak, she draped her arm over the toilet and lay on it, not giving a shit that it was a toilet.

She didn't last long in that position. Quinn wrapped a robe around her and pulled her back into her arms. Lacey opened her eyes long enough to make sure it was Quinn's slender fingers resting on her chest, letting her know she wasn't alone. Of course it was Quinn. Who else would it be?

Maybe BFFs were okay after all. Lacey slid her hand under Quinn's and intertwined their fingers. She stared at their joined hands until her eyelids got too heavy to keep open.

Lacey sat by her father's grave, wanting to be alone with him before they lowered him into the ground. Quinn hadn't left Lacey's side until that very moment. It killed her to do so, but she watched from a distance, giving Lacey the space she needed. She tucked her hands into her black wool coat and checked the sky again. Rain had been threatening all day, and she prayed the skies wouldn't open up before Lacey could say her final good-byes.

Amy walked up and stood next to Quinn. "How's she doing?"

"She's hanging in there."

"She was so strong up there, talking about her dad. I don't think I could do that."

Lacey had barely been able to say a few words at a time without crying, so when she said she wanted to speak at her father's funeral, Quinn was concerned, wondering if she'd be able to get through it without breaking down. "I owe it to him," she'd said.

Quinn, along with everyone else, watched in awe as Lacey courageously told her father's life story and also her parents' love story with such love and wit that she had the whole room laughing and crying with her.

"She's an amazing woman." Quinn gave Amy a sad smile. "Don't you think?" It was a dumb question. Amy was quite possibly Lacey's biggest fan.

Amy turned to her. "She's incredible, and I'm so happy you two found each other. It's better than any love story I've ever seen on TV or in the movies, because it's so real, you know?"

Quinn's smile faded. Amy didn't know the truth, that it was all a big sham. No one knew, except Jack. She forced a smile. "You really think so?"

Amy put her arm around her boss. "I've never seen you this happy, Quinn. Ever. And it's so obvious how much you love Lacey. It's written all over your face every time you look at her. And the way you're taking care of her? We should all be so lucky."

Quinn met Amy's gaze. "I do love her," she whispered, unable to deny it anymore.

Jack walked up and stood on the other side of Quinn, resting his hand on her back. "We need to get you two back in the limo."

"What's wrong?" Quinn looked around, wondering if the paparazzi had shown up. It was, after all, only a few days ago that the photos of them kissing had gone viral. Fake kissing, Quinn corrected herself.

"Just a few cameras."

"Just keep them back, Jack. She needs time alone with him."

"I'll try. What would you like me to do about Lacey's ex?"

Amy glanced behind her. "That's Lacey's ex? She's gorgeous!" She quickly tried to make up for her outburst by leaning in and whispering, "Not as pretty as you, of course." She glanced behind her again. "Oh God, she's coming this way."

Quinn didn't turn around. "Thank you, Amy. Will you make sure my mother gets home okay?" She folded her arms, steeling herself for whatever came next. "I'll handle the ex, Jack."

Amy and Jack walked away, passing Dani as they went.

"Quinn Kincaid, in the flesh. My life is now complete."

Quinn turned to find a beautiful young woman approaching her. "You must be Dani."

"Daniela Cordoza," she said, offering her hand. Quinn looked at the hand and reluctantly took it.

Quinn had been expecting this. She assumed Dani would attend the funeral, and Lacey had described her perfectly, although she didn't expect the strong Spanish accent. She took in the dark almond eyes, full lips, and long black hair before she pulled her eyes away from Dani and turned back to Lacey.

Dani stood as close as possible and folded her arms, mimicking Quinn's stance. "It's so sad that he's gone. He was like a second father to me. Did you have a chance to meet him?"

"Yes, I did. He was a good man."

Dani gave Quinn a sideways glance. "You're even more beautiful in person."

Quinn kept her eyes on Lacey. "Why are you being so polite? Surely you're upset that Lacey and I are dating."

"Yes, well, what you don't know is that I will always own Lacey's heart. And even though we've both had our little flings, our destinies will realign, and my princess, my future wife and the mother of our children, will come home. Of this you can be sure."

Quinn turned and gave the woman her best glare. "You know, you can say it with that Sofia Vergara accent all you want, but it's still just horseshit. I *know* what you did to Lacey's heart."

Dani gave her a closed lip smile. "I'd like to pay my respects now, and also my parents are here. It's time they met my future wife."

Quinn got in front of Dani, blocking her way. "That's not a good idea. This isn't the place."

Dani glanced over at two people standing by a limousine and waved them forward. "They would also like to meet their favorite TV star. Maybe get an autograph?"

Quinn's jaw flexed as she tried to control her anger. She wanted to rip this woman apart with her bare hands, or at the very least have the security guards Jack had hired drag her away. But that wouldn't help Lacey. "You do understand that Lacey is experiencing unimaginable grief right now, and your request for an autograph is both callous and wildly inappropriate. And the gall you have to expect Lacey to be polite to two people who refused to even acknowledge her existence…and on the day of her own father's funeral, is so far beyond the pale, I'm struggling to believe you have even one caring bone in your body."

Dani smiled again, seeming way too calm by Quinn's estimation. "Be nice to my parents. I'd hate for them to feel unwelcome at my fiancée's father's funeral."

"Fiancée?" Quinn wanted to grab the woman walking away from her. *Fiancée? What the hell? Is this woman totally batshit?*

Quinn watched helplessly as Dani sauntered toward Lacey. "Shit," she whispered. When she heard Dani's parents speaking Spanish behind her, she put on a fake smile and turned around. She could at least keep them at bay.

After posing for several photos and signing an autograph, and somehow convincing Dani's parents to get back in their car, Quinn went back to her own limo. "Tell me when they're gone," she said to Jack as she opened the car door. She took one more look at Dani and Lacey before she got in and laid her head back against the seat and closed her eyes. "I can't compete with that," she whispered to herself.

"No. I don't suppose you can. I learned that the hard way with your father. No matter how hard I tried, I could never be twenty-five again."

Quinn opened her eyes and found her mother sitting across from her in the stretch limo. "I didn't know you were still here."

Just then, Amy got in the limo. She gave her boss an apologetic grimace. "Mrs. Kincaid, are you sure you don't want the other driver to take you home?"

Margaret waved her off. "Shush, Amy, I'm talking to my daughter. Now, who is she, Quinn?"

Quinn took a deep breath. "Lacey's ex-girlfriend."

Margaret looked to Amy for answers, but Amy just shrugged. "Well, how nice of you to give them room to cuddle."

Quinn rested her elbow on the door and rubbed her forehead, ignoring her mother.

Margaret leaned forward. "Maybe you should tell me why you would let an ex-girlfriend who looks like that anywhere near Lacey. What the hell are you thinking?"

Amy's eyes widened as she nodded in agreement.

"Well, for one thing, I don't own her," Quinn snapped back.

Margaret scooted forward and grabbed her daughter's hand. "But you can own this moment. And that may sound dramatic, but you always liked a little drama in your life, so go take care of Lacey and put that little tramp in her place!"

Little tramp? Quinn had a feeling her mother wasn't referring to Dani so much as expressing her feelings about the woman that stole her husband. Quinn didn't move. It wasn't her place, no matter what everyone around her thought.

"Amy, talk some sense into my daughter."

"Um…" Amy cleared her throat. "She's the best thing that ever happened to you."

Quinn smirked. "Yes, I know you two are her squealing fangirls, but you don't understand."

"You think we're saying this because of her incredible career?" Margaret scoffed. "My darling daughter, we're saying this because of who you are when you're with her. If you can't see how happy she makes you, and how great you are together, then you're blind."

"She makes me crazy," Quinn muttered.

"The best kind of crazy," Amy gently replied.

Margaret narrowed her eyes at her daughter. "Amy, give me a moment alone with Quinn, please." She waited until Amy was out of the car and then said, "What's going on?"

"Nothing."

"Then go take care of your girlfriend. Her father is about to be lowered into the ground and you're going to let some other woman—"

"It's not real, okay?" Quinn blurted out. "We're not real."

Margaret straightened her shoulders. "I don't understand."

"I know you don't, Mom. It was Jack's idea. But it's over now. Lacey has done her part."

"Stop talking in riddles, Quinn."

"Our relationship, okay? I paid her to be my girlfriend to make the coming out process easier."

Margaret sat back in her seat, stunned by the declaration. "You paid her for—"

"Not that. Not sex."

"Well, that's a relief."

"And that's why I have no right to go over there and claim her as my own. She's not mine. She never was."

"I disagree," Margaret said. "Have you seen the way she looks at you? And unless my eyes have failed me, I believe it was your hand she held through the entire funeral."

"She doesn't have anyone else," Quinn muttered.

"Apparently, she does." Margaret forcefully pointed out the window. "But she chose you today. The worst day of her life and she chose you, Quinn. Now, get out there, because the worst day of her life isn't over yet. And if you don't, I will."

Quinn considered it for a moment, her eyes filling with tears.

"Do you love her, honey?"

Quinn didn't answer, but she did put her hand on the door handle.

"If you love her, it doesn't really matter how this thing between the two of you started. All the best love stories are complicated."

Quinn pulled on the door handle but didn't open the door.

"This sham…this charade…how does it end?" Margaret asked.

"We break up in a few months."

"And then?"

"Then I start dating for real. Find someone…" Quinn took her hand off the handle. "We have a plan. Jack has a plan. We need to stick to it."

"I see." Margaret smoothed her charcoal gray coat over her dress as she considered what she was hearing. "And you just forget about Lacey?"

"No." Quinn shook her head. "Never. She took care of me. She's become my best friend."

Margaret pulled her phone out of her purse. "I'm sorry, my

darling, but I don't buy it. These are not the words of someone who is just a friend."

Quinn put up her hand. "I know, Mom. I know she's texted you, but she was just saying what she had to say to keep up the charade."

"Really," Margaret said with a doubtful tone. She put her reading glasses on. "'Lacey, I'm so very sorry to hear about your father. I'm getting on the first plane out. See you soon, my darling.' And this was her reply. 'Thank you, Mrs. Kincaid. I feel so lost right now. Quinn is the only reason I'm still standing.'"

"That doesn't mean…" Quinn shook her head.

Margaret gave her daughter a stern look. "Let me finish." She scrolled down a bit. "'Quinn is a strong woman, Lacey. She gets that from me, whether she'll admit it or not. If you let her, she'll shine bright like a star in your time of need. She'll prop you up until you can stand on your own again. And I'll be there for you too. You're a part of us now, and the Kincaid women will not let you down.'"

"You really believe that?"

Margaret took off her glasses. "I may not say it enough. No, that's not right. I *haven't* said it enough, honey. But honestly, you haven't made it easy. You've kept everyone at arm's length for years. Including me. But Lacey has opened you up again, and yes, I can now see all of you in all of your glory and it's a beautiful sight. Now, do you want to hear what her reply was?"

Quinn nodded.

"Her grief was making her ramble, but just hear her out. 'Okay,' she says, 'before I met Quinn, I thought I knew what love was. It's funny how wrong we can be about our own lives. I wish you could've met my dad. He would've liked you and your honesty. I haven't been so honest lately. He would've been disappointed in me for that. Now, he doesn't have to know, and that's okay. He's with my mom now and that's the most important thing because he loved her so much. Life tears us to pieces sometimes, doesn't it? I hope we'll see more of you, Mrs. Kincaid. Family is so important.'" Margaret met Quinn's gaze. "Now I know what the dishonesty was about. She felt guilty that she'd lied to her father about her relationship with you."

Quinn took a tissue out of her pocket and wiped her nose. "She hasn't really said much at all to me since her dad died. Only the things she's had to say. Details about the funeral. Practical stuff."

"She's devastated, honey. Her thoughts, her feelings, they're all over the place. That text was a jumble of emotions, but one thing is clear—she sees you as her family. Now, am I going out there, or are you?" Margaret tucked her phone back in her purse and waited.

Quinn put her hand on the door handle again, this time she hesitated for only a few seconds before she opened the door and got out of the car. Margaret smiled in satisfaction. "That's my girl."

CHAPTER TWENTY-EIGHT

Quinn stood by the limo for a moment, praying for courage. Jack was keeping the paparazzi away and she couldn't see Dani's parents anywhere nearby. She looked to her left and found Amy, who gave her a reassuring nod. She slowly made her way back to the gravesite. Dani was sitting next to Lacey, an arm wrapped around her shoulders.

"It's time, honey." Quinn held out her hand to Lacey. She looked up with a vacant stare. She put her hand in Quinn's and stood up.

"Let her sit for as long as she wants." Dani stood up and grabbed Lacey's arm.

Quinn kept hold of Lacey's hand, completely ignoring Dani. "Tell me what you need. Do you want to be here when they lower the casket?"

Lacey shook her head. "I can't watch that again. When they threw dirt on my mom—"

Quinn removed the space between them and kissed Lacey's temple. "Shh…it's okay. I'll take care of it."

Lacey gripped the sleeve of Quinn's coat. "Let me say good-bye," she whispered. She went to her father's casket, keeping hold of Quinn's hand. She set her other hand on the casket and immediately started to sob again. She leaned down and kissed it, then turned and fell into Quinn's arms.

Margaret unrolled her window and tracked Dani as she walked away. "That's right. You walk away like a good little girl." Amy gave Margaret a thumbs-up. Margaret chuckled and returned the gesture.

Lacey leaned on Quinn as they made their way back to the limo. Jack opened the door for them, and Lacey met his gaze. "Thank you, Jack. For everything." He gave her a nod and offered his hand, helping her into the limo. He did the same for Quinn and Amy and then closed the door. He eyed Dani and her parents, standing by their car, watching everything as he tapped the roof of the limo, letting the driver know he could go.

"Thank you for coming, Mrs. Kincaid."

Margaret slid in the seat next to Lacey, wrapping her arms around her. "Call me Margaret, honey." Lacey rested her head against Margaret's and let her emotions go again. Her hand reached for Quinn's, finding it and squeezing it tightly.

Later that evening, Lacey opened her eyes and saw familiar wallpaper. Hotel. Dead father. Funeral. Quinn. Not ready to face any of it yet, she pulled the covers up around her face and closed her eyes again.

Half an hour later, Lacey's bladder woke her up. She pushed back the covers and got out of bed, never looking behind her to see if Quinn was anywhere in the room. When she came back out, Quinn was back in bed and lifting the covers for her. Lacey climbed back in and Quinn snuggled up behind, spooning her. Lacey kept her eyes open for a few seconds, soaking in the warmth of the woman behind her. She rested her hand on Quinn's arm and closed her eyes, refusing to care about what was real and what wasn't, because she didn't want any of the last few days to be real.

"Now's not a good time, Jack. It can wait."

Lacey opened her eyes when she heard Quinn speaking in hushed tones across the room.

"I don't care what she's saying, and my husband can go to hell. Ex-husband...yes, that's what I meant. Tell them I have no comment. Pictures? I was drunk, but I don't think anyone took pictures." Quinn turned around and looked at Lacey when Jack asked about her. "She's devastated. Just like we'd all be if we lost both parents that young."

Lacey squeezed her eyes shut, trying to fight back the tears again. She pulled the covers up over her head when her phone started ringing.

"I have to go, Jack." Quinn ended the call and walked over to Lacey's phone where it was charging on the desk. She saw Dani's name and pushed the red button.

Lacey threw the covers off her head. "Who was it?" She couldn't hide from the world forever.

"It was Dani."

Lacey motioned for Quinn to hand her the phone. She listened to the voice mail and sat up. She put her feet on the floor but didn't stand up. Quinn stood in front of her. "You're not going anywhere."

"I should shower." Lacey fell forward a bit, resting her forehead on Quinn's stomach.

"I could run a bath for you. Would that feel good?"

Would anything ever feel good again? Lacey had her doubts. She'd given up on trying to stop the tears that just kept coming.

"Lace?" Quinn ran her fingers through Lacey's hair. "Tell me what you need."

She needed time to stop and then reverse a few years. She needed to tell her dad to eat better and not work so hard. She needed to make healthy dinners for him, instead of making him fend for himself. She needed to give him more of her time, not just holidays and a few Saturday mornings where they would catch up over coffee. For so long, he lived with a broken heart and then he died of one too. She could've prevented that, couldn't she?

Couldn't she?

Lacey wrapped her arms around Quinn's legs and hung on for dear life as another sob exploded from her chest.

"I don't know what to do for her. She won't eat the room service food. And the tears, Mom—they're constant. If she's awake, she's crying."

"Where are you?" Margaret asked.

"I'm trying a different tactic. I'm buying her favorite junk food." Quinn grabbed a bag of Doritos and put them in her basket.

"Good idea. When are you heading back to L.A.?"

"Tomorrow morning."

"Quinn, honey, listen to me. You're doing everything exactly right. She'll probably want some space eventually, but right now, she needs your constant support. Don't leave her alone for very long. Be there for her, and in time, the tears will subside."

Quinn breathed a sigh of relief. She was starting to feel a little bit helpless in the face of such grief. "Thank you, for being at the funeral. I know Lacey really appreciated it too."

"Of course, dear."

Quinn put her basket full of snacks and drinks on the counter. "Mom, I have to check out now."

"Okay, honey. Keep me posted. And if I can help, you know I'm here for you both."

"I will. Bye, Mom."

Quinn was halfway down the hall when she suddenly slowed her pace, shocked at what she was seeing. Lacey had just stepped out of the hotel room, fully dressed. "Hey, what are you—" She stopped dead in her tracks when Dani walked out of the room behind Lacey.

Quinn hadn't been gone that long, had she? Maybe an hour at the most. Just long enough to make a few phone calls and pick up some food. She eyed them both and then said, "Going somewhere?"

Lacey adjusted the purse on her shoulder and stuffed her hands in her coat pockets. "Just for coffee."

A few awkward seconds of silence passed between the three of them. "You haven't eaten anything. You need more than coffee." Quinn held up the grocery bag. "I bought your favorites. Doritos, Snickers, ice cream…" Quinn trailed off.

Dani took Lacey's elbow. "I'll make sure she eats some real food."

Lacey took the few steps needed to be face-to-face with Quinn. "Thank you," she said. "The funeral. Everything you've done for my dad. I can't thank you enough." She gave Quinn a quick hug and walked away.

Quinn stood there, speechless. What was she supposed to say or do? Just before they turned the corner and disappeared, she shouted. "Lacey!"

Lacey stopped and turned around.

Stay with me. Quinn forced the words back down. "Eat something. Soup. Eat soup."

Lacey managed a smile and nodded. Dani put a possessive arm around her and urged her down the hall.

Soup? Fucking soup? Was that all Quinn had? What about *You're not going anywhere with her!* Or *I'm definitely not okay with you spending time with your ex.* Because even if this was all fake, they were still supposed to be acting like their relationship was real, weren't they?

Quinn tossed the bag of junk food on the bed and groaned in frustration. It was going to be a long evening.

CHAPTER TWENTY-NINE

Amy knocked on the door an hour before they were supposed to leave New York. Quinn let her in and went back to her suitcase. "I'll just be a minute," she muttered under her breath.

"Everything okay?" Amy knew her boss well, and there was definitely tension in the air and worry written all over her face.

Quinn didn't answer right away. She continued to fold clothes and tuck them into her suitcase. "I don't know where Lacey is. We'll have to go without her."

Amy walked over and picked up a sweater to fold. "We can hold the plane," she said, hoping Quinn would tell her what the hell was going on.

"No. She knows we're leaving, and if she wants to stay, I have to let her."

Amy put the sweater in the suitcase and rested her hand on Quinn's arm. "Why don't you tell me what's going on so I can help?"

Quinn pulled her arm away and went over to the window, her arms firmly wrapped around her body. "She's with Dani. She went for coffee with her last night and didn't come home...back...she didn't come back."

Amy shook her head in confusion. "Why are you so calm? And why the hell are you going to leave without her?"

"You don't understand."

"You're right! I don't!"

Seeming a little surprised by Amy's anger, Quinn turned around and shot her a glare. "Are you yelling at me?"

"Someone needs to! You don't even know where your girlfriend is? I'd be freaking out right about now! We should call the police! We should put out an APB! It's your *GIRLFRIEND*, Quinn! And this is *New York*!"

"I'm here."

Amy spun around and found Lacey standing at the door. She barely stopped herself from shouting *where the hell have you been?* She turned to Quinn, hoping she would yell the words, but she just stood there, staring at Lacey. The tension in the room was so thick, she decided she'd better leave. "Let me know what you want to do."

Amy tried not to make eye contact with Lacey as she brushed past her, but Lacey grabbed her arm. "Just give me a few minutes to shower and we'll go." Amy gave her a terse nod and walked out. Lacey turned her attention back to Quinn. "I won't be long."

Quinn ignored her, zipping up her bag and setting it on the floor. Lacey went into the bathroom, and when she came back out ten minutes later, Quinn was gone.

"I'm sorry I yelled at you," Amy said, breaking the silence in the limo.

Quinn stared blankly out the window. "It's okay. I think the person you really want to yell at is Lacey."

"You're right. I'm pissed at her. What the hell was she thinking going off like that? For all we knew, she could've been lying dead in the subway. Or bleeding out in Central Park, or…"

"Her dad just died." That was what Quinn had been telling herself. *She's fragile. Her dad just died. Don't make it worse for her.*

"I don't know how that relates to her staying out all night with her hot ex-girlfriend, but okay. I guess if you can forgive her, so can I."

That made Quinn crack a smile. She was lucky to have such a loyal assistant. "You've been incredible, Amy. The funeral was perfect. The flowers were gorgeous. None of that would've happened without you."

Amy swooned a little bit, tucking her blond curls behind her ears. "Thank you. I did my best."

"He seemed like a good man, didn't he? I wish…" Quinn took a breath. "I wish I could've spent more time with him before he died."

Amy's eyes misted over. "I should give her a hug when she gets here. I was rude earlier."

The door opened and Lacey slid in, moving Quinn's purse onto the floor so she could sit as close to her as possible. She kept her big sunglasses on and rested her hand on Quinn's thigh. "You're both amazing people," she said, her voice still shaky. "I'll never be able to thank you enough for honoring my father the way you have. And you should both know that I love you."

Amy's face contorted as she started to cry. She grabbed a tissue and nodded. "We love you too."

That was all Quinn needed. Those words and the hand squeezing her leg told her everything she needed to know. She wrapped her arms around Lacey, pulling her closer and kissing her temple. She breathed in the scent of her shampoo, a scent she'd grown to love. "Are you ready to go home?" she gently asked.

Lacey leaned her head against Quinn's. "Let's go," she whispered.

Quinn set a hot cup of tea in front of Lacey and gave Jack a bottle of water. She sat in between them at the kitchen table.

"I'm sorry we have to do this so soon," Jack said, eyeing both of them with concern.

Lacey wrapped her hands around the cup of tea. "It's okay. Thank you, for being at my dad's funeral, Jack. It meant a lot to me that you were there, helping with everything."

New York was kind of a blur for Lacey. She'd felt like a zombie, just going through the motions of living while trying to do right by the dead. But through it all, she knew who had been there for her, and Jack was on that list.

"Your father would be...was...is...very proud of you, I'm sure. You're a strong woman, Lacey. Every father should be so lucky to have a child show such strength, love and respect at their funeral."

"I had no one when my mother died." Lacey's eyes flicked between the two of them. They seemed surprised by her declaration. She took a sip of tea to soothe her dry throat. "My dad was too broken to be there for me. It took about a year before he could look at me and not see my mother. We looked a lot alike." She took another sip of tea, determined to say this. "So, I know what it feels like to grieve alone. And now, I know what if feels like to be surrounded by people who could take my burden and let me break down and cry for days on end. That's the only reason I was able to stand up and speak about my dad." She took Quinn's hand. "Because I knew once I was done, I could break down again and be weak and grieve. It means everything when you have that."

Quinn wrapped both of her hands around Lacey's. "You grieve for as long as you need to. Jack and I will handle things."

Lacey wiped her tears away. "No. I'm a part of this. Please don't shut me out."

Quinn turned to Jack and nodded. "Go ahead."

"Right now, everything is just rumor and a few paparazzi photos. We need to legitimize your relationship, and the faster we do that, the faster we can move on to the breakup and, Quinn, you can start dating for real, which has always been the goal, correct?"

Quinn glanced at Lacey. She didn't say it out loud, but she gave Jack an almost imperceptible nod.

Jack eyed them both over his reading glasses. "Is there something you're not telling me?"

"No," Lacey quickly said. She took another sip of her tea. "How do we legitimize our relationship?"

"There's always Twitter and Instagram, but nothing says you're a couple like walking a red carpet together. There are several charity events coming up in the next few weeks that would be good options. Of course, you'll get questions from reporters, so we'll have to work on your talking points. Beyond that, it's just a question of how far you want to take it. You could go on the late-night shows, do one-on-one interviews, that kind of thing. But honestly, if you're going to break up within a few months, I wouldn't take it too far. You might come off as shallow or experimental, Quinn."

"At the same time, getting on the late-night shows would be great for Lacey's career," Quinn replied.

Jack nodded. "They're all begging for both or either of you."

Quinn turned to Lacey. "We could keep it low key. Keep our answers vague. Not say out loud that we're in love. I mean, you know, we wouldn't have to gush about each other. As fellow actors, of course. Just not…you know."

"I could tell them how scared you were to shoot the love scenes," Lacey said, her voice small and sincere. "They'd laugh." Jack giggled. "See?" Lacey motioned with her head at Jack.

Quinn bit her lip, trying not to smile. "I wasn't scared."

Lacey huffed. "Right. And I didn't bite your pussy." Realizing what she'd just said and who she just said it in front of, Lacey's mouth fell open. "Oh God. Sorry, Jack. It was nothing. I just bit her panties a little…on the set…in front of everyone."

Jack put up his hand. "Don't worry about it. It's actually good to hear that sarcasm again. We missed it."

Quinn couldn't help but smile. It was the first time in over a week that Lacey had sounded like herself. "I guess we need to get our story straight. How we met. How you got cast on the show. How it happened."

Lacey tilted her head. "How what happened?"

"You know. How we fell in—"

"Fake love?" Lacey finished it for her. "Yeah. We need to make up a moment. The moment we fell in fake love."

They all eyed one another and then Jack stood up. "Let me know what event you'd like to attend first." He pulled a piece of paper out of his briefcase. "Here's a list."

Quinn took the list and walked Jack to the door. "Walk me to my car?" he suggested.

Jack stood by his car, smiling at Quinn. "What?" she asked.

"I'm getting a vibe."

Quinn folded her arms. "Oh yeah? What kind of vibe?"

"You love her."

Quinn glanced back at the house. The door was open, but they were far enough away that they couldn't be heard. "It's not like that. We care about each other. And I want the best for her. For her career. We have to do this right, Jack."

"Uh-huh." Jack bounced on his feet. "She loves you too. You know that, right?"

Quinn's gaze dropped to her feet. "I'm not so sure about that. She spent the night with Dani before we left New York."

"She WHAT? Why didn't you tell me? Did anyone see them? Photograph them? I have to talk to her."

Quinn grabbed Jack's arm. She was going to tell him he couldn't interrogate Lacey, but she wanted the truth as much as he did. And maybe Lacey would be more forthright with him. She let go and followed him back into the house.

Lacey put the teakettle on the stove and turned the burner on. Jack stood on the other side of the island. "Tell me about your night with Dani."

Lacey jumped at the sound of Jack's voice, not realizing he'd come back in the house. She eyed him and then looked at Quinn. "We went for coffee."

"For nine hours?" Quinn softened her tone. "I mean, you were gone for a long time."

Jack kept his eyes on Lacey, waiting for an answer. "I need to know where you went. If photos were taken. If you kissed in public. What time you left wherever you were."

Lacey looked at Quinn again and then lowered her gaze. "Do I really have to tell you everything? We weren't followed or photographed."

Jack turned to Quinn. She took a step forward. "Please just tell us, Lacey. It's important that we don't have any surprises."

Lacey sighed. "We were just going to have coffee. That was it. But then she took me somewhere else." Lacey turned away from them. Quinn put her hand up, gesturing for Jack to be patient. They waited and eventually, Lacey turned back around. "She proposed. In the middle of Times Square, Dani asked me to marry her."

Quinn's mouth fell open. "She...what?"

"Who saw?" Jack asked. He leaned on the counter with both hands. "Why am I even asking? Times Square? *Everyone* saw."

Lacey covered her face with her hands. "It wasn't like that. Dani isn't the type to get on one knee. No one was paying any attention to us. I swear." She took a breath. "You know how Times Square is—literally packed with tourists."

Quinn ran her fingers through her hair. "I should've stopped you. In the hallway, I should've stopped you. Why didn't I stop you?"

"Just so we're clear," Jack said. "You didn't actually accept her proposal, right? She isn't going to post a photo of your ring-clad hand on Instagram."

Lacey shook her head.

"And then where did you go?"

"Jack." Quinn gave him a look, hoping he wouldn't be so harsh.

Lacey looked at the ceiling, trying to hold back the tears. "I um... went to my dad's apartment and wrote him a letter."

"Oh." Quinn took Jack by the arm. "I think we're good here."

It was a stunning story and neither of them knew what to say as they walked back out to Jack's car. They stood there for a moment and then Jack said, "On the day of her father's funeral? Unbelievable. Who does this woman think she is?"

Quinn was kicking herself for not intervening somehow. She'd done everything she could to help Lacey deal with her grief and everything that goes with a loved one dying. But she couldn't protect her from Dani. It wasn't her place, she'd thought at the time. She wasn't Lacey's real girlfriend. She couldn't take her by the arm and insist that she not go out into the night with her ex.

That hadn't stopped her from pacing the floor all night like a real girlfriend would. She'd been worried sick and maybe a little bit jealous—the image of Dani taking Lacey by the elbow like she owned her playing over and over in her head. Also, her mother's words. Margaret would be so disappointed if she knew what had happened— that Quinn hadn't done the right thing the second time she'd had the chance to.

Jack didn't want to push, but he had to know one thing. "Have you watched the new episodes?"

Quinn shook her head. She'd seen a few of the scenes, but watching full episodes of her show wasn't something she enjoyed doing. She was too big a critic, noticing every little thing that she and her costars could've done better.

"You should watch them, Quinn. You'd see how good the two of you are together."

"Now you're a fan? I thought you didn't like Lacey."

"I never said I didn't like her. I said she'd give you a run for your money. And she has. In the best possible way. Even your mother can't get over the difference in you."

"My mother is a rabid soap fan. That's the only reason—"

"You're wrong. Your mother couldn't stop talking about *you*, not Lacey."

Quinn's gaze dropped to the ground. "She knows. My mom knows it's a fake relationship."

"I know. She told me. She also told me how proud she is of the way you handled the funeral. The way you took care of Lacey. The way you stepped up and did what needed to be done. She even shed a few tears when she talked about the day she met Lacey and how *she* did the same for *you*, standing up for you, defending you. She said it was so nice to see you with someone who seemed to have nothing but your best interests at heart."

Jack took a step closer, resting his hands on Quinn's shoulders. "Don't write her off just because keeping her in your life wasn't part of the original plan. I know you, Quinn. You make a plan and then you stick to it, no matter what. But don't forget—you trusted Lacey with your life when you broke your arm, and she didn't let you down. And if you'd just watch the episodes, you'd see that she's singlehandedly breathed new life into your show. Do you have any idea how many new Twitter followers you have?"

"I haven't looked lately."

"Well, it wouldn't hurt to tweet a photo of the two of you sometime in the near future."

Quinn nodded. "I'll keep that in mind. Thanks for everything, Jack."

Jack had to smile. "So far, so good. Even with the setbacks, you're almost where you want to be. We'll talk soon."

Quinn went back inside, but Lacey was gone. She found her out back, sitting in a sunny spot, sipping on another cup of tea. Quinn pulled up a chair and sat down, facing her.

Lacey kept her eyes on her cup. "I'm sorry I didn't tell you. I just didn't see the point."

"I hope you know you can trust me, Lace. With anything."

Lacey gave her a nod. "I know. I was just so embarrassed she'd pull a stunt like that. I mean, Times Square? It's like she doesn't know me at all."

"I'm so sorry."

"My father just died. And she took me to the most public place in the city, packed with tourists." Lacey shook her head in disgust. "And what's the goddamned rush, anyway?"

"She certainly let me know where I stand," Quinn said. "In no uncertain terms."

"What did she say to you?"

"Well, she intimated that you'd both had your little flings, but that she owned you. It sounds like she plans to take back that ownership." Quinn paused as Lacey's expression evolved into a look of disgust. "Lace, she called you her fiancée."

Lacey wanted to scream. She wanted to scream at Dani, but also at Quinn for not having the guts to say something in the hotel hallway that night. Just two words—*Don't go.*

If Quinn knew Dani's intentions and didn't even flinch when they left together that night, that meant something, didn't it? It meant that everything Lacey had been feeling was one-sided. They were friends and coworkers. Nothing more.

Quinn reached out and put her hand on Lacey's knee. "I got them to postpone production until Monday. That gives us two more days. What would you like to do? Do you need space? Or a long drive in the Maserati? We could drive up the coast. Whatever you need right now, we'll make it happen."

"What do *you* need?" Lacey knew the answer. Quinn needed them to break up so she could get on with her life.

"I need to know you're going to be okay. And anything I can do to help…"

Lacey stood up. "Pick a charity event for next weekend. I'll be fine to go."

Quinn also stood up. "We don't have to do it so soon."

"Don't we?" Lacey looked her in the eye. "Jack said the sooner we do it, the sooner we can break up." She handed Quinn her empty cup. "Just do it, Quinn." She headed for the guesthouse and slammed the door shut.

CHAPTER THIRTY

L acey was in bad shape. The week in New York had solidified in her mind that Quinn was the person she wanted to spend the rest of her life with. They'd spent every waking and even sleeping moment together, Quinn always by her side, even at the morgue when she said her final good-byes to her father. It was the most difficult week of her life and she didn't know how she could've gotten through it without Quinn there.

Even on the plane ride back to L.A., Quinn had held her close. It was only when they walked into the house that they went their separate ways, Quinn to her bedroom and Lacey to the guesthouse. Maybe Quinn was in desperate need of some alone time. It had been a hard week for everyone, after all. Lacey couldn't begrudge her that. But she couldn't sleep well, either. She'd sat on the edge of the bed for hours last night, not wanting to sleep alone. Not wanting to wake up alone.

But she did wake up alone. She stared at the ceiling for a while and then dragged herself out of bed. She sat at the little kitchen table alone and sipped on a cup of bad coffee, thinking about how wonderful a long drive sounded. It also sounded like torture, having to sit next to the woman she'd fallen in love with for hours on end. There wouldn't be a reason to touch her anymore. No cameras. No debilitating grief. Just them. Alone.

God, the more Lacey thought about it, it sounded absolutely horrible. No, it seemed best just to stay in L.A. and rest over the weekend. Find her bearings again. She had fan mail. More than she'd ever had during her career on *Light of Day*. Maybe she could sit and read the love mail and more than likely, a bit of hate mail.

❖

Quinn knocked on the guesthouse door and poked her head in. "Hey." She frowned when she saw the coffee cup. "Why didn't you come inside for coffee? I have breakfast waiting."

"I, um…" Lacey always went inside for coffee. That big espresso machine called to her, and Quinn knew how much she loved it. Any excuse she made for drinking the crappy coffee wouldn't be believed, so she didn't even try.

"Do you want to be alone?"

Lacey *was* alone, whether she liked it or not. She had no family, besides an aunt she barely knew who lived in Montana or New Mexico, she could never remember which. But she didn't want to talk about that. "Did you really cook breakfast?"

Quinn held out her hand. "Don't make me eat it alone."

Lacey took her hand and stood up. "Is it edible?" she joked, trying to lighten her heavy mood.

"Very funny." Quinn pulled Lacey into an unexpected hug. "Good morning. I missed you."

Lacey closed her eyes and inhaled Quinn's scent. It instantly comforted her and she relaxed into the hug, wrapping her arms around Quinn's waist. "Good morning."

"How did you sleep?" Quinn pulled back and cupped Lacey's cheeks, studying her face. "Not well, I see."

"Terrible."

"You're sleeping with me tonight. It's too soon to be alone. I don't know what I was thinking, leaving you out here like this." Lacey gave her a slight nod. "Good, then it's settled." She took Lacey's hand and led her outside. "It's a beautiful day."

Lacey shielded her eyes from the sun. "A good day for mountain biking?"

"A good day for flying." Quinn tightened her grip on Lacey's hand and grinned.

Lacey narrowed her eyes. "What are you talking about?"

Quinn pulled out a chair at the table for Lacey. "We're going to Napa, but we're going to fly there."

Lacey looked at her with big, questioning eyes. "Today?"

"Yeah. We'll eat breakfast and then we'll pack an overnight bag. And tonight, we'll have an excellent meal in the middle of a vineyard." Quinn put a plate of fresh fruit on the table and took the omelets out of the oven. She set one in front of Lacey. "It's your favorite. Spinach and Brie."

Lacey felt a little bit overwhelmed, but she held it together and smiled. "I can't believe you cooked for me."

"Don't get used to it," Quinn said with a wink. She picked up her fork and took a bite. A surprise moan escaped her mouth. "Not bad!"

Lacey took a small bite. "It's wonderful. You're wonderful."

Quinn picked up her coffee cup and grinned behind it. "So, you're in?"

Forget the fan mail. Forget their pending breakup. Forget everything else. Lacey only wanted to be with Quinn—for as long as she could have her. "Yeah. I'm in."

Lacey stepped out of the guesthouse looking as gorgeous as ever with her hair pulled back into a ponytail and her dark sunglasses on. She was wearing a low-cut white gypsy-style blouse with a denim miniskirt and wedge heels.

Quinn's breath caught when she saw her. "You look beautiful."

Lacey leaned in for a kiss on the cheek. "Thank you, honey. So do you."

While Lacey was showering, she'd decided she wouldn't hide her feelings anymore. If she wanted to kiss Quinn, she would. If she wanted to call her honey or another pet name, she would. She'd just be herself and whatever came of it—or whatever didn't come of it—she'd have to be okay with.

Life was too short, even if you were being paid to pretend.

On the small private plane, Lacey buckled her seat belt and immediately reached for Quinn's hand. She brought it to her mouth and kissed it. "I adore you for doing this for me."

"I couldn't leave you all alone out in that guesthouse. And this trip is for both of us. A change of scenery." Quinn mimicked Lacey's action, taking their joined hands to her mouth and gently kissing Lacey's. "And if you still need to shed a few tears, it's okay."

Lacey leaned in and relaxed, resting her head against Quinn's shoulder. "I love you." She closed her eyes, not caring what the reaction would be.

Quinn urged Lacey's head up and put a small pillow under it. "Just rest now. I'll wake you when we get there." Once Lacey was asleep, she snapped a quick photo.

❖

Quinn stared at the selfie she'd taken of the two of them. Lacey looked content and relaxed and beautiful sleeping on her shoulder. What surprised Quinn even more was how content she herself looked. Her blue eyes had a sparkle to them and her smile seemed so genuine. She looked happy in a way that she'd never seen in photos of herself before.

She gently kissed Lacey's head, being careful not to wake her up. *You're the reason.*

Quinn decided to send the photo to her mom—something she really never did—with a message.

Taking her to Napa. We both need the break.

It didn't take long to get a reply.

Oh, what an adorable photo. Thank you for telling me, darling. Have a wonderful time!

Quinn smiled at the reply and then decided to tweet the photo as well, with the following message:

She keeps me warm.

She sent the tweet and took a deep, cleansing breath. It felt good to keep her mom up to date on her life. That was new. It also felt good to have an amazing woman sleeping on her shoulder. It felt right and good and everything she'd always dreamed it would be. Quinn was gay. And now, she was out and proud. It could only get better from here.

After a hard, dreary week in New York City, the fresh, crisp air of a Napa Valley evening felt like heaven to Lacey. She closed her eyes and took in a deep breath.

"Your color looks a little better tonight." Quinn reached across the table and filled Lacey's glass with a full-bodied merlot.

"Have I been pale?" Lacey touched her face, wishing she'd touched up her makeup before dinner.

"A little bit. The color in your cheeks is back."

"The walk felt good."

They were literally in the middle of a vineyard, having dinner on a small wooden platform with only enough room for a table and two chairs. Tiki torches and candles lit up the space, creating a very romantic atmosphere.

Lacey had assumed they would be staying in a hotel, but they drove straight to the winery and were greeted by the owners with hugs and kisses. Friends of Quinn's, apparently. They were given the key to a cozy guesthouse where they freshened up and then went for a long, slow walk around the property. They had total privacy, which Lacey was very grateful for. She wasn't looking forward to being in public with Quinn again just yet. That would come soon enough.

They'd walked hand in hand, taking in the beauty of their surroundings. Quinn had carried the conversation and Lacey nodded and smiled when appropriate. Now that they were seated for dinner and she'd had a glass of wine, Lacey was feeling a little more talkative. "I want to make a scrapbook."

"A scrapbook? Like one of those storyboards on your phone?"

"No," Lacey replied with a firm shake of her head. "Like a real scrapbook with real memories in it. Something I can hold in my hands and turn the pages and remember. I have two boxes full of photos, postcards, and letters that my parents collected, and I think I'd like to turn it into something tangible, you know?"

"I thought you weren't very crafty. Isn't scrapbooking a crafty hobby?"

"Why are you busting my balls about this?" Lacey picked up her glass and took another good, long sip.

"I'm not busting your—" Quinn pushed the charcuterie board across the table. "Have some food with that wine."

Lacey threw a few cashews in her mouth. "So what if I couldn't Bedazzle your damn sling. That doesn't mean I can't put a scrapbook together. How hard can it be?"

"Fourteen thousand likes," Quinn blurted out. She seemed instantly relieved she'd gotten that off her chest. She also threw a few nuts in her mouth and nodded just to punctuate her point. "So far."

Lacey swirled the wine in her glass and narrowed her eyes. "What the hell are you talking about?"

"Twitter."

"Did you change the subject? I was talking about a scrapbook. For my deceased parents."

"And I fully support you in that effort. I'll even help. We'll watch YouTube videos. Take classes. Whatever it takes, okay?"

"Thank you," Lacey said, feeling slightly better about the conversation. "I can't forget their faces. Or the sound of their voices."

"So, back to the digital album?"

"We'll do both," Lacey said. "But we'll have to hire a professional for that one. I'm technologically inept."

Quinn rolled a small piece of melon in a slice of prosciutto. She stabbed it with a fork and offered it. "Agreed. Now, try this."

Lacey took the fork. "Are you trying to shut me up?"

"Never." Quinn smiled. "I love talking about scrapbooking."

"You hate it. And this is delicious." Lacey washed it down with more wine. "Now, what's this about Twitter?"

"I thought you'd never ask." Quinn was so excited it was bubbling out of her. "I posted a photo."

"And it's gotten fourteen thousand likes?"

"And counting." She reached down and took her phone out of her purse. "It's a photo of us."

Lacey frowned. "When?"

"You were asleep. Oh my God. Fifteen thousand and counting. The comments are awesome."

"Wait." Lacey leaned forward. "I was asleep? What the hell, Quinn?"

Quinn handed over her phone, watching Lacey closely for her reaction.

"She keeps me warm." Lacey looked up and searched Quinn's eyes. All she saw was a look of satisfaction for a job well done. Quinn pumped her fist as Lacey pushed her chair out and stood up, setting the phone on the table. "Good job. Jack will be very happy." She turned and stepped off the platform, disappearing into the darkness.

She didn't get very far. Once she was a few feet away from the torches, it was so dark she couldn't even see the rows of vines that surrounded them. She stood still for a moment, hoping her eyes would adjust. Hoping her heart wouldn't break in two right then and there.

She looked up at the clear night sky, wishing she believed in God. Wishing someone could make sense of this mess she was in. Wishing she could call her dad. She hadn't called him enough since she'd moved in with Quinn. It was awkward, telling him half-truths. Lying to her own father. God, how she wished she'd handled it differently. The whole thing, she'd handle differently, given the chance.

It wasn't worth all this heartache. Being so goddamned in love with someone who only saw her as a means to an end. Not being there for her father during the last months of his life. No job, no amount of money was worth it.

The darkness was fitting. Lost in the inky blackness, barely able to see her own hand. That seemed okay. She wanted to disappear for a while. Maybe forget to breathe and just...float away.

"Lace? Honey, come back."

Lacey didn't turn around. She wrapped her arms around herself, needing protection from that voice. "You should post it on Instagram too." She hoped if Quinn posted the damn photo enough places, maybe they could avoid having to make a public appearance and just end this fucking charade ASAP.

"I meant it. Those words I wrote. You keep me so warm."

"It's my job," Lacey said, her voice cracking. She desperately did not want to cry. *Not right now.* She turned around, her arms still tightly wrapped around her body. Quinn was a silhouette backlit by the torches. She couldn't see the expression on her face, and maybe that was for the best, since she didn't want to lie anymore.

Lacey was over it. Done with this farce. Yes, she'd fulfill the terms of her contract. She'd stand by Quinn's side and smile for the cameras. But she wouldn't spend one more second denying how she really felt. If her dad were still here, she knew what he would say. *Tell her.*

And what better place to admit that you'd fallen in love when you weren't supposed to, when you'd sworn to yourself that you wouldn't, when you'd laughed it off and told Quinn she was arrogant to even think such a thing could happen, what better place, than in a pitch-black vineyard, where the woman you love can barely see you as you say it?

"It's not just my job." Lacey lowered her gaze, still gripping her stomach. "It stopped being a job a long time ago, and I know you don't want to hear this, but—"

"I love you too."

Lacey froze. She played the words over in her mind, making sure she'd heard right. Lifting her gaze, she squinted in the darkness. Why was it so damned dark out? Where was the damn moon when she needed it? Because now, she needed to see Quinn's face more than she needed air.

Quinn took a few steps forward, making her even harder to see as the darkness enveloped her. Lacey took her by the hand and led her back onto the platform. She held her by the shoulders and said, "Say it again." Quinn opened her mouth, but Lacey put her fingers over it, preventing her from saying the words. "Wait. This isn't just because my dad died and you think I need to hear it."

Quinn shook her head, the hand still on her mouth.

"Or because I'm feeling sorry for myself now that I have no family."

Quinn shook her head again.

"Or because—"

Quinn took Lacey's hand away, keeping hold of it. "Stop trying to find reasons other than the real one—that I fell in love with you a long time ago too."

"Real. Not fake?" Lacey's voice sounded so unsure. And it was. Her heart, her mind, her soul—none of them were ready to accept this truth.

Quinn took a step back and held out her hand. "You said I couldn't just hold out my hand. I also had to tell you that I love you. And even though I've fought it and thought it would be one-sided. And even though I was scared to death to feel anything for you, because there was always Dani, and your life back in New York. And even though you might break my heart because you're bigger than life and your career is going to explode now—even with all of that, I would be an absolute fool to keep those words inside for another second. So, yes, honey. I love you. And I want you, if you'll have me."

Lacey took Quinn's hand, still trying to process all of it. "None of that BFF stuff?"

Quinn shook her head. "No. I mean, I hope you'll always be my best friend, but you'd make a shitty maid of honor."

Lacey dramatically swiped her hand across her forehead. "Whew! What a relief."

"For me too. Peach really isn't your color."

"Not to mention that you really shouldn't want to fuck your maid of honor." Lacey paused, realizing what she'd just heard. "Peach?"

Quinn removed the space between them and wrapped her arms around Lacey's waist. "Do you think you could maybe stop with the banter and the whole not kissing me thing, and maybe…"

Quinn whimpered when Lacey's lips hit hers. The electricity between them was immediate and even more powerful than it had been on the set. "Oh God," she whispered into Lacey's mouth.

"Yeah," Lacey whispered back, right before she deepened the kiss. As her tongue found Quinn's, a hand slid from her back down to her ass. She giggled. "I knew you were obsessed with my ass."

CHAPTER THIRTY-ONE

Everything. Quinn was obsessed with everything. Her hands were everywhere, squeezing Lacey's ass, gripping her back. There were way too many clothes. She pulled away, her eyes dark with lust. "Let's take this inside."

Lacey grabbed Quinn's blouse and pulled her back. She worked her way over to Quinn's ear, kissing her cheek, her jaw, her neck. She ran her tongue over her ear and said, "You need to be sure. Are you sure? Because I can't hold back everything I feel for you anymore. You'll have all of me after this."

Quinn's panties were wet. Her body was on fire. And Lacey whispering in her ear was making her crazy with lust. She wanted her naked. She wanted to taste her and know what she sounded like when she came. She wanted to make up for all the times she didn't tell her how beautiful and funny and sexy she was. She wanted to own Lacey Matthews's heart. "God yes, I'm sure."

Lacey grabbed the bottle of wine off the table and put out her hand. "Let's go."

Quinn was pushed up against a wall, her clothing slowly being stripped from her body. Her chest was heaving, her eyes were tracking Lacey's every move. It would happen soon. Lacey's mouth would be on her— "Oh God." She ran her fingers into Lacey's hair and closed her eyes, pressing her breasts closer, needing more pressure.

She'd imagined this so many times, the things Lacey's mouth would do. Her tongue, flicking and sucking. Her warm hands gripping her waist, like they were right now. Quinn needed them lower. She took Lacey's hands and placed them on her ass. Yes. That was better.

Lacey urged Quinn to turn around and face the wall. Quinn gasped when she felt the bite on her shoulder. Lacey's hands reached around and cupped her breasts as she sucked on the spot she'd just bitten.

Quinn's breaths were excited and shallow. She couldn't wait to see where Lacey would go next. Zipper. They would go to the zipper next. "You're so beautiful," Lacey whispered as she let Quinn's pants fall to the floor. She turned her back around and pressed their bodies together. Her hands slid into Quinn's panties and squeezed her ass as her tongue found Quinn's again.

"I need to see you," Quinn whispered. She pulled Lacey's blouse over her head and tossed it aside. Then unzipped her skirt. Lacey stepped out of it and Quinn stared in awe. She'd seen Lacey in her bikini, but this—seeing her in a sexy pink bra and matching thong? Good God, Quinn couldn't take it anymore. She pushed the straps off Lacey's shoulders and pulled the bra down. "Oh my God," she whispered as her fingers trailed down Lacey's chest and over taut nipples.

Lacey took Quinn's hand and led her to the bed. She unhooked her own bra and then Quinn's, leaving them both in just their panties. She urged Quinn onto the bed and straddled her hips, putting them in the same position they were in when they shot the love scene, minus the bras. "I should finish what I started," Lacey said. She kissed Quinn soundly and then worked her way down her body, kissing and sucking as she went.

Quinn pushed herself up onto her elbows, needing to watch Lacey's every move. Just before she got to the edge of Quinn's panties, Lacey looked up and gave her a sly grin. "You want this so bad, don't you?"

Quinn nodded. "Ever since that day."

Lacey ran her tongue over the panties and looked at Quinn again. "Me too." She sat up. "But I really should take these off." Quinn put her legs together so Lacey could slide her panties off. "Ohhhh..." Lacey breathed out slowly as she got her first real look at Quinn's waxed pussy. She ran the back of her finger over her slit. "Fuck, you're gorgeous."

Quinn's wide eyes shuttered closed at the touch. When she opened them again, Lacey was staring at her. "I love you, Quinn." She didn't wait for a reply. She bent over and wrapped her arms around Quinn's legs as she took her first taste. "Mmm...God, you're wet."

Quinn fell back on the bed, unable to hold herself up on her elbows anymore. Lacey took her time, tasting every part of Quinn and dipping her tongue inside. When Quinn started to shudder, Lacey grabbed for her hand and held it tightly.

Quinn was on the verge. She was grabbing at the sheets with one hand and squeezing Lacey's hand so tight she was leaving fingernail marks. She came with a force she'd never known before. It was explosive and loud and she would've felt embarrassed, except Lacey didn't give her time to think about it too hard. She was on Quinn, holding her face and looking into her eyes as her breathing calmed down. She kissed Quinn's forehead, her nose, her lips, her chin. "That was amazing," Lacey whispered. "You're so beautiful. And so gay."

They both giggled as Quinn pushed Lacey's hair back and cupped her cheek. She wouldn't wait another second to touch Lacey everywhere she'd fantasized about. She wanted inside. She wanted to feel Lacey's warmth. Taste it. Get lost in it. And she wanted it now. "My turn."

Did it really happen? Lacey glanced behind her, just to make sure. Beyond the white linen curtains that were gently blowing in the breeze, she could see Quinn lying naked in bed, still fast asleep. Yes, it really happened. They'd made love. Sweet, sexy, beautiful, passionate love. She turned back around and relaxed into the patio chair, taking in the early morning air. The birds were out in full force, singing their morning songs. It was a perfect moment. One that Lacey wanted to burn into her memory and hold close forever.

Her heart felt almost full again. There was still an emptiness from losing her father that would never go away, but she'd been down this road before. She knew the pain would fade and life would go on, just like it had after she'd lost her mother. The difference between today and yesterday was that she felt excitement for the future. She wanted a future with Quinn, and it was definitely looking good on that front.

"Hey."

Lacey turned around and grinned from ear to ear. "Hey." Quinn was lying on her stomach, propped up on her elbows, looking all sexy with her messy blond hair and rosy cheeks.

"Should I get up or are you coming back to bed?"

Lacey stood up. "Oh, I'm definitely coming back to bed." She sauntered back into the room and untied her robe, letting it fall away behind her. She pushed Quinn onto her back and settled on top of her. "Good morning, beautiful."

"Good morning." Quinn ran her hands down Lacey's back and wrapped her legs around her, holding her close.

Lacey gently placed a kiss on her nose and cheeks. "Any regrets?"

"Only that I didn't stop you from going off with Dani that night in New York. I knew what I wanted and I should've shown more courage."

"Me? You wanted me?" Lacey teased.

"I wanted to be the one you leaned on. I wanted you to need me, not her."

"You," Lacey ran her finger over Quinn's soft lips, "are everything to me."

Quinn rolled them onto their sides and possessively wrapped her leg around Lacey. Her eyes raked over Lacey's body, her hand gently running up and down her torso. "It was everything I imagined it would be."

"Sex with a woman?"

"Sex...with you." Her hand came to rest over Lacey's belly button. "You're everything to me too, you know."

"So, you're not upset that you won't be able to sow your wild lesbian oats?"

Quinn pulled back. "What?"

"Oh, come on. I know you fantasized about dating L.A.'s finest."

Quinn rested her hand on Lacey's cheek. "I'm going to. She's lying right here with me."

Lacey squeezed her eyes shut, fighting back the tears. "That was a really good answer."

"Honey..." Quinn leaned in and gently kissed her lips. "Look at me." Lacey opened her eyes. Quinn wiped away a tear that was making its way down her cheek. "What can I say or do to make you believe I want this as much as you do?"

Lacey took Quinn's hand in hers and kissed it. "I don't know. I guess I just need some time to let it sink in...you know...that it's real. That your words and your kisses are real. And that you won't regret not dating Ginny Strong."

"Oh, God." Quinn held Lacey's face, forcing her to look her in the eye. "That's what you're worried about?"

Lacey hated feeling this insecure. She wanted to be strong and confident, but it worried her that Quinn had an obvious crush on someone else. "Kind of," she said under her breath.

"What if I shout it to the world that I want to date you and only you? And what if from now on, I always introduce you as my girlfriend? Would that help?"

"You would've anyway. That was the plan."

Quinn's hand slid lower. "This wasn't part of the plan."

"Mmm...no, it wasn't. Oh, God." Lacey's hips bucked.

Quinn entered the wet warmth with two fingers. "And this wasn't part of the plan."

"No." Lacey's eyes shuttered closed. "Definitely not." Quinn pushed in a little deeper. "Oh, God." Lacey opened her legs and lifted her hips. She needed this—for Quinn to be deep inside her. She needed the connection, and she didn't mind begging. "Fuck me, Quinn. Please."

"Tell me," Quinn urged as she pushed in harder. "Look at me and tell me you know this is real. That this is us. Not a contract. Not a sham."

Lacey covered Quinn's hand with her own, pushing it in deeper. She wanted to feel Quinn in her very core. She wanted to become one with her and create a bond that would never break. She opened her eyes and met Quinn's gaze. "I know."

Quinn didn't stop. Not until Lacey was writhing underneath her. Not until Lacey shouting Quinn's name echoed in the room as she climaxed. Only then did Quinn slowly remove her hand and wrap her arms around Lacey, burying her face in her long hair. "God, I love you. I love you so much. And I love saying it out loud."

CHAPTER THIRTY-TWO

L ace?" Quinn stepped into the guesthouse. "Hey, where's my girlfriend?" If the happy grin on Quinn's face was any indication, she loved saying that out loud as well.

"Bathroom!"

They'd had an amazing overnight stay in Napa, each of them posting a photo on Instagram before they left. Lacey's was a photo of Quinn, sitting across the table from her with the tagline—*Lucky me.*

The comments from fans were overwhelmingly positive, which was a huge relief to Quinn. They'd be shooting the final episode next week, followed by a two-month break. Everything had come together as planned. And then some.

"There you are." Quinn stepped up behind Lacey and kissed her shoulder, looking at her in the mirror. "Jack is stopping by in a few minutes."

"Jack? Why?"

"I'm not sure. He just asked that we both be here." Quinn looked around and noticed that Lacey still hadn't packed up her things. "When are you moving into the main house?"

Lacey tied off her braid and turned around, leaning on the bathroom sink. "I thought I'd work on it tonight."

Quinn stepped closer, tucking her finger into the waistband of Lacey's jeans. "Why the worried look?"

"I don't know…I guess I'm not sure you're going to enjoy sharing a closet with me. Or a bathroom. Or a house. Maybe I should stay out here for a while longer."

"You kept my house extremely tidy when I couldn't." Quinn tucked a loose strand of hair behind Lacey's ear. "I really don't think it's going to be a problem."

"I did that for you, because I knew it was what you expected."
Lacey lowered her gaze. "Can't I just keep my things out here? We
don't have to rush into this."

Quinn lifted Lacey's chin. "I know what I'm getting myself into.
I've imagined you stripping your clothes off at the side of the bed and
then crawling under the covers. Even right now, I know your toothbrush
is on one side of the sink and the toothpaste is on the other. It's fine."

"You've imagined that, huh?" Lacey sat on the counter and pulled
Quinn in between her legs. "What else have you imagined?"

"Waking up in your arms. I really want to wake up in your arms.
And I don't want you rushing out of our bedroom to get ready in the
morning. I want you right there with me in that big bathroom with the
double sinks." Quinn put her hands on Lacey's waist, caressing her
stomach with her thumbs.

She'd imagined touching Lacey like this so many times and had
kept herself from actually doing it on a daily basis. Little touches, like
when Lacey was making dinner and Quinn walked past her to get to the
fridge. She often wanted to stop and kiss her shoulder. Put a hand on her
hip and thank her for another incredible meal.

So many missed opportunities. But not anymore.

Lacey loosened a button on Quinn's blouse, revealing a little more
cleavage. "What about the closet, where everything is perfectly spaced
and the shoes are all shiny and all the bras have matching panties?"

"Why, Lacey Matthews, did you go rifling through my underwear
drawer when I was in the hospital?" Quinn joked, because when
Lacey said it like that, she felt embarrassed that her little world was so
structured and controlled.

Lacey's eyes were locked on Quinn's cleavage. "The only thing
I'm willing to admit right now is that I want to rip this blouse off
you." She leaned forward and pressed her lips against Quinn's neck.
"Mmm…you smell so good."

Quinn tilted her head back and put her hand on Lacey's head,
loving what those warm lips did to her insides. "You can rip it off
me later, if you want. In fact, I insist on it." She couldn't believe how
much she wanted Lacey. It had never been like that with her husband
or her previous boyfriends. Sex wasn't something she craved. Not
until Lacey.

Her phone rang and she pushed a button, letting Jack in the gate,
then tucked it back in her pocket. "Come on, honey. Let's get this
meeting over with." She pulled Lacey's face to hers and kissed her,

letting their tongues touch. She pulled away before Lacey could deepen the kiss. "Promise me you'll move in with me tonight."

Lacey buttoned Quinn's shirt back up. "Let's go talk to Jack, and then you can beg me to move in with you. Which, of course, will turn me on. And then…"

Quinn pulled Lacey off the counter. "You are such a pain in my ass. Let's go talk to Jack." She slapped Lacey's butt and pushed her out of the bathroom.

So many times, Lacey had imagined walking arm in arm with Quinn, the way they were right now. How many times had they walked along this beautiful swimming pool from the house to the guesthouse, and vice versa, never touching one another? Keeping a safe distance between them? She pushed her hand a little deeper into Quinn's back pocket. "Does it feel different with me?"

"What do you mean?"

"Well, you've only been in relationships with men, so I'm just wondering if it feels different."

Quinn smiled, a look of contentment washing over her face. "It's hard to describe how I feel right now. Blissful is probably pretty accurate. Validated—that I was right about my sexuality. And proud of myself for taking this huge risk. It's certainly paid off handsomely."

"Are you calling me handsome?" Lacey joked.

"Uh-oh." Quinn stopped at the open sliding glass door. "Jack doesn't look happy," she mumbled through her teeth. She stepped into the house and greeted him with a bright smile. "Hey, Jack! Your usual?"

Jack stopped pacing by the sofa. "That would be fine." He eyed Lacey closely as she walked into the room. She furrowed her brow, wondering why he was looking at her that way.

Quinn pulled three beers out of the fridge and slid one across the kitchen island for Jack. She opened one for Lacey and handed it to her, then opened her own and took a sip while keeping her hand on Lacey's back. Jack took a sip, his eyes focusing on Quinn's hand that was now wrapped around Lacey's hip. He set his beer down and said, "If you two are really together now, this is going to be worse than I thought."

Quinn glanced at Lacey and grinned, which caused Lacey to grin so hard she almost giggled. "We are," Quinn confirmed. "No more faking it." She turned her attention back to Jack. "Now, what the hell are you talking about?"

He set his stare on Lacey. "I got a call from your ex-girlfriend. She has a story to tell and she's going to start telling it if you don't take her calls."

Lacey's smile faded. "Dani? What story?"

"What story?" Jack repeated, incredulously. "Are you really going to deny telling her all about our little agreement?"

Lacey shook her head in confusion. "What? I didn't. She couldn't possibly know."

All the happiness drained from Quinn's face. She removed her hand from Lacey's body and moved away, out of arm's reach.

Lacey's face paled. "Quinn..." She swallowed hard, her throat constricting. Getting no reaction from Quinn besides an angry glare, she turned to Jack. "What did she tell you?"

Jack ignored Lacey and kept his eyes on Quinn. "I don't think I need to tell you how bad this could get."

"No," Quinn said. "I'm very aware."

Lacey put up her hands. "Wait! Both of you, just stop! I didn't tell Dani a damn thing! Whatever she's saying, it's bullshit!"

"She knows how much you've been paid. She knows WHY you've been paid. That's not exactly bullshit, Lacey." Jack's jaw flexed, he was so angry. "And as of this moment, I am no longer your publicist. My only concern right now, is helping Quinn."

Lacey's head was spinning. "She couldn't possibly..." She grabbed her head, trying to remember if in her state of grief over the death of her father, she'd shared details she shouldn't have. It didn't seem possible, but the night she left the hotel with Dani was all kind of a big blur.

"Get out," Quinn said, her voice low and hard. Her arms were folded tightly and her eyes were on the floor.

Lacey turned to her. "What?"

Quinn's face was turning red and her eyes were burning with tears. Lacey made a move toward her, but Quinn put up her hand. "Don't." She took another step backward.

"Don't do this, Quinn. Not after..."

Quinn finally met her gaze, her eyes filled with anger. "How could you?" she growled, her teeth clenched.

"I didn't! That's what I'm trying to tell you!" Lacey took another step toward Quinn but stopped, her chest deflating. "I haven't betrayed you. I love you."

Lacey was trying to remain calm. She desperately wanted to tear into Jack for his false accusations and for dumping her like trash. But that wouldn't help her case with Quinn. And Quinn was the only thing that mattered right now. "Please, Quinn. Let me find out what's going on. Let me talk to Dani. I've been ignoring her calls after what she did, dragging me to Times Square, but I'll call her. I'll fix this. Just…don't shut me out."

"That doesn't change the fact that she already knows." Jack said, behind her. "And I can guarantee you, someone will pay her a lot of money for this story. Damnit, Lacey, why—"

Lacey whipped around. "Shut up, Jack! You're not helping!"

"He's right," Quinn said. "You broke the nondisclosure agreement. Not to mention my trust. And God knows what she'll do with it. Blackmail me, maybe? Or you? She sounds like a real peach, this girlfriend of yours."

"Oh, God! This again? We're going to fight about Dani?" Lacey cringed at her own words. "I'm sorry. That was…"

Any tears that were in Quinn's eyes had dried up. There was only contempt there as she stared Lacey down. "I guess this explains why she was so arrogant at the funeral, calling you the mother of her children. She knew all along that we were in a fake relationship."

Lacey's world was crashing down around her and she was helpless to stop it. She sucked back her emotions, but a tear still managed to fall. She quickly wiped it away. "Do you really want me to leave?" Quinn didn't say anything. "You have to say it." Lacey ventured a step toward her, whispering, "Quinn, I love you."

She got a hand on Quinn's arm, but it was quickly snatched away. "Just go." Lacey didn't move. "Go!" Quinn shouted.

Lacey managed to get outside before the tears really started. She ran to the guesthouse, and once inside, she grabbed her head and paced around, wondering what the hell to do. She was being kicked out again. Everything they'd shared the last few days—Quinn was just going to throw it all away. Pretend it never happened. So, what—they'd go back to being business associates? Was that even possible? How were they supposed to keep working together?

Lacey didn't have the answers, but she knew that trying to stay in Quinn's house against her will wouldn't solve anything. So she packed an overnight bag, grabbed her keys, and went out the side gate. She got to her Range Rover and stopped. She looked at her keys and then gently set them on the hood of the car. She walked out the gate on foot and called for a car.

❖

Jack watched her go and then sat on the sofa next to Quinn. "There are only three people who know the kind of detail Dani gave me, and two of us are sitting here."

"I know." Quinn hadn't moved much. She was in a state of shock, unable to even comprehend the betrayal that had just been exposed. She couldn't cry, she couldn't yell. She didn't want to feel anything yet. Half an hour ago, she'd been basking in her belief that she'd found real, honest, deep love with Lacey. The kind she'd always longed for. She was ready to stop living her life alone behind those big gates, keeping everyone at arm's length. She was so ready to live out loud and let the world see how happy she was.

That was gone now. In the blink of an eye, it was all gone.

Jack wrung his hands together. "I'm sorry for the things I said the other day—encouraging you to give Lacey a chance. I was wrong about her. Wrong from the beginning, I guess."

"How do we contain this, Jack? If this gets out…" Quinn gasped for air and covered her mouth with her hands, the fear of what could happen hitting her full force. "I brought her on my show. If the producers find out, they'll think I planned the whole thing from the beginning."

"You couldn't fake a broken arm. Surely they'll get that." Jack rubbed his forehead, trying to come up with a plan.

Quinn stared at the front door. A part of her wanted Lacey to walk through it. Yes, she'd yell at her for being so stupid, but at least she'd be in the room. Quinn doubled over herself, wrapping her arms around her stomach, which was roiling so hard she felt like she would vomit.

"We need Lacey to contain this. It can't get out. Period," Jack said. He pulled Quinn up off the sofa. "She's on the road, waiting for a taxi. Go talk to her. Tell her she has to do whatever it takes to keep this under wraps."

Quinn stared at the door again but didn't move.

"Look," Jack said. "Lacey's a hell of an actor, but she's not that good. From what I just saw, I'd say she's really in love with you."

"Does that even matter now?" Quinn couldn't hold back the tears. She wiped her eyes, but they just kept falling. And then, without any forewarning, a violent rage boiled up inside her. She lunged for a vase sitting on the coffee table and with all her might, she threw it against the wall. "Aaagh!" she screamed as the pain ripped through her arm.

Jack tried to grab her, but she pushed him away. Her eyes were full of fury as she stared him down. "You too," she growled out. "Get out of my house."

Jack reached for her again. "Quinn…"

"No. You did this, Jack. You and your STUPID ideas!" She balled up her fists and yelled as loud as she could, "GET THE FUCK OUT OF MY HOUSE!"

Jack put his hands up. "Okay. I'm going." He got in his car and sat there, trying to come up with a solution he could take back inside to Quinn. A plan of some sort. After a while, he gave up and drove away.

Lacey opened the hotel room door, looking less than pleased to see her guest.

"Thanks for seeing me."

"Do I have a choice?" She closed the door and leaned against the wall with her arms folded. Jack could say whatever he needed to say, and then she could go back to the bottle of whiskey sitting on the bedside table.

"I don't know who looks worse, you or me," Jack joked. Lacey didn't laugh. Of course she didn't laugh. Her whole life had just been blown up. Again.

"Look," he said. "I know I could've handled that a lot better."

Ya think, Jack? "Let me guess. Quinn fired you." Lacey sat on the bed and poured two fingers into a glass. She offered it to Jack. He sat on the other bed and downed it in one gulp.

"I don't know yet. She kicked me out before we could talk about options."

"Options," Lacey scoffed, and took a sip of her own drink. "At least you have some."

"How did this happen, Lacey? Why would you break the contract?"

God. Jack still thought she'd purposely broken the contract. After everything—months of being right by Quinn's side, helping her heal. Saving her goddamned show—because even if Quinn couldn't admit it, her ratings had been dipping. Even after all of that, neither of them had a single ounce of faith in her.

"I want nothing more than to go back to New York and figure that out, Jack. But we start shooting the season finale tomorrow." She downed the rest of her drink and wiped her mouth with the back of her hand. "I can't go anywhere. Not yet."

"What do you mean, you want to figure it out? Are you saying you really didn't tell Dani?"

Tears welled up in her eyes. She tried to blink them away. "I would never betray Quinn like that." Just the thought of it made her want to vomit. She put her hand on her stomach and slowly breathed out, letting the wave of nausea pass. "I have no idea how Dani found out. I only saw her…" Lacey met Jack's gaze. "Oh, God." She stood up. "Oh, God."

"What?" Jack also stood up. "Tell me."

Lacey's eyes searched the room for answers. "She must've seen the contract in my suitcase." Realizing it was her own fault, she sat back down. "God, that must be it."

Jack sat next to her, putting his hand on her forearm. "What, Lacey? Tell me."

"Quinn was questioning whether or not I should stay in the guesthouse. She thought maybe I should move out before everything was set into motion—with the show—with us. I got angry." Lacey covered her mouth with her hands, realizing this was the only explanation.

"What happened after that?" Jack asked.

"I packed everything up and went back to New York. I needed to rent out my apartment and I asked Dani to stop by and pick up some of the things she'd left behind." Lacey turned and looked Jack in the eye. "The rental agent came by at the same time. I was with him for an hour while Dani was in the bedroom, packing up her things. That has to be it. She must've gone through my suitcase."

Jack seemed to breathe a sigh of relief, but the look on his face told Lacey he was still angry with her. It was careless. She knew it was careless. "You have to call her," Jack implored. "You have to contain this. It can't get out."

"Do you believe me?" Lacey desperately needed someone to believe her, even if it was her fault. "Will Quinn believe me?"

"I don't know. She's locked herself up in that big house and won't take my calls."

Lacey picked up her phone. "I should call her."

"No, you shouldn't." Jack took the phone and set it back on the table. "Let her calm down. You'll see her on the set tomorrow."

Lacey's eyes widened. "We can't wait until we're in a public place to figure this out!"

"Yes, you can. Quinn is a consummate professional. What you

need to focus on is containing your ex-girlfriend. Tell her that you'll go and see her as soon as you can. Keep her quiet, Lacey."

Lacey huffed at that. "Pardon me if I don't trust your advice anymore, Jack."

"You're still under contract. That hasn't changed. You're Quinn's fake girlfriend for a few more months, whether you like it or not. So, how about you use those acting chops you're so proud of? Convince everyone that everything is just peachy and we might get through this in one piece."

Lacey couldn't believe what she was hearing. "My father just died! And the woman I love just dumped me! And my ex-girlfriend is blackmailing me! And you want me to..." Lacey's expression went from complete disbelief to understanding. "Oh. You want me to save your sorry ass because this was all your fucking idea. Is that it, Jack?"

Jack headed for the door. He went to open it and then stopped and turned around. "Save Quinn. If you really love her, then save her."

CHAPTER THIRTY-THREE

Lacey hadn't slept. And she couldn't convince her legs to get out of the car and walk into the studio. She hadn't seen any of these people since her father's death. Or since Quinn had sent that tweet, outing them to the whole world. She imagined everyone would want to express their condolences first, followed by their congratulations on her relationship with Quinn.

Fuck, what was she going to do? "Get your shit together," she whispered to herself. *And keep it together.*

The last episode had been kept a secret, so she didn't even know what to expect. Would she have to kiss Quinn? Perform another love scene? She couldn't do it. She'd break down in the middle of the scene. Cry her eyes out right then and there. Beg Quinn for forgiveness in front of everyone.

She couldn't do it.

Just as she was putting the car in reverse, Amy opened her door. Her eyes scanned the car, but she didn't question why Lacey was driving a rental, thank God. "Hey. They've already started the table read. Quinn was worried. She sent me to find you."

"She…did?"

"Yeah. I have a cart. Come on."

It was slow going, but Lacey collected her things and locked up her car. She sat next to Amy and held on tight, knowing Amy would take the corners at full speed.

"How are you doing?" Amy asked. "Quinn said you two had a wonderful time in Napa."

God. Apparently, Quinn was already in full-on acting mode. Lacey forced a smile. "Yeah, it was great."

"Good. You needed it after…you know." Amy looked at her and frowned. "Sorry for bringing it up."

"It's okay." Lacey grabbed her stomach as they raced around the last corner and lurched to a stop. She took a breath, trying to fight the nausea she'd had all morning.

"You look gray. Are you sure you're okay? I didn't drive too fast, did I?"

Amy was such a sweetheart, Lacey couldn't do anything but smile. "Would you mind getting me a cup of tea for the reading? Nice and hot?"

"Sure. Give me your stuff and I'll put it in Quinn's trailer."

Lacey handed over her tote bag. She took a deep breath and let it out slowly as she walked into the studio. Some of the crew were there, milling around. A few of them greeted her with a gentle hug and offered their condolences. She managed not to cry.

By the time she reached the conference room, her lip was quivering but she held strong as she opened the door. Everyone went silent as they turned and looked at her. She forced a smile. "Hey, everyone. Thanks for delaying so I could bury my father." She had to get the words out fast or she wouldn't be able to say them at all.

"Of course." Dan stood up and gave her a hug. "Quinn said it was a beautiful tribute to a good man. I'm sorry we all couldn't be there for you."

All Lacey could do was nod and hope she could hold it together. The only empty seat was the one next to Quinn. She couldn't look at her. Not yet. Not until she was seated could she look Quinn in the eye. And really, not even then. She kept her eyes on the script sitting in front of her, but she could feel everyone's eyes on her. She took a quick look around the table. All familiar faces, except one. A pretty girl with short brown hair sat across from her. The girl smiled when their eyes met. Lacey quickly looked away.

And then, she felt the tug of Quinn's arm as it wrapped around her shoulder and pulled her close. And soft lips gently kissing her temple. And two words spoken in her ear. "Hey, babe."

Babe. Definitely not something Quinn had ever called her before. The arm wrapped around her shoulder felt real. The kiss felt real. But that pet name—not real.

Lacey kept her eyes down. "Hey." She still couldn't look at Quinn. Didn't want to look at Quinn. Because then, she'd know for sure how fake this little scene was.

Everyone quickly got back to business. A few minutes in, Lacey was relieved to see that there would be no love scenes. Not even a kiss. And it turned out that the pretty girl sitting across the table from her would be playing Selena's ex-girlfriend. They were going to end the season with a great big cliffhanger, which everyone was excited about. Everyone, except Quinn, it seemed.

Even though she was only using her peripheral vision, Lacey could tell Quinn's expression hadn't changed much through the read. Just a hint of a smile to placate everyone, Lacey imagined.

She couldn't take it anymore. Lacey had to look. She had to see Quinn's eyes, even though she didn't think she'd find anything real there. She waited until everyone was preoccupied with a story Dan was telling, and then she slowly turned her head. Quinn was looking at Dan, but her gaze fell to the table, and then slowly to Lacey.

Pain. Pain, pain, pain. That's all Lacey saw. She couldn't help herself. She reached for Quinn's hand and held it tight. *I didn't betray you*, she wanted to scream. *I love you!*

But the moment was lost. Chairs were pushed out and jokes were made. J.J. made his way over to them, and Quinn pulled her hand away.

"We're on a tight schedule because of the delay, so we're going to go ahead and shoot some scenes today. I hope you got the message?" They both nodded and he put his hand on Lacey's shoulder. "I lost my dad last year, so I know what you're goin' through, kid. Just hang in there and eventually, the pain will subside."

Lacey gave him a grateful smile. "Thanks, J.J. Someday, you'll have to tell me about your dad."

"We'll hang out and do just that," he said with a wink. "Thank God you have Quinn to hold you up. My wife was my saving grace that day, and every day since."

Lacey pursed her lips together, trying to fight back the tears. She gave him a quick nod, and luckily, he walked away before the first tear fell. Quinn's hand landed on her knee, but she pushed it away. "You don't have to do that," she said, standing up.

"Lace."

Lacey looked at her. She saw empathy in those ice blue eyes. She didn't need empathy. Her dad was dead, so fucking what? That hadn't mattered to Quinn yesterday when she kicked her out.

"I know this is all just for show. I'll do my part." Lacey rushed out of the room, tears streaming down her face. She needed to get somewhere private, and fast. She couldn't go to Quinn's trailer. She couldn't go to the dressing room she shared with three other people. She turned a corner and saw a door. Having no idea where it went, she pushed through it and landed in an alley. An empty alley. She wanted to scream out the pain and sob until she had no more tears left, but that would bring unwanted attention. She slid down the wall, landing on her butt, and covered her face with her hands. Silent tears would have to do.

Amy opened the trailer door. "Found her! She's in the back alley where people take their smoke breaks."

Quinn took off her reading glasses and stood up.

"She's crying, Quinn. Hard."

Quinn pushed past her and Amy followed on her heels. The new girl was headed toward the door with a pack of cigarettes in her hand. Quinn stopped her. "Hey, can I have one of those?"

Amy watched in horror as the new girl gave Quinn a cigarette and also her lighter. "Oh, God," Amy whispered. "Everything's going to hell in a handbasket."

Quinn lit the cigarette and handed the lighter back to the girl. "Don't be so dramatic, Amy. And make sure we have some privacy."

Quinn pushed the heavy door open, and Amy stood in front of it, blocking the new girl. "Sorry. It's going to be a minute." The girl rolled her eyes and walked away.

Quinn leaned against the wall and took a long drag and then another. "Thanks for showing up today. I don't know how I would've been able to explain what's happened—after I'd lied all morning, telling them everything is great."

It had been a hellish morning, dealing with everyone's questions about their new, budding relationship. Quinn had lied through her teeth over and over, and when Lacey finally walked through the door, a huge sense of relief washed over her because at least now she wouldn't be alone in the lie anymore.

It was such a mixed bag of emotions she was feeling. Her love for Lacey hadn't diminished. Only her trust. And yet, somehow that was still there, to an extent. Even after the big betrayal, she had a feeling that Lacey would come through for her, and she had been right.

"Since when do you smoke?" Lacey asked, keeping her eyes on her shaky hands.

"I used to smoke. It was a stupid kid thing. Defying the parents bullshit. I quit years ago." Quinn flicked the ashes and offered it to Lacey.

"No, thanks." Lacey laid her head back against the wall. Her eyes were red and puffy. Too red to work, Quinn thought. She wondered what the hell they'd do about that. Laura was good, but she wasn't that good.

"I guess this was always the risk, wasn't it? Someone finding out the truth?" Quinn paused long enough to take another drag. "I never should've listened to Jack."

"We both knew it was a shitstorm just waiting to happen."

Quinn chuckled and then coughed. "God. Now I remember why I quit." She flicked the cigarette away.

Lacey pushed herself up the wall and brushed off her butt. "Let's get this stupid episode over with."

Quinn reached for her arm, her hand sliding down to Lacey's wrist. "And then what?"

"I'm going back to New York. I still have to deal with my dad's apartment. And…Dani."

"She had flings," Quinn said, keeping hold of Lacey's wrist. "Dani admitted it to me at the funeral. She hasn't been pining away for you all this time. It's all just a game with her." Quinn didn't want Lacey getting back with Dani, just to keep her quiet. There had to be a better way. She just hadn't come up with it yet.

"I never thought she was pining away for me, Quinn. She broke up with *me*, remember?"

"I'm just saying…"

Lacey pulled her hand away. "I don't know what your point is, but as long as we're giving each other advice on love, you should probably know that Ginny Strong kissed me. Yeah, she took me outside at Nobu and laid one right on me."

What the hell? "You said it was a French actress who kissed you."

"I lied. I didn't want it to be a big deal. And then you revealed your true feelings for her, so I couldn't really tell you, now could I?"

Fuck. That cut a little too deep. If Lacey was trying to hurt Quinn, she'd just succeeded. "What else have you lied about?"

"Fuck you, Quinn." Lacey made a move to leave, but she stopped suddenly and pushed Quinn up against the wall, holding her there by the arms. "I never lied to you about anything else. All I did was take care of you. I saw to your every need, and I was loyal. And then I fell in love with you. You're the one who fucked it up, Quinn. And now, you get to live with it."

Quinn winced. "My arm, Lace. You're hurting my arm."

Lacey immediately let go and backed up. Her chest was heaving, her expression one of anger and regret. "You don't get to throw me away, Quinn. Not so easily, as if I never meant anything to you. It makes you no different than Dani. And it means I can't trust you to let me make whatever sin I've committed, right." Lacey sucked in air, feeling like she was going to hyperventilate. "You have no idea the damage you've done. I didn't even know it until right this second."

"I was hurt." Quinn reached for her, but Lacey stepped out of her reach. "You told Dani about us, for God's sake."

Lacey shook her head. "No, I didn't. She dug through my suitcase and found the contract. And why was the contract in my suitcase in New York? Because you'd decided my moving out might be a good idea. Just toss me aside whenever you damn well feel like it."

Quinn crumpled against the wall. "I'm sorry."

"I'm sure you are. And so am I, about all of this. I never should've…" Lacey sucked in air. "I never should've let myself feel something for you. I should've stuck to the contract. No romantic interactions. No sex. Fuck!" Lacey kicked a coffee can that people had used as an ashtray. They both silently watched the ashes fly.

"Lace." Quinn finally found her voice, not sure what to say next.

"No." Lacey turned back around. "I'll fulfill the terms of the contract. We can pretend we're together for a while longer, but then we're done. You think you can't trust me? Well, guess what…I can't trust you, either."

Quinn tried to reach for her again. "Lace, just give me a second." This couldn't be the end of them. God, why did Quinn have to react so harshly? Why was her first reaction in any stressful situation to push people as far away as possible? Make them feel worthless?

"My father died." Lacey glared at her with a look so full of pain, it crushed Quinn. "I have no one now. Did you not consider what losing you so soon after losing him would do to me?"

Quinn went pale. "I'm sorry," she whispered.

"Sorry isn't good enough." Lacey opened the door. It slammed shut behind her.

❖

Lacey stood on her mark and adjusted her blazer. J.J. stood in front of her. "Laura performed her magic. You look great," he reassured her.

"She's a miracle worker." Lacey's hair was pulled back in a tight ponytail and she was wearing her black glasses—Laura's solution to the bloodshot eyes.

"Let's roll, people!"

J.J. sat in his chair in front of the monitor and waited for the marker. "And action!"

Selena stepped up to Jordan's assistant's desk. "Is she here? I got a text saying she didn't need a ride this morning."

Lisa pointed at her own arm. "The cast came off today. She's like a new woman, I swear. I mean, when does she ever get me coffee when she gets her own?"

"Never?" Selena guessed as she stared into Jordan's office.

"Until today. I almost fell off my chair."

The door opened and an older gentleman walked out with Jordan right behind him. "Thanks for the heads-up, Jordan. I owe you one."

"And you know I always collect, Jim."

Lisa stood up. "I'll walk you out, Mr. Jensen."

Jordan watched them until they were out of sight. "My office, Selena." She walked back into her office. "Close the door, please."

"So, no more cast?" Selena asked, shutting the door behind her.

"Just the sling. And only if my arm gets tired." Jordan stood behind her desk, looking pensive. "Selena..."

"Can I talk first?" Selena asked.

Jordan nodded.

"The other night shouldn't have happened. I know that."

Jordan shook her head. "No, it shouldn't have."

"But it did. And it was amazing. And when I got your text this morning..."

"Selena, stop." Jordan held on to her desk with her fingertips to steady herself. "I apologize for what happened between us. You're my employee and it was highly inappropriate of me to behave in such a manner."

"You regret it?" Selena asked, barely above a whisper. "You regret sleeping with me?"

Jordan remained stoic, her head held high. "I regret putting either of us in that position."

"You didn't," Selena said, taking a step forward. "I kissed *you.* I'm the one who started it."

"Stop." Jordan's gaze fell to her desk. "Our time together is over. I won't be needing your services anymore."

Selena frowned. "So, that's it? That's all you have to say to me?"

Jordan looked up. "I hope you consider it time well spent." Her voice was softer now. "I hope you come away from this having learned something."

"Yes," Selena said. "I learned that Jordan Ellis thinks I'm disposable."

"Selena!" Jordan shouted as her office door slammed shut.

"And cut! Perfect, ladies. One more scene and we're done! Let's move, people!"

J.J. noticed that Quinn hadn't moved. She was standing dead still behind Jordan's desk, staring straight ahead. He followed her line of sight and caught Lacey just as she turned into the dressing room. "You okay, Quinn?" He walked up to her and stood on the other side of the desk. "Your hair needs to be down for the next scene."

Quinn's eyes met his, but she still hadn't moved. "Yeah. Okay."

Quinn never went into the dressing rooms. She always changed in her trailer. That was why every head turned when she walked in. Everyone's except Lacey's. She was chatting in the corner with the new girl.

Amy walked up to Quinn. "You're in casual wear for the next scene. Well, casual for Jordan."

Quinn kept her eyes on Lacey. "Where's the outfit?"

"In your trailer, like always."

She watched as Lacey took off her clothes in front of everyone. God, that body. The things she did to that body in Napa. She wondered if Lacey remembered that she had a small love bite on her stomach, right next to her belly button. *I did that.*

"Lace?" Her voice wasn't working very well. It came out as more of a whisper. No one heard her but Amy.

"Lacey!" Amy said a little louder.

Lacey turned and looked. She put up a finger and then put her T-shirt and jeans on. She walked over barefoot. "What's up?"

Amy turned to Quinn. "I'll go get your clothes."

Quinn reached for Lacey's hand, holding on to one finger—just enough for some contact without forcing the issue. "I get it," she whispered, barely able to hold back the tears. Lacey's words in the alley, and the scene they'd just performed, had cut Quinn to the core. She knew how deeply she'd hurt Lacey. She also knew there might not be any coming back from it, but she had to try.

Before Quinn could say anything else, one of the hairdressers was pulling her away. "Sorry, but I need Quinn. We have to get that hair down."

"Don't leave," Quinn said. "Please."

Lacey didn't reply. She just stared at Quinn as she was being pulled away.

CHAPTER THIRTY-FOUR

D id you find her?"
Amy shook her head.

"Shit." Quinn pinched the bridge of her nose and willed herself to calm down. The last scene didn't require much acting on her part, but she couldn't look as anxious as she felt. Lacey hadn't stayed like she'd asked her to, and she wasn't answering Quinn's text messages. "Are they ready? What's the holdup?"

"Trouble with the cat. They're bringing in a different one." Amy eyed Quinn's shaking hands. She sat down next to her and put her hand on her knee. "Maybe you could tell me what's really going on between you and Lacey?"

Quinn stood up, needing space. She was wearing dark trousers, a turtleneck sweater, and boots when it was seventy-five degrees outside. She wanted to rip the clothes off and go running naked through the lot, screaming at the top of her lungs, that's how wound up she was. She went to run her fingers through her loose hair, but Amy shouted, "AH! Don't ruin your hair!"

She was stuck there, helpless, and Lacey was probably getting on a flight to New York, since her scenes had been shot already. Lacey was done for the season but Quinn still had at least three more days of work.

She had so much to say. So many apologies to make. So many hugs and kisses to give. So many professions of her love. *Real* love.

Was it too late?

She didn't know.

And it was killing her.

A loud knock on the door made them both jump. "We need you in five!" someone shouted.

Amy stood up. "It looks like they found a cat."

"Amy?" Quinn couldn't believe these words were about to come out of her mouth. "Can you drive me home tonight? I need…" *Just say it. Let someone in. It's time. It's long overdue. Stop hiding.* "I need to tell you everything."

"And action!"

The apartment door opened and Jordan quickly dropped the bouquet of flowers to her side, hiding them behind her back. "I'm sorry, I think I must have the wrong apartment."

"Jordan Ellis, right?" The woman picked up her cat, and that's when Jordan's eyes narrowed in on the beautiful gold watch on the woman's wrist.

"Cut! Okay, let's get a close-up of the cat and the watch." J.J. stood behind Quinn and helped her remove her overcoat. "All done for the day, kid."

Quinn turned around and gave J.J. a tight hug. She held on for longer than she normally would. "Thank you, J.J."

"It's gonna be a great ending to a great season, and this show isn't goin' anywhere."

Quinn pulled away and nodded. "I know. Everyone killed it. We should have a nice cast party. Maybe at my house?"

J.J.'s mouth fell open. "I'd love to see your new digs. Lacey said you did an incredible job on the renovation."

Guilt tugged at Quinn's heart. She'd kept everyone at a distance for so long. That needed to change. "I'll get Amy to plan something fun. We'll include the kids too. I have a huge pool that needs to be played in."

"Sounds fun!" Amy said, walking up to them and taking Quinn's coat. "Let's go, hon. I've ordered some fabulous Indian food for dinner."

Amy twirled a lock of her blond curly hair as she paced barefoot by the pool. "That bitch!" she exclaimed for the third time. "I knew I didn't like her the minute I saw her at the funeral."

"Do you want to take these leftover samosas home to Trent?" Quinn held up the plate.

Amy waved her off. "Nah, he hates Indian food."

Quinn leaned back in her chair and sipped on her wine. It felt good to tell someone the whole, sordid story. She felt a little lighter. And Amy was such a good listener, asking questions but not judging.

"So that's why you wanted to smoke this morning?" Amy didn't wait for an answer. "I guess it makes sense. I mean, I think I'd probably want to kill myself if I literally had Lacey Matthews in my bed and then I fucked it up."

So much for not judging. "Aren't you straight, Amy?"

She stopped pacing. "I'm fluid."

"Fluid?" Quinn asked with a chuckle. "What the hell is fluid?"

"Fluid, Quinn. It depends on the person."

Quinn put up her hands in defeat. "Okay. You're fluid."

Amy sat down and leaned on the table, suddenly looking very serious. "Is Lacey a wonderful lover? She is, isn't she?"

Quinn groaned. "I can't talk about that."

"You can," Amy said with an encouraging nod. "You really can."

Maybe she could say a few things. No details, of course. "Napa was wonderful. So romantic. So different than it ever was for me with a man. It felt right, you know? Just...so right." Amy looked like a hungry puppy dog, waiting for another treat. Quinn chuckled. "Okay, yes. Lacey is...sexy and passionate and..." Quinn sighed as a feeling of euphoria washed over her. "Yeah, she's goddamned amazing in bed."

Amy clapped her hands in excitement. "I knew it." Her expression fell when Quinn buried her face in her hands and started to cry. "Shit."

It had been one of the longest flights of her life. The woman sitting next to Lacey had talked through most of the flight to New York, leaving her feeling even more exhausted than she already was. She desperately needed a bed and a good night's sleep.

Her phone beeped several times after powering back up. Texts from Quinn.

Where are you?

I was hoping we could talk.

Please call me.

She couldn't stay at the studio like Quinn had asked. Her brain and her heart were both running on overload, lights flashing red, warning of imminent failure. What she really needed was time to think things through. The woman sitting next to her had prevented that, along with the nap she'd hoped to take.

And then there was Dani. What the hell was she going to do about

Dani? Lacey didn't have the first clue how to handle it. She could worry about that tomorrow. Right now, she needed to find a bed and catch up on some much-needed sleep.

Lacey turned the key and paused before she opened the door to her dad's apartment, trying to brace herself for the onslaught of emotions that were sure to hit her full force. The scent would hit her first. It was a unique mixture of her father's cologne and the old, rare books he collected. Spicy and musty.

The photos would be next. Family. Lacey's life. Daria Matthews.

She opened the door and kept her head down—eyes on the floor. She dropped her suitcase and found the nearest chair. It was too late at night to fall on her knees and wail at God again for leaving her parentless. It would disturb the neighbors. She huddled at the small dining table, afraid to lift her gaze.

And then she saw it—the letter she'd written to her dad after his funeral. It was sitting on the table, right where she'd left it a week ago. She slid a shaky hand across the table and pulled it to her.

Dear Dad,

No, she shouldn't read it. Not tonight. Not when she felt so broken inside. But then, a name popped off the paper, about halfway down the first page. *Quinn.*

Lacey gripped the paper with both hands.

Dear Dad,
You're gone. I hope you're not sad about that. I hope you and Mom are dancing together the way you used to. I hope you're happy again.
We celebrated your life today. Some of your students were there. They cried right along with me. They said you were their favorite professor. Not just a teacher, but also a friend. I already knew that about you, but it was nice to hear.
I can't really function right now, but I'll try to get back on my feet. I know you would want that for me. You always pushed me to do my best and be my best. I'll keep trying to honor your memory.

Quinn is here with me. I lied to you about her. I guess we both lied to each other about certain things. I'll forgive you if you'll forgive me. Scratch that. I forgive you, Dad. I miss you so much. Life is pretty terrible without you right now. I mentioned that Quinn is here with me. I think I'm in love with her. She's everything, Dad. And I know it's a lofty goal, but I really think we could have a love like you and Mama had. I just have to say those words out loud. But it's scary.

Lacey folded the letter up. She couldn't read anymore. She laid her head on the table and closed her eyes.

Quinn didn't want to move. She stared at the curtains blowing in the breeze, not even caring that she'd left the guesthouse door open all night. It reminded her of that morning in Napa, when she woke up and saw Lacey sitting just beyond the curtains. "Am I getting up, or are you coming back to bed," she whispered.

Of course, there would be no reply this time.

After she'd seen Amy to her car, Quinn had wandered back to the guesthouse, longing to feel closer to Lacey. Some of her things were still there. Most of them, actually. She'd torn off her own shirt and bra and put on one of Lacey's T-shirts. Then she'd fallen into her bed and hadn't moved until her alarm went off.

That was fifteen minutes ago.

She needed to get up and get to work. She checked her phone again, just in case Lacey had texted back in the last three minutes.

"Give her time," Amy had said. "Let her sort this thing out with Dani. She'll call if she needs you."

That was Quinn's fear; that Lacey wouldn't ever call. She sat up and put her feet on the floor, the pain and regret hitting her hard again. She grabbed Lacey's pillow and held it tightly, breathing in the remnants of her scent.

Lacey zipped up her coat, trying to keep the wind out. She had her dad's Yankees cap on her head and sunglasses covering her eyes. She didn't want to take the chance of being recognized. Not today.

She waited, impatiently, on their favorite bench in Central Park.

She didn't want to have this conversation in a coffee shop, in case it got ugly. She hoped it wouldn't come to that today, but Dani wasn't known for her discretion. She wasn't known for her punctuality, either.

Lacey was just about to send a where-the-hell-are-you text when she saw Dani's feet. She looked up, but didn't smile. "Thanks for meeting me here."

"Let's walk. I need a coffee." Dani gave Lacey a sideways glance as they walked. "It looks like you're hiding from the world."

Lacey pulled the faux fur hood up over her baseball cap. "I am."

Dani threaded her arm through Lacey's. "It's good to see you."

"Is it? Because you're blackmailing me, Dani. You're ruining my life again. Taking away my livelihood. Not to mention your inexplicable actions last week on the day of my father's funeral. How could you possibly think this is a friendly visit?"

"You're right. I shouldn't have asked you to marry me on such a painful day."

Lacey let out a cynical laugh. "Could you imagine ever being able to celebrate our engagement anniversary? Yay! My father died on this day two years ago, three years ago, four years ago..." Lacey yanked her arm away. "I don't even know who you are anymore."

God, how did it get to this point? Dani was Lacey's heart and soul at one time. Her beginning, and the person she thought would be her middle and end too. Now she barely recognized the person walking next to her. "Why, Dani? Why do you want to ruin me? Is it one of those 'if I can't have you, no one can' things?"

"I'm not trying to ruin you. How is that considered ruining you? I just want us to be who we were always meant to be. A family. Parents. Grandparents, one day."

Lacey shook her head in disbelief. Was Dani really this dense? And how had she missed it all this time? Had Dani's academic intelligence overshadowed her emotional immaturity? "And what do I tell our children when they ask about our wedding? Mama held a gun to Mommy's head? Blackmailed her?"

Dani stopped and grabbed Lacey's sleeve. "You tell our children that Mama was so in love with Mommy, she'd do anything to keep her."

Lacey's whole body tensed up. It was like talking to a psychopath. "No. Mama dumped Mommy, remember? She didn't do a damn thing to keep her. And now...it's too late, Dani. I refuse to be tossed to the side until you deem me worthy of your love again. I refuse to be that person to anyone. It's over. You need to move on."

Dani looked away for a moment. "It's her, isn't it?"

"Who?"

"You know who. Quinn Kincaid. She was so rude to me at the funeral, treating me as if I didn't belong there. I was your father's student. Of course I belonged there."

Hearing those words transported Lacey back in time to the day they'd met. She'd brought lunch to her father's office on campus. They'd almost collided as Dani walked out of his office. Lacey was instantly smitten. The accent. The face. Her smile. She was Dani's from that day forward. And now, almost five years later, here they were.

"You brought your parents to the funeral," Lacey said. "We both know why, and so did Quinn. You brought them to meet her. Get her autograph. Take a damn selfie." Lacey threw her hands in the air. "For someone who claims to be so Catholic, you sure have an interesting way of showing respect for the dead."

Dani sighed. "They wanted to meet *you*, my love."

"Bullshit. How long were we together? How many times did your parents refuse to meet me?"

"I'm sorry, okay? How many times do I have to apologize for one little lapse in judgment?"

Lacey couldn't believe what she was hearing. "How many times? You haven't yet. Not for the funeral. Not for Times Square. Not for this ridiculous threat, and certainly NOT for dumping me after I lost my job."

Dani threw her hands in the air. "I just did! I'm sorry, Lace. Now, can we please go get coffee and talk about our future?"

"DANI!" Lacey snapped back. "You are literally ruining my life. Do you understand that? Do you understand how much that makes me hate your ever-loving guts? I *hate* you, Dani. Please tell me you understand what I'm saying. Please tell me you're not some sick psycho who believes love can be manipulated. This isn't a fucking soap opera! Sarah Covington isn't going to marry her blackmailer to save the woman she loves from a little public humiliation!"

Lacey stepped back. She'd never had the urge to hit someone before this very moment. She just wanted to slap some sense into Dani. Wake her up and make her see who she'd become. She took her cap and sunglasses off and unzipped her coat. Either it had warmed up quickly or she had worked herself into a fervor. "I can't look at you anymore, Dani. Have a good life." She turned and walked away, having no idea if her words had sunk in. No idea if Dani would stay quiet. But she had nothing left to say. Nothing left to give the woman she once loved.

"Shit!" Lacey stopped, her hands clenched in her coat pockets. If only it were that easy. Just walk away and never see that beautiful, horrible face again. Live every day with a hope that Dani had too much pride, too much goodness in her heart to ever make the contract public.

Nice dream.

Lacey turned back around and shouted, "Daniela!"

Physical pain almost seemed better. It didn't numb the emotional pain, but it gave Quinn something different to focus on. Her throat was raw. Her legs were on fire. Her arm—she didn't want to think about how much it would ache when she stopped. The constant push and pull—the braking—the jarring dips and bumps in the trail—her arm would be trashed. But she didn't stop.

She'd sent another text before her ride.

Please call me. Text. Anything. I'm begging now.

Nothing. Fucking nothing.

As the security gate closed, Quinn let go of her bike, letting it land wherever it cared to. She shed her helmet and shoes before she got to the side gate. Her gloves were dropped at the gate. Everything else—shorts, shirt, underwear, sunglasses—all dropped on the way to the pool. She stepped over the edge into the deep end, letting herself sink to the bottom.

Quinn deserved all this pain. She was so quick to doubt. So quick to hit back. So quick to run. So quick to hurt the woman she loved. She came up out of the water sputtering and gasping for air. A cry from deep inside made its way out. She swam to the edge and held on as all the pain and regret poured out of her.

Lacey wasn't coming back.

CHAPTER THIRTY-FIVE

Three weeks later, Lacey was packing when she heard a knock on the door. She brushed the dust off of her T-shirt and looked through the peephole. "Oh, God. You found me."

"May I come in?"

Lacey opened the door. "Knock yourself out." Jack looked different. His hair was longer. His year-round tan had faded. "What brings you to New York?"

Jack laid a garment bag over the back of the sofa and looked around. "Hello to you too, Lace." He zeroed in on one of the family photos on the wall. "You're as beautiful as your mother."

Lacey continued packing books into a box. "Sucking up, Jack? What the hell do you need from me now?"

"Not at all." His voice was gentler than normal. "I'm just not sure what to say to you, standing here in your father's apartment." He pointed at the box. "Can I help with that?"

Lacey's shoulders relaxed. Jack wasn't the enemy. In fact, he could be a good listener when he wanted to be. She set the books down and gave him her full attention. "I'm sorry. How are you, Jack?"

"I'm okay." Jack shoved his hands into his pockets. "Worried about you and Quinn. Hoping I didn't ruin everyone's lives."

Lacey's already sad expression turned into one of pain as she frowned. "I think the verdict is still out." She couldn't look at him. She turned back to her box of books.

Jack stood next to her, wrapping an arm around her. "What can I do?"

Lacey gripped the book in her hand, trying to keep her emotions at bay. She didn't want to cry in front of Jack, but she'd never felt so alone in her whole life. Her dad was gone. Quinn was...gone. She'd been all alone in that apartment, trying to decide what of her father's things to keep and what to give away. Everything held a memory. Even her dad's ties were special—mostly because she'd picked them out for him. But what good would it do to pack everything up and store it away for years on end? No, it would be best to give most of it away, if she could just muster up the courage.

It surprised them both when Lacey buried her face in Jack's chest. She let go of the book and gripped onto the lapel of his jacket. Jack ran his hand over her long hair. "Shh…it's okay. It's going to be okay."

Jack took a swallow of the beer Lacey had found in the fridge for him. "It's a surprisingly nice view out here."

Lacey leaned on the metal balcony. "It gets the afternoon sun, and if you lean out and tilt your head just right, you can see the river."

Jack eyed Lacey closely for a moment. She had calmed down some. Even joked about how claustrophobic New York apartments felt to her now. She also apologized for the big, wet stain on his jacket, and followed that up with how ugly the jacket was anyway. Typical Lacey. Which was what he'd hoped to see. He took another sip of beer and said, "Quinn's in town." He tried to look casual as he waited for a response.

Lacey stiffened. "Why?"

"She's going on *The Not So Late Show* tonight."

She turned away from him, looking out at the view. "Oh."

"She'll be promoting the season finale."

"Yeah. Of course. Makes sense."

"I'd like you to show up and surprise her. Johnny Falcon's always up for a good surprise. They wanted both of you anyway, and this makes it more fun."

Lacey squeezed the metal railing with both hands. "You haven't asked about Dani."

"I assume you've done all you can, short of marrying her, of course." Jack grinned showing off his very white smile. Lacey reached over and whacked his shoulder. "Hey! What was that for?"

"Because it's not funny, Jack."

"Hey." Jack reached out and squeezed her shoulder. "Whatever happens with her, we'll deal with the fallout. No one blames you anymore."

"There won't be any fallout. I'm doing what has to be done. I was going to contact you anyway so I could get the name of the lawyer who wrote up the original contract."

The worry lines in Jack's forehead deepened. "Oh, God. Is she blackmailing you?"

"No." Lacey shook her head. "I'm going to use the money Quinn gave me to pay off Dani's student loans. In exchange, she'll sign whatever kind of gag order I need her to sign."

"So, she *is* blackmailing you." Jack wasn't so sure about this little plan.

"It was my idea, not hers. She just wanted *me*, and that's not going to happen."

"And she agreed? Just like that?"

Lacey's gaze fell. She found a spot of peeling paint on the railing and picked at it. "Just like that." She took a breath and looked at Jack. "She has a lot of growing up to do, but I have no doubt she'll make a difference in this world one day. I'm fine with it."

Words. Those were just words. Jack could see in Lacey's eyes how hurt she was. He considered it for a moment and then said, "Let me handle the contract. I'd rather you didn't ever see her again. In fact, I'll put that in the deal as well. No contact. Period."

Lacey gave him a nod. "Thank you, Jack. I'll tell her to expect your call." She turned and leaned against the balcony with her arms folded. "So, you want me to show up and surprise Quinn on Falcon? What does that get us?"

"Lots of airtime. Especially if you kiss her. And ratings for the show, which are great, by the way."

Lacey lowered her gaze and furrowed her brow, looking worried. "I haven't answered Quinn's texts."

"She's aware."

"I don't have anything to wear. All those nice clothes Shauna picked out for me are in California."

Jack opened the door. "Let's go inside." He set his empty beer bottle down and unzipped the garment bag. "I went to see Shauna before I left." He pulled a beautiful, and rather short, maroon dress out of the bag. He held it up with a pair of black strappy heels. "You'll knock everyone off their chair wearing this."

Lacey put a hand on her hair, smoothing it down. "I'll need help with…"

"Just say the word and I'll have hair and makeup here in half an hour." He checked his watch. They didn't have a lot of time.

Lacey ran her fingers over the dress. "It'll be good for the show."

Jack grinned and then cleared his throat. "Yes. Right. Good for the show."

"And you swear this isn't a setup? Quinn knows nothing about this?"

He put up his hands. "I swear. It'll be a total surprise. And Lacey, I'm still your publicist."

Lacey smirked. "Gee, I thought you dumped me."

"Let's just say Quinn and I were both a bit hasty."

Lacey rolled her eyes. "Hasty? God, Jack. You both threw me out on my ass. I still have the bruises."

They didn't have time to rehash the past. He'd apologize profusely later. He tapped his watch. "We're on the clock, here."

Lacey threw her hands up. "Okay. Let's do it."

He pulled out his phone, tapped a button, and put it to his ear. "It's a go."

Jack opened the door, letting Amy into the green room. She screamed and jumped up and down when she saw Lacey. "Shhh," Jack said, giggling.

"I'm sorry. I just…can I hug you?"

"Of course!" Lacey opened her arms.

"I don't want to ruin your dress. It's so pretty."

"You won't. How are you, Amy?" Lacey had missed Amy's sweet, joyful demeanor.

Amy pulled back from the hug and looked Lacey up and down. "My God, that dress. She's gonna die! For so many reasons, she's just gonna DIE!"

"Only if I make it out there without breaking my neck. Look at these heels!" Lacey kicked up a heel behind her.

"They're hot! And you look gorgeous. I love what they did with your hair."

Lacey touched the soft curls that framed her face. She didn't usually wear it this curly, but it seemed to suit the dress. "Yeah, I kinda like it too."

Amy bubbled up with excitement, clapping her hands. "I can't believe this is happening. Quinn is so sad without you." Everyone in the room stilled, including another guest and her assistants. "I mean, because you've been in New York," Amy quickly clarified.

Jack opened the door. "It's time."

Amy wished Lacey good luck and gave her a thumbs-up, then she turned to the TV monitor. *"And we're back with Quinn Kincaid."*

Jack led Lacey to the edge of the stage and stood there in the dark with her. "You doing okay?" he whispered.

Lacey grabbed his hand. She was nervous as hell. What if she froze up when she saw Quinn and things got awkward? What if the hug was weird? What if she couldn't find anything nice to say to Johnny? She took a deep breath and tried to imagine what this moment would be like if the whole thing with Dani hadn't happened. If they were still madly in love and nothing had come between them. If she had actually moved into Quinn's bedroom. What would that be like?

Lacey looked at the small monitor hanging on the wall next to them. She focused on Quinn. God, she looked stunning in that blue dress. *What is that, turquoise?* Lacey smiled, remembering the first day she met Quinn. Shades of blue—that's what Quinn was to her. Including the saddest shade of blue, but she couldn't think about that right now. She needed to focus on the positive, like how cute Quinn's hair looked parted down the middle and tucked behind her ears. It was simple and beautiful and shorter than it had been before, barely grazing her shoulders.

"You're gonna do great," Jack whispered.

Lacey closed her eyes and took a deep breath. This was it. Make or break. They'd either come off looking crazy in love, or completely awkward and barely able to look at each other. Lacey took a step back. Maybe this was just another one of Jack's stupid ideas. She clasped her hands together and bowed her head like she was praying. Is was too late to run. *Focus, Lace. Focus on the good stuff. Focus on Napa. Her lips. Her laugh. Her scent. The way she—* Lacey opened her eyes and looked at the monitor again. *The way she makes love.* Lacey smiled. That was a memory she could hang on to.

Johnny Falcon thrummed the desk with both hands, then leaned in toward Quinn. "Okay! The studio sent over a clip of the season finale of *Jordan's Appeal*, so why don't you set it up for us?"

Quinn crossed her legs and clasped her hands over her knees. "Sure. So, Jordan is defending a murderer…"

"A murderer! Wow. That doesn't sound like the clip I saw."

"It doesn't?" Quinn looked at the audience and then at Johnny.

"Let's show the clip!"

Lacey's panty-covered ass showed up on the big screen and the audience roared. They played about ten seconds of their love scene, most of it Quinn watched through her fingers. Once it was over she looked at Johnny and said, "That wasn't the season finale."

"It wasn't?" Johnny tapped his cheek. "I wonder what happened."

"That was last week's episode," Quinn said, giggling.

"And it was HOT, HOT, HOT!" Johnny stood up and gave her a standing ovation, the audience joining in.

Quinn covered her face with her hands as she turned bright red. Lacey looked at Jack and they both giggled.

Johnny sat back down. "Seriously, though. Where's Lacey tonight?"

Shit. This was it. Lacey smoothed down her dress and straightened her shoulders. "We're still in love," she whispered to herself. "Everything's fine."

Quinn hesitated slightly before answering the question, but she quickly recovered. "She's here in New York. We shot the last episode and then she came back here to take care of some family business."

"Have you seen her yet?" Johnny asked.

"No. I flew in right before the show."

"Do you miss her?"

Quinn didn't hesitate at all before answering that question. "Terribly."

The whole audience gave her a collective *Awww.*

"Thank you!" Quinn said. "Thank you for sharing my pain."

"They're good people." Johnny looked at the audience. "Should we help her out, folks?"

Jack put his hand on Lacey's back. "You're on."

Lacey walked out onto the stage and the audience went crazy. She stopped and waved to them. Quinn turned around and gasped. She stood up and covered her mouth with her hands.

Lacey focused on the step she had to take up onto the stage, making sure she didn't trip and fall. Then her eyes met Quinn's, and time stood still for a second. The words she was going to say were long gone. Her mind was blank. Those blue eyes had taken her in and she was lost.

Quinn reached out for her, taking her hands. "Lace."

Hearing her name brought everything back into focus. And words she never planned on saying came pouring from her mouth. "Hey, beautiful. I missed you too." She reached up and cupped Quinn's cheek. "Can I kiss you?"

The audience went crazy again, having heard the question.

Lacey didn't wait for an answer, she leaned in and gave Quinn a sweet, gentle kiss, then pulled away. It wasn't enough for Quinn. She grabbed Lacey's face and laid one on her.

The audience went insane.

Quinn took Lacey's hand and led her over to Johnny. He kissed Lacey's cheek and went back behind the desk. Lacey sat next to Quinn on the sofa.

Johnny giggled, pointing at Quinn. "Look at you, you're so happy."

Quinn put her hand on Lacey's crossed knee, grinning from ear to ear. "Wouldn't you be?"

The audience went wild again.

Lacey covered Quinn's hand with her own. "I'm the lucky one, Johnny."

"So, do we get to hear how all of this came about?"

Lacey looked at Quinn. "Can I tell the story?"

Quinn gave her a nod, even though there was a flicker of fear in her eyes. "Sure."

"We met in a Starbucks. Quinn is a *huge* fan of *Light of Day*."

Quinn pursed her lips together as she silently giggled.

"That's the daytime soap you were on," Johnny clarified for the audience.

"Yes. So anyway, Quinn recognized me and introduced herself. We quickly became friends and when she had her mountain biking accident and broke her arm, I happened to be staying in her guesthouse."

"So, you were there when that happened," Johnny said.

"Lacey was a godsend," Quinn said, breaking into the conversation. "It was a bad break and I was a mess for weeks."

Before Quinn could say anything else, Lacey continued with her version of the story. "Yeah, and they were scheduled to start shooting the next season of *Jordan's Appeal* in less than two weeks, so we came up with a storyline that would include her broken arm. The writers ran with it, and that's how I ended up on *Jordan's Appeal*."

Johnny gestured with his finger at both of them. "Doing love scenes with Quinn Kincaid. Was that part of the storyline you came up with?"

"No!" Quinn quickly clarified. "That was all the writers."

"I think we have the first kiss. Do we have that? Let's show that," Johnny said.

They watched the first kiss scene and the audience whistled and hollered. Johnny cleared his throat. "So, was there a lot of practice getting that scene just right?"

Lacey shook her head and Quinn joined in. "No," Quinn said. "That was our very first kiss."

Johnny's mouth fell open. "We have your very first kiss on tape?"

Lacey leaned in. "She gave me a little tongue, Johnny." She looked at Quinn. "Or, did I give you tongue?" Quinn turned bright red again. "Anyway," Lacey said with a shrug. "There was a little tongue."

"And the rest is history?" Johnny asked.

Quinn intertwined her fingers with Lacey's "Off the market."

Johnny gestured at them with a sweeping move. "Quinn Kincaid and Lacey Matthews, ladies and gentlemen."

Quinn got out of the car behind Lacey. It had been an awkwardly quiet ride to Lacey's apartment. Not even Jack and Amy's excitement over how well the show had gone could cover up the fact that Lacey had nothing to say to Quinn once they were off stage. It was as if a switch had been flipped, turning off the light in Lacey's eyes.

But it wasn't all just an act. The kiss was real. Lacey had kissed Quinn back. She had gripped her waist and held on to her during the kiss. Just like the first one, Quinn realized. Lacey's kisses had never been fake. And Quinn couldn't let it end like this. She had to try.

"A huge soap fan, huh?" Quinn asked as she followed Lacey to the apartment building. She hoped she could break the ice. "Now I'm going to have to watch old episodes just so I'll know what's going on, in case anyone ever asks."

"Yeah, well, you deserved it," Lacey said, not stopping or turning around.

"I'm sure I deserve a lot of things, including the silent treatment I got in the car. But, Lace…"

Lacey stopped at the door and turned around.

"Jack told me about Dani. I plan to repay you, whatever amount you end up giving her."

Lacey shook her head. "No. It feels better this way." She sighed deeply. "More honest. Less dirty."

"Lace," Quinn whispered. "Please…just give me a minute." She looked around to see if anyone was near enough to hear. "I know I've said it over and over in emails and texts, but I need to say it in person." She took a step closer. "I'm so sorry I doubted you. After everything we went through together...the way you took care of me..." She sucked in a breath, trying to hold back the tears. "I should've handled it so much better than I did. I should've—"

"Given me a chance to fix it," Lacey interrupted. "Which I have."

"I know. And I will never doubt you again."

Lacey hesitated. "Okay," she said. "Are we done?"

"I hope not. God, I hope not." Quinn reached out her hand. "Lace..."

Lacey stared at the hand and then her gaze met Quinn's. She faltered again, but then straightened her shoulders. "I can't." She turned to open the door.

"I have a brother!" Quinn exclaimed.

Lacey slowly turned around. "What?"

"I have...a brother." Quinn was embarrassed to say the words. "A half brother. I want to meet him, but I can't do it alone. Will you go with me?"

Lacey shook her head in confusion. "You have a brother...and you've never met him? How old is he?"

Quinn kept her eyes on the ground.

"How old is your brother, Quinn?" Lacey's voice had a little more force behind it now.

"They live in Connecticut. Will you go with me to see my dad and my brother?"

Lacey turned back to the door and punched in the security code.

"Lace, I can't do it alone. I won't."

"Wow," Lacey scoffed. "This feels like emotional blackmail." She folded her arms and looked Quinn in the eye. "You don't need me by your side to meet your own brother, and you don't need me by your side when you tell your father that you've finally forgiven him. You're so much stronger than you think, Quinn."

"He's eighteen." Quinn lowered her gaze, embarrassed that she had a brother she'd never bothered to get to know.

A look of disbelief crossed Lacey's features. She started to say something but stopped. In a softer tone she said, "And you're his cool celebrity sister. Just plan on being all over his Instagram."

"You don't think he'll hate me for never..." Quinn looked away.

"He'll love you. No matter what, he's gonna love finally knowing you."

A glimmer of hope flashed across Quinn's face. "You really think so?"

Lacey pointed at the building with her thumb. "I need to go. I have a lot of packing to do."

Quinn looked up at the building, trying to remember which floor Lacey's dad's apartment was on. "Since we're giving out advice, do you mind if I give you some?"

Lacey punched in the code again, ignoring Quinn.

"Don't sell it."

Lacey turned back around.

"Don't sell your dad's apartment, Lace. I mean, what's the rush?"

"It'll just sit empty."

"Not really." Quinn took a step closer. "Everything you have left of your parents is in that apartment. It can be your New York pied-à-terre."

Lacey chuckled at that. "Yeah, I guess it could." A wave of sadness crossed her features.

Quinn wanted to wrap her arms around Lacey and take away the sadness. Or, better yet, offer to go up and make coffee and talk all night, so she wouldn't have to be in that apartment all alone. She was grasping for ideas. Anything to keep her in Lacey's orbit a little longer. But the look on Lacey's face told her that wouldn't be welcomed. "Thanks for what you did tonight. I think I was boring Johnny to death before you showed up."

"Well, technically I'm still under contract, so…"

"So, you'll go with me to visit my dad and meet my brother? You know…as my supportive girlfriend?" Quinn knew she was pushing it, but it wouldn't hurt to try one more time.

"Nice try, but you're on your own with that one." Lacey lifted her chin toward the car. "Jack and Amy are—"

"Getting paid. Don't worry about them."

Lacey smiled, and this time it made her eyes sparkle. "You'll be the death of me, Quinn Kincaid."

Quinn snorted. "How many times have you said that in your head over the past year?"

"Too many to count." Lacey reached out and pushed Quinn's hair behind her ear, then cupped her cheek. "We managed to have a few laughs, didn't we?"

Quinn covered Lacey's hand with her own. "Too many to count."

"Take care of yourself. Don't ride that bike too hard." Lacey stepped away and punched in the security code.

"Too late."

Lacey went still but didn't turn around. The big sigh had Quinn hopeful for a few seconds. So did the slight shake of Lacey's head. It was okay, she could be disappointed, disgusted, whatever—so long as she turned back around. *Yell at me, Lace. Yell at me for riding too hard. Yell at me for everything! Just don't walk away.*

The door opened. A couple came out of the building and walked the other way. "That wasn't our first kiss, Lace."

Lacey held the door open and turned her head, but didn't look at Quinn. "I know."

"I wanted to kiss you back that night. I wanted..." Quinn sucked in air. "I wanted to do more than that."

Lacey met her gaze. "You should have."

The door closed, leaving Quinn standing on the sidewalk alone. She stared at the door, tears welling up in her eyes. Jack took her arm. "Come on, sweetie." Quinn didn't move. Jack tugged again. "Come on." He wrapped his arm around her and led her back to the car.

CHAPTER THIRTY-SIX

L acey walked into the production offices trying to portray an air of confidence she didn't actually feel. Forty-four days was a long time to go without contact when the whole world still thought you were a couple.

Then there was the table read they were about to do. Would they have the same chemistry on-screen? Could they sell it the way they had the first time around, or would everyone know the truth the second Lacey walked into the room?

"Hey, Quinn! There she is!"

Lacey stopped dead in her tracks as the young man made his way toward her.

"Hi, I'm Brax."

It was like looking at the male version of Quinn. Same blue eyes. Same blond hair. Same smile that could light up the world. Quinn came around the corner and their eyes met. "Hey, honey," Quinn said, her voice full of hesitation.

Okay, so they were going to perpetuate the lie a little longer. Lacey quickly pulled herself together and said, "Hey, babe." She looked at Brax. "You must be the brother."

"Braxton, this is Lacey." Quinn stood next to Lacey and put a hand on her back, barely brushing her blouse. "Lace, this is my little brother. He's staying with me until he moves into his dorm next month."

"UCLA," he added, his voice full of pride. "And it's great to finally meet my sister's girlfriend. She really can't stop talking about you."

"Yeah." Lacey glanced at Quinn and then offered her hand. "It's nice to meet you too, Braxton."

"Well, I should get out of your hair for a while. Amy said she'd show me around some more and then take me to lunch. See you for dinner tonight? I'm manning the grill."

Quinn leaned in. "Seriously, he makes the best grilled shrimp. You'd love it."

"Oh," Lacey said, not sure what to say next. "I just got back in town…" They both just stared, waiting for her to accept the invitation. "I guess…maybe…I could swing that." She could always back out later. Jet lag. Headache. She'd come up with something.

Quinn smiled from ear to ear. "Good. Amy and her husband will be there as well. One last celebration of our freedom before we're back to long shooting days."

Lacey tried to hide her surprise. Quinn didn't entertain in her home. It was her "private refuge."

"See you tonight!" Brax jogged away, leaving them standing there alone.

"It's good to see you," Quinn looked Lacey up and down. "You look as beautiful as ever."

Lacey turned and slowly led them to the conference room. "So do you." She kept her eyes forward, wondering if it would help to tell the truth. Maybe if it was out in the open, her heart would stop trying to hammer its way out of her chest. "I'm nervous about this table read."

"Why?" Quinn kept her hands behind her back as they walked.

"What if we've lost it? What if everything the audience saw and loved last season is gone? And when are you going to announce our breakup to the world?"

She didn't mean for that last part to come out, but every day, she'd woken up expecting to see an email from Jack with the press release he'd be sending out later in the day. *Quinn Kincaid and Lacey Matthews remain good friends, blah blah blah.*

But that email never came.

Lacey had said it kind of loudly too, and the way Quinn was glancing around to see if anyone had heard made her regret blurting it out like that. "Sorry," she whispered.

"No, it's okay." Quinn started walking again. "Braxton wanted to see the set. I hadn't really thought about his reaction to seeing you here. You don't have to come to dinner tonight. I know it'll be awkward for you."

"Oh, yeah? And what excuse will you make for your girlfriend this time? I can imagine there have been some real doozies in the last two months."

"I tell everyone the same thing—that you're in New York, settling up your life so you can move out here with me."

Lacey stopped and turned to her. "We have to stop this charade, Quinn. What good does it do anyone to keep living this lie?"

"I know." Quinn folded her arms and looked at the floor. "Can you give me another week? I just need to figure out how to tell the world that I managed to fuck up the best thing I've ever had."

The door opened and a production assistant waved them into the room. "We're ready to go, ladies. Welcome to season seven!"

Lacey didn't share the woman's excitement. Yes, she was so happy to have a job, but she was seriously concerned about their on-screen chemistry. Everything was riding on it still being there. She gestured with her hand to Quinn. "After you."

"Okay, scene five," one of the writers said. "Just a refresher on where we left the Jordan slash Selena arc last season—Jordan told Selena it was over! Oh no!" he joked. "But Jordan went to Selena's apartment to apologize and who was there but Selena's supposedly ex-GF, wearing the watch Selena and Jordan had shopped for together. Leaving all of America wondering what the hell would happen next. That brings us to scene five, ladies and gentleman. Jordan is waiting outside the courtroom for Selena. Selena walks out and..." He motioned for Lacey to continue.

Lacey found her spot in the script and cleared her throat. "I wondered when we'd casually run into each other and act like nothing happened."

Quinn peeled her eyes from Lacey and looked at the script. "Casual? You think I just happened by today? In all the time we spent together, did I ever just *happen by* someplace?"

"I guess not. How are you?"

"Well, let's see. You left a resignation letter on my desk, took your old job with Hamilton & Nye, which makes my blood boil."

"They're a good firm. The best in town...next to yours."

"Good save."

"I was really talking about your arm, anyway."

"I didn't come here to talk about my injuries—physical or otherwise."

"Why *are* you here, Jordan?"

"Because..." Quinn looked up, her eyes finding Lacey's across the table.

One of the writers cleared his throat. "Is there a problem, Quinn?"

"No. Sorry." Quinn found her place in the script again. "Because I can't stop thinking about you, Selena. We have something special. And if another day goes by without me telling you what an amazing lover you are...or how much I appreciate what you did for me while I was healing..."

"Um..." J.J. looked at the script. "Quinn, it's lawyer, not lover." A few people at the table giggled.

"Right." Quinn wanted to crawl under the table and disappear. "Lawyer. I'll just..." She glanced up at Lacey but her eyes were focused on the script. On any other day, Lacey would've been all over that, giving Quinn provocative looks and teasing her relentlessly. Not today. Probably not ever again. Quinn focused on the script again. "Let me just redo that." She took a breath. "Because I can't stop thinking about you, Selena. We have something special. And if another day goes by without me telling you what an amazing lawyer you are, or how much I appreciate what you did for me while I was healing, well, that would make me truly unworthy of even being in your presence."

"I appreciate that, Jordan," Lacey said, reading her line. "I know that was hard for you to say, and I really appreciate it."

"May I ask you if you're still with...the cat owner?"

"No."

"No, I can't ask or..."

"We broke up, remember? She dumped me because I forgot her birthday, at least that's what I tell myself. It's easier to think it was just the one time I screwed up."

"I see. So, why did you give her that watch, then?"

"It was a consolation gift, I guess. Thanks for putting up with me for so long sort of thing. I don't know...it just felt like the right thing to do. How did you know?"

"Flowers, apologies, cats...it was awkward. We don't really need to talk about it, do we?"

"No. We don't. It was good seeing you again, Jordan. Don't be a stranger."

Everyone turned to the next page in the script and the assistant director said, "Selena walks away, and when she's almost at the door, Jordan yells to her and catches up."

"Selena! Since you don't work for me anymore, maybe we could start over…do this the right way?" Quinn looked up again, but Lacey was still keeping her head down.

"Are you asking me out, Ms. Ellis?"

"Don't make me say the actual words, Selena. You know I hate to beg."

"Then we have Jordan walking away, and Selena says—"

"Thank you, Jordan…for finally figuring out why I quit. I'll pick you up at seven."

"Any changes?" the head writer asked, looking around the room. He didn't get a reply, so he tossed his copy of the script on the table. "Excellent! We're good to go."

Lacey collected her things and stood up. Quinn did the same. She wanted to follow Lacey and get a final confirmation that she'd be at her house for dinner, but something stopped her. She stood there, at the table, waiting for everyone to clear the room. When they had all left, she grabbed onto the table with one hand as the realization gripped her again. There would be no second chances for her. Lacey was done. Quinn had seen it in her eyes during the table read—the emptiness. There was no love left for Quinn in them. It was over. God, it was really over.

"Quinn?"

Quinn stilled and then turned around.

"Are you coming?"

She nodded at Lacey. "Yeah." She tried to suck up her emotions as she grabbed her purse and stuffed the script into it. She stilled again when she felt Lacey right behind her.

"They're out there, Brax and Amy," Lacey said, her voice low and close. Quinn felt goose bumps form on her neck. "I thought it would be best if we walked out together."

"Of course." So that was the only reason Lacey had come back for her? It was okay. It would be okay, Quinn told herself. All was not lost. They'd still be working together for a while. When all was said and done, they'd still be friends.

They would, right?

She looked up and met Lacey's gaze. She wanted to grab her around the waist and rest her head on Lacey's chest while she begged for forgiveness. She wanted to convince Lacey that she wasn't Dani— she was better than Dani, even though her actions said otherwise. But those eyes were still empty—still void of the love they once held.

Quinn followed Lacey out of the room. Amy spotted them and waved as she jogged over. "We missed you!" she said as she wrapped her arms around Lacey's shoulders. She held on tight for a few seconds and then released her. "You look amazing. What's different?"

"I didn't look amazing before?" Lacey joked. "And I missed you too, Amy. You're good for my ego."

Amy narrowed her eyes as she stepped back. "You put little highlights in your hair. It's gorgeous, the way they frame your face."

Lacey shrugged. "Thought I'd try something new."

"And those jeans..." Amy wagged her finger up and down Lacey's body. "So sexy."

"Okay, Amy." Quinn gestured with her head toward Braxton.

Braxton grinned. "No, she's right, sis. Your girlfriend is smokin'."

Quinn wanted to take a step closer and wrap her arm around Lacey's waist, claiming her. But Amy knew the truth, even if Braxton didn't. She felt embarrassed, putting on a show for them. And then she felt an arm wrap around her waist, pulling her closer. "Just trying to keep up with my superstar girlfriend," Lacey said with a smile. The smile was for Amy and Braxton. She didn't look at Quinn. And then she did. "See you later, babe?"

The "babe" nickname. Quinn knew it wasn't real when she'd said it, and she knew it even more so when Lacey said it. But at least it was preceded by something good. "Yeah. See you tonight." She leaned in for a kiss and Lacey gave her a cheek. It was better than nothing.

Amy poured a glass of wine and handed it to Quinn. "Take this to your girlfriend." She motioned with her head toward the sliding glass door.

"She's not my—"

"God, Quinn." Amy pushed her toward the door. "She never will be unless you try."

"She's done. Can't you see it? The way she looks at me...all dead-eyed?"

"It's not dead, silly. It's sad. She looks at you with sad eyes. Because she lost you too, ya know."

They'd sat at opposite ends of the table during dinner. To everyone else, it probably looked like two heads of the household entertaining their guests appropriately, but Quinn knew better. Lacey had purposely chosen the seat farthest away from her. Every time their eyes met,

Lacey would look away, finding a sudden interest in the painting on the wall or her own hands.

Quinn got through dinner pretending they'd had a big fight before their guests had arrived, but they'd work it out later, in bed. It was the only way she could sit there and not tear up the stairs to her bedroom in a fit of tears.

The pretending helped, but it also broke her heart, because how perfect would it be if it were true, that her wife might be a little bit miffed at her for inviting people over without any notice, but she was still her wife, and she'd still be there in the morning.

Quinn stepped outside, two glasses of wine in hand. She glanced back at Amy and got a finger pointed at Lacey. "Fine," she whispered. Quinn watched as Amy folded her arms and smiled, looking all proud of herself. *Damn assistant, assisting where she shouldn't be.*

She gulped down some wine from her glass and slowly made her way over to Lacey. "I thought you might like another glass, since you took a cab here tonight." There was a slight breeze blowing through Lacey's hair. She looked absolutely stunning standing there in the dimming light. She looked like summertime in her white linen pants, blue gauze blouse, and flat sandals. Quinn's mind immediately went back to Napa—Lacey trying to wrap her mind around the fact that Quinn loved her for real. God, how could she have let it all go so wrong? How could this gorgeous woman not still be hers?

Lacey took the glass and turned back toward the setting sun. "I forgot how much I loved this—watching the sunset."

"I always knew where to find you at dusk." Quinn stood next to Lacey, leaving a little bit of breathing room between them. "Thanks for showing up again. I can't thank you enough for making me look like a decent person to my brother."

Lacey took a sip of wine and cradled the glass on her folded arms. "He's a nice kid, your brother."

"Yeah, he is." Quinn glanced over at Braxton, who was sitting on a lounge chair, chatting with Amy's husband. "He said if I hadn't gotten in touch with them, he would've sought me out when he moved to L.A."

"And your father? How did that go?"

"Eh," Quinn said with a shrug. "It went okay. It wasn't easy, seeing him again."

"I'm proud of you." Lacey turned around, facing the house. "This place was a mausoleum when I moved in, and now you're having cast parties…dinner parties…"

"You heard about the cast party?" Quinn shook her head as she giggled. "God, this place was a mess. Blood on the patio, food everywhere—"

Lacey raised an eyebrow. "Blood?"

"J.J.'s eight-year-old slugged Laura's ten-year-old right on the nose. Got his little ass grounded for most of the time you were gone. It was ugly for a while, but we all pushed through it and came out the other side better people. Mostly me—I'm a better person now," Quinn quipped. "That corn cob that's been stuck up my ass is a little looser now."

Lacey giggled. "Good to know."

"Vera cleaned up the blood, but not before I put crime scene tape around it." Quinn glanced at Lacey. Yeah, she was surprised to hear Vera's name. It made Quinn smile. "We're tight now, me and Vera. She made the salsa that everyone devoured tonight."

Lacey took another sip of wine while she eyed Quinn, appearing to give her the once-over to see if she could be trusted.

"So, how about you, Lace? How did it go in New York, with your dad's apartment?"

"It seems we both took each other's advice."

"You're keeping the apartment." It wasn't a question. More of a statement of satisfaction that Lacey had taken Quinn's advice to heart.

"I am. For now, at least. I'm selling my place as soon as the renters' lease is up. It's even smaller than my dad's, so I won't really miss it."

"So, you're really moving out here?" Quinn asked, hopefully.

"My job is here. And my agent is getting movie scripts for me now…so one way or another, I hope to keep working in L.A." Lacey turned back around toward the ocean. "Then I won't have to give up this," she said, lifting her glass to the sunset.

They were both quiet for a moment as they sipped their wine and enjoyed the view. "I should get the rest of my things." Lacey said, breaking the silence.

"They're in the guesthouse, right where you left them. And the Range Rover is yours, Lace. Please take it."

"Brax isn't staying in the guesthouse?"

"That's your space," Quinn said, perplexed by the question. "He's staying in the house with me." She took a breath and the words almost spilled out of her mouth. *I love you, don't you know that?* "It's just like you left it. I mean, I slept in your bed a few times…" *More than a few.* Quinn felt Lacey's eyes on her. She couldn't meet her gaze. Not with guests here to witness a total breakdown.

"Quinn…"

The tone in Lacey's voice was one of annoyance. She obviously didn't want to have this conversation in front of guests any more than Quinn did. Or probably at all. She was done. Why couldn't Quinn get that through her head? "It's okay. I know it's over." Quinn covered her mouth with her hand to keep her lip from quivering. "Thank you for coming tonight." She ran into the house, leaving Lacey standing there.

Lacey helped Amy clean up the kitchen. Surprisingly, Amy didn't ask why Quinn had gone to her room and not come back out. She'd just quietly helped and then hugged Lacey good-bye when she left with her husband.

During dinner, Lacey had noticed that Amy and Quinn seemed closer now. They'd caught her up on the latest storylines happening on *Light of Day*, almost as if they'd watched the soap together. And Amy knew exactly where everything was in the kitchen, which wasn't how it used to be. She'd hardly spent any time in Quinn's house before Lacey had arrived.

Things were different, and that was a good thing, Lacey supposed.

She got a bottle of water out of the fridge and leaned against the counter. Needing to hydrate so she wouldn't have a headache in the morning with all the wine she'd consumed before, during, and after dinner, she took a long swallow.

Braxton was still outside on a lounge chair with earbuds in his ears, jamming away to his music. Lacey set the half-empty bottle on the counter and went back out there. He quickly pulled the earbuds out. "Do you need help with anything?"

"No," Lacey said. "I just need to get a few things out of the guesthouse."

"Sure…um…do you think it would be okay if I had another beer? I only had one at dinner."

Lacey thought it was sweet he would even ask, so she gave him a nod, even though it wasn't really her decision. "Just one more." She turned and stared at the guesthouse, wondering why her feet had stopped working. She should go out there and collect her things. This new version of Quinn would most likely invite more guests to stay with her. And very soon, the charade would be over, which meant Margaret would probably show up to comfort her daughter after her breakup, whether Quinn liked it or not. Lacey liked Margaret. Yeah, she could be a little pushy, but her heart was in the right place, and there was no question she loved Quinn very much.

Lacey should go get her things. She should definitely not go back into the main house. And yet, she turned and went inside. She stood at the bottom of the stairs knowing what she should do. It did not include staring at the stairs, wondering how many times she'd climbed them to get to Quinn. To take care of her. Love her, even when she wasn't supposed to. Sneak little peeks at her gorgeous body. Lust after her, if truth be told.

Stop, Lacey. Stop while you still can. You've been so strong. Just go back to that hotel room and drink away the pain.

Two steps.

Braxton is here. What if you say the wrong thing and Quinn yells at you? What will that poor kid think? He won't think anything. He's drinking a beer and listening to music.

Two more steps.

God, Lacey. How many times are you going to give yourself to someone who throws you to the curb whenever the mood strikes them? HOW MANY TIMES?

Good, you've stopped halfway. Now, turn around and collect your things and leave. Just leave. You'll see her tomorrow at work. You'll make more small talk. Everything will be fine. Better than fine. You have a good job. You'll find a nice place to live. And as soon as Quinn gets the fucking balls to officially break up with her fake girlfriend, you can start dating. There are a ton of beautiful women in this town. Go and date them!

Well, if you can't go down the stairs, at least sit down. Good. Take a breath. Breathe, Lace. In and out. Now, go back downstairs...

"Lace?"

Too late. Lacey squeezed her eyes shut. Shit, she should've gotten out of there while she had the chance. "Yes, Quinn?"

"Where's Brax?"

Lacey glanced over at Quinn as she sat down next to her. She looked like hell, with her mascara-stained eyes and messy hair. "He's outside. I hope it's okay, he asked if he could have another beer and I said yes."

Quinn shrugged.

"Have you seen Ginny Strong?" Lacey cringed inside, her jealousy of that woman, rearing its ugly head and barreling out of her mouth at exactly the wrong time.

"You were right about her," Quinn said, dejectedly. "She's dating someone half her age and twice as tall. Okay, maybe that's an exaggeration, but you know what I mean." She scrubbed her face with her hands. "Thanks for warning me about her. I didn't want to believe it at the time, but I'm glad I didn't go there." She got up and started down the stairs. "I need a drink. Want one?"

"No. I'm good." Lacey stayed where she was, sitting on the step.

"Suit yourself." Quinn got to the bottom of the stairs and turned back around. "Did you need something?"

"No," Lacey said, her eyes meeting Quinn's. God, she looked broken. *Did I do that to her? No. She did that to you, remember?*

"Okay. It just looked like maybe you were headed upstairs."

Lacey shook her head. "No." A damn lie. And not even a good one.

Quinn nodded and went into the kitchen. Lacey listened as Quinn took a glass out of the cupboard and poured herself what Lacey assumed was a glass of whiskey—because she heard the ice cubes hit the glass—two of them. Quinn rarely drank anything hard, but when she did, it was Jack poured over two ice cubes. Lacey laughed the first time she'd seen it. "It's like drinking in college," she'd said. She never could figure out how Quinn could have such expensive taste in wine and still buy cheap liquor.

Get up. Get your stuff and get the hell out of here. She'll be fine. You'll be fine. This isn't your home. Never was.

"But it feels like home." Lacey mouthed the words. The huge lump in her throat was preventing her voice from working. "Quinn?" She whispered the name, testing it out. She licked her dry lips, swallowed hard, and tried again. "Quinn?"

Quinn appeared at the bottom of the steps, looking every bit the hot mess with streaked makeup and a tumbler of whiskey held loosely in her right hand. "Yeah?" She replied with so little feeling in her voice Lacey was sure she'd completely given up hope. There was no joy in her "yeah." No dream of a future. She almost seemed bothered that Lacey had even said her name. She stood there, looking up the stairs at Lacey, waiting for something to come out of her mouth. When it didn't, Quinn's gaze dropped to the floor.

"I was just thinking…" Lacey covered her mouth with her hands. Was she really going to do this? She waited for Quinn to lift her gaze again. "I was just thinking that since I don't work for you anymore…" A ray of hope flashed across Quinn's face. The tumbler hit against her thigh, causing the ice to hit the side of the glass, filling the silence. "Maybe we could start over," Lacey whispered, barely able to get the words out. "Do this right," she said, a little louder.

Quinn set the glass down on the first step and put one foot on that same step. She grabbed hold of the banister, looking determined to climb, but staying where she was. "Are you asking me on a date, Ms. Matthews?" she asked, repeating the line from the script.

"Don't make me say words," Lacey said through her tears. She couldn't hold them back now. She wiped them away, but they just kept falling. "God, I'm so scared."

"Lace." Quinn climbed a few steps and knelt down in front of Lacey, taking hold of her shaking hands.

"I can't make myself leave. Why can't I leave?" Lacey's chest was heaving as she gasped for air.

Quinn sat next to Lacey and pulled her into her arms. "Because you belong here, honey." She kissed Lacey's head and whispered, "You belong here with me. We'll figure it out. We'll work it out. Just stay, Lace. Just stay."

Lacey cried in Quinn's arms on that step. Then she cried some more in Quinn's bed, the pain finally coming out in a way Lacey hadn't let it before. She'd needed Quinn there, to take it from her and fill the void with something else—her love.

And she did.

CHAPTER THIRTY-SEVEN

Lacey woke up around midnight, still in her clothes. She took them off and climbed back into bed in just her underwear and slept for another four hours. She woke with a start, knowing they had to be at the studio at six. She could hear the shower running, so she decided to go out to the guesthouse, where she had clothes and toiletries.

Quinn was telling the truth when she said she'd left everything just as it was in the guesthouse. The photo of Lacey and her mother was still on the wall. Her go-to flip-flops were still by the door. The book she'd bought to read by the pool was right where she'd left it, on the kitchen counter. It was comforting somehow, knowing the place hadn't been wiped clean of her existence. She tidied up a bit and then got in the shower, letting the hot water run on her back.

After her shower, Lacey threw on a pair of running pants, a T-shirt, and flip-flops, and wrapped her wet hair up in a bun. It was just starting to get light outside as she walked the length of the pool. She couldn't help but smile, remembering all the times she'd done this in the past.

The fancy coffeemaker got a kiss. "Hello, my friend." She made the coffee and filled two travel mugs, then buttered a toasted bagel, wrapping it in a napkin. Quinn made her way down the stairs. Lacey smiled at her. "Good morning."

"Good morning."

They were running a few minutes late, so Lacey wasted no time handing Quinn her favorite travel mug. They headed for the garage—Lacey's keys to her Range Rover were hanging on a hook by the door, right where they always were. She grabbed them. "I'll drive as long as you don't bitch about how fast I'm going."

"I won't bitch if you stay in your lane."

"Fine."

"Fine." Quinn stopped short when Lacey turned around at the door. "Is something wrong?"

Lacey hesitated, her eyes locked on Quinn's lips. "No. We'll kiss later." She tried to turn back around, but Quinn caught her arm.

"We'll kiss now."

It was a sweet kiss. They both tasted like mouthwash. Quinn hummed her approval and deepened the kiss as much as she could with hands that were full with coffee mugs and handbags. Lacey's were full too, so they fought for dominance for a moment before Lacey pulled back. If she kept going, coffee mugs would eventually crash to the floor and clothes would be tossed aside and desperate, hot sex would be had, but none of that was a good idea with an eighteen-year-old brother in the house, not to mention a call time in less than an hour. "Later," Lacey said, her chest heaving and her heart so full it wanted to burst wide open.

Quinn nodded. "Yeah." She licked her lips and sucked in a breath. "God, you turn me on. Always have."

"From day one." Lacey said as she pushed the garage door open with her bum. She set the travel mug on the roof and opened the car door, but didn't get in. She looked at Quinn across the hood of the car and raised an eyebrow.

"Fine," Quinn acquiesced. "From day one. Are you happy now?"

Lacey bit into her bagel and grinned. "Ecstatic."

Amy pulled up to Lacey's car in her little cart, surprised to see Quinn in the passenger seat. "Good morning, ladies."

"Morning, Amy," they said in unison. Quinn sat next to Amy in the cart and Lacey sat in the back.

She eyed them both closely and then took off at full speed. "Trent is taking Braxton surfing this afternoon. He thinks your brother is awesome."

"Oh, yeah? Brax will love that, I'm sure," Quinn said.

Amy gave Quinn a look, her eyes wide as she motioned with her head at Lacey. Quinn smiled and patted Amy's leg. They pulled up to Quinn's trailer and Lacey jumped out of the back of the cart. She had to get to hair and makeup as soon as possible. She turned around and walked backward, winking at Quinn. "See you later." As soon as she was in the building, Amy squealed.

Quinn sat there, grinning from ear to ear. "I think maybe we'll be okay."

Amy grabbed Quinn and hugged her. "I can't believe it!"

Quinn patted Amy's arm. "I'm not going to risk losing her again."

"What?" Amy pulled back. "What does that mean?"

Quinn hadn't slept much. Not at all, really. She was scared to death that she'd wake up and Lacey would be gone. Change her mind. Come to her senses. Whatever. About an hour before the alarm went off, she got out of bed and sat in a chair watching Lacey sleep. She looked so beautiful with her hair splayed all over the pillow. Quinn's pillow.

She'd fallen in love with Lacey so slowly, she didn't even realize it was happening. Every day, they'd laugh a little more and argue a little less. Touch a little more, just because they could.

Her broken arm did that—forced them to be together 24/7. It was a blessing in disguise.

On set, they'd found a rhythm, just like they'd done at home. It was magic, how well they worked together. The best of both worlds. How many couples could say that?

And then, tragedy struck. A death. A funeral. Inconsolable grief. And that's when Quinn knew that her heart—as hard as she'd tried to fight it—belonged to Lacey.

A gift she threw away.

That would never happen again.

Quinn turned to Amy and looked her in the eye. "I'm going to ask Lacey to marry me."

"What?" Amy was frozen, gripping the steering wheel as she watched Quinn walk away. "WAIT!" She got out and slowly made her way over to Quinn. "Hon...are you sure that's the best..."

"I refuse." Quinn pursed her lips together as her eyes misted over. "I don't care if it seems reckless, or too soon, or whatever other reasons you come up with, Amy. I don't want to live another second of my life without her."

Amy nodded. "Okay." She slid her arm through Quinn's. "We'll pick out the ring together. It needs to be big. I prefer a solitaire. Or maybe emerald cut."

Saturday morning came, but not soon enough for Quinn. They'd had late nights and early calls all week. By the time they got home, they were both too tired to do anything but spend a few minutes with Braxton and then fall into bed. The same bed.

Quinn had bought a new toothbrush and set it next to her own. When Lacey saw it, she smiled, but she had yet to use it, always going out to the guesthouse in the morning to shower and dress.

Quinn had put in writing what she wanted to see happen with *Jordan's Appeal*. After one more season, she hoped they'd be open to a spin-off with Lacey's character as the lead. Quinn would agree to several guest appearances per season if they kept Jordan and Selena in a happy, committed relationship. She was ready for something different. Something that would give her more time to spend at home. When the time was right, she'd email her desires to the producers and hope for the best.

"You hauled me out of bed at the ass crack of dawn to do this?" Lacey bent over, trying to catch her breath. "There better be a gourmet breakfast at the top of this damn hill."

Quinn giggled. Lacey looked so cute in her spandex shorts and racerback top, her skin glistening with sweat. Quinn literally had to pull her out of bed by both arms. Lacey hadn't stopped moaning about it since. "We're almost there."

"That's what you said two hours ago."

"You were still in bed two hours ago."

"As it should be." Lacey motioned with her hand. "Give me that water." She took a long sip and gave Quinn a stern look. "Are you trying to kill me? You know I'm not a mountain girl."

No. I'm trying to marry you. Quinn could see the little piece of red fabric Amy had tied on a tree, indicating where she should get off the trail. They were close. She took the water bottle back and slapped Lacey's butt. "Come on. We're almost there."

They hiked several hundred more feet and came to an opening that looked out onto the valley. Lacey stopped, putting her hands on her hips. "Well, this is gorgeous."

Quinn took her hand. "It's even better from right up there." They climbed a little higher and came to a flat spot where a picnic had been set out on a big blanket.

Lacey gasped. "I was kidding about the gourmet breakfast! What the—"

It was the perfect spot. Completely private. Beautiful view. Quinn tried to get her breathing under control, but it was hard. She was out of breath from the hike, but she was also nervous as hell.

"How did you get all of this up here?" Lacey asked, looking at the champagne bottle sitting in the ice bucket and the pillows strategically placed on the blanket.

"I had help." Quinn handed Lacey a cold bottle of water from the basket. "Are you hungry?"

Lacey gulped the water down and wiped the sweat from her brow. "What's going on? It's not my birthday. Or, your birthday."

"No, it's not." Quinn kicked at the dirt with her toe. Maybe this was the worst idea she'd ever had in her whole life. On a list of a million bad ideas, this would be number two, right behind Jack's let's-get-you-a-fake-girlfriend idea.

Lacey pushed her sunglasses on top of her head. "It must be something special for Amy to haul her ass all the way up here with an ice bucket."

Quinn laughed. "Yeah. She's already texted to let me know she'll be getting a bonus for that one." She kept her eyes on the rock she was working hard to dislodge from the ground.

Lacey stepped closer, putting her finger under Quinn's chin and meeting her gaze. "I'd love to crash on one of those pillows and drink champagne, but I'd prefer to know what we're celebrating."

"You're beautiful," Quinn whispered, saying the first thing that came to her mind, her voice a little shaky.

"That's what we're celebrating?" Lacey ran the back of her fingers over Quinn's cheek. "Because I think we'd be celebrating the wrong face."

"You didn't let me finish." Quinn took a step back and reached for Lacey's hand. Her own hand was shaking but she held on tightly. "I know what it feels like to love you. I also know what it feels like to lose you. I prefer the first one. Because the second one almost killed me." She took a breath, trying to calm her nerves. Her words were coming out too fast now and she needed to slow down. "I want to love you forever. My whole life. And I want to do it knowing that you're mine and I'm yours and no one can take that away from us."

She reached into the small pocket in her spandex shorts and pulled out a very large diamond solitaire ring. She tried to read Lacey's expression. Surely, she'd stop her if the answer was going to be a negative one, but Lacey's expression was only one of disbelief. Her mouth was slightly open and her brow was furrowed, but Quinn had no idea what she was thinking. She didn't want to say the words if they would be rejected. It would hurt too much.

"Aren't you going to…" Lacey pointed at the ground.

"Oh, right." Quinn got down on one knee. She had no choice. She'd have to say the words, come what may. She reached for Lacey's hand again and tried to breathe, but her chest felt like it was slowly being crushed.

Lacey squeezed Quinn's hand and whispered, "Say it."

Quinn took that as a positive sign. Also, the fact that Lacey was still standing there meant something, right? Instead of saying yes, she wouldn't say that after all they'd been through, they should wait. See how it went. Be a real couple for longer than a day. They'd only had one night together, unless you counted the last week of falling into bed after work. And now, this? Crazy, right? Insane. Worst idea ever.

Except it wasn't. They'd spent almost a year together. They'd seen each other at their best, and they'd seen each other at their worst. Quinn struggled to think of a person in her life who'd failed to notice how Lacey made her a better person. By the time the craft services guy mentioned it, Quinn was pretty sure they were all on to something. Maybe it wasn't such a bad idea after all.

Quinn squeezed her eyes shut and imagined their wedding again. She'd been planning it all week. It wouldn't be small and private. The opposite, actually. She wanted the big wedding her mother would love to help them plan. She would include everyone important to them. She would invite someone from the press to cover it. Give an interview. Tell the world how happy she was. All of this would of course only happen if it was what Lacey wanted as well.

Lacey. She was waiting. Quinn opened her eyes. "Lacey Matthews." Quinn swallowed hard. "Will you marry me?"

Her voice and gaze were both steady this time as she waited for an answer. It didn't take long. Lacey gave her a nod and whispered, "Yes."

Quinn couldn't get the ring on her finger fast enough. She pressed against Lacey cupping her cheeks. "You said yes." She kissed her soundly and giggled. "You said yes."

Lacey wrapped her arms around Quinn and picked her up off the ground, turning them in a circle. "Of course I did." She set Quinn back down, keeping her arm around her waist, and looking at her ring. "I'm going to be your wife," she said, a disbelieving tone in her voice.

"Mrs. Kincaid." Quinn twisted the ring, making it sparkle in the sunshine.

"Matthews." Lacey said. "Matthews Kincaid." She picked Quinn up by her waist again and carried her to the blanket. "I think I'll have my way with my fiancée."

Quinn tried to wiggle her way loose. "Not out here!"

"Oh, yes. Out here." Lacey got Quinn down on the ground and knelt over her. "Unless you're worried about drones."

Quinn pulled Lacey to her, holding her face. "Shut up," she said, right before kissing her fiancée.

Jack hadn't been surprised by the tweet—a photo of Lacey with her arms resting on her knees, showing off an engagement ring, along with a message—*She said yes.*

Quinn had warned him of her intentions. He didn't try to dissuade her, even though he'd been somewhat concerned about Lacey's response.

Margaret was very surprised when she'd received the same message in text form. Surprised and overjoyed for her daughter.

Amy hadn't stopped crying tears of joy ever since.

They all sat in the front row, dressed in their finest. Amy wasn't the only one crying anymore. Did Jack always carry a cloth handkerchief in his coat pocket, or just at weddings? Amy took his hand and squeezed it, offering support. She reached over and took Margaret's hand in hers as well. It was only when Quinn kissed her bride that Amy let go and cheered, louder than anyone else.

When the emcee announced the first dance, Lacey stood and held out her hand. "That's our cue."

Surprised, Quinn took her hand. "But we didn't talk about a first dance."

"We didn't?" Lacey led her out to the dance floor. "I swear we discussed it on the way home from dinner that night, remember? You talked about having a cheesy song?"

"But…" Quinn's jaw slacked as the sounds of a piano filled the air. "I never told you what it was."

Lacey pulled her in close. "You didn't?"

"Oh. My. God." Quinn held on tight and they began to sway. She didn't know whether to laugh or cry. "Lace, you realize I picked this song when I was twelve, right?"

"Shh…dance, baby."

They swayed a few more moments with the crowd hooting and hollering. Quinn giggled. "TMZ is going to have a field day talking about how cheesy we are. You know that, right?"

"Quinn Matthews Kincaid!" Lacey paused, letting the feel of her wife's new name roll around on her tongue. "I don't care what they say. TMZ didn't see your face when you talked about your wedding song. There's no way I'd deny you that."

Lacey pulled back and guided Quinn into a spin, quickly pulling her back into the embrace. "The song is true," she said. "Everything I do…"

"You do it for me?"

Lacey raised Quinn's hand to her lips and kissed her wedding ring. "From day one."

Quinn's throat tightened. "Could I possibly love you any more than I already do?"

"Probably not," Lacey said with a grin. "Besides, we are slow-dancing the fuck out of this song."

"That we are, honey. That we are."

About the Author

Elle Spencer is the author of *Forget Her Not* and *Casting Lacey*. She is a hopeless romantic and firm believer in true love, although she knows the path to happily ever after is rarely an easy one—not for Elle and not for her characters.

Before jumping off a cliff to write full-time, Elle ran an online store and worked as a massage therapist. Her wife is especially grateful for the second one. When she's not writing, Elle loves a good home improvement project and reading lots (and lots) of lesfic.

Elle and her wife split their time between Utah and California, ensuring that at any given time they are either too hot or too cold.

Books Available From Bold Strokes Books

Captive by Donna K. Ford. To escape a human trafficking ring, Greyson Cooper and Olivia Danner become players in a game of deceit and violence. Will their love stand a chance? (978-1-63555-215-7)

Crossing the Line by CF Frizzell. The Mob discovers a nemesis within its ranks, and in the ultimate retaliation, draws Stick McLaughlin from anonymity by threatening everything she holds dear. (978-1-63555-161-7)

Love's Verdict by Carsen Taite. Attorneys Landon Holt and Carly Pachett want the exact same thing: the only open partnership spot at their prestigious criminal defense firm. But will they compromise their careers for love? (978-1-63555-042-9)

Precipice of Doubt by Mardi Alexander & Laurie Eichler. Can Cole Jameson resist her attraction to her boss, veterinarian Jodi Bowman, or will she risk a workplace romance and her heart? (978-1-63555-128-0)

Savage Horizons by CJ Birch. Captain Jordan Kellow's feelings for Lt. Ali Ash have her past and future colliding, setting in motion a series of events that strands her crew in an unknown galaxy thousands of light years from home. (978-1-63555-250-8)

Secrets of the Last Castle by A. Rose Mathieu. When Elizabeth Campbell represents a young man accused of murdering an elderly woman, her investigation leads to an abandoned plantation that reveals many dark Southern secrets. (978-1-63555-240-9)

Take Your Time by VK Powell. A neurotic parrot brings police officer Grace Booker and temporary veterinarian Dr. Dani Wingate together in the tiny town of Pine Cone, but their unexpected attraction keeps the sparks flying. (978-1-63555-130-3)

The Last Seduction by Ronica Black. When you allow true love to elude you once and you desperately regret it, are you brave enough to grab it when it comes around again? (978-1-63555-211-9)

The Shape of You by Georgia Beers. Rebecca McCall doesn't play it safe, but when sexy Spencer Thompson joins her workout class, their nonstop sparring forces her to face her ultimate challenge—a chance at love. (978-1-63555-217-1)

Exposed by MJ Williamz. The closet is no place to live if you want to find true love. (978-1-62639-989-1)

Force of Fire: Toujours a Vous by Ali Vali. Immortals Kendal and Piper welcome their new child and celebrate the defeat of an old enemy, but another ancient evil is about to awaken deep in the jungles of Costa Rica. (978-1-63555-047-4)

Landing Zone by Erin Dutton. Can a career veteran finally discover a love stronger than even her pride? (978-1-63555-199-0)

Love at Last Call by M. Ullrich. Is balancing business, friendship, and love more than any willing woman can handle? (978-1-63555-197-6)

Pleasure Cruise by Yolanda Wallace. Spencer Collins and Amy Donovan have few things in common, but a Caribbean cruise offers both women an unexpected chance to face one of their greatest fears: falling in love. (978-1-63555-219-5)

Running Off Radar by MB Austin. Maji's plans to win Rose back are interrupted when work intrudes, and duty calls her to help a SEAL team stop a Russian mobster from harvesting gold from the bottom of Sitka Sound. (978-1-63555-152-5)

Shadow of the Phoenix by Rebecca Harwell. In the final battle for the fate of Storm's Quarry, even Nadya's and Shay's powers may not be enough. (978-1-63555-181-5)

Take a Chance by D. Jackson Leigh. There's hardly a woman within fifty miles of Pine Cone that veterinarian Trip Beaumont can't charm, except for the irritating new cop, Jamie Grant, who keeps leaving parking tickets on her truck. (978-1-63555-118-1)

The Outcasts by Alexa Black. Spacebus driver Sue Jones is running from her past. When she crash-lands on a faraway world, the Outcast Kara might be her chance for redemption. (978-1-63555-242-3)

Death in Time by Robyn Nyx. Working in the past is hell on your future. (978-1-63555-053-5)